Dear Mystery Reader:

First a major celebrity in Cleing national attention for his acclaimed Milan Jacovich P.I. series. In his eighth adventure, our favorite Cleveland P.I. lands himself right in the middle of a murderous international crime ring.

Joel Kerner, a hotshot lawyer from Cleveland, is killed while jogging on the pristine sands of the Caribbean. Enter Milan Jacovich. Flown in to investigate the murder, he finds himself up against everything from the local police to sex-starved women to back-alley bandits. Upon his return to Cleveland, things manage to get worse. There he finds himself up against a notorious labor leader and a local mobster who will stop at nothing to keep Milan from the truth.

Whether you're a native Midwesterner or taking your first trip to Cleveland with Roberts, one thing's for sure: after reading THE CLEVELAND LOCAL, you'll never want to leave.

Yours in crime,

Joe Veltre
St. Martin's Press DEAD LETTER Paperback Mysteries

Other titles from St. Martin's **Dead Letter** Mysteries

Dead Letter is also proud to present these mystery classics by
Ngaio Marsh

St. Martin's Paperbacks Titles
by Les Roberts

Collision Bend
The Cleveland Connection
Pepper Pike

THE CLEVELAND LOCAL

LES ROBERTS

St. Martin's Paperbacks

To the late Barry W. Gardner,
To newlyweds Neal and Peggy Barnes Szpatura,
To Dawn Pierce,
and
To Samuel H. Miller:

To deserve friends like these, somewhere and sometime I must have done something awfully good.

THE CLEVELAND LOCAL

Copyright © 1997 by Les Roberts.

Library of Congress Catalog Card Number 97-20581

ISBN 0-312-96678-4

Printed in the United States of America

St. Martin's Press hardcover edition/November 1997
St. Martin's Paperback edition/December 1998

10 9 8 7 6 5 4 3 2 1

Acknowledgments

The author wishes to thank Joan Kalhorn, Noreen Koppelman Goldstein, Tom Simpson, and Jill Acquaviva, without whom this novel would still be on the hard drive.

Appreciation also to Dr. and Mrs. Mark Levine and Mr. and Mrs. Sam Scaravelli.

And as ever, warm thanks and hugs to Dr. Milan Yakovich and Diana Yakovich Montagino.

CHAPTER ONE

It was a black-and-white-movie morning when I opened my office, looked out the window down the Cuyahoga River, and saw the angry thunderheads hunkered over Lake Erie. It was one of those mornings we get in Cleveland at the end of April. We've been looking at gray skies and fastening our coats and jackets up to the top button for almost eight months, and the longing for a spot of sunshine and warmth to burn through the pewter-colored overcast becomes as urgent and palpable as the throbbing of an infected hangnail.

It doesn't matter that we've already sprung forward into daylight saving time, because the Tribe is playing night baseball at Jacobs Field, the hoods of their undershirts pulled up over their heads, making them look like ski racers. Dillard's is trumpeting their big spring sale, and it's been much more than six weeks since Punxsutawney Phil, neighboring Pennsylvania's groundhog, saw his shadow at the beginning of February. We still have little to look forward to; we know that within a few days of its turning balmy and sixtyish the temperature will soar up toward the eighties and nineties and every car window will be closed tight to keep the cooled air from escaping—and we'll have once more missed spring.

I spooned three scoops of Maxwell House into the filter basket of my Braun, opened the sports page of the *Plain Dealer*, and waited for my nine o'clock client to arrive.

There are many reasons clients come to a private investigator, and almost none of them are happy ones. Some people have lost something or someone and want it found, some want their suspicions allayed or confirmed, some are seeking redress or protection or succor. In any case, the decision to seek out members of my profession stems from some sort of disquiet that has reached a point of crisis.

As a result, clients tend to walk into my office with any one of a number of attitudes. Some are almost pathetic, some nervous, some defensive to the point of being obnoxious, some angry, and many just plain frightened.

Patrice Kerner came to me at promptly nine o'clock on a Tuesday, nodding a rather formal good-morning. She sat down opposite me in one of my leather client chairs, crossed her legs, cleared her throat self-consciously, and started to cry. Hard.

The tears didn't creep up on her gradually; there was no preliminary quivering of her chin or reddening of her nose or filling up of her eyes. They came like a sudden gully washer on a sunny day, spilling down her cheeks and taking her mascara with them. She'd seemed so cool and self-possessed when she'd called for an appointment, and even more so when she came in that morning, the kind of person one might imagine only wept at funerals.

Somewhere in her early forties, she was short and compactly built, with dark curls. An attractive woman, looking all business in a fawn-colored wool power suit just right for the kind of chilly Cleveland spring day when rain, snow, sunshine, or even a tornado are all reasonable possibilities. She'd walked in with a slim ostrich-leather folder tucked under one arm like a bird colonel's swagger stick, and the long strap of a Gucci purse slung over the other shoulder. She divested herself of both, shrugged her coat off into my hands as if I were a servant, graciously allowing me to hang it in the closet, and sat down, and then the waterworks surprised us both, messing up her careful makeup.

I keep a box of tissues at the ready for just such emergencies. I pushed it across the desk at her. She went through seven before she was done, blotting and blowing and dabbing. I'd known her for exactly two minutes, not long enough for a kindly series of murmured there-theres, so I simply waited, looking out my office window across Collision Bend, that particularly treacherous hair-pin curve of the Cuyahoga River, at Tower City beyond. Finally she got herself together enough to tell me what she was there for.

"My brother has been killed," she said at last, in a voice sur-prisingly flat and well modulated, issuing as it did from a tear-streaked, reddened, puffy face. She might have been giving the sports scores.

"I'm very sorry, Ms. Kerner."

"Perhaps you read about it in the newspapers."

"No, I'm afraid I didn't."

"It doesn't matter," she said, but the disapproving thrust of her jaw indicated it did. "What matters is that there's someone out there who's gotten away with murder."

It's an ugly word to just toss out on the table like that. I shifted uneasily in my big executive chair, not exactly relishing the idea of hearing the rest of the story. When an unexplained fatality oc-curs, family members often let their grief overtake their com-mon sense.

"Are you so sure it was murder?" I said.

Her mouth twisted into a sneer; she was in full control once more. "What would *you* call a shotgun blast to the face, Mr. Ja-covich?" She even said my last name correctly, with the J sound-ing like a Y—*Yock*-o-vitch. I wondered how she'd do with my first name. I pronounce it the Americanized way, *My*-lan, although most people trying it for the first time fancy it up as Mi-*lahn*, like the Italian city, or *Mee*-lan. That's what happens when you have an ethnic name. Nobody ever mispronounces Fred Wilson.

"This is kind of a touchy area, Ms. Kerner," I said. "Private in-vestigators like myself aren't allowed to investigate ongoing cap-ital cases. There's a law against it. The police don't like it, and it could cost me my license."

"The police are the ones who recommended you," she said. "A Lieutenant Meglich, I believe."

That would be my oldest friend in the world, Marko Meglich—who prefers being called Mark these days—the number-two man in the Cleveland PD's homicide division. Our friendship began when we bloodied each other's noses in the schoolyard in fourth grade; neither one of us remembers why. But most of our adult arguments have been about my butting into his cases when they happen to dovetail with mine. It was hard to believe that he'd given this woman my name to investigate her brother's murder.

"Why would Lieutenant Meglich recommend me to work on a murder case when he knows that by law I'm prohibited from becoming involved with it?"

"My brother wasn't killed in Cleveland," she said. "It happened when he was on vacation. In San Carlos."

It took a few moments to pinpoint San Carlos in my mind, but I managed to remember that it was a small island country in the Caribbean that wasn't famous for much of anything except secret numbered bank accounts, jerk chicken, steel drum music, and a couple of overpriced luxury resort hotels that feature white sand beaches, shockingly clear water, and killer rum drinks.

"When was this?"

"About ten weeks ago."

I didn't like that; trails grow cold. After ten weeks, one can be completely obliterated. "What do the San Carlos police say?"

Patrice Kerner's spine straightened slowly, one vertebra at a time, and her face composed itself into a hard mask. "They're no damn help at all."

In her anger, she seemed to gain even more frighteningly icy control. She leaned forward aggressively in her chair, the only remnant of her recent crying jag a slightly reddened nose. "They don't have the manpower or the expertise to handle anything as sophisticated as murder. Or enough interest, for that matter, when a gringo dies." Her mouth puckered, as if the words even tasted bitter. "They're calling it 'death by misadventure at the hands of a person or persons unknown.' Frankly I think that's a load of bullshit."

I took a sip of my coffee. My older son, Milan Junior, had bought his caffeine-addicted father an electric mug-warmer for Christmas, so the coffee was still nice and hot. "I'm not sure what you want me to do for you, Ms. Kerner."

She uncrossed her legs and then recrossed them the other way.

"I should think that's obvious. I want you to find out who's responsible for my brother's death. And I want them to pay for it."

It sounded easy the way she said it, but I knew damn well it wouldn't be. These things never are. "Let's be clear, Ms. Kerner," I told her. "I don't take money for hurting people, and I'm not going to get you information so that you can. I understand your need for revenge, but whatever you do with what I find out, you'll have to stay within the law."

She looked offended again. She had a wider range of unpleasant facial expressions than Laurence Olivier came up with when playing Nazis late in his career. "Do I strike you as the vigilante type?"

"How are vigilantes supposed to look?"

She stared at me, or rather through me, with eyes like those of a basking crocodile. "I just want to know," she said.

"Then I'm going to need a little more to go on."

She unzipped the ostrich-leather case, pulled out a stack of documents an inch thick, and dropped it on my desk. I was embarrassed at the little cloud of dust and minuscule particles of cigarette ash that arose from the surface. Housekeeping is not one of my strong suits.

"I've put together a dossier of everything I think you'll need," she said. "My brother's name was Joel Kerner. Junior." She tapped the stack. "I've got his photograph here, and where he worked, his bank accounts, credit card numbers, a list of his friends, and . . ."

She faltered, grabbing for a fresh tissue and dabbing at her nose with it. The used ones were in a wad the size of a softball on the desk in front of her.

"There are copies of two newspaper stories about his death in there too," she continued, her voice a little shakier now. She added the most recent tissue to the collection. "One from the *Plain Dealer* and the other from a San Carlos paper. You won't get very much out of those, I'm afraid."

"I won't get much out of any of it unless you and I talk some more," I said. "That'll be more help than any of this." I pointed to the documents.

The flock of gulls circling outside the window must have been a lot more fascinating than I was. She followed their progress closely as they swooped and darted and wheeled over the river. "I have a limited amount of time this morning," she said, apparently addressing the gulls. "I have to be at work."

"Would you like to come back when your time isn't so limited?"

She took her eyes from the gulls and zipped up the leather case again, the first in a series of those brusque, businesslike movements people make when they're getting ready to leave. "I have clients of my own, Mr. Jacovich. I'm an attorney."

I nodded. Somehow I'd known that.

"It runs in the family. My father, my brother. Joel was a partner in Kalisher, Kerner and Keynes. It was kind of a family joke. We used to say Joel was a big shot in the KKK." She tried for a smile, but it wasn't a very good try. Her expression disintegrated into a grimace; her face flushed and there was a white line around her lips, but she didn't cry anymore. She was in control now and wasn't about to relinquish it.

I shuffled through the papers she'd given me. The photograph of Joel Kerner was a rather formal black-and-white portrait, the kind a partner in a law firm would have had taken to put in the brochure or the financial report—pinstriped suit, muted tie, a snowy white shirtfront and a fifty-dollar haircut. He'd been handsome in a kind of weak-chinned way, younger, darker and more Semitic-looking than his sister, with distinguished sprinkles of gray at his temples and sideburns. I noted the photographer was one of Cleveland's best-known and highest-priced portraitists.

Further down in the pile I found photocopies of two newspaper articles, both illustrated with the same formal picture. I read the piece from the local paper; the one from San Carlos was in Spanish.

Joel Kerner Jr. of Cleveland had been shotgunned in the face while jogging on the beach behind the San Carlos Inn some ten weeks earlier. The body had been dragged off the sand and into a small oasis of scrub pine and bushes. His running shoes, which the story identified as Nikes, had been taken, as well as his wallet and a Movado wristwatch. A couple of kids playing on the beach had found him just after nine o'clock in the morning. The local coroner had estimated he'd been dead about three hours.

Putting the article down on top of the pile, I looked up at my prospective client. She was perched on the edge of her chair, the ostrich-leather case in her lap and her purse strap on her shoulder, as if waiting for the starter's pistol.

"Your brother died ten weeks ago," I said. "Why did you wait this long? The more time elapses, the harder it is to solve cases like this."

She didn't flinch; indeed, she was almost defiant. Patrice Kerner didn't like being put on the defensive. "We couldn't even think about it. Our first reaction was grief. We were in shock, of course."

"We?"

"The family. My parents and myself. It took us a while to realize we weren't going to get any satisfaction from the San Carlos authorities. My father naturally contacted the police here, but they told us it was out of their jurisdiction and they couldn't do anything about it. That's when Lieutenant Meglich suggested I see you." Her jaw set stubbornly. "We need some sort of closure."

"We could be looking at a simple robbery."

"For a watch and a pair of shoes?"

"People have been killed on the streets of Cleveland for a lot less."

She shook her head. "I don't buy that."

"Why not? San Carlos is a poverty-stricken country. What that watch is worth, a poor man in San Carlos could live on for six months."

Her lips clamped shut and her shoulders went rigid with impatience. She shook her head resolutely, making her dark curls dance; she was having none of it.

I sighed. "All right, then. Did your brother have any enemies?"

Her mouth turned down at the corners, making her face look like a classic mask of tragedy. "He was a lawyer. Lawyers make enemies. Of course he had enemies."

"Like whom?"

"I don't know," she said, evidently unimpressed with my achingly correct grammar. "We weren't that close. He didn't talk to me about his practice. You'll have to ask his associates."

"And they are . . . ?"

She gestured at the stack of papers under my hand. "It's all in there." Then she pointed a finger at me and sighted down the length of it. "Look, I need to know right now if you'll help me or not. If you won't, please tell me so I can make other arrangements. You come highly recommended, but I can't force you to do what you don't want to."

"I'll help you," I said. "And I understand you have somewhere to be this morning. But I really need to talk to you some more."

Fishing a discreet gray business card out of her purse, she dropped it on the stack. I saw that she was with one of the high-profile law firms in Terminal Tower. "Call my secretary for an appointment," she said, as though I were the one asking for help.

"This may run into some money," I warned her. "I may have to go to San Carlos. Don't you want to know my rates?"

Her hand fluttered at me, like a bird flushed from cover and flying away. Or like her money taking wing. "It's not important," she said. "Results are important. Is there something for me to sign, or what?"

I got out one of my standard contract forms and passed it across the desk to her. She put on a pair of glasses shaped like cat's eyes with rhinestones at the corners of the aqua frames, and unlike most of my clients, read the document very carefully before giving me a curt nod and signing it with a gold Cross pen that she took from her purse. Then she wrote me out a retainer check and was gone, the ghost of her White Diamonds perfume lingering in the air. I rather liked it; it masked the stale smell of cigarette smoke.

Outside the sky was growing darker; we were apparently in for some rain. The winter had been a long one, with near record-breaking snowfall, and although a heavy rainstorm tends to dampen the spirits, at least it wasn't a blizzard.

I poured myself some fresh coffee and sat down to more carefully go through the papers she'd left. Her parents, and Joel's, were listed as Mr. and Mrs. Joel Kerner Sr., with an address on South Park in Shaker Heights. Somewhere in the recesses of my brain a warning light flashed; nobody who lives on South Park shops at Kmart, and I remembered her saying that it had been her father who had contacted the Cleveland police. We were evidently dealing with Leading Citizens here.

I sighed. Leading Citizens make me tired.

I pulled an empty file folder from the drawer, wrote Patrice Kerner's name on the tab, and wrapped it around the stack of documents.

Swiveling around in my chair, I faced my computer. I'd had it for almost a year, but it was not yet user friendly, at least not to me. I'd reluctantly joined the computer age at the same time I'd bought the building where I now have my office, aided by a modest inheritance from my late Auntie Branka, my *tetka,* but just as I was unused to being a landlord and having a big, efficient, well-equipped office in which to work, I wasn't yet comfortable with the technology. I didn't have an e-mail address, I was barely able to send a fax, and surfing the net still sounded to me like something the Beach Boys might have sung about in the sixties.

The screen saver was on, displaying flying stars. I created an electronic file for Patrice Kerner and input the essential data contained in her sheaf of papers.

Input the data. A plastic pocket protector would be next.

Joel Kerner Jr. had lived in an expensive apartment he owned in the east tower of Moreland Courts near Shaker Square. His law offices were in the Leader Building, one of Cleveland's older and more architecturally interesting downtown office structures, once the home of a now defunct daily newspaper. His law partners were listed as Daniel Kalisher and Robert Keynes; they were not among the scores of attorneys whose paths I had crossed in the course of my own business.

Patrice had included a laundry list of her brother's friends and acquaintances, along with two of his former girlfriends, Lois Scaravelli and Patt Wolfe—that's Patt with two *t*s. There was also a page of organizations to which Joel had belonged, some of them with their roots in the legal community, and some prestigious social clubs like the Cleveland Skating Club, the Rowfant Club, and the University Club. He'd served on the boards of a local library Friends group, a film society, and a ballet company, as well as that of a shelter for homeless women and children. Joel hadn't lived long enough to attain the rarefied social heights scaled by the older and more powerful players in town, like membership in the Union Club, but he had definitely been a young man on the way up.

I scrolled through what I had typed, then leaned back in my chair to finish my coffee. There was a lot to do here, much spoor to follow on a trail already grown cold, but at the moment all of it was just words on paper to me. I wanted to talk to Patrice Kerner sometime when her concentration wasn't elsewhere and she didn't keep looking at her watch—and I wondered what the real reason for the ten-week delay was, why it had taken so long before she got interested, and why her very real tears had been followed by such impatience.

My first priority, though, was to find out about Joel Kerner Jr.'s last vacation.

The rain finally hit, big, hard drops beating on the old roof of my building. Snakes of water ran down the windowpanes, and the wind squalled loudly and blew sand and gravel around in the parking lot. The surface of the river was choppy. A good day to stay inside and think about your options.

I called Lieutenant Mark Meglich and invited him to lunch.

CHAPTER TWO

The pretty blond hostess who greeted us at the door of Piccolo Mondo on West Sixth Street turned her twinkly brown eyes on Marko Meglich and addressed him by his rank. He in turn called her by her first name, and I could see his considerable charm with women kick into over-drive. She was in her very early twenties, which meant that she was fair game for Marko, who rarely dated anyone over a quarter of a century old.

My coat was soaked across the shoulders and my hair had been mussed by wind, but Marko looked as if his valet had just handed him out of his dressing room, as if the rain wouldn't dare wet him.

In a gray three-piece suit just a tad too tight for his ever ex-panding chest and gut and with the Tom Selleck mustache he'd cultivated since he'd become single again, he cut a striking fig-ure. I must have made quite a contrast beside him, with the gap between my two front teeth and the receding hairline many Slovenian men are plagued with, which he had somehow dodged. His wife had divorced him at about the same time mine had divorced me, although they'd had no children while I had two boys. Everybody in town knew Marko, because he'd learned early in his career how to play and enjoy the depart-mental political games that had intimidated me right off the force and into private practice. It was generally understood that when his boss retired at the end of the following year, Marko would get his captain's bars and the number-one slot in homicide. He'd come a long way from that little-boy fight in the schoolyard.

As the hostess led us to our table, Marko worked the room like a politician, shaking hands with important people, waving to others not so prominent, nodding to those he didn't know. We were seated in the front room, where the bar is, in a corner by the window, so that we could see everyone who came in and everyone who happened to walk by outside too. It was a pretty parade—nearly everyone who comes to West Sixth for lunch from the nearby office towers is well turned-out, Cleveland's best and brightest.

I started with a beer—a Stroh's, which has been my drink of choice since college. Marko, in the middle of a duty shift, righteously opted for some fancy bottled water with a quarter of a lime floating in it. We didn't start talking about Joel Kerner until the drinks were served.

"The reports we got from San Carlos didn't say much more than the story in the *Plain Dealer*," he told me. "The guy was on vacation—some sort of package tour—and he'd been there four days. He went out for an early morning run along the top of a big high sand dune and never came back. Some kids playing on the beach found him a few hours later. The San Carlos police sent photographs, too. It wasn't pretty."

"A shotgun in the face never is," I said.

He sipped at his designer water, the lime slice bumping against his mustache. "When the sister came in to see me, there wasn't anything I could do for her. It's not only out of our jurisdiction, it's out of our country."

"You must have a read on it, though."

"My crystal ball's in my other suit." He picked up the menu but only glanced at it. I think he knew it by heart. Then he waved at a waiter who hovered nearby.

"I'll get *your* waiter for you," the young man said pointedly, and hustled off.

I sighed. Everyone's a specialist.

"Think about it, Milan. In a country where ninety-eight percent of the citizens are at or below the poverty level, along comes a rich *turista* with an expensive watch and shoes and probably a bulging wallet. Figure it out."

Our waiter was even bigger and stockier than the first one. He dutifully recited the specials of the day and congratulated us on our choices, like a high school guidance counselor whose advice we'd taken on college majors. Then he went away again.

I looked around to see whether anyone else was smoking, but no one was, and I didn't want the two Ann Taylor–clad older women at the next table to yap at me about my poisoning their air with secondhand smoke, so I left my Winstons in my pocket. The country's values are changing, and my cigarette habit is beginning to make me feel like the main attraction on *America's Most Wanted*.

"It doesn't sit right, Mark," I said. "The robbery angle. It doesn't fit with a shotgun blast in the face. A guy gets robbed, okay. He gives the thief shit and he gets killed, it happens. But someone blows his head off? That's sending a message. That's a hell of a lot of anger."

"You try raising a family of seven on eighty bucks a month," he said. "And then you see a guy running on the beach with the equivalent of the gross national product on his wrist and his feet and in his hip pocket, you'd have a lot of anger too. And Kerner probably did put up a fuss."

"That's the way you see it?"

"That's the way the San Carlos police see it. And the way our safety director sees it too."

"The safety director?" That's what Cleveland calls the official who in other cities is the police commissioner. "What's he got to do with it?"

"He always gets his fingerprints on the high-profile cases. You know that. Kerner's father is a heavy-duty labor lawyer—he's been on retainer for several of the big industrial locals over the years, and he's golfing buddies with everyone from city hall to the statehouse. He didn't bother with us peons at first—he went right over our heads, right to the top. But the SD kicked it down to me like he always does, with a recommendation to stroke the guy and kiss away his tears, but don't put too many man-hours into it."

He spread his big hands wide—when he was flawlessly catching passes at Kent State, his teammates called them soft hands. They, along with his belly, were the only things about Marko Meglich that had ever been called soft. "I take orders," he said. "It's what I get paid to do."

"So you turned the Kerners over to me."

He preened his mustache. "You ought to thank me. I figured you wouldn't mind making a buck." The hostess led a party past our table into the back dining room. Marko smiled and wrinkled his nose at her. The effect was not nearly as adorable as he must have hoped.

"What's the story on the sister?" I said. "One minute she's crying her eyes out, the next she acts like she's leveraging a buyout."

He made the kind of face a five-year-old boy affects when his mother puts lima beans on his plate. "She's a tough cookie. I didn't get to talk to her much, but my sense of it is that she's that new breed of lawyer with Dom Perignon in her veins and a cash register behind her eyes."

"I thought that was the old breed of lawyer," I said.

"These lawyers today, they've got no heart, that's the trouble."

"I hate to be the one to tell you this," I said, "but Clarence Darrow is dead."

"You gotta have heart in this world, and compassion, or else you're a piece of crap just taking up space." His expression turned wistful. "You've got heart, Milan. That's what made you such a good cop. If you'd stayed with the department—"

I held up a stop-sign palm. "Please," I begged, "not today, all right?"

I'd heard this song before, many times. Marko had talked me into a blue uniform when I'd come back from Vietnam, and it broke his heart when I resigned. After grammar school and all the high school and college football together I think he'd fantasized about us as the Butch Cassidy and Sundance Kid of the Third District, although I had the feeling he'd have wound up being both Butch, the charming, charismatic brains of the outfit, and steely-eyed, quick-drawing Sundance. Either way, he'd never forgiven me for kicking over his dream.

"And did you say 'heart'?" I asked. "You're not getting mellow on us, are you?"

He looked almost sheepish. "Y'know, you hit forty and your perceptions change, along with your priorities. You don't have to prove how tough you are anymore."

Then he leaned toward me, lowering his voice to a warning rumble. "I'm not getting *too* mellow, though."

I laughed. For all his sartorial elegance and political posturing, in his heart and his gut Marko Meglich would always be a tough cop.

We stopped talking as our lunches arrived, and I waited until our waiter went away to wherever waiters go when they aren't asking you how everything is when your mouth is full. "So what are we going to do about Joel Kerner?" I finally said.

"*We* aren't going to do anything. *You* can do whatever you want."

"It's that easy for you to blow it off?"

"I'm sorry about the guy and sorry for his family, but I'm not the world's policeman." He dug into his lunch with zeal. "There's always a murder someplace—Los Angeles. Kansas City. Miami. Detroit. It's too bad, but I can't get hot and bothered about all of them. I get paid to take care of things right here in town, which is enough to do. Too much, in fact." He poked at his salad, speared a chicken strip. "A murder of a U.S. citizen in a foreign country like San Carlos has international implications. I stick my nose into that, pretty soon I've got the FBI and the State Department sitting on my face. I can't fool with it, Milan." As the first waiter sailed by, Marko jerked his head at him, looking almost apologetic. "It's not my table."

"That's disappointing," I said. I took a bite of my pasta; it was perfectly al dente, just the way I like it. "But you know stuff I don't, so help me out here. What about Joel Kerner the elder?"

"He's a piece of work," Marko said around a mouthful of chicken. "Kind of a legend around the courthouse. At the beginning of his career he was in the pocket of some of the less savory union organizers. They had quite a little sting operation going. The local union rep would go into a small shop, sometimes no more than eight or ten people, and try to organize the workers. The owner would naturally have a fit. So then Kerner would come along, offer his services, and charge the owner big bucks to chase the union away. All that took was a phone call—by pre-arrangement the union would back off, Kerner would collect a fat legal fee from the business owner for saving his ass, and then kick back a chunk of it to the union guy."

"Not exactly looking out for the rank-and-file, is it?"

"No, except it wasn't common knowledge, and nobody bitched about it, so he got away with it."

"And you let him?"

"It was a long time ago. Besides, I'm a homicide cop. Call the bunco squad."

"And that bought him a mansion on South Park?"

"That was just chump change. But the union bosses took care of him, too. Now he gets his income via big retainers from those same unions, and he's known far and wide as the workingman's friend. How's that for irony?"

"Was Joel Junior a labor lawyer too?"

"No," he said. "Personal injury stuff. They advertise on TV, usually in the middle of the night. You're the insomniac, I'm surprised you haven't seen them."

I am an insomniac, but I don't watch television all night; the only things on are cheesy soft-core porno movies and those half-hour infomercials, and I don't want to spend three hundred dollars on cosmetics or buy a plastic upper-body-toner that will break in three weeks. "And what about Patrice?" I said.

He shrugged. "I don't know much about her except that she's on the partnership track in a big downtown law firm. My guess is her specialty is corporate law. What's the difference?"

"I don't know. I guess I'm just making conversation. But isn't your cop's soul just a little bit curious?"

"My cop's soul can't afford to be. A guy gets himself shot two thousand miles away, there isn't much I can do about it from here anyway."

"Maybe I can," I said.

◦　◦　◦

Lunch was over and so was the conversation about Joel Kerner. I took a last swig of beer. "Well, thanks for the referral, Mark. I'll keep you posted."

"Don't do me any favors," he said.

I paid the check, tucking the receipt away in my wallet to present to Patrice Kerner later. Out on the sidewalk it had stopped raining. The asphalt was slick and shiny, and minirivers flowed merrily in the gutters. Marko and I exchanged the *abrazo* of good friends who don't see each other often enough, and he headed off toward the Justice Center a few blocks away. I crossed the street to the parking lot where I'd left my Pontiac Sunbird, ransomed it for almost as much as I'd paid for my lunch, and pointed its nose eastward toward the suburb of Beachwood.

The Beachwood Travel Center, where Joel Kerner had booked his final, fatal trip, occupied a storefront in a strip mall it shared with a real estate company and a shop that sells baby clothes on Chagrin Boulevard near Warrensville Center Road. When I went inside, a discreet *bing-bong* announced my presence to four women sitting at metal desks in a large room festooned with garish travel posters of exotic places. Three of the women were middle-aged and overweight; the fourth, the one with the sexy, willowy figure and her nose in a travel magazine, was in her mid twenties. She wore too much makeup and her blond hair was teased and permed into a kinky fright wig. A heavyset, prematurely bald young man with the faded remnants of a winter suntan sat at a desk in a glassed-in cubicle under an enormous full color poster of the Eiffel Tower, working two phones at once. He wore no jacket but a flowered tie was knotted under the collar of his plaid shirt. Even from across the room I could see that his upper lip perspired a lot, just like Nixon's, and there were dark half moons of sweat under his arms.

"I'm looking for Janice Futterman," I announced.

The blonde looked up; she had the kind of sleepy, pouty good looks that made her appear uninterested in everything. After a cursory glance she decided I was no one she had to concern herself with, so she went back to her magazine. From the upside-down headline I gathered that she was studying an article about low-cost packaged tours to Singapore, that vacation paradise. I supposed getting your ass whipped with a bamboo cane cost extra.

One of the older women said, "Hi, I'm Janice."

I introduced myself and gave her one of my business cards.

After studying it, she said, "Oh, you're the one that called about the Joel Kerner thing." She was wearing a thick gold wedding ring that looked heavy enough to drag a fishing trawler to the bottom of the ocean.

Off in a corner of the room a printer was clacking away, another machine was spitting out airline tickets, and one of the other women was telling someone on the phone that she could book them to Los Angeles on Northwest but there'd be a change of planes in Minneapolis with a ninety-minute layover.

"You should really talk to Josh—that's him inside there," Janice Futterman said, indicating the glassed-in cubicle. "He's the boss around here. We'll just wait until he gets off the phones."

We just waited. I sat down and we listened to the printer printing, looking at each other in silent mutual discomfort until Josh got off the phones.

When we finally gained entrance to his inner sanctum, I learned that Josh's last name was Borgenecht, which rhymed with circumspect, and that he and his mother were the owners of Beachwood Travel. And he wasn't at all happy about what had transpired with Joel Kerner in San Carlos. As a matter of fact, he was in something of a dither about it.

"Janice told me you'd called," he said in a high-pitched voice. "We'll naturally do what we can to help you—the Kerner family have been some of our best clients. But we're anxious to avoid any negative publicity. I mean, it was hardly our fault what happened, and it certainly wouldn't do our reputation any good if the word got out that on one of our tours—"

"All I want," I said, "is a list of the other people that were on that excursion package with Mr. Kerner."

His facial muscles went stiff. "I'm afraid I can't give you that information. It would violate our clients' trust."

"Why? You think one of them killed him?"

What was left of his vacation tan went a few shades paler. "Certainly not!" he said.

"Then what's the problem? Or is a travel agent like a priest, you're sworn to keep the secrets of the confessional?"

Now he flushed. "There's no need to be sarcastic. I'm just doing my job."

"One of your best clients has been murdered while on a vacation trip that you set up. I'd think you'd want to help."

"I do," he said, "and I'll tell you what I can. But I can't release that list to you."

"In fairness to our other clients," Janice Futterman added.

"I just don't want negative publicity." He stuck his little jaw out bravely.

"Well, I could get a subpoena," I bluffed. I knew damn well no judge would sign a subpoena, especially not for a private detective and especially not when the crime had occurred in another country, but I was betting Josh didn't. "Or maybe it'd be easier if I just called up my friend Ed Stahl at the *Plain Dealer*— and have him come over and ask you why you're being so uncooperative. He'd probably love to do a column on it."

He puffed himself up, his Adam's apple working double-time under his second chin. I thought I discerned some muscle tone under the flab—maybe Josh had been a pretty good physical specimen before too much home cooking and too many years away from the gym took their toll on him. "That's not fair."

"Fair is in baseball, Mr. Borgenecht. This is real life." I smiled at him. "So? What do you think?"

He pursed his lips in a peculiarly prissy fashion. "I think you're not a very nice person, Mr. Jacovich."

I held my hands up in a kind of mea culpa. "Just doing *my* job," I said.

I'd leaned on him harder than I'd intended, but I can't stand officious, self-important people who go through life being obstructionist just because they can. Who'd rather just say no than think about it. Who get off on making things just a little bit tougher for everyone else. And who, like Josh, cave in completely when anyone stands up to them.

It was two thirty in the afternoon, so when he put on his coat and left after a few more minutes I assumed he wasn't going out for lunch. He seemed too upset, anyway. I didn't have much sympathy for him. Everybody needs an afternoon off once in a while, and when you're the boss you get to take them.

Janice Futterman and I took over his office. She sat in his chair with a printout of Joel Kerner's covacationers on the excursion package to San Carlos, rattling off the Cliff Notes on their biographies while I made rapid squiggles in my notebook that I'd probably be hard-pressed to read later that evening. They don't pay me for penmanship.

"The Altmans are a nice young couple," she said, sounding like a docent guiding a tour through a two-hundred-year-old cemetery. "Jay and Hillary. I think this might even have been their honeymoon—if people still do that." She tried to stifle a girlish giggle. "They even came in together to book—you don't see that much anymore. Mr. Lipsky is a professor of business and economics at Cleveland State. Um, Dalma Levine and Teri Levine are mother and daughter—they live in Shaker Heights, just off Fairmount Boulevard. Harry Channock is an executive with Republic Oil."

The little recitation took about fifteen minutes and didn't get much more interesting. I took dutiful notes anyway. When she was through I said, "Are all these people steady clients, like the Kerners?"

"Mr. Channock is, certainly. And the Levines. The others I'm not sure of—except the Altman couple. I know they were new."

"And why would they all want to go to San Carlos?" Her eyebrows arched. "As opposed to Jamaica, say, or the Virgin Islands?" I added.

She winked knowingly. "It's a bargain vacation. Except for the shopping, you can get the same thing in San Carlos as in Jamaica for half the price. Nice hotel, nice beach, balmy temperatures, tropical moon, the whole mishegas. And the San Carlos Inn is actually owned by a corporation here in Ohio—Tropic Inns, it's called, out of Akron. And you know how Clevelanders are, always wanting to give their business to locals."

I reached over for a copy of the printout. "I know how Cleve-landers are. Thanks, Ms. Futterman. You've been very helpful. I can't say as much for your boss."

"Don't think too badly of Josh," she said.

"Why not?"

"Can I be honest with you?"

"I wouldn't have it any other way."

She took a deep breath, her ample bosom rising and falling. She glanced at the door to make sure Josh wasn't coming back in. Then she said, "This is Josh's last shot at making something of himself. His first business was a small ad agency that did direct-response marketing—you know, like those commercials for old records you see on TV and you're supposed to call an eight-hundred number. It went out of business after eighteen months. The second one was a gift shop he opened on Larchmere, and that went under in less than a year. He bought some downtown real estate and now that's looking shaky. His mother keeps fi-nancing his business ideas and he keeps running them to the ground. He was a hotshot quarterback when he went to high school—Shaker High, actually—but that was a long time ago, and ever since then whatever he's touched has shriveled up and died on him. So you can't blame him if he gets nervous some-times."

"I get nervous too," I told her. "When someone commits a murder and gets away with it."

"Oh dear," she said, looking nervously toward the door as if afraid Josh Borgenecht would return and kick her out of his chair. "This has been very hard on everyone here. I mean, someone you know getting killed like that." She rose, pushing her glasses up on her nose with one finger. "Nothing personal, Mr. Jacovich, but I think it'd be better if you didn't come back here again. I know you'll understand." She stood looking down at me with the Eif-fel Tower poster behind her.

I put my notebook back in my pocket and got to my feet. "We'll always have Paris," I said.

CHAPTER THREE

Republic Oil Company was listed in the telephone directory as being in the industrial section of the Flats, just five blocks from my own office. Since the day was winding down and it was on my route, I figured I'd stop by there on my way back. I'd never heard of Republic Oil, never gassed up in one of their service stations, if indeed they had any, so my curiosity was piqued.

The building was probably ninety years old, a dusty reddish-brown stone construction on the side of an embankment overlooking the Cuyahoga that looked in imminent danger of toppling off its foundation and crashing into the water. There wasn't much of a view across the river, unless you happen to think mountains of slag and iron ore are scenic.

Since the vintage elevator looked none too trustworthy, I climbed the stairs to the top floor. The pattern on the worn linoleum was probably one they stopped making somewhere around 1952, about the same year the walls had last been painted. The stairwell smelled of mice and mildew.

Four offices occupied the third floor, but only one seemed to be in use. The gilt letters spelling out REPUBLIC OIL on the frosted glass pane seemed at least a half century newer than the door itself. I turned the knob and went in.

It was a one-room office, no bigger than my living room, painted an institutional dirty cream. A slightly battered Venetian blind was half-open over the single window, admitting the meager light from the gray sky. Geological maps affixed to the wall with yellowing transparent tape were peppered with colored push-pins, most of them in the area of South America. The heat emanating from the clanking radiator made the room stuffy and close. The only artificial light came from a single gooseneck lamp, which cast a pool of buttery illumination over the disarray of papers and charts on the desk. On a rusting metal stand under the window was an improbably bright red IBM Selectric II. Someone here was even less computer-literate than I.

The man behind the desk clutched a telephone to his ear with age-spotted hands, and he cast a startled but not displeased look at me when I walked in. He was doing a lot more listening than talking, and he wigwagged his fingers at me that he'd be off the phone momentarily and I was to wait. I looked around. The only unoccupied seat was a fragile-looking faded green canvas director's chair with a wooden frame. A defensive lineman in high school and at Kent State, I'm no lightweight; I opted to remain standing.

I estimated him to be in his late sixties. He was in white rayon shirtsleeves and a tie that defined nondescript, and his pleated trousers were held up several inches above his navel by baby blue suspenders to cover his comfortable paunch. The suntan probably acquired ten weeks earlier in San Carlos had faded to a jaundiced yellow. He'd combed a few strands of white hair across a freckled scalp, and his teeth were whiter and more even than nature could make them; they looked as if he'd bought them out of the kind of mail-order catalogue that also featured whimsical dish towels embroidered with geese, barbecue aprons that beseech you to kiss the cook, and battery-powered door chimes that play "Jesu Joy of Man's Desiring."

He finally finished his conversation, put the receiver back in its cradle, and looked at me with hope and smiling uncertainty. "What can I do you for?" he said. I hadn't heard that one in twenty years.

Introducing myself, I handed him one of my business cards, which he scrutinized as if it were one of the Dead Sea Scrolls.

"Are you Mr. Charnock?"

"That's what it says on my driver's license." A comedian-in-training. " 'Milan Security,' " he read aloud from my card. "Are you here to sell me a security system?" He gestured around the mean little office. "What do I need with a security system? What's there in here anybody besides a junk dealer would steal?"

"I'm not here to sell you anything. I'm a private investigator."

"Sam Spade, huh?"

I ignored that. I had long ago tired of such remarks. I'll bet when an attorney tells someone his profession, people don't say, "F. Lee Bailey, huh?"

I said, "I'm inquiring into the death of Joel Kerner, who was killed in San Carlos when you were there a couple months ago."

He frowned. "Oh, yeah. That was an awful thing. I don't know if I'll ever get over that. A dirty shame." He sighed. "I guess if you live long enough, you experience everything—but who could imagine something like that? It cocked up my vacation, I'll tell you that much." His eyes met mine and he suddenly sobered. "I'm sorry, that was pretty insensitive. Sometimes you don't know exactly what to say. . . ."

"That's all right," I assured him. "Did you know Joel Kerner well?"

"How well can you get to know someone in four days?"

"Did you talk to him at all?"

"Thirty-two people on a week-long excursion, it'd be pretty hard not to talk. Yeah, sure. We even had a drink one evening."

"You remember what you discussed?"

He raised his eyebrows, and deep horizontal furrows appeared on his high forehead. "Nothing momentous. He talked about cars—he had a Porsche, he told me—and women. I talked about my granddaughter and my ulcer." He waved at the chair. "Sit down, for Christ's sake, you make me nervous looming over me like that."

"I hope I don't bust your chair," I said, and lowered myself into it gingerly. The wooden frame gave an ominous creak. "Did Mr. Kerner seem nervous to you? Or anxious?"

He laughed. "I don't know what he was usually like, so how could I tell if he was nervous? He seemed okay to me. A little uptight, maybe, but he was a lawyer. That's part of the job description."

"How about his relationships with the rest of the tour group?"

He made a clucking noise in the back of his nose; I think he was trying to clear his sinuses. "Listen, my friend. I'm sixty-seven years old. My wife died three years ago and this was the first vacation I ever took alone in my life. Beautiful beaches, big white moon, pretty young girls with no tan lines running around in thong bikinis. You can just imagine how much attention I paid to Joel Kerner." He smiled sadly. "Who knew somebody was going to kill him?"

"Anything you can think of that was unusual or out-of-the-way? No matter how small. Any arguments with anybody?"

He screwed up his face, thinking. "There was some little girlie on the tour he was kind of putting the moves on."

"You remember her name?"

"I wouldn't even remember *his* name if he hadn't gotten killed."

"Did it come to anything?"

"How should I know? Do I look like I peek at keyholes?"

"What's your educated guess?"

"My guess is that they never got around to it, but that was because the girl had her mother along, and the old lady watched her like she was the Crown Jewels." He scratched his head, his fingernails leaving white furrows in his bare scalp. "Go figure. You save up your money to go to one of the most romantic places in the world. There's only two reasons to do that—one is to find romance and the other one is you bring it with you. So what does this girlie do? She schleps her mother along!"

"How about the rest of the group? No personality conflicts with Kerner?"

"No, if you're not counting the girl's mother. The way she fussed over her and demanded her attention, you'd think the kid was fifteen instead of in her late thirties."

"They argued? Joel Kerner and the mother, I mean?"

"Not that I saw. But I could tell Momma was pissed off at him. If looks could kill . . ." He winced. "Jesus, another foot in my mouth. I'm sorry—I've never been this close to a murder before."

"Don't worry about it," I said.

He cast a meaningful glance at his wristwatch. "As charming as this has been, my friend, I gotta get on the phone and raise some money. If I don't raise money, I don't make money. You wouldn't be interested in investing six hundred thousand dollars in a Venezuelan oil-drilling operation, would you?"

"Not this week, Mr. Channock. I'm a little short."

"My luck," he said to whichever god it was that lived just above the ceiling.

"Just a minute more, and then I'll be on my way. Where were you when Joel Kerner was killed?"

"What, I'm a suspect now? Me? A grandfather? I don't remember where I was, as a matter of fact. I remember where I was when I heard about it—having breakfast and reading the paper in the coffee shop. But he got killed early in the morning, I think. So I must've still been in bed."

"Was anybody with you?"

He couldn't quite suppress the laughter. "From your mouth to God's ear," he said.

I drove the few short blocks to my office and headed up the stairs. The firm on the first floor, which had been there for eighteen years before I bought the building, manufactures and sells ornamental wrought iron gates and window grilles, and they were banging away happily. I wasn't yet comfortable in the role of landlord—I take it personally when they bitch about a leaky faucet or a loose window that lets in the gusts of winter. But now, whenever I make a mortgage payment I feel as if I'm investing in myself.

My other tenant, the surgical supply company across the hall from me on the second floor, had closed up fairly early, so I had the entire floor to myself. Big deal, like I was going to do something I didn't want anyone else to see. I unlocked the wrought-iron security door my downstairs tenants had installed for me, opened the two locks on the inner door, which was made of two-inch-thick oak, and went inside.

I hadn't left any lights on, but as I let myself in, the enormous windows that looked out onto the river provided all the illumination I needed in the spacious, high-ceilinged room. I hung up my coat in the little closet, went across to the den-size refrigerator built to look like an old-fashioned safe, and pulled out a can of Stroh's. I took it back to my desk and sat down, switching on the lamp.

The light on my answering machine was blinking, and I pushed the play button. Two of the calls were hang-ups, resulting in a recorded message from the operator telling me what to do if I'd like to make a call. The third was from Patrice Kerner. I called her at the office but her secretary said she'd left for the day. I asked if I could make an appointment but was told I had to talk to Ms. Kerner in person.

Round and round we go, I thought.

I had lucked out with Harry Channock, but I knew that most people who worked for a living couldn't very well be bothered at their places of business, so I took a chance and tried to set some interviews for that evening, since I didn't have anything else to do.

Who am I kidding? I never have anything else to do.

Lois Scaravelli, one of Joel Kerner's ex-girlfriends, wasn't in and, wonder of wonders in our age of electronic technology, didn't have an answering machine or voice mail, so I couldn't leave a message. The other one, Patt-with-two-*t*s Wolfe, had just gotten home from work when I called. After I told her what I wanted she suggested I come by at eight o'clock.

I finished my beer and shut the office. With a couple of hours to kill, I figured I might as well go home.

Home is a rambling apartment at the top of Cedar Hill where Cedar Road triangulates with Fairmount Boulevard in the eastern suburb of Cleveland Heights. It's right across the street from Russo's market, and just up the block from Nighttown, an Irish pub-style restaurant that's one of the few places on the east side that serves dinner past ten o'clock at night. I'm three minutes from University Circle, ten minutes from downtown and my office, and twenty minutes from where my two sons, Milan and Stephen, live with their mother and her boyfriend. Cleveland has long styled itself "the best location in the nation," and I think I'm in the best location in Cleveland. The most convenient, anyway.

There wasn't much in the pantry or the refrigerator by way of dinner. Since I'd enjoyed pasta for lunch at Piccolo Mondo's, I didn't feel like having it again, so I fried up some hard salami and onions, slapped it between two thick slices of Orlando Ciabatta bread slathered with hearty brown Stadium mustard, both locally produced, and ate it at my kitchen table, washing it down with another Stroh's while I read the latest *Newsweek*. Just to make it feel not quite so lonesome, I put on a CD of Tony Bennett singing to the accompaniment of Bill Evans's piano. The old stuff is the best, I think—Irving Berlin and Cy Coleman, the great songs of an era I was too young to have enjoyed the first time around.

After dinner I brushed my teeth and rinsed my mouth with Listerine—eating salami and onions right before going to meet a witness probably wasn't such a good idea. Then I drove ten minutes to South Euclid and the duplex where Patt Wolfe lived.

It was on a side street and backed into a pretty stand of woods which, if viewed from the right angle, could make you forget you were in the middle of one of America's largest urban areas. The wide front porch served two front doors; Wolfe's was the one on the right. I pushed her bell and she appeared after the first ring.

More than a foot shorter than I—about five one in the pink and white running shoes that matched her designer sweatsuit—Patt Wolfe was probably flirting with forty. She was pretty in an unspectacular way, and her dark curly hair was worn a little too long for her age and stature. But she had a great smile and the kind of warm personality that probably won friends easily. She had set out a plate of cookies made with chopped macadamia nuts and hunks of white chocolate, which was enough to win my heart, and she poured us each a cup of strong coffee from a thermal carafe before we sat down in her small comfortable living room to talk.

"Of course I was shocked," she said. "And very sad. Joel and I hadn't been—dating—for almost a year, but we stayed friends, we stayed in touch. And when someone has been in your life like that and then . . ." She rubbed her upper arms as if she was cold. "That's a first for me," she said ruefully. "All the other men I've slept with are still alive."

Goose bumps sprang up on my arms too. "When was the last time you saw Joel?"

"Three weeks before he died—maybe less. I could look up the exact date if you need it. We had lunch at Johnny's Downtown. He was all excited about his upcoming trip to San Carlos. He was pretty much a workaholic, and this was the first vacation he'd taken in a long time." She drank some coffee, using both hands to lift the cup. "He certainly never took one with me. Other than a weekend here and there, you know, to Chicago or something."

"How long were you together? As a couple, I mean."

"Less than a year." She sighed. "For singles in this day and age, that's not a bad run."

"I know," I said, and reached guiltily for a second cookie. "I don't mean to pry, but why did you break up?"

She waved her hands in front of her. "Who knows? Things like that just end. It wasn't as if we were in love. I mean, it was exciting for me to be with someone who was so well known around town. Or whose father was so well known, I guess. It was just . . . good times. When the times got to be not so good, we stopped."

Been there, done that, I thought, and wondered why the times had gotten to be not so good. "While you were together, or even afterwards, did he ever mention anyone who had a grudge against him?"

She bit her lip. "Joel had a certain—well, some people might call it arrogance. I always thought of it as self-confidence. And I found it attractive, obviously. I'm sure there were those who didn't." She anticipated my next question. "But I don't know who they might be."

"Other ex-girlfriends?"

"Look," she said. "Joel got killed fifteen hundred miles away. Isn't that where you should be asking your questions?" She took a cookie from the plate and bit off a tiny crescent. "Sorry. I didn't mean to tell you how to do your job."

"That's okay. What about his business? His practice, I mean."

She nibbled delicately on the end of one long tapered red finger-nail, which was probably acrylic. "When he won a case, usually the only ones mad at him were insurance companies."

"And when he lost?"

"He didn't lose very often. At least when he did, he didn't talk about it."

"Are you an attorney also, Ms. Wolfe?"

"Call me Patt, please. Everybody does. No, I'm a regional sales manager with a machine-tool firm out in Solon."

"How did you meet Joel Kerner?"

"At a singles dance at our temple."

"Did he go to that sort of thing often?"

"I don't know. That's the only time I ever saw him at one of them."

"You go a lot, then?"

"When I'm—between involvements, yes. It beats hell out of hanging out in bars." She put her hands to the sides of her head as if she was in pain.

"I'm sorry," I said. "I know this is hard for you."

She took her hands down and folded them in her lap. "Sure it is—but it's not like I'm exactly grief-stricken. I'm sad, sure. Joel was a friend. But I did my crying ten weeks ago. Besides, we hadn't been an item for a long time, and even though I miss the high-profile parties, I've gone on with my life."

I decided to go ahead and pry. "Your breakup was amicable, then?"

"As amicable as those things get. We didn't have a major fight or anything. It's just that—well, he got very moody and sullen toward the end. Difficult to be with. It was as if he was angry about something he wouldn't talk about. I finally got tired of the moods. A relationship is supposed to enhance your life, not be a pain in the ass."

"There wasn't another woman in the picture?"

"If there was, I sure didn't know about it." She tossed her hair away from her face. "More coffee?"

"No thanks," I said.

She poured some for herself from the carafe. "Whatever was

going on with Joel, I don't know about." Her eyes turned sad. "We weren't that close anymore."

"But you had lunch with him three weeks before he went to San Carlos?"

"I have lunch with a lot of people," she said. "But I don't know whether there's anyone who wants to kill them."

"I guess not." Unable to stop myself, I took one more cookie. Then I stood up. "I appreciate your seeing me," I told her.

She stood up too. The top of her head came to just below my chin. "I wish I could have been more helpful."

"Just one more question?"

She had to look up at me.

"What's with the two *t*s?" I said.

It brought laughter back to her sad brown eyes. "I used to have just one. My college roommate was also named Pat, and we kept getting each other's messages—and sometimes each other's boyfriends. I added the second *t* to avoid confusion. My numerologist says it was a mistake, that I'd be more successful and be luckier in love if I dropped it, but that's who I am now, so . . ." She shrugged. "Two *t*s."

I smiled. "A girl can't have too many."

She smiled back, and took two more cookies and wrapped them up in a paper napkin. "Here," she said, thrusting them at me. "In case you get hungry later."

"Two Tees, you're a wonderful human being."

I put on my coat and pocketed the cookies, and she went with me to the door. "I'll tell you this," she said; she'd obviously been thinking it over and decided to share one more piece of information. "Joel was a risk taker. He'd walk around downtown at night and never even look over his shoulder. He thought he was invincible, that bad things happened to other people."

"A lot of us are like that," I said.

"Maybe it was the brown belt."

"Joel Kerner had a brown belt?"

"It's not as good as a black one, from what I understand, but he'd only been at it a short while. In tae kwon do. That's like karate."

I knew what it was—a Korean martial art that loosely translated means "kicking and punching." Marko Meglich had a black belt in tae kwon do of which he was inordinately proud. "Where was his *dojang*?"

"His what?"

"The place where he studied. Where he worked out."

"I don't know," she said. "He never mentioned it. Someplace downtown, I'd imagine."

I nodded. "You've been more helpful than you know, Ms.—"

"Patt," she corrected me.

"Patt," I agreed. "With two *t*s."

I didn't feel much like going home right away, so I cut across Green Road and wound up at the Cooker, a restaurant located in the La Place shopping center on the corner of Cedar and Richmond in Beachwood, where I had two more Stroh's and did some thinking.

A lot of people study martial arts, especially well-to-do yuppies who think it a way to be macho and fashionable and politically correct at the same time. But some take them up because they really want to be able to defend themselves in a tight spot—as if they'd need it someday. I wondered which category Joel Kerner fit.

And whether he had realized that martial arts wasn't much of a defense against a twelve-gauge shotgun.

When I got back to my apartment I could see light seeping out from beneath the door, and I heard the soft droning of the television. Disturbing, because I tend to watch my pennies and I was pretty sure I'd turned everything off before I left for Patt Wolfe's.

I paused for a moment. I don't usually walk around armed unless I think I'm going to find trouble, so there was no question of my blasting in there waving a gun like someone out of a *Lethal Weapon* movie. There was no sign of forced entry, and I didn't think I'd done anything within recent memory that would cause anyone to want to break into my apartment and wait for me with a lead pipe or an AK-47.

And if they were going to, they certainly wouldn't leave the lights on and watch television.

In for a penny, I thought, and opened the door with my key.

There was no one in the living room. I walked into the den; my older son, Milan, was sitting in my big leather chair watching the Cavs' game. Next to him on the end table were the remains of a Subway sandwich and salad, and a half-finished bottle of Snapple.

"Hey," he said, and stood up. At seventeen he was almost as tall as his old man, with a broad silhouette that plunged in a V from his wide shoulders to a slim waist. His hair, complexion, and disposition were all dark, all inherited from his Serbian mother, my former wife Lila; his younger brother Stephen had gotten his fair Slovenian looks and mild temperament from my side of the family.

"Hey." I went over to him and tried to hug him, but he moved away.

"Come on," he said.

"I haven't seen you in a week and a half," I said. "Don't I get a hug?"

He sat back down and focused on the basketball game. "You'd want a hug even if you'd just gone to Russo's for groceries."

I went back into the living room and took off my coat, pondering the truth of that. I felt happy. My divorce agreement stipulated that I get to spend a day and night with my sons every other Sunday. Of course now that Milan had a car he could pretty much call his own shots. "You spending the night?" I called over my shoulder.

"Is it okay?"

"Sure it's okay. If it's okay with your mother."

"It is."

"I hope so. Otherwise I'm the one that'll get into trouble with her." I hung my coat up in the closet, took out the wrapped cookies, and went back to the door of the den. "To what do I owe the honor?"

"I dunno."

I went into the kitchen and put the cookies on the counter, then got myself a Stroh's from the refrigerator and took it back into the den. I sat down on the slightly lumpy sofa that hardly anyone ever uses. "How's school?"

"It's okay. I miss football," he said.

"Me, too," I said. After his high school graduation, which was only a few months away, he was heading for my alma mater, Kent State University, and I knew he was worried about making the freshman team.

"Shouldn't you be studying? Don't you have a physics exam Monday?"

He nodded. "I'm taking a break tonight. I think I'm okay in it. I'll probably get a B or a C—if I'm lucky."

"How's Mr. Barr?"

He laughed. "The same," he said.

Mr. Barr had been my physics teacher at St. Clair High, too—a feisty, funny iconoclast with an Alfred E. Newman haircut who groused about the paperwork that kept him from doing the teaching he loved, and who preached ethics and morality and self-determination. He had an elaborate ham radio setup in his basement, and his kindly wife had a limitless supply of cupcakes and hard candies put by for any of his students who wanted to come over in the evening and fool with it. I'd learned a hell of a lot from him—not much physics, although I could have learned that too. After he'd had my son in class for five weeks he'd called me to tell me Milan had a greater aptitude for science than I'd ever displayed. It was just one more of the many ways in which my firstborn and I differed; my strong suits in school had been English and history and economics, where there were few absolutes.

We watched the game quietly for a while. Danny Ferry, who'd been signed by the Cavaliers for a lot of money and had spent several years trying to find the range, was on fire this season even though it was generally acknowledged that nobody was going to catch up to the Chicago Bulls again.

Milan squirmed around in his chair to face me. "You weren't a real great student in high school, were you Dad?"

"I was okay. Not so good in physics, as I'm sure Mr. Barr will tell you."

"He did tell me." He picked at the label on his Snapple bottle. "You ever cheat?"

"What do you mean?"

"On an exam. Did you ever write the answers on the back of your hand or anything?"

The hair on my arms stood up straight and did a wave, but I didn't let on. "I thought about it—especially in Barr's class. But I never did."

"That's what I figured. You're such a straight arrow."

Coming from a seventeen-year-old, I didn't know whether that was approbation or criticism. I shrugged. "It's a curse."

He subsided into a silence that might have been characterized as tense. I focused on the TV set and decided to let it go for a while.

Cavs coach Mike Fratello called a time-out and the station went to a commercial. A little bald man was having a loud conversation about carpets with a cartoon figure of himself.

Milan said, "One of the guys got hold of a copy of Barr's test."

"Oh? Who?"

He shook his head.

"How'd he get the test?"

"I don't know." He chug-a-lugged the rest of the Snapple and wiped his mouth with the back of his hand. "He said he was gonna get a few questions wrong on purpose so it wouldn't look suspicious."

I wanted a cigarette badly, but my son is a child of the nineties and disapproves of smoking. I thought about getting Patt Wolfe's cookies from the kitchen, but I didn't want to leave the room just then, didn't want to disrupt what had suddenly become a delicate balance between us.

My son cleared his throat. "He said he'd sell it to me for ten bucks."

"How do you feel about that?"

"I dunno."

"Are you asking my permission?" I said. "I won't give it to you. But I'm not going to tell you no either." His eyes got wide as he stared at me. "You're only a couple of months away from college—you can make decisions like that on your own."

"It's not like I'm going to be a physicist or anything."

"No, it isn't. It's up to you. But if you do cheat, don't tell me about it."

He shifted his butt around in the chair. "I thought you said I should tell you everything."

"I did," I said. "But if you're going to cheat on a test, you might as well cheat on me too."

A louder commercial came on for a local optician; for some inexplicable reason the guy who owned the company was dancing—or moon-walking. A middle-aged guy trying unsuccessfully to look cool. We both watched him until he finished.

"If you write your answers on the back of your hand, you might be able to fool Mr. Barr," I said. "And when you bring your A home you might even be able to fool your mom and me. The trouble is, the one whose head you'll really be messing with is the one guy you never should try to fool—yourself."

The game came back on; the Cavs got the ball and scored within twenty seconds.

"If you cheat now and get away with it, that'll make it easier for you to cheat in college," I went on. "And for the rest of your life. Some people get into the habit and cheat whenever they can. And then what've you got?"

Milan was silent for a moment. Then he leaned forward to watch the game more closely. "Okay," he said. I don't think he was talking about basketball. Obviously, the subject was closed.

I ached for him, having to make the decision that was his alone. And I was disturbed by the whole question. But I'd said what I had to say and I figured it was better to keep my mouth shut.

Climb Mount Everest, discover a cure for the common cold, hit major league pitching, become president—they're all a piece of cake. If you're looking for challenging, if you're looking for tough—try being a parent.

CHAPTER FOUR

By the time I woke up the next morning, Milan was already showered and dressed, sitting in the kitchen reading the sports section, drinking coffee that he'd brewed, and eating Lucky Charms, which I always keep on hand for when my boys visit. He raised his head and said good morning to me in his deep, silky voice, and I looked at him there, his black hair still glistening from the shower, his shoulders wide and powerful under his T-shirt, and something painful and wonderful twisted around inside of me. This nearly grown man had actually come here to ask advice of his father, to wrestle with one of the first big ethical issues of his young life, and to eat my Lucky Charms.

Behold my son, I thought, in whom I am well-pleased.

I was a little less pleased when he found Patt Wolfe's white-chocolate-chip cookies and devoured both of them as I watched helplessly.

"You're the only guy I've ever seen who has dessert after breakfast," I said.

"I needed the carbos," was his excuse.

When he left for school I filled my mug and sat down with the sports section. He didn't make bad coffee either.

I made my phone calls, took a shower, put on my camel's hair sports jacket over a reddish tie and blue shirt and headed off to begin my day; it looked as if it was going to be a long one. The sun was fisting its way through the haze, but storm clouds darkened the western sky.

Not everyone who lives in Shaker Heights is a millionaire. Dalma Levine lived in a two-story Cape Cod colonial just off Fairmount Boulevard. It was painted a quiet gray that captured some of the stingy warmth of the morning sunshine, and there were rhododendron bushes on either side of the door and a dogwood tree surrounded by a circle of bricks in the middle of the lawn. In another few weeks it would be blooming, unless we had one of our Cleveland May blizzards.

The woman who came to the door was only a shade over five feet tall, but she carried herself almost regally. She had startling white hair pulled back into a chignon, piercing dark chocolate eyes under heavy brows, and a chin like the bucket of an earthmover. She wore a straight dark skirt and a long-sleeved white blouse buttoned to the neck. At her wrists jangled a lot of jewelry, heavy gold bands and chains on the right hand, a shimmering watch of rolled gold and two other bracelets on the left. When she spoke there was the barest trace of a European accent. Her gaze was proud and level, almost penetrating.

"I have to confess I have reservations about talking to you," she said as she led me into a dark-paneled living room full of antiques. The furniture had blue and white flowered upholstery, and the floor was covered with braided rugs. "Obviously the entire incident is disturbing and distasteful, and one we wish to put behind us as quickly as possible."

"I'll only take a few minutes," I said.

She indicated a chair for me and sat down on the curving sectional sofa, spine very straight and knees and ankles tightly together. A quick glance around the room confirmed that there were no framed photographs anywhere, almost as if the people who lived there had not been born into a family but had somehow evolved through parthenogenesis. The coffee table was bare except for a large art book on the works of Ben Shahn; there would be no coffee and cookies forthcoming here.

"I'm trying to speak to everyone who was on that vacation excursion with you, Mrs. Levine. I understand that in San Carlos, Joel Kerner had been paying a good deal of attention to your daughter."

"That unfortunately is correct," she said. "Unwanted attention, I might add."

"Oh?"

"There were no other young or attractive single women booked on the tour, so I guess it was natural. But Teri wasn't interested. She certainly wasn't interested in a one-night stand or a week's fling."

"Are you sure that's all Kerner was offering?"

She raised her eyebrows. "What else could it have been?"

A lot of things, I thought, but it wouldn't have done any good to tell her what they were; Mrs. Levine was obviously a woman who was very much in love with her own mind-set. "So you didn't like him?"

"I didn't dislike him. He wasn't significant to me one way or the other. At least not while he was still alive."

"And after he was dead?"

"He became another character in a long nightmare." She took a deep breath, as if steeling herself for something. "In the first part of my life, Mr. Jacovich, tragedy and brutality and death was as normal and everyday as the sun coming up. I've spent fifty years trying to insulate myself from it, and my daughter as well. Mr. Kerner's unfortunate death churned up a lot of ugliness for me that I've tried hard to forget."

Setting her prominent jaw firmly, she pulled up the right sleeve of her blouse and jammed the gold bracelets and chains up toward the crook of her elbow so I could see the crudely tattooed blue numbers on the inside of her arm.

"I'm sorry," I said, the inanity of it echoing shamefully in my head.

"For three, nearly four years of my childhood, a day didn't pass when someone I knew or loved didn't die—often right before my eyes. By some miracle I survived. And I determined to surround myself for the rest of my life with beauty and kindness and things that were life-affirming, and to shut out everything else. So you can well understand that a murder right under our very noses is something I don't choose to dwell on."

"Of course."

"But I realize the Kerner family's need for closure, so I'm willing to speak with you about it. For a while, at least."

"I appreciate that. Were you aware of what Mr. Kerner did while he was in San Carlos? How he spent his days? Or nights?"

She pushed her jewelry back down around her wrist with more force than necessary, and her shoulders dropped very slightly. "I didn't really pay much attention. He was always in bathing trunks during the day. And I recall seeing him once with diving equipment—one of those air tanks you strap on. I suppose he went swimming and windsurfing and parasailing like everyone else did. There's not much else to do in San Carlos."

"What did you do?" I said. She didn't seem like the parasailing type.

"I brought several books with me, so I mostly sat on the terrace overlooking the Caribbean and read. I'm a little too old for strenuous recreation."

It occurred to me that she could have caught up on her reading in Shaker Heights and saved herself a lot of money, but I didn't say so. "Did your daughter swim and dive as well?"

Mrs. Levine gave a soft, put-upon sigh. "Of course. That's why she went. She's a normal young woman and she does things people her age like to do."

Like taking your mother along on a tropical vacation, I thought. "What were Mr. Kerner's relationships with the other people on the tour? Was he particularly close with any of them?"

She shook her head gravely. "It was a small group," she said. "Thirty or so. Most of us were older, except for one newlywed couple who kept pretty much to themselves, as you might imagine. I think Mr. Kerner shared his time with all of them equally." She raised her head, facing defiantly into a nonexistent wind. "Except for my daughter Teri, of course, and he had an entire agenda where she was concerned."

"What about you, Mrs. Levine? Did he spend much time with you?"

She cocked her head at me as if the entire idea were out of the question. "If you were trying to take advantage of a young woman, would you make friends with her mother?"

"Isn't 'take advantage' kind of strong? Maybe he was just being friendly."

"You must be a very kind man, Mr. Jacovich, because you don't look like a stupid one." She shook her head resolutely. "I'm old enough to recognize an attempted seduction when I see one. Mr. Kerner knew I was on to him from the very first day, and he gave me a wide berth."

"Did you and your daughter know Joel Kerner before the tour?"

Her head quivered slightly. "I knew *of* him. Rather I knew of his father." She cleared her throat politely. "My late husband was a vice president of the International Ladies' Garment Workers local. Everyone in the labor movement knows of Joel Kerner."

"So Mr. Levine knew him?"

"I didn't say he knew him!" she snapped. "I said that we were aware of him."

"I'd like to speak to your daughter too, Mrs. Levine."

The dark brown eyes became obsidian. "I hardly think she can add anything to what I've already told you."

"You never know," I said. "Everybody remembers things just a little bit differently, from their own personal perspective."

"Teri and I are very close. We usually share a perspective."

"I'd like to talk to her just the same."

She stood up; for a short woman, she bore an unsettling resemblance to the Statue of Liberty. "As you wish, Mr. Jacovich."

Getting hurriedly to my feet, I said, "Where can I reach her during the day?"

"I think I'd prefer it if you spoke to her in my presence," Dalma Levine said. "You may call her here after six o'clock." I thought I noticed a malicious flash behind her eyes as she added, "If she'll talk to you."

"Any reason why she wouldn't?"

She lifted one bony shoulder. "We'll have to see."

I stopped in at Jack's Deli on Green Road across from Heinen's supermarket and had my favorite breakfast, matzo brie, looking at the Hirschfeld caricatures of famous stars on the wallpaper while I ate and trying to see how many I could name. On the way out I got some corned beef to take home with me so the cupboard wouldn't be bare the next time I had to scare up dinner. I also bought a piece of halvah; I love the stuff—I'd eat it every day if I wasn't afraid of turning into a six-hundred-pound gorilla.

I used the pay phone in Jack's vestibule to call Joel Kerner at his office, but his secretary told me he hadn't been coming in lately. "He's had a tragedy in the family, you know," she said in hushed, respectful tones.

I called his house and got his voice mail, but I didn't leave a message. Since I was so close anyway, I decided to drive over there and see if he was home but for some reason wasn't answering his phone. After all, I figured, everybody's got to be somewhere.

And if one has to be somewhere, it might as well be on South Park. The homes are as close to mansions as you can find these days, set far back from the street on gently rising lawns. I looked through a locked wrought iron gate at the Kerner's sprawling Tudor. The lawn was about the size of a football field, and tentative stirrings of spring had turned it emerald. An early robin, my first sighting of the year, was stutter-stepping along the grass looking for a worm breakfast, oblivious to both the chill of the morning and to the noisy power mower being run not thirty feet away by a cheerful-looking Asian man wearing a floppy fishing hat.

A wrought iron fence about eight feet high ran along the perimeter of the property. It wasn't high enough to keep out anyone who was really motivated to get in, but the electric wire along the top would probably discourage any unwanted visitors very nicely.

The last setup I'd seen with security like this had belonged to a top-level mob capo living in the hills just above Youngstown. It made me wonder a little.

I pulled into the driveway, stopping with the nose of my car against the gate, and watched a video camera swivel in my direction. A red light on the brick gatepost switched on, and I rolled down the window so I could communicate with the little black speaker box.

"Yes?" a disembodied voice crackled.

"My name is Milan Jacovich," I said. "I'm a private investigator, working for Ms. Patrice Kerner. I don't have an appointment, but I was wondering if I could speak with Mr. or Mrs. Kerner for a few minutes."

"Hang on," the voice said, and the red light went off.

I hung on. The power mower's drone bounced off the trees that surrounded the house as it decimated the tall spring grass and dandelions in its path. Cleveland is known locally as the Forest City because of its many trees—the nickname even appears on the red-white-and-blue signs designating its corporate limits—and behind the main house it appeared as if Joel Kerner had his own personal forest, a densely wooded stand of white oak and catalpa and sugar maple.

When the red light came on again the voice said, "Come up to the front door," and the gate swung inward.

I started up the long arc of driveway, glancing at my odometer; it had gained more than an eighth of a mile when I pulled up at the portico of the big house. The electronic gate clanged shut behind me as I went. To the right and behind the house was a four-car garage; a late-model BMW sedan was parked in front of one of the bays. Beneath the portico was a two-year-old Lincoln Town Car in which a big battered-looking man sat. He was wearing mirrored sunglasses and a leather bomber jacket over an Irish cable-knit sweater, and his cheeks showed the ravages of childhood acne. He looked like that character in all the old western movies—the obscure member of the Jesse James gang whose name we never know, who always gets killed first and the audience doesn't care. He gave me a long, hard look as I got out of my car and approached the front steps.

I returned it. I'm no slouch at hard looks myself.

When I rang the bell, the door was opened immediately by a wide, weathered man in his early sixties wearing an open-collared dress shirt with the sleeves rolled up to reveal a tattoo of an American eagle on a forearm the size of a gas main. The collar was turned up in the back so it looked like the kind Queen Elizabeth the first wore to have her portrait painted. His gunmetal hair was worn in a brush cut, and his face looked like a bombed-out city. A vertical white scar bisected his left eyebrow and there was another scar at one corner of his mouth. His nose had been flattened so that the tip sprang up almost unexpectedly above his upper lip. I noticed that the knuckles of his right hand were also flat and irregular. He looked a lot more like a boxer who had engaged in about ten fights too many than like a butler.

"You got some identification?" he said in a voice that was almost a gargle. It was the same voice I'd heard over the intercom at the gate, but then I'd assumed its scratchy quality was caused by defective electronics. I revised my estimate—it was the guy's throat that was defective.

I produced a photostat of my business license. He looked at it carefully. "Anything with your pitcher on it?"

Annoyed, I handed over my driver's license, which he examined closely, looking first at my photograph and then at my face. Apparently my bona fides were satisfactory, because he handed them back to me and treated me to a smile as crooked as the rest of his face.

"Lift 'em," he said with a gesture.

"Are you kidding? Come on!"

"Lift 'em or leave," he said. "I could give a shit less."

Now several degrees beyond irritated, I raised my arms and he patted me down expertly and none too gently. I was carrying nothing more lethal than my keys.

"Just a minute," he said, and disappeared up the sweeping staircase, leaving me to guess from what employment agency the Kerners hired their house servants. I couldn't help wonder why an attorney like Joel Kerner Sr. needed this kind of security in his own home, but I didn't think I would find out by asking my broken-nosed friend.

The central entrance hall was enormous. A domed ceiling soared two stories above, tiny fragments of quartz glittering in the rough stucco finish. To my right was a dining room with a table big enough to comfortably accommodate the diners at the Last Supper.

After about two minutes, Elaine Kerner descended the stairs. She was what some might call a handsome woman. Taller than her daughter, with silver-streaked hair permed into a curly cloud around her head, she wore a simple shirtwaist dress and no makeup. There were dark circles beneath her eyes.

"Of course, Mr. Jacovich," she said when I'd introduced myself. "Patrice told us she'd engaged you. I hope you won't be offended if I say my husband and I strongly disapprove."

"Why is that, Mrs. Kerner?"

She lowered her eyes. "Wounds never have a chance to heal when you pick at them."

She led me into a big antique-filled living room. There were large picture windows on either side of the white brick fireplace, but the drapes were tightly drawn. "I wish you had called first and let us know you were coming," she said.

I didn't tell her that I had called and no one had answered. Instead I said, "I'd really like to speak to both you and your husband, if that's possible."

She blinked rapidly. "Why don't you make yourself comfortable, then? I'll tell him you're here—but he's with somebody, now. I don't guarantee he'll want to see you."

She disappeared, leaving me standing there feeling too large for the room. I sat down in a high wing chair, which was several degrees from making myself comfortable, and looked around at the antique globe, the worn but expensive furniture, the cherry-wood music stand, the mahogany grand piano displaying photographs of both the Kerner children at various ages from childhood through the present. Since I had nothing better to do, I counted them; there were eight of Joel and six of Patrice, plus two featuring both of them. One had been taken when they were children, approximately eight and eleven, with a solemn-eyed Patrice sitting at that same piano and Joel standing at her side holding a violin, stiff and little-boy-like in a suit and tie. The other, with both of them in preppie casual wear, I estimated was taken about ten years later.

A stately old grandfather clock stood against one wall, and I was very cognizant of its ticking, as the moments of my own life tumbled by while I waited in someone else's empty living room. I watched as its spear-shaped minute hand moved from 11:14 to 11:21, and then I heard several pairs of feet coming down the stairs.

Joel Kerner Sr. was about seventy, but he looked ten years older; his clothes—khaki pants and a dark green cardigan over a black polo shirt—hung loosely on what once must have been a robust frame, and the skin on his face seemed slack over a firm jaw. He had a large, noble head covered with white hair that looked as if it had not yet been brushed this morning, and the unshaven white stubble on his cheeks and chin added to the impression of a tired, broken old man.

What scared me most were his eyes—watery blue and totally without light or sparkle. Dead eyes, like a basking snake's.

The man with him was about ten years younger. Short and bull-necked, with a deep tan that could only have come from a sunlamp and a brown suit that was right off the rack at Value City, he had a bushy mustache and wore glasses with plastic rims and a toupee so patently false-looking I found it hard not to laugh. The front of it had been styled into the kind of exaggerated upswept pompadour favored by old-time country singers.

"Hello, Mr. Jacovich," Kerner said as if each word caused him physical pain. "This is a friend of mine, Pat Stranahan."

Stranahan nodded his head at me; the toupee didn't move at all. It looked as though it had been molded out of vinyl. Then he looked at Kerner.

"Two months, Joel," he said. There was the barest lilt of a brogue in his speech. "That's at the outside. There are people I have to answer to, you know."

"I'll do what I can," Kerner answered.

"You'll have to do better than that. Two months is giving you a break."

Kerner nodded, his wide shoulders slumped.

"We understand each other then, do we, Joel?"

"We understand each other, Patrick."

Stranahan nodded in a self-satisfied way, then turned to kiss Mrs. Kerner on the cheek. "Lainie, darlin'," he said. "No matter what else happens, remember—I love *you*."

He turned and went out the door. After a moment the Lincoln's big engine could be heard turning over, and then the sound receded.

Joel Kerner gave me a limp, diffident handshake and then sank heavily onto the sofa with a wheeze. The soft cushions nearly engulfed him. His wife stood behind him with her hands clasped at her waist, as if she was about to toss off a Wagnerian aria.

"Jacovich," he said. "What is that, Slovenian or Croatian?"

"Slovenian," I said."

His hand flopped loosely on his wrist. "When you're involved in the labor movement in this town, half the people you know have Eastern European backgrounds. You get to know the names. Slovenian, Croatian, Polish." He had a wonderful rumbly baritone.

"I'm very sorry about your son," I said. "I know how hard this must be for you."

"Thank you—but I wish Patrice hadn't come to you," he said. "Poking around in the ashes of my son's life isn't going to bring him back. It's not going to do any good at all."

"Your daughter thinks it might."

He shook his massive head. "She wants it to, and she thinks wanting will make it so. It's a waste of time and money, you ask me. What happened was a robbery that got out of hand, that's all. For all its luxury hotels and fancy prices, San Carlos is the Third World. Joel probably shouldn't have gone out on the beach by himself so early. . . ." His voice quivered and threatened to break, and he lowered his chin and spoke into his chest.

"I'll make you a proposition, Mr. Jacovich. Whatever Patrice is paying you to look into Joel's death, I'll pay you double not to. How does that sound?"

"Unethical, sir—and you know it. I have a contract with your daughter."

He snorted. "I make and break contracts all the time," he said, a harsh edge to his voice. He raised his head and filled his chest with air. "I'm good at it."

"I'll bet you are. But I'd think you'd want every effort made to find out the truth about what happened that morning."

"What I want," he said, "is to heal. We've done our grieving—now it's time to go on about the business of our own lives." He wagged his head back and forth. "God only knows how you're supposed to do that. To outlive your own child—you can't imagine."

With two sons of my own, I didn't *want* to imagine.

Joel Kerner put a hand over his eyes as if the sun was too bright, although the shades were drawn and the light from a floor lamp near the window was the only illumination. "You have so many dreams for your kids," he said, his voice hollow. "It's the only reason for having kids, I think—the dreams."

The grandfather clock ticked some more in the overstuffed silence.

"Your son was a personal injury lawyer, wasn't he?" I said.

Kerner nodded, uncovering his eyes. "It wasn't the branch of law I would have picked for him, but he knew what he wanted, right out of law school. He was a fine attorney. He had a way of getting people to do whatever he wanted, and that included judges and insurance companies. The sky was the limit for him."

"Is there any chance—no matter how remote—that what happened to him might have had something to do with his business?"

"I don't see how," Mrs. Kerner offered tentatively from behind the sofa.

Her husband glanced over his shoulder at her with what might have been annoyance before he answered. "Not in that kind of practice. In tort law, if a client thinks he didn't get enough money and blames his lawyer, he might throw a punch in the parking lot outside the courthouse. If he were really pissed off he might take a baseball bat or a crowbar to the attorney's car. Not that anything like that ever happened to Joel," he added. "His clients were blue-collar people for the most part. I hardly think any of them would be sophisticated enough to follow him down to a place like San Carlos and . . ." He pressed his lips close together.

"Did he gamble?"

"Not that I knew about. Oh, everybody bets on the Super Bowl and things like that, but Joel was too careful with his money to waste it gambling. Gambling is a sucker's game."

"He bought Super Lotto tickets sometimes," Mrs. Kerner said. "But only when the jackpot was over twelve million dollars."

Her husband threw another irritated look over his shoulder. "Not exactly what they call a high roller."

"What about his personal life?" I said.

Kerner raised his head to look at me. "What about it?"

"He was single. He dated a lot of women. Maybe someone he broke up with stayed angry."

The old man stood up and jammed his hands into the back pockets of his khakis, thrusting his head and shoulders forward. "And they're all very nice, decent women too," he said, starting to move across the room toward me, "just in case you're building a fatal-attraction scenario in your head. You're not wearing a wedding ring, Mr. Jacovich. Are *you* single?"

"Divorced."

"How long?"

"Ten years or so."

Mrs. Kerner went over to the window, turning her back on us and facing the drapes as if she was looking outside.

"Do you date a lot of women?" Kerner demanded.

"Not a lot."

"More than one?"

"At the moment, not any."

He advanced on me, and for a moment I could imagine him in his heyday, wearing a three-piece suit of litigation gray, the old fire in his eyes and in his belly, the sheer force of his personality scorching his adversaries across the bargaining table. He removed his right hand from his pocket and jabbed an index finger at me. "When you break off a relationship with a woman, does she get homicidal about it?"

"Of course not, but—"

"Of course not—*no* buts! So on behalf of Joel's friends—his women friends—I'm insulted by your suggestion." He drew himself up to his full height.

"It wasn't a suggestion, Mr. Kerner. It was a question that had to be asked."

He shook his head resolutely. "None of this has to be asked. It has to be put away, put behind us."

"Is that the way you feel too, Mrs. Kerner?"

When she turned to look at me, I could see the whites of her eyes all around her pupils. She drew a breath as if she was about to say something.

"Obviously I speak for both of us," her husband cut in.

He hovered over me for a moment longer, his jaw thrust aggressively forward, a small fleck of saliva at one corner of his lower lip. Then all at once he seemed to deflate, and he turned and sat heavily back down on the sofa. He put his hands on his thighs, fingers splayed, and looked at them as if he'd never seen them before. The right one twitched a little, and he made a concerted effort to hold it still, looking up at me to see whether I had noticed.

"This has just taken the guts out of me," he rasped.

"I'm sorry to have bothered you," I said, moving toward the door. "Thanks for seeing me. I don't want to intrude any more."

"So what's the deal, Jacovich?" he asked huskily, leaning forward. "Will you give this up so we can start to heal, Joel's mother and me? Let us go on somehow, the best way we can?" He cleared his throat. "Will you in the name of God be kind?"

"I always try to be kind, Mr. Kerner."

"Then you'll accept my deal? Double pay for no work?"

I tried to say it gently. "I can't do that. Your daughter hired me, and I'll stay on the job until she fires me. It's just how it works—it's how I am."

His smile was bitter. "A tough guy, huh? I know about tough guys. I used to be one myself." He was silent for a few seconds.

The good-byes were awkward. When I'd reversed the procedure of navigating down the driveway and getting out through the electronic gate, I drove down South Park past homes even bigger than the Kerners', until it turned into Fairhill Road and plunged down the hill into Cleveland.

When I got to my office I put the corned beef into the little refrigerator and hoped I'd remember to take it home that evening. Then I sat down at my desk, took a packet of three-by-five cards from the drawer, and started filling them in, one for everybody I'd already talked to and one for everyone I hoped would talk to me. It's a method that helps me put things in perspective; I can move the cards around into various configurations and perhaps see who fits where. But so far, in the matter of Joel Kerner, nothing seemed to dovetail anywhere. Was it a simple case of robbery, of a young man being where he shouldn't have been, on a deserted beach early in the morning?

I opened the hunk of halvah and started eating it slowly, doodling on a yellow pad with my free hand. Since I was about ten years old I've always doodled an empty noose hanging from a gallows. I don't know why—I'm not a particularly morbid guy. I suppose a shrink would have a field day with it.

By the time I was finally able to get Patrice Kerner on the phone, I'd just about filled the page with unoccupied gibbets. I made an appointment to see her at four o'clock that afternoon at her office. She sounded extremely businesslike.

I went through my mail without much enthusiasm. I used to like getting mail, but in these days of the Internet, the civilized art of writing letters has become a lost one.

The telephone chirped loudly at my elbow. More technology— now telephones chirp, whistle, oscillate, or bing-bong like Avon calling. Whatever happened to just plain ringing?

"Milan Security," I said into the receiver.

The voice on the other end was small and tentative. "Is this Mr.—Jacovich?"

I said that it was.

"This is Teri Levine."

I sat up a little straighter. "Ms. Levine, yes," I said. "I was going to call you this evening."

"I just spoke to my mother—she said you'd been at the house."

"That's right."

"Uh, I think I'd rather talk to you when she's not around," she said. "Would that be possible?"

"Sure."

I heard her breath catch in her throat. "She—she won't have to know about this, will she?"

"Of course not," I said. "Would you like to come to the office?"

"All right. What time?"

I looked at my watch; it was nearly twelve thirty. "Would two o'clock be convenient?"

I heard pages turning. She was probably checking her Filofax. "That's fine," she said.

I told her how to get there and hung up thoughtfully. I was glad we were going to be able to talk without the specter of Dalma Levine haunting us. Things were looking up.

I'd just about covered another page of yellow legal paper with my doodles, and there were several things sticking in my throat that had nothing to do with halvah.

Joel Kerner Sr. had started out by leaning on a personage as exalted as the safety director and demanding an investigation into his son's death, and now he didn't want anybody poking into it—why?

Instead of trying to bribe me out of the case, why didn't he just talk to his daughter and get her to fire me?

And if he was so anxious to put the tragedy behind him and get on with living his own life, why after ten weeks of mourning was he still not going into the office?

I leaned back in my chair and lit a Winston, my first of the day, figuring that within the next few weeks I would probably find out.

CHAPTER FIVE

Teri Levine arrived in my office on time, just five minutes after the rain had started. I admired her as she took off her raincoat and rain hat and shook out her shoulder-length dark brown hair. She was considerably taller than her mother, slim and extremely pretty, with strong high cheekbones, very dark blue eyes, a dimple in her left cheek, and a regal carriage.

And a very full mouth. A mouth that begged to be kissed. Some women just have mouths like that, and they drive me crazy.

I'm sure some men have kissable mouths too. I just never notice.

There was an unsure, vulnerable, almost bruised quality about her that contrasted with her expensive white linen suit and shoes, her jewelry. The probationary way she sat on the edge of the chair as if poised for flight, her eyes downcast, the slight hesitancy when she spoke in her soft, small voice, the reluctance to make meaningful eye contact with me, and her refusal of coffee or a soft drink because, she said, she didn't want to put me to any trouble, all led me to believe that, as pretty as she was, Teri Levine was in dire need of some self-esteem.

As she recounted the story of her San Carlos vacation, I realized that she'd almost gotten some from the late Joel Kerner.

"I was flattered," she told me. "At Joel's paying all that attention to me. I didn't really take it seriously. I was the only unattached woman his age on the tour. But getting—courted, I guess—doesn't happen to me that often, and I'd be a liar if I said I didn't enjoy it." Then she frowned as though she was afraid that I'd think badly of her, that for an attractive unmarried woman to enjoy the attentions of a man was somehow less than admirable. "In an abstract way," she added, as though that made it all right.

"I can't believe you don't get—courted—a lot, Ms. Levine," I said, hoping to get her to relax. "You still have your San Carlos tan. It looks good on you."

She allowed herself a self-deprecating smile, shaking her head. "No, it's starting to fade now. I'm surprised it lasted this long. It's been a long, cold winter. But on the trip I was out in the sun just about every day."

"Were you sunbathing, or were you into the more active water sports?"

She crossed her long legs, and her nylons whispered distractingly. "There aren't a lot of choices in San Carlos. I'm a little too hyper to lie in the sun. I windsurfed and scuba-dived every day—scuba-dove?"

"Either way," I told her.

"I'm an architect. You don't get much fresh air or exercise at a drafting table, so when I'm on vacation I usually take advantage."

I searched for just the right words. "You brought your mother along on your vacation. You two must be very close."

Her eyes flickered and went blank for a split second. "She brought me, actually. I mean, she paid for the trip." She breathed in through her nose and exhaled loudly through her mouth. "I work too hard, she says. She's probably right. I never would have taken time off to go if she hadn't insisted."

"Everybody needs some time off," I said. I didn't add, even from their mothers.

"Mother hasn't had an easy time of it," she went on. "Ever since my father died, I try not to exclude her from things. She lost all of her family during the Second World War—in the camps. I'm all she has left." The smile that came next was tight and forced. "So we went on the trip together. I swam in the Caribbean every day, and she put on her big sunhat and sat by the pool and read her books. She had a good time."

"Did you? Have a good time?"

Her brows knit and lowered. "Up until Joel Kerner got killed. After that, I don't think anybody had a good time."

"You got to know him pretty well?"

"No, not really." She slid down in her chair, onto the end of her spine, as if she was self-conscious about her height. "On vacation tours like that, everything is kind of—it seems to look bigger, move faster, be more intense. Like you're under a magnifying glass and moving at warp speed. So we talked, sure. The way strangers talk when they're thrown together. I didn't really get to know him." She picked at the hem of her skirt. "I think my mother kind of intimidated him."

"Did that bother you?"

"If you go on a trip with someone, it's kind of lousy to spend all your time with someone else," she said, her soft voice wavering a bit. "I didn't want Mother left alone all week."

"But you liked him? Joel Kerner."

"He seemed like a very nice person. Too nice for something like . . . " She looked away.

"His family wants to know what happened," I said. "They've asked me to help. So maybe you can help me. You can never tell when some little detail that might not seem important to you is the one little piece that make all the others fit together."

She nodded. "I'll try."

"Good. Did Joel say anything while you were in San Carlos that might lead you to think he was worried or nervous or frightened about something?"

"No . . . not—worried, exactly."

I waited.

"Sad, kind of."

"He was sad?"

"Well, no. I mean, he was having a good time, swimming and surfing. He was pretty reckless sometimes. He went diving by himself in this little cove when everyone told him not to. They kind of encourage the buddy system when you dive, in case your equipment malfunctions or something, or you catch a cramp. It's a lot safer."

"But nothing happened to him?"

"No. And he always swam out past the buoys even when the lifeguards warned him he shouldn't. He seemed to relish the danger. But still there was a kind of sadness about him. Or maybe anger."

"Anger?"

"I don't know. He didn't *say* anything about it."

There are all sorts of ploys men use to get close to a woman, I thought, drumming my pencil on the edge of the desk. Perhaps Joel Kerner's had been to show off and act reckless and make her worry about him. Or to act sad so she'd feel sorry for him. Or maybe he really was sad and angry.

"Did he tell you anything about his business?"

She shook her head. "Only that he was a lawyer. Of course I already knew that—I've seen his commercials on television."

Maybe she was an insomniac too. "The morning he got killed, Ms. Levine . . ."

"Yes," she murmured.

"Anything out of the ordinary about him?"

"I didn't see him that morning," she said quickly. "We talked the night before. Out on the terrace outside the cocktail lounge. He asked me to go jogging with him the next day, early. He ran every morning. I said no."

"You're not into jogging?"

"Well, but—Mother and I had breakfast together every morning before I went out to the beach. She would have been . . . Anyway, I said no. I said no to a lot of things." A tremor shook her whole body. "Maybe if I'd gone with him he wouldn't have gotten killed."

"And maybe you both would have," I said as gently as I could. "Don't blame yourself."

Both her hands were resting on her thighs, and she tapped her fingers on her knees. "Well. That's all conjecture."

"Did you ever see Joel Kerner talking to anyone who wasn't on the tour with you? Anybody local?"

"I don't think so," she said. "Oh, waiters and bartenders and the cabana boy, people like that. You know, you're at a resort hotel for the better part of a week, you get to know the staff."

"How about the other hotel guests? The ones who weren't on your tour?"

She looked out the window. Having such a great view was beginning to seem like not such a good idea after all—visitors spend more time looking at the scenery than at me. "Not that I remember," she said. "I wasn't really paying that much notice."

"Even to a man whose attentions you admit flattered you?"

She flushed rosy red and shifted uneasily in her chair. "I suppose . . ." she began, and then closed her mouth tight and shook her head.

"Did Joel pay attention to any other women on the tour?"

"He was charming and friendly to everyone. He was very outgoing." She lifted one shoulder and cocked her head against it, as if she had an earache. "He was probably just being gracious to me too."

"I don't think so," I said. "I wouldn't have been. There's a difference between being gracious and flirting."

"Are you being gracious now, Mr. Jacovich?"

"Trying to be," I said. "Under other circumstances I might be flirting."

"I don't date much," she said, "so maybe I can't tell the difference."

"Would you have dated Joel Kerner?"

Her lipstick was all chewed off now, but she kept gnawing at her lip anyhow, the way someone will suck on the ice cubes at the bottom of a glass even when every trace of the drink is gone. "I don't know. He was—slick, I guess would be the word."

"And you don't like men who are slick?"

"It just seemed so—practiced. Like he did it all the time. I suppose he did."

"Well, did you and he make plans to see one another again when you got back to Cleveland?"

Her eyes filled with tears. "We never got that far," she said.

"Are you sure you wouldn't like something to drink?" I said. "I'm going to have a soda."

She shook her head. I went to my refrigerator, took out a can of Pepsi, brought it back, sat down, and looked at her while I clawed it open. "Ms. Levine, why did you call me? Why did you come here?"

She blinked. "I don't understand."

"You've been telling me for the last ten minutes that you have nothing to add that will shed any light on what happened to Joel Kerner, yet you made a special point of calling me to make this appointment. Why?"

She studied her fingernails, which were blunt-cut and covered with clear polish. "I wanted to help."

I sat down, took a gulp of Pepsi, and gave her an inquiring look. She squirmed a little. Neither of us said anything for a while, until it became obvious that if I didn't break the silence we'd sit there like that until the vernal equinox.

"Was it on account of your mother that you and Joel never got any further than—gracious?" I said as gently as I could.

She begrudged me the assenting nod.

"You want to tell me about it?"

Her exhalation was shuddery. "You already know about it, I think. You've met Mother."

I agreed that I had.

"She's—formidable. She's scared off every man who's ever come near me. I guess she doesn't believe that old saw about not losing a daughter but gaining a son. She wasn't really mean to Joel—but she certainly let him know that she'd be happy if he kept away from me. We talked about it, Joel and I, on that last night, before—" She hiccupped a stifled sob. "He was quite annoyed about it. Angry, really. It frightened me that he got so upset."

I reached for the box of tissues, but I saw she wasn't going to need them.

"Maybe it could have come to something. Something." Her sigh was ragged. "That would have been . . . nice."

It wasn't until she'd stood up and buttoned her coat that she finally looked me in the eye. "He said something that last night that's really stayed with me. I was crying, because my mother was being so impossible and so rude to him. He told me not to feel too bad about it, that you can pick your friends but that whoever you wind up with for parents, that's the luck of the draw."

The downtown law firm where Patrice Kerner worked went beyond mere elegance. Occupying the upper floors of Terminal Tower, its territory included the historic and architecturally dazzling Greenbrier Suite, originally built of oak, marble, and crystal in English Gothic style as their private downtown apartment by the Van Sweringen brothers, the legendary developers and railroad tycoons of the early twentieth century, whose names are familiar to every Clevelander. The law firm restored the suite as a conference and reception center and gave the city back one of its architectural wonders, and on the ledge outside its leaded windows, the town's two favorite wild pets, peregrine falcons Szell (named after George Szell, the great conductor and one-time leader of the Cleveland Orchestra) and Zenith, raised their fledglings a few years ago in full view of closed-circuit TV cameras and the entire North Coast.

Patrice Kerner didn't entertain me in the Greenbrier, however, but in her office two floors down, which had a view northward toward the lake that was blocked by several other tall buildings. She seemed small and harried behind a mahogany desk stacked high with file folders and law books. Dressed today in a gray and black pinstripe suit with a hemline some four inches above the knee, she didn't look quite as imposing as she had the day she came to see me, perhaps because a tendril of dark hair had somehow escaped from its silver clip and was hanging down below her ear.

And she was mad at me.

"My mother called in hysterics this morning," she said, her look disapproving and frustrated, "which with my workload I didn't need. Your visit upset my parents a lot. I wish you hadn't approached them until you'd checked with me first."

"You mean I have to get your permission every time I talk to someone? I don't work that way."

"There's no need to take that tone, Mr. Jacovich," she said, and I got a petty satisfaction out of having flustered her. "They are my parents, and I want to protect them as much as I can. They've been through a lot."

"Is that why they have all the security at their house? The TV cameras, the electronic gates, the butler who looks like he used to fight cruiserweight."

"The butler? You mean Carl?"

"The beat-up old guy who answered the door."

"He's not the butler." She tried to laugh gaily and didn't quite make it. "He's just a friend of my father's, from the old union days. He's retired, he needed a job, so they keep him around as kind of a handyman. He drives for them too sometimes."

"And Patrick Stranahan?"

She clicked her fingernails on the desktop as if she were practicing her piano lessons. "Why do you ask about him?"

"He was at your parents' house."

"They're old associates. Good friends. Uncle Pat is the business manager and treasurer of Local 696—has been for years."

"Construction," I said.

She pushed the rebellious tendril of hair back behind her ear. "How did you know that?"

"My father was a millworker all his life, a solid union man."

"And you don't know Pat Stranahan?"

"My father's been dead for twenty-two years, Ms. Kerner."

"I'm sorry," she said. "Pat Stranahan has been active in the union movement in Cleveland for forty years. He did it the way you're supposed to. Came up through the ranks, held various union offices, shop steward and so on, and now he's secretary-treasurer and business manager. He's in line to be the president, I guess."

"What about the security gates and all? At your parents' home."

She squared the corners of a stack of papers on her desk and flicked away a mote of dust, just in case the inspector general should pay a surprise visit, wearing his white gloves. "They put all that in about two years ago. It's just a precaution. Labor lawyers make enemies. But I don't see what it's got to do with what happened to Joel."

"I don't either," I said. "But it's my job to ask."

She settled back in her chair and put her hands together in front of her prayerfully. "Isn't everything you need in that folder?" she said. "I thought it was very complete. What more do you need to know?"

"Subtleties," I said. "They're sometimes more important than facts."

"Such as?"

I pulled out my notebook. "When did your brother get interested in martial arts?"

The question seemed to take Patrice Kerner by surprise. "I'm not sure. About a year, year and a half ago."

"Do you know where he took his instruction?"

"I never bothered to ask," she said. "I assumed it was a phase. Joel went through phases. I guess everybody does."

"Kind of an unusual phase for someone who played the violin." Her eyebrows shot skyward and I added, "I saw the picture of the two of you at your parents' house."

"Oh, that. Joel hadn't touched his violin in years. When we were growing up, nice Jewish kids took music lessons. It was the thing to do."

"Do you still play the piano?"

"I have a piano," she said. "But I'm too busy to play it anymore."

"You listed two of your brother's ex-girlfriends—Patt Wolfe and Lois Scaravelli."

"Uh-huh."

"I've talked to Ms. Wolfe already. What about Ms. Scaravelli? Was Joel with her before or after Ms. Wolfe?"

"After," she said. "They went together for about five months. I think they stopped seeing each other right before the holidays." She made a wry face. "Single people do that sometimes, so they don't have to buy Christmas presents."

"Whose idea was the breakup?"

"I never asked."

"Weren't you interested?"

"Not really. Joel dated a lot of different women, and I can't remember him being particularly serious about any of them, so his ending a relationship wasn't exactly news." She shook her head. "He was a nice person and a good lawyer, but he could be very immature sometimes."

"Is that a big sister talking?"

"No—I'm trying to be objective. In a lot of ways Joel was still the Little Prince. He never grew up."

I wondered if I wasn't hearing a manifestation of classic sibling rivalry, and the results of the patriarchal desire for a male child to carry on the name while pretty much consigning the female child to a pat on the head. "What was he like as a kid?"

She shrugged. "Like any other kid. He was a pretty good student, which made him a little different, I guess. He liked Elvis and the Beatles, but he liked classical music too, especially the Russians. He was a Browns fan—it cut him up a lot when the Browns deserted Cleveland. I don't know. He was your normal kid."

Not hardly, I thought. "Athletic?"

"No. Not so much." She watched me scribble something in my notebook. "What are you writing there?"

"It seems that in the last few years of his life Joel changed a lot. He was into all sorts of sports, tae kwon do, scuba diving . . ."

"And you find this significant?"

"I don't know yet."

"I can't imagine how his taking up martial arts would shed any light on who killed him—or how talking to my parents would, either. This is a waste of time."

"It's your time. You're free to fire me."

"I don't want to fire you," she said impatiently. "I want you to start looking in the right places."

"Would San Carlos fit your definition of the right places?"

"I suppose it would."

"Good. I'd like to go day after tomorrow, if you're willing to pay for it."

She managed to force a smile, but there was no good humor behind it. "A little break from the spring doldrums in Cleveland?"

"I'm not a beach person. San Carlos isn't my idea of a vacation paradise."

"Where do you go on vacation then?" she said, making it almost a challenge.

The question stopped me cold. For a moment I took a pretty hard look at the way I'd been living since becoming single. "I haven't taken a real vacation in about twelve years," I admitted with wonder and dismay.

"No wonder you're so uptight. If I didn't take a vacation every six months the top of my head would blow off."

I took a breath. I hadn't thought I *was* uptight. "The partnership track is rough, huh?"

"You do what you have to do," she said, and reached for the cream-colored telephone console on her desk. "Shall I have our travel agent make a booking for you?"

"That's all right," I said. "I'll take care of it."

"How long are you planning to stay there?" she asked, drawing her hand back.

"Probably two days."

She sighed. "It'll cost a fortune, booking on such short notice."

"I promise you," I said, "I won't have a good time."

CHAPTER SIX

If newspapers ever die out in this country, as the Cassandras often predict, Ed Stahl, who writes a daily column for the *Plain Dealer*, will be one of the last survivors. A throwback to the days of wear-out-your-shoeleather journalism, Ed is several years older than I, dour-looking with his Clark Kent horn-rims and ever present malodorous pipe, and his wardrobe pretty much consists of two out-of-date suits, a half dozen shirts that began life as white, and a small collection of ugly ties, few of which match or complement either of the suits. A life-long bachelor who would never dress that way if there was a woman in his life to stop him, he's a workaholic, doesn't suffer fools gladly, drinks Jim Beam neat as if defying his ulcer to make a fuss about it, and never mentions the Pulitzer he won about thirteen years back for investigative reporting. His columns are pithy, sometimes funny but more often filled with cranky outrage, and have made or broken more than one reputation on the North Coast.

Ed and I have been pals for a long time now, ever since I was a rookie cop. Our friendship endures not because he's such a lousy poker player, although his perpetual losing cements our bond a bit, nor because he can usually cadge prime tickets to sporting events on short notice, and not even because he knows everything about everybody who's anybody in Cleveland and is often willing to share his knowledge and expertise with me when

I need background on a case. It endures because I genuinely like his company.

We were at the bar at Nighttown, the James Joyce–inspired Irish pub two blocks from my apartment on Cedar Hill and only six blocks from Ed's house. The foul emanations from his pipe had already caused two well-coiffed Cleveland Heights matrons out on the town for a cocktail to move ostentatiously to the far end of the bar and reestablish themselves under the TV set, where the Indians could be seen whaling the tar out of Detroit.

What with the expanded playoff structure in major league baseball and the season starting earlier than ever, the Indians sometimes play April home games in near freezing temperatures. Tribe third baseman Jim Thome stepped up to the plate and pointed his bat at the pitcher, sighting down the length of it as if he was aiming a rifle. You could see his breath. The boys of winter.

"I remember reading about young Kerner getting himself whacked somewhere in the Caribbean," Ed said, his eyes fixed on the ball game.

"San Carlos," I told him.

"Senseless." He tapped his pipestem against his front tooth. "As if all killing isn't ultimately senseless. Where do you come into the picture?"

"His sister wants more answers than the San Carlos cops provided," I said. "Mark Meglich suggested she come see me, since obviously the local police are out of it."

"Lieutenant Meglich wouldn't have wanted to interrupt his relentless pursuit of the perfect Lolita to investigate it himself anyway."

As always, it made me uncomfortable to hear Ed run Marko down. "I'm going down to San Carlos the day after tomorrow," I said to change the subject.

He pointed the pipestem at my beer bottle. "Lucky you. But don't count on them having Stroh's down there."

He was right, so I took a swallow, hoping I wouldn't miss it too much while I was away. "You ever run into Kerner, Ed?"

"Junior? Only in the middle of the night on his tedious television commercials. Other than that, we nodded to each other across restaurants. I don't know much about him. He made a good buck, I think, and he was as philanthropic as his income allowed. And I seem to remember he dated a lot of different women. Otherwise he was your run-of-the-mill hotshot lawyer on the way up. He knew most of the right people, mainly because of his father."

"Ah, the famous Joel Kerner Senior."

"A big-time labor lawyer with very deep pockets and very heavy friends. Lives on South Park in Shaker Heights."

"I know, I was at the house. Lots of security, electronic gates, and some elderly muscle at the door. I felt like I was trying to break into San Quentin."

"That's the trouble with you, Milan—you're a screwup. People don't try to break *into* San Quentin." He sucked at his pipe, which had gone out. He knocked the bowl against his palm, spilling the wet dottle into a convenient ashtray. The acrid odor made my nose prickle.

"The old man seems to have a hard-on about me being hired to find out who iced his son," I said. "He said he just wants to grieve and heal."

"Sounds reasonable to me."

"Not to me. And not with all the security."

"Don't be paranoid. Kerner rubs elbows with some very rough-hewn folks in the course of his practice, and I imagine some of them might not care for him or his ways. So he plays it safe. The elderly muscle you speak of is probably Carl Cavallero, who once was a headbreaker for one of the construction unions Kerner represented. I guess they've been friends for forty years, and when Carl got squeezed out because of his age, Kerner put him on the payroll and gave him a little apartment over the garage. He used to be a pretty bad actor, but he's got to be close to seventy now, and he's probably not as tough as he looks."

Jim Thome lined a screaming double off the wall in right center field, and the frozen capacity crowd managed to holler. Sandy Alomar Jr. stepped to the plate and laced a single through the hole between second and short to score Thome. All I could think about is how much it must have hurt their hands to hit the ball that hard in thirty-eight-degree temperatures.

"This is a labor town," I said. "It always has been. Do the union big shots all live behind guarded fortress walls?"

"No. But they don't all handle the kind of money Joel Kerner Sr. does, either."

"What do you mean, handle money?"

"Pension funds." Ed refilled his pipe with vanilla-scented tobacco from a hoary leather pouch. I've never understood why pipe tobacco is so fragrant until you light it; afterward it smells as if the sink backed up. "The unions don't just sit on those pension funds. They invest them. That's where Kerner the elder comes in."

"I thought unions had treasurers to do that for them."

"They do. But a guy who's spent thirty years puddling steel or tightening lug nuts on Buick Electras gets elected a union officer because everybody likes and trusts him and because he stands for the beer after work. He's not necessarily a financial wizard. What he usually knows about investing is a passbook savings account. Kerner, on the other hand, moves very comfortably between the rank-and-file and the high rollers who run this town. He has his finger on the pulse and knows who's looking for capital, and why. He's been known to set up some of those investments for his union buddies."

"Is that legal?"

"Sure. And it's good business for the unions, as well as being very civic-minded."

"How do you mean?"

Ed struck a wooden match and began sending smoke signals toward Nighttown's ceiling. Brendan, the genial Irish manager, caught a whiff and frowned down the bar at Ed. But there wasn't much he could do about it—it's a tavern, after all, not the First Church of Christ.

"In recent years," Ed said, "a lot of the trade unions around here have been investing in the rehabbing of some of those beautiful old buildings down in the Flats and the warehouse district that were slated for demolition, or else just being allowed to rot. So it's a boon to the preservationists who don't want all of downtown leveled to make room for parking lots, it's increasing the tax base and the incentives for businesses to move back downtown, and it makes pretty good practical sense too. Who do you suppose does the rehabbing—all the carpentry, masonry, plumbing, and electrical work?"

"The unions."

He poked me in the chest with a knuckle. "You're still sharp as a tack. So in a way, it's like the unions are investing in themselves as well as the city. Buildings are saved, money makes money, and the members get jobs and overtime. Win–win."

"And Kerner acts as a kind of broker?"

Ed nodded. "And not pro bono, either."

"He gets a slice?"

"A slice or a straight fee, I don't know exactly how they work it. But he's making his. How do you suppose he can afford to live on South Park?"

"Not too many lawyers live in the projects on East Fifty-fifth and Quincy."

Ed took a gulp of Jim Beam and grimaced as it hit bottom, stoking the fires of his ulcer, no doubt. "What's the big deal? Everybody's got a scam."

"What's yours, Ed?"

He grinned wickedly. "A lot of the guys in the sports department owe me favors. You want to go to the game Tuesday night? Boston's in town."

"I'm not sure I can make it," I said. "Better get somebody else." I hardly ever turn down tickets to a ball game, but I didn't know where the Kerner investigation was going to take me. Besides, I knew I'd probably freeze my ass off.

"You want to go to San Carlos?" Janice Futterman said. "Tomorrow?"

"And come back Sunday, yes."

She fiddled with the black knob on her Rolodex and the wheel spun slowly like a hamster's treadmill when the poor little guy finally figures out he's not going anywhere no matter how fast he runs.

"I don't know," she said, glancing into the glass cubicle. Josh Borgenecht was taking it easy this morning, only talking on one telephone at a time. "It's awfully short notice."

"I'd prefer an aisle seat on the plane," I said, ignoring her. "And I'll want a room for tomorrow night at the San Carlos Inn as well. Nothing fancy. I don't need an ocean view, unless they happen to have one available." I smiled easily at her, figuring her usual clients were a lot more demanding.

Josh had spotted me through the glass, and his frown darkened all of his wide, fat face; it looked like he was trying to cut his phone conversation short.

"I doubt they'll have anything available," she said, licking her lips. "People don't usually go to Caribbean resorts on twenty-four-hour's notice."

"I figured since you send so many Clevelanders to San Carlos, you'd be the people to come to."

"Yes, well . . . " She twisted the Rolodex wheel some more, looking at Josh, and then began thumbing through the cards.

Josh hung up the phone, took off his glasses with a sweep of his pudgy hand, and marched out of his cubicle.

"I thought you were asked not to come back here, Mr. Jacovich," he puffed, using the hard *J*.

I corrected him. "I'm just here as a customer. I've asked Ms. Futterman to get me a flight to San Carlos."

"We don't need your business."

"Oh," I said. "It's because I'm black, isn't it?"

He blinked stupidly. "You're not black."

"You mean if I were, you wouldn't do business with me?"

"Of course not," he stammered. "I mean, I wouldn't not do business . . ."

"Well then, you must be discriminating against me for some other reason. Because I'm Slovenian, is that it? Or is it just that I'm not Jewish?"

The flush on his face was a deep cardinal red now and had spread to his ears and his throat. I was getting a kick out of making him feel uncomfortable.

"There probably won't be anything at the last minute anyway,"

Janice Futterman said too quickly, proving at least that hope springs eternal.

"If I go to another travel agent and find out there is, I'm going to file a complaint," I said. "You know how the government is with discrimination suits. It's going to cost you a fortune in legal fees."

Josh wiped the sweat from his upper lip. "Oh for God's sake, Janice, book him his effing flight."

He stomped back into his cubicle and felt around on the desk for his glasses.

Janice Futterman poked at her computer, placed a few phone calls, and made my travel arrangements with what under the circumstances would have to be classified as good grace. When she handed me the bill, I couldn't help wincing. It was more than a week's salary, even though I was flying coach—my salary, that is, not Patrice Kerner's, who was, after all, going to be paying for it.

"Have a nice trip," Janice told me as I walked out the door clutching my tickets. But I didn't think she really meant it.

The tae kwon do school, or *dojang*, was on St. Clair Avenue in the east Twenties, in a large room facing the street. Its proximity to downtown and the youngish attorneys and rainmakers who work there was probably its biggest recommendation. The floors were covered with red vinyl padding, and all along one wall a floor-to-ceiling mirror was a constant reminder of what you were doing wrong and how you needed to lose another fifteen pounds.

Nine or ten thirty-plus men and three younger women were out on the mats wearing protective body pads like a baseball umpire's chest protector, being put through their paces by a wiry, flat-nosed Asian who was screaming at them as if they were boot camp recruits, except he seemed to be doing it in Korean.

I had spent the better part of the morning phoning martial arts schools all over town to see whether Joel Kerner Jr. had been enrolled, hitting paydirt on my eleventh call. There is apparently a crying need for martial arts instruction in Cleveland.

The man who welcomed me was a few years older than I am and wore white duck pants, white cloth slippers, and an exquisite black silk jacket with a multicolored Asian dragon embroidered on the back. His sandy blond hair, blue eyes, and craggy, pasty white face led me to conclude that he wasn't Korean. His name was Steve Kovalchek, which confirmed it. He asked if I'd mind taking off my shoes before I walked on the mat-covered floor.

"Sure I knew Joel," he said, arranging a line of chairs against the wall and not even looking at the class in progress. "Like I told you over the phone, he'd been studying here for about ten months or so. He was a good pupil—very dedicated, very hardworking. I wish all my people were that committed."

"Did he ever say why at nearly forty years of age he decided to study martial arts all of a sudden?"

"The same as anyone. It's dangerous out there on the streets, and more and more people are realizing it. And by the way, the older you get, the more you need to learn to defend yourself. Age doesn't matter that much."

"Did he mention whether he had been mugged or attacked before he signed up?"

Kovalchek grinned. There were a couple of teeth missing from his lower right jaw. "That's a common thing with a lot of older students. Kind of locking the barn door after the horse escapes. But if that was the case with Joel, he never said anything to me. I think he just enjoyed it." He scratched his chin, which bore a deep horizontal scar running parallel to his lower lip. "I know he did."

The students began lunging and kicking and grunting "Hai!" a lot. I waited until their sequence was finished.

"What makes you say that?"

He straightened his shoulders.

"I spent twenty-five years in the Marine Corps, mostly as a hand-to-hand-combat instructor. And I never saw anyone who loved the actual contact so much. There were even times when Joel would get a little bit too enthusiastic and I had to talk to him about it. I was afraid he might hurt someone."

"Isn't that the idea?" I asked. "To hurt someone?"

"Not in class," he said sternly. "We stress discipline and control."

"Sounds like Joel was working out some anger."

"Everybody's angry about something." Kovalchek shrugged. "With Joel, though, it was a little different."

"Why?"

He rubbed at a smudge on the mirror with his sleeve. "You ever in the military, Milan? Is it all right to call you Milan?"

"Sure," I said. "Yes, I was an army MP."

His grin was a little cockeyed. "Army," he murmured.

"Sorry about that."

"It doesn't mean you're not a good guy. An MP, you say?"

I nodded. "I used to call myself the deputy sheriff of Cam Rahn Bay."

"You must be able to handle yourself pretty well, then."

"Carrying a billy club helped."

His eyes glittered a little "A tae kwon do master could take that billy club away from you and shove it up your ass in about two seconds."

"Probably," I said.

He moved so fast that he was a blur. All of a sudden he was down on the mat and had my legs between his own in a scissors hold, his shin behind my knees. With the exertion of the slightest amount of pressure he would have had me flat on my face. I didn't move. The students had stopped to watch.

"See?" he said.

I looked down at him and made a pistol out of my thumb and forefinger, pointing it at him. "That's why we carried side-arms too."

He released his hold and came to his feet in one fluid motion. "Right. Did you ever think about learning martial arts? A big fella like you probably has lots of guys getting in his face all the time just to make their bones."

Kovalchek was considerably smaller than I am, and in other circumstances he probably would have liked to try me, just to prove he could win. I shook my head. "I spend my life avoiding trouble, not looking for it."

He took in my once-broken nose. "Looks like you don't always succeed."

"Win a few, lose a few."

"I hear you," he said. "Listen. In Nam, did you ever run into guys who just didn't give a damn? Who were so reckless and wild that you got the feeling they didn't care whether they lived or died? The ones who'd volunteer for the most dangerous duty, the most suicidal missions?"

"Sure," I said. "The lifers. The ones who stayed in the service because there was always a chance they'd get to go in and kill somebody sometime—or be killed. They were the scary ones."

"Scary, yeah. Those were the kind of vibes I got from Joel. It was almost like he was hoping for somebody to fuck with him so he could take them out."

This didn't exactly jibe with the image I had of young Joel Kerner, the unathletic, violin-playing A-student. "Are you saying he was the kind of man who goes looking for a fight?"

"I don't think so, no," Kovalchek said. "I mean, we teach non-violence here—unless there's no other way. But I doubt if Joel would ever have backed off from anybody. He took a lot of chances. Crazy chances. When he first started with me, before he got any good, he was always getting himself banged up in class."

"Was he ever badly hurt?"

"Not really. But that's only because the people he practiced with were just beginners too. He got the wind knocked out of him a few times, though."

"And that didn't slow him down?"

Kovalchek's chest expanded with what I took to be pride. "It just made him more determined than ever."

"Did he ever say anything about thinking he was in some kind of danger? That anybody was out to get him?"

"He wasn't the type to mention it. He'd have just taken care of it himself."

He rubbed his right hand with his left, and I could see the heavy ridge of calluses along its edge, probably acquired by breaking bricks and two-by-fours for fun, the way other men might shoot hoops or whack a golf or tennis ball to burn off their excess energy.

"In the corps we called guys like that death eaters," Steve Kovalchek said.

CHAPTER SEVEN

Somewhere in the memory bank where I store all the useless information I've compiled in my lifetime is something about a primitive tribe that designated certain unfortunate individuals to eat the sins and deaths of others, but I couldn't recall the details well enough to bring them up into the light. The philosophy, as I remember, is somewhat akin to Jesus dying on the cross for the sins of the world—some sufferer has been elected to pay for what everyone else does. It certainly fits in with the "victim mentality" under which we labor these days, the idea that if someone commits a murder or rape or armed robbery, we can't really blame them because they had a rough childhood.

Everybody had a rough childhood. Being a kid is tough by definition; everyone is bigger than you, older than you, and can tell you what to do. And while parents who are abusive, roaring mean drunks, or zonked-out druggies are fortunately not in the majority, half of all marriages end in divorce, like mine, and the other half sputter along on two cylinders most of the time. So when I hear people moaning about the dysfunctional families from whence they sprung, I challenge them to show me a functional one.

My own father, Louis Jacovich, who was born in Ljubljana and emigrated to this country to work in the steel mills, sat around most evenings in his underwear, leaning in toward the old family Philco to catch Herb Score broadcasting the Indians games, and the only time I ever saw my mother dressed in anything but one of several shapeless housedresses was on Sundays when she generally wore her church outfit all day, even to cook. I used to watch the Cleavers and Ozzie and Harriet and wonder what was wrong with my family.

And now I was trying to figure out what went askew with Joel Kerner Jr., a studious young man who played the violin and dutifully went to law school in his father's and sister's footsteps and smiled sincerely on his TV commercials. Why he'd turned into a foolhardy risk taker and an angry man. And whether that recklessness and rage had in some way caused his death on a foreign beach. Whether he was really a death eater.

When I went downtown to the Leader Building and put the theory to one of his law partners, Daniel Kalisher, he didn't seem to think so.

"That's a crock," he said, leaning back in his huge leather chair, which was carefully designed to resemble a throne. "Joel was no more angry than anybody else. He was a little bit off the wall in court sometimes—but it generally worked for him. He did his job—did it well—and the rest of his time, his spare time, he pretty much enjoyed himself."

Kalisher, according to the brochure I'd read in his waiting room under the gimlet eye of his attractive receptionist, was the managing partner of Kalisher, Kerner and Keynes. He was about half a foot shorter than I, had thinning brown hair which he wore a little too long and combed straight back, and the sharp features of an unpleasant marionette. On his desk was a triple picture frame displaying photos of a pretty woman in her late thirties and two little girls who fortunately looked just like their mother. Kalisher's expensive suit was gray worsted with a large windowpane check, his shirt was dark blue silk, and his yellow, red and pink tie fairly screamed for attention.

"I'm not saying everybody loved him," he went on. "He had an attitude that some found arrogant and elitist. But he was rich, successful, kind of a local celebrity because of the commercials . . ." He ducked his head in mock humility. "We all three of us are, I guess. I even get asked for my autograph once in a while. It proves people do watch the damn things."

He waited for me to tell him I'd seen his commercials too. He's still waiting.

"How long had you worked together, Mr. Kalisher?"

"Joel joined the firm right out of law school—he went to Cleveland Marshall—and I put his name on the door about eleven years ago. He earned it. He brought a hell of a lot of money into this firm, and a lot of clients, too—mostly union contacts from his father." He looked past me. "I think there were issues there . . ."

"Yes?"

Kalisher toyed with a sterling silver tennis ball holding down a stack of papers on his desk. "When you're the son of someone like Joel Kerner, you have to push just that much harder to get out of the old man's shadow." He smiled. "I guess most guys have issues with their fathers. Mine sold women's clothing—ladies' ready-to-wear, they used to call it. He never had two nickels to rub together or the guts to stick his neck out and try something else. I suppose I went to law school because I wanted to be something better than he was, to show him that I could be."

That seemed a little mean-spirited, but I didn't care why Daniel Kalisher had made his career choice. "What issues between Joel Kerner and his father are we talking about?"

"The usual ones. Trying to establish your own identity in a field where your father is already a legend."

He sat forward suddenly, the huge chair-back coming forward like the top of a giant clamshell. "He grew up in a house that had pictures of Senior with Truman and J.F.K. and Walter Reuther all over the place. Jackie Presser would come to dinner one night and the governor the next. And Joel went into his old man's profession in his old man's town. So did his sister. That's a heavy load of water for Jack and Jill to haul up the hill."

I refrained from pointing out that Jack and Jill went up the hill to *fetch* water, that it was when they tried to carry it down that they fell and broke their crowns. "Are you saying Joel wasn't a happy man?"

"I'm saying that it was tough being a junior, that's all."

Uneasiness ran up my spine as I thought of my own elder son and wondered whether my naming him after myself had been wise, or the act of an egoist. "Had Joel been working on anything that might conceivably have put him at risk?"

"Not to my knowledge."

"You knew about all his cases?"

"That's how it's supposed to work, yeah. I'm the managing partner."

"Supposed to?"

He squeezed the silver tennis ball, his knuckles whitening. "He could be a maverick. He'd go off and do things on his own hook sometimes, without consulting Bob and me. Bob Keynes, our other partner. He's taking depositions today."

"That made you angry?"

He looked at the paperweight in his grip and put it down self-consciously. "Irritated. Certainly not enough to shoot him. Besides, I was in court that morning. You can check."

"I wasn't asking for your alibi."

Kalisher opened the top drawer of his desk, took out half a roll of antacid tablets, and thumbed one into his mouth. "Then I'm not certain what you want. I understand Joel's sister wanting answers, but you won't find any here. We were as surprised and shocked as anyone." He chewed up the tablet until it disintegrated into little white specks on his tongue. "Joel was difficult to get along with sometimes. Most really brilliant people are. But Bob and I liked and respected him, or we wouldn't have made him a partner, would we?"

"I don't know. All those juicy workman's comp cases from union members might make arrogance and recklessness taste a whole lot better."

Kalisher leaned back in his chair again, his little paunch straining the buttons of the blue silk shirt. "This is a business, okay? We're here to make money. Sure, Joel's father's union contacts were attractive, and sure the cases were lucrative. So what? Hollywood hires Schwarzenegger and Stallone to be in their movies instead of some schmuck who drives a beer truck because it makes good fiscal sense. We gave Joel a partnership for the same reason."

He waved a hand around his office. "This firm employs fifty-eight people full time. We buy tables at most of the benefits, give to all the charities. So I think we're contributing to the local economy and to society as well. We don't operate on retainers—we collect fees from our clients only if we win judgments for them. And a lot of that is because Joel had union contacts. I think we're to the point where Joel's death won't make any difference to our billings, thank God, but I make no apologies for anything— certainly not for his partnership." His brow furrowed. "Now if you want to start making accusations, go ahead and take your best shot," he said darkly. "Personal injury isn't the only kind of law I'm good at, if you understand my meaning."

"I understand, Mr. Kalisher. What I don't understand is why you're being so confrontational when I'm trying to find out who killed your partner."

He slumped in his chair and it nearly engulfed him. "I'm sorry. It's been hard. For all of us. I've never known anyone who was— who died that way. Nobody knows quite how to handle it. I didn't mean to get in your face."

"That's okay. It's probably what makes you a good lawyer. Joel could probably be confrontational too."

"Well, that's a funny thing, actually," Kalisher said. "When Joel first got out of law school, what impressed us most is that he could win his cases without engendering any hard feelings. He was a very reasonable guy, a charming guy. Insurance companies would smile while he was pulling their pants down. It's only in the last, oh, two years, maybe—that I could really characterize him as being tough."

"What do you think happened?"

"I don't know." He smiled with only one side of his mouth. "Maybe we all get cranky when we get older. I know I have."

"Me too," I said.

I made some more phone calls when I got back to the office and was finally able to reach Lois Scaravelli, who told me to come over at nine o'clock that evening. It was one more interview I could get out of the way before heading off to the Caribbean in the morning.

Before I went home I stopped off at a little restaurant over on Taylor Road, the Sun Luck Garden. It's in a dreary-looking strip mall, next to a bagel shop, but Annie, the owner-chef, serves some of the best and most inventive Chinese food in town. I had spicy mussels drenched in a sauce so delicious I would have licked the shells had I been somewhere private.

Feeling full and satisfied, I started thinking about my trip on the drive home. I didn't know what to pack. My wardrobe isn't exactly geared toward beach resort wear. I couldn't remember the last time I'd seen an ocean.

I finally hung a pair of slacks, a sports jacket, and two dress shirts in my battered garment bag, along with a tie, two days' worth of socks and underwear, a pair of shorts, and two pullover shirts with tiny polo players stitched on the breast. Then I added sneakers, a pair of white gym socks, and some rubber flip-flops I hadn't worn in years.

At the last minute I remembered to put my passport in the outer pocket of the bag; as had been pointed out to me often, San Carlos is a foreign country.

Then I headed out for my appointment with Lois Scaravelli.

Like most single Clevelanders, Joel Kerner Jr. had not dated outside his own neighborhood. It's rare that east-siders and west-siders get together romantically. It's more than the geography, it's a whole different approach to life. Lois Scaravelli lived in a red brick Georgian condo on the boundary of Pepper Pike, just off Chagrin Boulevard, a ten-minute drive from Joel's place in Moreland Courts. It was dark when I got there, and the light rain made it even harder to see.

Lois Scaravelli came to the door wearing a short-skirted tan suit with a deep blue scarf around her neck. I understood why Joel had been attracted to her. Probably a few years past thirty, she had blond hair, green eyes that sparkled, a spare, willowy figure, and a sort of brittle elegance about her.

"You're prompt," she said, glancing at her watch. "I like that in a person."

"I really appreciate your giving up your Friday evening for me."

She brushed her shoulder-length hair away from her face with the back of her hand. "Friday night is no big deal. Frankly, it was either you or paint my toenails. Hi-ho, the glamorous single life."

She led me up four steps into the living room, gripping the railing as she went; she seemed a little unsteady on her feet.

The furniture was all done in pastels and off-whites; the large oil and acrylic canvases on the wall were abstract and, to me, incomprehensible. There was a half-empty glass of white wine on the glass coffee table, and an ashtray overflowing with lipstick-imprinted butts. I sat down on the sofa.

"Join me in some wine?" she said.

"If it's no trouble."

She disappeared into the kitchen and came back with another glass and half a bottle of chenin blanc, which might have explained the twinkle in her eyes. She poured my drink, gulped down the rest of hers, and refilled her glass, clinking it against mine.

"To absent friends," she toasted gaily. I thought under the circumstances it was kind of morbid.

She sat opposite me on the off-white sofa. "I'm not the person to talk to about Joel, I don't think."

"His sister said you were dating."

"I wouldn't call it dating. I mean, there was no romance." She made a vague, circular motion with her hand. "How can I put this in a genteel way?"

"I get the picture," I said.

"We went out together—frequently. But I think Joel was just looking for a pretty arm decoration."

"I'm sure you're a lot more than that."

"Thanks. But for Joel, Im' the wrong brand."

I waited for clarification.

"A shiksa." From the way she pronounced the Yiddish word, I don't think she much cared for it. "Joel would never get serious about a woman who wasn't Jewish. We've known each other practically forever—our fathers were friends—but he never even looked at me until last summer. Then he started inviting me out whenever there was a party or a benefit dance or something where he needed a companion. And we'd go to movies at the Cedar Lee—Joel liked arty foreign films. That's it. No love affair, no hot, sweaty kisses."

"Is your father a lawyer, too?"

She shook her head. "He was a labor negotiator. He died about four years ago. He thought Joel's father was the workingman's messiah. It never really occurred to me to date Joel, though. I was as surprised as anybody the first time he asked me out to a big society party." She smiled crookedly and took a big sip of her chenin blanc, lowering its level by almost half. "I live in a slower lane."

And a damn good thing, I thought, if she drank like that all the time.

"So Joel and I were friends and that's it."

"Did you want it to be more?"

"Sure—at first." She waved the glass at me, sending the wine sloshing over the rim. "Joel was what you'd call a good catch. But he wasn't interested, so I just went along for the ride. I got to go to a lot of neat parties, meet a lot of politicians. Judges."

"Did you ever see him argue with anybody at these parties?"

"No. I was there having fun—so was everyone else. Having fun and being seen." She drank some more, flicking her tongue over her upper lip to catch what hadn't gone into her mouth, and sort of fell against the sofa cushions, showing me a lot more leg than she'd perhaps intended. "Oh, wait," she said. "He did have a shouting match one time. With his father."

"When was this?"

She screwed up her face trying to remember. "It was warm, because they were out on the patio when it happened. Yeah, it was a Labor Day party one of the union presidents gave at his house."

"What were they fighting about?"

"I don't know. I didn't really care," she said, "other than being embarrassed. When they started yelling, everybody went into the house and closed the sliding doors, so they had the patio to themselves."

"Did they come to blows?"

"No. You don't hit your dad—that's the rule. They were just yelling." She polished off the rest of her wine. I'd only taken a sip or two of mine, so when she held out the bottle to me I shook my head.

"More for me," she said philosophically, and upended the bottle, emptying it into her glass. She put the bottle down on the table, carefully holding her brimming glass level. "One dead soldier," she pronounced.

"What happened afterwards?"

"Afterwards when?"

"After they had the argument."

"Not much. Joel came back in, had two quick drinks, and took me home."

"Did he say anything about the fight?"

"I'm not sure. I had a lot to drink myself that night. I think he said his father was an asshole." She tried to contain a giggle without much success. "That's all I can remember."

If she had much more to drink, she wouldn't remember her name. "Would you say Joel was the kind of guy who took a lot of risks?"

She snorted an unpleasant laugh that caught in the back of her throat and made her choke. "Not with me, he didn't," she gasped. The coughing fit left her red-eyed and teary, and she gulped more wine.

I could see she was getting too high to be useful. I got to my feet, more than ready to escape. "Thanks for seeing me, Lois. And for the wine."

She stood too, swaying. "Why don't you stick around? I'll open another bottle."

"No, thanks. It's a school night." I started for the vestibule.

"It's Friday!" she protested.

"I have an early morning plane to catch." I went down the steps to the door and she followed, tripping on the second one and banging into me, spilling quite a bit of her wine onto the tile floor.

"Careful," I said.

"What's the fun in being careful?" She put one hand on the back of my neck. "Please stay. You won't be sorry."

She pulled my head down to hers and kissed me. Her tongue tasted of wine and cigarettes.

I disengaged myself gently. "Not tonight, Lois. Maybe we'll see each other again."

She stepped back. Her mouth was slack, her lipstick smeared. She looked unbearably sad. She put one fist on her hip, talking more to herself than to me. "I'm too damn pretty to get rejected *all* the time, you know?"

"You're not being rejected," I lied. "Call this a rain check."

I opened the door, letting in a blast of damp air. The rain hissed on the walkway outside.

"It's always raining," she said in a tiny voice.

I drove home with the wipers providing off-rhythm accompaniment to WCLV's classical music, feeling a little sad. Lois Scaravelli was a very attractive woman; I didn't know whether she drank that way all the time or if I'd just caught her on a bad night. But I had enough problems of my own without taking on someone else's addictions.

I wondered why young Joel Kerner had gone out with a terrific-looking woman like that for more than six months without ever trying to get romantic. And I was as curious as hell about his very public shouting match with his father on Labor Day. I wished Lois had paid more attention to it at the time, because I sure as hell wasn't going to get the answer from Joel Kerner Sr.

CHAPTER EIGHT

My flight was at 7:20 the next morning. I drove to the airport through a cold, penetrating drizzle, allowing myself time to go through the elaborate security procedures put into effect when TWA flight 800 blew up and they started to worry about terrorists again. First it was metal detectors. Then they made you show photo ID and swear that no mysterious stranger had given you a package to carry on the plane. Now they can open and inspect your luggage if they feel like it. Pretty soon air travel is going to require a note from your mother.

Sometimes it feels like the bad guys are winning. It makes me angry.

Everyone in the waiting room seemed dazed and bleary-eyed at that early hour. I'd brought along a book to read on the plane, but before boarding I decided to check that morning's *Plain Dealer* to see what was going on in the world and in Cleveland. In his column Ed Stahl bitched about the football stadium being built for the new "Browns," none of whose yet-to-be-named players would engender the kind of affection the town had lavished on Bernie Kosar or Ozzie Newsome or Jim Brown, and for its inaccessibility, money-wise, for the working-class fans who kept the old team alive for forty years. I shared with Ed the feeling that when we finally do get pro football back on the North Coast, the people who attend the games, men and women alike, will be the kind who wear gray suits and power ties.

The first leg of the journey was between Cleveland and Miami, and I fell asleep as soon as we were airborne. Happily the flight attendants didn't wake me up to offer me what the airlines laughingly call breakfast.

Refreshed from my nap and with more than an hour to waste between planes, I went through the security procedures again, this time showing my passport, and then wandered the wide concourses of the Miami terminal, noting that more than half the passengers there were Hispanic. They called the flights bilingually too.

The plane to San Carlos was an aging DC-9 that took off twenty-five minutes late, and the cabin attendants told us in English and Spanish about our seat belts and oxygen masks and pointed out the emergency exits with two fingers of each hand the way they always do. I once asked a flight attendant I met at the bar at Nighttown if she had been specifically trained to do the two-fingered point, and she looked at me as though I was insane. Everyone is in denial about something these days.

As we made our approach, I caught a glimpse of the island republic of San Carlos out the window. It was configured like an egg that had been dropped into a frying pan from a great height, full of little coves and inlets. The sky was aquamarine, with a few clouds scudding across its face to the east. About a mile offshore, a coral-colored reef shimmered through the water, for all practical purposes ringing the island, and I knew why San Carlos wasn't a more popular tourist destination—no big luxury cruise ship could get anywhere near it.

The plane hit the runway and bounced to a stop. When I stepped out into the midday tropical sunshine, the heat struck me like a fist.

I didn't have to wait for the baggage to be unloaded; I'd only brought along a carry-on. It did take quite a while to clear customs, however; they didn't seem to be terribly well organized. And the customs shed wasn't air-conditioned either.

Neither was the taxi I was hustled into at the curb in front of the terminal. There were only two others. Mine was a Chevrolet Nova of uncertain years, its wheel wells and fenders pitted with rust, its interior shabby and worn, with stuffing oozing from several rips in the seat cushions. The kind of car you see up on blocks in front of ramshackle houses in rural America. Junker cars on the front lawn are poor people's answer to the middle class's pink flamingos.

The driver was young, short, and skinny, his almost blue-black head shaven bald. He wore a collarless striped shirt and there was a rhinestone stud in his right earlobe.

"You a big man," he said. "Big hombre." He slid in behind the wheel and turned the key; the engine coughed and sputtered, then caught. Idling, it sounded like a twenty-year-old Kenmore washing machine.

He grinned when I told him I was going to the San Carlos Inn. "Nice place," he assured me. "You have a good time there."

We pulled out into traffic. The highway from the airport was two lanes of patched, uneven blacktop that made the taxi rattle and shake. It was lined with small restaurants, a few gas stations, and some auto and boat repair shops. Most of the parking areas were unpaved. A haze of powdery gray dust hung in the air.

"American?" the driver wanted to know.

"Uh-huh. I'm from Ohio."

"O-hi-yo." He bobbed his head.

"Lots of people from Ohio come here for vacation?"

"Sometimes," he said with an upward inflection.

"You remember a man from Ohio—a turista—got killed on the beach a few months ago?"

He nodded again and crossed himself, glancing quickly at a white plastic figurine of the Virgin Mary mounted on the dashboard with a suction cup. "Very bad."

"Did you know him? The man who got killed?"

"I think I see him," he said slowly, as if choosing his words. "I don' know, though."

"They never found out who did it, did they?"

He threw a look in the rearview mirror. "You his frien'?"

"Sort of. That kind of thing happen here a lot?"

"Never happen before."

"Never?"

"No, señor. Not turista. Local people sometime, but never before a turista."

The road turned suddenly residential. None of the houses had seen a coat of paint since the seventies, and all were tiny and ramshackle. Children played in the dirt outside their homes. Beyond the houses were vast stretches of fallow fields, randomly dotted with shrubs and lonely trees and outhouses. I remembered Joel Kerner Sr. characterizing San Carlos as a Third World country, and I guessed he was right.

We passed through Ciudad San Carlos, which was full of quaint reconditioned buildings, little cafés, and touristy curio shops that probably sold souvenirs of San Carlos manufactured in Taiwan. There were a couple of large, expensive-looking restaurants. The sidewalks were crowded with visitors carrying cameras and wearing garish and unattractive resort clothes.

On the far side of town, the road became rural again, with more agricultural fields stretching off toward the horizon. White-clad workers in broad-brimmed straw hats labored among the rows of plants.

About eight miles from the airport the taxi veered off to the left, and in a few minutes we were on a well-paved road cutting through a densely wooded area. Palmetto bushes, jacaranda trees, plumeria, and what looked like weeping willows lined either side of the highway, and the warm, muggy air turned heavy with the fragrance of frangipani. The sky was bluer here, crisscrossed by large birds that soared in the sunshine, borne on currents of tropical air.

"Is the San Carlos Inn far from here?" I asked.

"Oh, yes. Far."

I'd never have known. My driver might have been taking me the long way around, but there wasn't much I could do about it. I settled into the lumpy, rump-sprung back seat and enjoyed the ride as best I could. Taxis, I suppose, are rattletrap almost everywhere.

Fifteen minutes later we emerged onto a road hugging the side of a hill that wasn't quite a mountain, which overlooked the sun-dappled sea. On the left was a sheer drop of about eighty feet, on the right a wall of dense tropical shrubbery. The driver didn't seem perturbed by the possibility of our rocketing off into thin air, so I tried not to be either.

"You travel alone?" the driver said.

"Uh-huh."

"Gets lonesome, no?" His eyes flashed at me in the mirror again. "You like some company? Nice young lady?"

"No thanks."

"Pretty lady," he added. "Young."

"I don't think so."

He reached back and handed me a creased, grubby business card. "You change your min', you call me at the taxi office. I am there alla time."

The name *Eladio* had been scrawled across the card in pencil. I put it in my shirt pocket. San Carlos apparently offered all the comforts of home.

The air blowing in the taxi's open windows had taken on a salty tang. Below us a sprawling stucco hotel complex hugged the hillside, fronting on a white-sand beach. Lacy surf churned at the shoreline. The resort was a large red-tile-roofed building painted an eye-aching pink, with several free-standing cabanas scattered around it like afterthoughts. On the water were several sailboats and power launches, surrounded by windsurfers and parasailers. Closer to shore swimmers tried to avoid one another as they cavorted in the gentle waves. It was Saturday, and the San Carlos Inn was crowded with fun-seekers.

The road wound down and around the main building, and the taxi came to a stop on the red brick driveway under the portico. Eladio jumped out and held the rear door open for me; on his feet sandals made out of old automobile tires with leather straps threaded through them. As he rescued my bag from the trunk he said, "I am sorry about your dead frien', señor."

The clerk at the desk was a young brown-skinned woman wearing typical hotel-clerk attire, a blue blazer, white blouse, and red foulard, and her smile dimmed a bit when she looked up my reservation and found I was only staying one night. It lost a little more wattage when I asked to speak to the manager.

"He is at lunch, señor . . ." I think she was about to give my last name a try but decided against it. "He will call you when he returns."

"Muchas gracias," I said, exhausting most of my Spanish vocabulary. A beefy man wearing tan cords and a short-sleeved white rayon shirt with a brown tie was watching me openly. The security man, I figured—they don't call them house dicks anymore.

A young boy of about twelve, whose white shirt was badly frayed at the collar and worn without the ugly tie, rushed to take my bag. He led me down a long corridor to my room. I tipped him two dollars, and his face lit up as though I'd given him a hundred.

"What's your name?"

"Heriberto, señor." His voice cracked with approaching puberty. Apparently the child labor laws were a lot more lax in San Carlos than they are in Cleveland.

"Well, Heriberto, I need somebody to show me around here a little bit. Can you come back at . . . " I looked at my watch; it was twenty past one. "At three o'clock?"

"Sí, señor," he said happily, and practically skipped out the door.

The room was large and airy, with a king-size bed and furniture made of processed wood in a quasi-Spanish style. A small basket of fruit and a welcoming note were on the dresser. Behind it hung a gilt-framed mirror with most of the silvering gone, and over the bed a garish blue-green seascape, the kind they turn out by the hundreds each day in a factory. The bathroom was the most elegant of the accommodations, with all the modern amenities and a pinkish basin in the shape of a seashell, so lavishly out of place that anyone with a smidgin of sensitivity would hate to spit in it when he brushed his teeth.

A lizard skittered out from behind the commode and into the bedroom. He was a cute little fellow, probably a skink. I chased him across the floor, opened the sliding glass door and let him out onto the balcony, where he disappeared over the edge. My view wasn't of the beach but overlooked the hill I'd just been driven down, and I was once again aware of the dense scent of frangipani. My room shared the little balcony with the room adjoining; only a waist-high fiberglass partition separated us. I wondered if my neighbor might turn out to look like Michelle Pfeiffer, but I've never been that lucky.

I stripped off my traveling clothes and put on a pair of shorts, one of the pullovers, and my flip-flops and was about to head out to find lunch when the phone on the desk jangled like a fire alarm.

"Mr. Jacovich?" a cultured male voice said with only the hint of a Spanish accent. His mispronunciation of my name was unique—he turned the *J* into an *H*. "This is Mr. Ybarra, the hotel manager."

"Yes, Mr. Ybarra. Thank you for calling."

"You left a message for me. Are your accommodations satisfactory?"

"Yes, quite. I wonder if I might come and speak with you?"

There was only a breath of hesitation. "Of course. Is now a convenient time?"

"I'll be right there," I said. I took one of my business cards from my wallet and put it in my pocket, and went back down the hall to the lobby, where the desk clerk directed me to a glassed-in office behind the desk. MANAGER was lettered on the door.

Mr. Ybarra wore an unmistakable air of self-importance that immediately got my back up. He had round, chubby cheeks and was dressed in a cheap gray suit with flakes of dandruff on the shoulders, a white shirt, and a plain gray tie. When I came in, he rose from his desk and extended a slightly damp hand.

"Please sit down, Mr. Hacovich," he said.

I corrected him this time.

"My apologies," he said, accompanied by an unctuous bow. "In Spanish the *J* has the sound of an *H*." He waited until I was seated. "May I offer you something? A beverage?"

"No thanks. I won't take up too much of your time."

"Of course you want to get out to the beach." His smile

widened. "I looked at your registration card. You're from Cleveland Heights, Ohio? I don't imagine you have sunshine like this in Cleveland right now."

"You know Cleveland?"

"I know Chicago. I went to school at Northwestern. I know the weather of the Midwest."

"It was cold and rainy when I left," I admitted.

"Then you will enjoy the endless summer of San Carlos."

The weather of the Midwest. The endless summer of San Carlos. I think he'd read *For Whom the Bell Tolls* one time too many.

"Mr. Ybarra, a few months ago a man from Cleveland, Mr. Joel Kerner, was killed on the beach here."

His smile went out like a halogen lamp when somebody trips over the cord and pulls the plug out. "Yes?"

I gave him my card. "Mr. Kerner's family has engaged me to look into the matter."

He knit his brow. "In what way?"

"They'd like to find out what happened. And why."

"But I can add nothing beyond what the police must have told the family. He went for an early morning run on the beach and someone shot and robbed him. It was very unfortunate." His frown deepened. "Tragic," he amended.

"Was Mr. Kerner a good guest?"

"I don't understand . . ."

"I know that some hotel guests can be difficult. Demanding. That they can be rude or unpleasant to the staff. Would you say Mr. Kerner was someone like that?"

"Certainly not!" he huffed.

"So his relations with your personnel were pleasant?"

"I don't think there were any 'relations.' Our staff is not allowed to fraternize with the guests."

"I understand. I just wondered if anyone here at the hotel particularly disliked him."

His brown eyes turned to slits in his pudgy face. "I hope you are not suggesting someone in our employ was responsible for what happened."

"It's my job to ask," I said.

"And it is my job to maintain the very high reputation of this resort." His words were clipped, precise.

"Would you know if Mr. Kerner had any visitors during his stay?"

"Visitors?"

"Besides any of your other guests. A young woman, perhaps. A local woman."

He stiffened with moral outrage. "You mean a—a prostitute?"

"Mr. Kerner was a single man, here alone. It can happen."

He shook his head resolutely. "Not at the San Carlos Inn. Many families stay with us here. Things like that are not permitted."

"They're hardly permitted anywhere. But they happen."

He shot his cuffs. "San Carlos is a small island. Such women of the town are known to our staff and are not even allowed in the building or on the grounds. Ever."

"I noticed several cabanas separate from the main building. Isn't it possible that . . ."

"No, señor. We have a full-time security staff, twenty-four hours a day. Besides, Mr. Kerner was not in a cabana. He stayed in room 237."

"How do you happen to recall his room number nearly three months later?"

"We've never had anyone murdered at our hotel before. I am not likely to forget what happened in that room." He made a big show of looking at his watch.

"If you think of anything else that might be helpful," I said, "anything at all, I'll be around until tomorrow afternoon. And you have my card—you can call me in Cleveland, collect."

"I do not believe I will think of anything," he said stiffly by way of dismissal. "Enjoy your stay at the San Carlos Inn, Mr. Jacovich."

I didn't think I would. I did, however, enjoy a late lunch in the dining room—ackee rice, cooked with fruit, and jerk chicken. It wasn't the kind of fare you found at Nighttown or anyplace else in Cleveland. I looked out the big picture window at the terrace, where several people about Dalma Levine's age lay slathered with sunblock reading books or magazines under their umbrellas. Beyond, down at the water's edge, bathers leaped around in the surf and bumped into one another.

I went back to my room, where the pink shell basin didn't inhibit me from brushing my teeth, looked around for my little lizard but didn't find him, and went out on the balcony for a smoke.

I understood Ybarra's reluctance to talk about Joel Kerner just as I had Josh Borgenecht's reticence and lack of cooperation. Having a guest murdered while he was enjoying your hotel's hospitality didn't exactly build public confidence. So I was going to have to get my information the hard way.

On the other half of my shared balcony the sliding glass door opened and a tall middle-aged man came out wearing tiny black bikini swim trunks that barely covered his genitals. He was bald except for a long fringe of dark hair that went around the back of his head from ear to ear. About thirty pounds overweight, his stomach and love handles slopped over his bikini and were matted with the same dark hair that covered his back and legs.

"Bon jour," he said in a high, piping voice. French. I said hello.

He flapped his beach towel over the edge of the balcony a few times to get the sand out, and draped it over the railing to dry in the sun. Then he took a deep breath of the sea air, nodded at me, and went back inside.

So much for Michelle Pfeiffer.

At two minutes after three, Heriberto was at my door, smiling and eager.

"Three o'clock," he announced.

"Good, Heriberto, thank you. I've never been here before, so I was hoping you could show me around a little, tell me where everything is." I took two ten-dollar bills from my wallet and watched his eyes grow huge. It was probably more than he made in a week.

"Is too much, señor," he said.

I stuffed the bills into his shirt pocket. "It's okay," I said. Then I went to my bag and took out the photograph of Joel Kerner.

"Heriberto, do you remember this man? He was at the hotel about three months ago."

He look at the picture and blinked nervously. He nodded. "Es muerto."

"Do you know anything about what happened to him, Heriberto?"

He shrugged bony shoulders. "I think somebody shoot him. I don' know who."

I put the picture in my hip pocket. "Okay, let's go," I said. "I want the grand tour."

Smiling happily once more, he led me back down the corridor into the lobby. Piped-in music was playing a little too loudly, an unfamiliar tune with a macarena rhythm. Caribbean Muzak.

"Dining room," he said, pointing to where I'd eaten lunch. "The food is okay, I think." He took a few more steps and indicated a smaller doorway right next to it, done up in bamboo and rattan and wicker, with a blue neon sign that read EL TRÓPICO arching over the entrance.

"The bar. You have a drink now, señor?"

"Not right now," I said. The kid really knew how to hustle, I had to give him that. He led me across the lobby to another alcove that had seemingly been added as an afterthought. It was about the size of a master bathroom in an expensive tract home. A young woman sat behind a counter surrounded by ashtrays, mugs, mummified iguanas mounted on wooden plaques, cigarettes, toothpaste, and minor first-aid accoutrements.

"Gift shop," Heriberto informed me.

"Very nice," I said dutifully.

He marched me out to view the terrace and the vivid turquoise swimming pool. Two other boys close to his age and dressed similarly scuttled around passing out towels and wiping sweat and tanning oil from vinyl-covered loungers. There was a bar in a small open shack at one end of the pool, and a white-jacketed attendant with light brown skin and jet black hair, self-confident in the way only very handsome young men can be, stood behind the beer spigots openly ogling two thirtyish women in skimpy swimwear who lounged at poolside. They sipped apathetically at tall pink drinks while they worked hard on their melanomas. One was slim, dark-haired, and rather pretty, tanned to the color of old leather. The other, a blonde, was a little more obvious—more bust and hips, less swimsuit. There was a hard, bitter look around her mouth, and the pinkish tinge to her pale skin suggested she'd have a painful sunburn that night. They both sat up a little straighter and thrust out their breasts and sucked in their stomachs as I walked past them, and the dark-haired one gave me a fluttery smile.

"The pool," Heriberto told me proudly. "Five o'clock the steel-drum band comes."

We went around behind the bar and down a paved walkway to another pink stucco building about the size of a two-car garage. Against an outer wall were stacked several surfboards and para-sails, and I noticed a couple of two-person paddle boats and three Jet Skis behind the building. The glass doors were open, and inside a young man bobbed to the music coming through the headphones of the Walkman he wore.

"Dive shop," Heriberto said. It seemed the kid never stopped smiling.

I nodded. "Let's look around."

We went inside, where all sorts of scuba tanks, masks, swim fins and snorkeling tubes were neatly displayed. The air-conditioning made the little shack almost chilly. When the attendant saw us he whipped off his headphones. I could hear the music, tinny and indistinct, from across the room.

"Buenos días, señor. You wan' to dive today? Snorkel, maybe?"

"No—I'm just looking right now."

He lost interest and put the headphones back on.

"Scuba," Heriberto said, stroking a compressed air tank lovingly. "You wan', I show you the best place to go. Little cove down the beach. Better if you go with somebody," he added gravely.

Nodding, I went back over to the attendant, who yanked off his headphones once more in evident irritation. I pulled Joel Kerner's picture from my pocket and showed it to him.

"You remember this man?"

His eyes widened, then narrowed in suspicion as he gave me a glum nod.

"He went scuba diving?"

"Scuba, windsurfing, Jet Ski—everything."

"Did he go with anyone?"

"Solo. Always. If he meet someone outside, I don' see him. Always he go alone from here." He turned the music off.

"You ever see this man argue with anyone here. One of the guests? Or an employee?"

He shook his head.

"How about you, Heriberto?"

"No, señor."

To protect the top of my head from getting sunburned through my thinning hair, I bought a baseball cap with the hotel logo on it, which made the dive shop attendant marginally more friendly. Then we stepped outside into the heat of the day, which was almost a relief after the artificial coolness of the dive shop.

"You wan' go on the beach now?" Heriberto asked.

"I want to go see where they found the turista's body."

CHAPTER NINE

We descended a flight of thirty-four steep stone steps from the terrace to the beach. I counted them. A stiff breeze was blowing down by the shore, but it was still early enough in the afternoon to be balmy and pleasant. I slipped off my sandals and the warm sand toasted the soles of my feet. The sun was baking the fair Slovenian skin of my nose, arms and legs, but I hadn't packed any sunscreen—it wasn't like Advil or toothpaste, something I usually had on hand in my Cleveland apartment.

Heriberto scampered ahead of me along the surf, playing tag with the waves and laughing. Poor little guy, he lived right by the ocean but probably had few opportunities to play in it. I wondered how many hours a week he worked at the San Carlos Inn.

A large dune, about forty feet inland, ran almost the entire length of the hotel's property, forming a natural windbreak. At its crest it was about twelve feet wide and some sixteen feet high, and it was easy to imagine Joel Kerner Jr. jogging along the top of the ridge, arms pumping, breathing deeply, waiting until he got into the dedicated runner's "zone." I wondered if the shooter had come up from the ocean side of the dune or from landward.

Or if Joel, in his running reverie, had even known what hit him.

We walked along the crest until we saw a little natural rise on the beach ahead of us. It was marked by a scraggly stand of palm and palmetto and a few skimpy deciduous trees I couldn't identify and skirted with beach grasses, sea oats, and shrubs that looked like dormant geranium bushes. Heriberto stopped short about fifty feet from the greenery, his heels leaving little skid marks in the sand, and pointed a finger. "They find him there."

"Let's go look, okay?"

He hung back and shook his head. I couldn't blame him; I wasn't anxious to visit a scene of violent death, either.

"All right," I said. "I'll go myself."

He grinned relief and set off down the beach, searching for shells or sand dollars or perhaps buried treasure. I put my sandals back on and trudged toward the palm grove. It was an arduous walk in the soft sand—and a long way to drag a dead body.

I stopped in the middle of the little patch of green. It was probably fifteen yards from one end to the other, and twelve or fifteen feet wide. The grasses were waist-high; from the rest of the beach and the hotel it would be easy to miss anything hidden here. If the kids who found Joel's body hadn't come along and virtually stumbled over him, who knows how long he might have stayed there while insects and crabs picked at him.

I'm not a mystical person—Slovenians tend to the practical side. I don't believe in tarot cards or psychics who say they can read my aura, and I hadn't even thought about my astrological sign until the social mores of the seventies forced me to consider it so I could answer the inevitable question of the times. But here where a young man had died violently, something sorrowful and brooding came crawling up my spine and elbowed its way forcefully into my consciousness, some spiritual connection between Joel Kerner and me. I was glad Heriberto wasn't there to see, because I was seized with a violent shudder.

I knew that after all this time there'd be no visible sign of what had occurred here, no bloodstains or telltale footprints, but I looked around anyway. It was unlikely the killer had dropped a wallet with his name and address in it, but I'd come a long way and felt obligated to search. A mournful wind whistled through the palms.

I turned back the way I'd come, walking up to the top of the dune. If the shooter had been on the seaward side down by the water and firing upward, the big ridge of sand would have muffled and absorbed the sound and the wind and surf would have masked it from the hotel. If, however, the shot had been fired from the top of the dune, it would have echoed all over this side of the island in the quiet of an early morning.

But no one I'd spoken to remembered hearing the discharge of a shotgun.

Calling to Heriberto, I walked down the side of the dune and joined him at the surf. The cold spray was a salty delight against my face.

"You see it?"

"I saw it. Now—where is this cove where el muerto went diving?"

"You don' go down there by yourself, señor. Take somebody with you."

"I'm not going diving. I just want to see it."

Clearly puzzled that anyone would come all the way to San Carlos and not want to go in the water, he gamely led me down the strand and around a sand spit extending out into the sea.

The cove was almost a perfect three-quarter circle, as if a giant had taken a bite out of the land. Protected from the waves, the seemingly fathomless waters of a crystal lagoon tiptoed up to gently lap a shell-encrusted beach. About fifty yards from the water's edge the sand was ringed with tall palms. Beyond the seaward end of the lagoon, flashes of sunlight sparkled like mercury on the surface of the water. It was postcard-beautiful.

"You don' wan' to dive?"

I did want to, very much. I wanted to immerse myself in the warm lagoon and swim lazily to its floor, explore the formations of coral and the starfish and mollusks, and chase the brightly colored fish that darted in and out of the sensuously waving beds of kelp. I wanted to come out refreshed and dripping, let the sun bake me dry, and make love on the white sand to a beautiful woman I'd never actually seen but had imagined many times.

But the best I could do was dip a tentative toe into the lagoon. Then I stepped in with both feet, up to my ankles. It was the temperature of bathwater.

"Any sharks in here, Heriberto?"

He shook his head, his big eyes grave. "Not so many. Jellyfish sometimes—not sharks."

I stepped back out of the water, my alacrity making my young companion snicker. But a jellyfish sting wasn't something I wanted to take home with me.

"Do a lot of people from the hotel come diving out here early in the morning? Or jogging, the way Señor Kerner did?"

"Not so many," he said again.

That made sense. Although some people, type-A personalities like Joel, might want to squeeze every available moment out of their vacations, most people like to sleep in, take things easy, and not push themselves the way they do back home when careers and marriages and children and social lives take up every spare moment. I made a crude outline sketch of the lagoon in my notebook. Something about the place was tickling the inside of my head.

"Heriberto," I said, "you know a cabdriver named Eladio?"

He nodded.

"Did Mr. Kerner know him too?"

The boy shrugged. "Maybe he bring el señor to the hotel from the airplane—but I don' know."

We started back toward the beach. Heriberto hung back to walk with me, but I could tell he was itching to run and jump.

"Why don't you see if you can find us some nice flat stones we can skip over the water, okay?"

His face lit up and he was off down the beach, every so often stopping to pick something out of the sand. By the time I caught up with him he had quite a collection. We spent the next few minutes skimming the stones out across the tops of the waves; he was a lot better at it than I was.

By the time we ran out of flat stones, the sun was lying low on the horizon and the sea wind had turned colder. We started back for the hotel.

"The man who died?" Heriberto said. "The American? The night before he got shot . . ."

I looked down at him. His face was screwed up in consterna-
tion, and he chose his words carefully. "That night—he leave the
hotel. Go into town, I think."

"Where did he go?"

He shook his head.

"What time did he leave?"

"I don' know. Maybe nine o'clock."

"What time did he come back?"

He turned up his palms. "I go home then," he said.

I thought about that for a while, rubbing my nose where the
sun had kissed it hard. I figured in three or four days it would be
peeling.

We continued on up to the terrace. All the pool rats had gone
in for the afternoon. An elderly man was sitting in a lounge chair,
reading through what looked like prescription sunglasses, a blan-
ket draped over him from the waist down. He wore a toasty-
looking zippered sweatsuit with a hotel towel wrapped around his
neck and tucked in like a muffler. On his head was a checkered
driving cap. He was dressed warmly enough for Cleveland.

I clapped the boy on the shoulders. "Muchas gracias, Heriberto," I said. "You've been a big help and I appreciate it."

He was almost the same age as my son Stephen, and being
with him made me miss home, even though Stephen was reaching that stage where hanging out with his old man was cruel and
unusual punishment. I knew Heriberto was only spending time
with me because I was paying him, but I chose not to think about
that even as I slipped him another ten-dollar tip.

As he bubbled his thanks and skipped off around the side of
the hotel, I noticed the beefy security man standing just inside
the door to the terrace, glowering like a thundercloud.

I walked the long corridor to my room, showered the sand off,
put on slacks and a dress shirt open at the collar, and slipped on
my jacket. Then I searched in the pocket of the shirt I'd worn on
the plane and retrieved the card the cabdriver had given me.

It was twenty minutes to six. I picked up the old-fashioned
black rotary phone on the dresser and dialed the number.

"Eladio, por favor," I said to the gruff-voiced man who answered.

From the loud clunk that assaulted my eardrum I figured he had dropped the receiver on his desk. I could hear shouting back and forth in Spanish, and then the taxi driver got on the phone.

"Sí, Eladio."

"Eladio, this is the man you brought from the airport to the San Carlos Inn this morning. From the U.S.A. Ohio?"

"Oh, sí," he said, suddenly animated. "El hombre grande."

"I'm not *that* big, but Eladio was small, and I suppose everything is relative. "I've changed my mind," I said. "I am lonesome."

He cackled.

"Can you bring a young lady to see me?"

"Oh no," he said. "At the inn it is not allowed. You got to come to town."

Ybarra had told the truth about that, at least.

"Can you come and pick me up then?"

"Okay, hombre! Cost you sevenny dollars U.S.," he said. "For the girl and the cab ride—both ways."

I gritted my teeth, imagining submitting an expense report to Patrice Kerner for the services of a hooker. "All right," I said. "One thing, though. The girl. I want the same girl as my friend from Ohio. The one who died on the beach."

His breath rushed into my ear through the receiver. After several moments of silence he asked, "Why?"

"Do I have to have a reason?"

"No. Seem funny, tha's all."

"You can do this for me, Eladio?"

Another moment of silence, this one not quite as long. "Sure. You be in front of the inn nine o'clock," he giggled. "You gonna have a good time."

I doubted it.

A burnt-orange sun hovered over the Caribbean as I arrived at the hotel bar, which boasted a breathtaking view of the beach. As promised, the steel-drum band was playing on the terrace, although I could discern no recognizable tune. It was simply infectiously joyful rhythm.

In honor of my surroundings I ordered a piña colada, removing the little paper umbrella from it almost before the bartender had set it down. I wondered who had come up with the bright idea of decorating drinks that way; probably an enterprising soul who somehow got stuck with a surplus of little paper umbrellas.

It was like drinking a milk shake. The sweetness made my teeth ache. The band launched into what might have been "Fly Me to the Moon" as the two young women I'd noticed by the pool earlier walked in and sat down two stools away from me. They both wore backless, low-cut sundresses that ended six inches above the knee, the brunette's with big red flowers on a black background, the blonde's a slinky, too-tight turquoise. They both showed plenty of skin, and the blonde's was all a painful-looking pink. I imagined she'd spend the night plastered with Noxzema.

"Hi," the dark-haired one said, flashing a smile as wide as a mail slot. Her too red lipstick emphasized her very white teeth. "I'm Lissa. This is my friend Ann."

Ann, the blonde, had a smile not nearly as broad. When she leaned forward around Lissa to see me, her hair fell into her eyes. She didn't push it out of the way with her hand but instead threw her head back to toss it over her shoulder, in much the same way certain Cleveland-area women do when they're telling you they come from Shaker Heights.

"Hi. My name's Milan."

"Milan?" Lissa's blue eyes widened. "I don't think I ever heard that name before."

"It's not an uncommon name in Cleveland."

"Cleveland?" Ann made a face; she obviously knew nothing about my city beyond the now outdated jokes Johnny Carson used to tell. Her loss. She had a pinched, little-girl voice I was sure would become irritating in no time.

"You lost your football team, poor baby," Lissa said. Ann and I are Skins fans. We're from Washington."

"D.C.," Ann added helpfully, in case I might otherwise think that it was Tacoma or Spokane that had a football team called the Redskins.

"Actually," Lissa said, "we live in Arlington. But we work in the District."

"For the government?"

"Good guess." I tried to detect sarcasm, but she beamed at me as though I'd just come up with Rumplestiltskin's name. "We're in Commerce."

I took that to mean that they worked for the Department of Commerce and not that they were prostitutes.

"What do you do, Milan?"

I didn't want to get into it. I didn't want them to mention Sam Spade or say they never met a private investigator before and ask how I happened to get into that line of work and did I ever shoot anybody and tell me they knew about private eyes because they'd seen *The Big Sleep* and always watch *Harry O* on cable. "I'm a consultant," I said.

They both nodded knowingly; federal employees understand about consultants.

"We saw you walking on the beach this afternoon, didn't we, Ann? And I said to her, my God, where did that gorgeous man come from?"

"Now you know. Cleveland."

Lissa squeezed my bicep with a red-taloned hand. "And there's so *much* of you, too."

In nobody's wildest imaginings could I be considered a gorgeous man. I'm too big, I weigh too much, and I'm losing my hair. It might work for Sean Connery—it doesn't for me. But it was kind of nice to hear anyway, although for all I knew, she went home from the Department of Commerce every evening, had a lonely glass of white wine, and played with her cat. Maybe, like so many other people, vacationing in a foreign country had transformed her into a sexual predator.

I asked if I could buy them a drink, because it was expected of me. Lissa ordered a grasshopper, Ann something called a godmother. It was just punishment for my drinking piña coladas.

"When did you get here, Milan?" Lissa said.

"Just this afternoon."

"All by yourself?" She moved over onto the stool next to me. "You're gonna love it. We've been here since Wednesday. But we have to go home the day after tomorrow. Duty calls." She did a Shirley Temple pout. "Just when we're getting to know you, too."

We sat and talked for a while, the steel drums finally becoming irritating as they launched into a beguine-flavored version of "More." Ann chain-smoked Virginia Slims and had moved to close the gap between Lissa and herself; otherwise she looked as if she'd rather be back in Washington. She kept dipping a finger into her godmother and licking it with the tip of her tongue. I wasn't impressed, but I think the bartender was.

My next-door neighbor, the Frenchman with the hairy back, came into the bar, stopping at the entrance to look around. This time he had his clothes on, a mocha jacket over dark gray slacks and a black sports shirt open at the neck. His eyes found us, and he hurried over.

"Ann chérie," he said. "I've been looking for you for two days."

Ann's expression, never very open to begin with, slammed shut like a screen door in a tornado. "Hello, Jean-Paul," she said. Her voice dripped contempt, and she didn't look directly at him, but at his reflection in the mirror behind the bar.

Jean-Paul was buffeted by the gust of frigid air. He stiffened, then glanced at Lissa. "Good evening, Lissa," he said. Then he looked at me. "Sir."

I nodded back at him and watched as he spun around and marched out into the lobby, his back ramrod straight. Captain Dreyfus after he'd been stripped of his epaulets.

"Asshole," Ann murmured, and knocked back what was left of her drink.

"Ann went out with him the other night," Lissa confided, leaning closer to me than she had to; her breath was grasshopper-minty and tickled my ear. "He was a total washout."

"I thought Frenchmen were supposed to be romantic."

Without moving her body, Ann turned her face toward me so

I could get the full benefit of her sneer. She held her thumb and forefinger about two inches apart, rolling her eyes.

"Oh," I said.

"He said he was some big-shot munitions dealer," Ann whined. That got my attention. "Munitions dealer?"

"Big nothing, if you ask me. And I'll bet he's married too."

"You aren't married, are you, Milan?" Lissa purred, putting a hand on my arm.

"Not anymore, no." I was still thinking about Jean-Paul being an arms dealer.

"I didn't think so. Married men have a kind of—look."

"And I don't?"

She shook her head, pink tongue between her lips. "You have the look of a hunter."

I almost laughed. If anything, I was the hunt-ee.

I bought them another drink apiece, the steel drum ensemble packed up and disappeared, and the sun dipped down into the sea and went out. The three of us decided to eat together, and moved into the dining room to a table by a picture window overlooking the beach. Jean-Paul was at a small booth against the wall; as soon as we were seated he called for his bill, signed it, and left without looking at us.

Lissa and I ordered the specialty of the house, a shrimp dish in a piquant red sauce. Ann had a salad Niçoise at which she half-heartedly picked, smoking two cigarettes in the process. Each of them had two more drinks.

Halfway through the meal a combo appeared on the small stage at the rear of the room and began playing forties dance music. Their fourth selection was "Fly Me to the Moon," apparently a San Carlos favorite.

By the time the coffee arrived—dark, strong, and bitter—they were playing Jerome Kern. Kern was losing by two touchdowns.

Lissa stood up and held out her arms. "Dance with me, Milan."

There were two couples already out on the tiny dance floor, both in their sixties, doing joyless fancy dips and turns as if they'd been dancing together for so long that the spice and novelty had gone out of it. "I'm a lousy dancer, I'm afraid."

"Prove it."

I allowed her to lead me out onto the floor, feeling as awkward as a trained bear. I don't like to dance. I don't believe most men do. Dancing is a girl thing, I think; they perceive it as romantic, almost like foreplay. I think it looks kind of silly—unless it's Fred Astaire.

Lissa draped an arm around my neck—no small feat since I was about eight inches taller than she—and leaned into me. She wasn't much of a dancer, either, but she swayed nicely to the rhythm, and she felt good against me.

"Mmm," she said into my chest. Apropos of what, I didn't know. I held her a little closer because I think she expected me to. The band segued into "Long Ago and Far Away." Same composer, same result.

When the music mercifully stopped, I started back to the table. Lissa put a firm, grasping, almost possessive hand on my arm.

"I'm not finished with you yet."

"Don't you think it'd be polite if I asked Ann to dance, too?"

"Fuck her," she said. She pulled my head down close to her mouth; her breath still smelled like the grasshoppers she'd been drinking, sweet and cool. "I think we ought to go back to your room, don't you?"

A lot of men might have been flattered. A lot would have taken her up on it. But she'd come to the tropics to find a little non-committed romance only to discover that most of the men at the resort were thirty years older than she and had brought their wives; there were only two nights of her vacation left, and I was single and simply available.

Nothing flattering about that.

"Sorry, Lissa. I have an appointment at nine o'clock."

Her lower lip came out like a change drawer at a gas station on the turnpike. "Can't you break it?"

I shook my head. "Business."

Skepticism leaked out of her blue eyes. "At nine o'clock on a Saturday night?"

"A consultant's work is never done," I said.

Just before nine I left them both at the table. Ann had been sulking since the moment I met her, and now Lissa had jumped on that particular bandwagon too. Not the best company for a Saturday evening. It was the second time in two days an attrac-. tive albeit slightly drunken woman had made me an offer I couldn't refuse—and I'd refused them both.

I just couldn't seem to get it right.

* * * * * * *

CHAPTER TEN

* * * * * * *

Eladio's taxi came for me at nine o'clock on the dot, chugging up to the main entrance of the San Carlos Inn trailing an effluvium of purple smoke. He had on a nylon shirt with big red hibiscus all over it and had knotted a white scarf around his neck, probably because he thought it made him look dashing. I got in and we set off with a lurch that almost gave me whiplash.

"Change your mind, eh?" Eladio seemed happy about it—his eyes twinkled in the rearview mirror. "Good. You don' be sorry."

"I hope not," I said, meaning something else entirely.

We started up the narrow road that banded the side of the hill, Eladio navigating it with ease and confidence, the transmission groaning. After about fifteen minutes the jungle thickened on either side of us, and outside the narrow beam of the taxi's headlights the darkness was almost total. Eladio stopped the car, turned his head and spoke over his shoulder.

"You got the money?"

"Sure."

He reached out his right hand, palm upturned. "I think you better give it to me now."

"Half now, half later."

"No, señor. Tha's not how we do it."

In the middle of the jungle with no other transportation and a slim-to-none chance of getting picked up by a passing car, I was in no position to argue. I reached into my pocket. "How do I know the girl is going to get any of this money?"

"You don', man. You don' know shit. You pay for somethin', you gonna get it. Tha's all you got to know."

"How do I know it's the right girl? The one who was with el turisto from O-hi-yo?"

" 'Cause I tell you so. I don' lie to you." he said, sounding wounded, aggrieved.

I sighed and peeled off three twenties and a ten, passing them over the front seat. "Gracias, señor," he said, inclining his head politely, and tucked the bills into his shirt pocket.

He put the car in gear again. The heavy, sweet smell of tropical flora was almost overpowering. The headlights seemed woefully ineffective to me, but Eladio seemed to have no trouble finding his way.

It took us about twenty mintues to get to the center of Ciudad San Carlos. It seemed tackier at night than it had that afternoon, meaner, with too loud music coming from scruffy bars. Not so many tourists now, after dark, but mostly locals, men, lounging on the sidewalk holding beer bottles.

We stopped in front of a three-story hotel that wasn't as crummy as I'd imagined it would be. It looked kind of like a Caribbean Days Inn.

"Okay," Eladio said. "You see down there, block an' a half, at the corner?"

I leaned forward and peered through the dirty windshield. Several taxis were lined up at the curb where he was pointing.

"When you finish, go over there an' get in a cab. Any cab, is okay." He took another of his business cards and wrote something illegible on the back. "Give the man this, he take you back to the inn. Yes?"

"All right." I pocketed the card. "Where do I go?"

"Room 201, secon' floor."

"And that's the girl who was with my friend?"

He nodded vigorously. "From O-hi-yo. Her name is Luz." He grinned widely. "Have a good time, señor."

I got out and shut the door, and he peeled off from the curb before I'd taken two steps.

I might have been suckered. There might be no Luz, no room 201, and the Spanish he'd scribbled on his card might have read, *Take this moron out and dump him in the jungle.*

Then again there might be a room 201—with three big guys in it, waiting to lighten the weight in my pockets.

I went through a glass door into a brightly lit lobby that smelled of equal parts disinfectant and barbecue sauce. The only thing tropical about the decor was a woeful potted palm at the edge of a sisal rug. A TV set with the world's lousiest reception played to an empty room. It could have been a cheap hotel in downtown Youngstown.

Off to the right was a dingy little lounge with a long wooden bar and several tables at which parties of three and four men, mostly Anglos looking as if they'd just wandered in from the barroom scene in *Star Wars,* huddled in doubtlessly clandestine conversation—which might have been why the blatant Latin jazz was played so loud, so that no one could be overheard.

Straight ahead of me was a staircase that had once been grand and elegant. Its maroon plush carpeting was threadbare, and the banister wobbled when I put my hand on it. Several steps creaked a noisy protest as I climbed.

The second-floor hallway was dim, its stucco walls painted a deep beige more suitable for outdoor trim. The same maroon carpeting covered the floor, and the smell of disinfectant was even stronger.

Room 201 was at the far end of the corridor. Tinny music emanated from behind several of the closed doors as I passed.

I knocked on the door, listening for male voices, for any suspicious movement; all I heard from inside was a small, tentative "Sí?"

"Eladio sent me," I answered, never having felt quite as dumb.

After a few seconds the door was opened by a young girl. Short and slim with skin the color of coffee with lots of cream, she wore a simple shift that was obviously her only garment and low-heeled shoes with no stockings. Her long black hair was pulled back at the sides by two mismatched barettes. She couldn't have been more than sixteen years old, but it was sixteen the hard way.

"Luz?"

Her eyes were small and very dark. "You from Eladio?"

"That's right."

She smiled a smile she didn't mean a bit of and stood aside so I could come in, closing and locking the door behind me. The bed was queen-size and looked surprisingly clean. At least it had been neatly made. In the corner was a washbasin. She went to it, turned on the water, and wet a washcloth. "You wan' take your pants off now?" She picked up a bar of soap.

"No," I said. "I just want to talk to you for a while."

That was all right with her. She put down the soap and washcloth and dried her hands. Then she moved over to me, reached down to the hem of her shift and began pulling it up.

"No, don't do that," I said. "I just want to ask you a few questions."

Clearly puzzled, she sat on the edge of the bed, hands clasped between her knees, completely passive. This was going to be easier than she'd thought. "You got to make it fast, man. Eladio gets mad."

"This won't take long." I sat down next to her. Removing Joel Kerner's photo from my jacket pocket, I held it out to her. She didn't look at it.

"About ten, eleven weeks ago. This man. American, like me. He was here. You remember?"

She still hadn't glanced at the picture. "I see many men."

"Look at him. You remember him? About my age, maybe a little younger?" I tried not to let my impatience show. "Look at it, Luz. Por favor."

She took the photo with two hands, and I thought I detected a change in the pattern of her breathing, "Okay."

"He was here to see you, wasn't he?"

A long time passed before she answered. "Maybe."

"He was, wasn't he?"

Small, reluctant nod.

"Tell me what happened."

She stood up angrily, throwing the picture down on the bed and moving to the other side of the room. "What you think happen, man? Why you think men come here?" She whirled around to me, her dark eyes dancing fire. "You want hear about it? Eladio tell me maybe you kin' of funny."

"I don't mean that," I said. "Tell me what he was like. Was he sad? Angry? Did he act scared?"

"I don' remember," she said, but she wasn't very convincing.

I took a twenty-dollar bill out of my pocket. "Luz, it's important. This man got killed the next morning. Somebody shot him on the beach."

Her face contorted in real panic. "I don' know nothin' about it!"

"I know—but I want you to tell me what he said, what he was like. If he did anything unusual."

"Un-u-su-ull?"

"Funny." I held out the twenty. She stared at it, then took it and put it in a drawer in the night table.

"You remember, don't you, Luz?"

She sniffled, nodding.

I waited.

"When he firs' come," she said haltingly, "he act like he was mad."

"Mad at you?"

She shook her head. "Jus' mad. He keep cursing. 'Son of a bitch!' he say. Lotta times. An' then after . . ." She colored a little and looked down at her shoes.

"It's all right. What happened after, Luz?"

She took a deep breath, then raised her head and met my eyes. "After—he cry. Like a baby. He jus' cry in my arms."

I walked down the seedy stairway of the hotel, ideas churning in my brain. I was no closer to finding out who killed Joel Kerner, but I was a little closer to Joel himself, the man he had been. A very troubled man, I thought—and wondered why.

As I crossed the lobby I heard Ahmad Jamal's version of "Poinciana" coming from the jukebox in the adjoining bar. Jamal, a jazz legend in the fifties, isn't heard so much anymore, although he gave a concert in Cleveland a few years ago. He's a piano player's piano player, one I didn't expect to hear on a jukebox in one of San Carlos's less felicitous hotels.

When I glanced in at the bar I got an even bigger jolt. Jean-Paul, my next door neighbor at the Inn and Ann's date from hell, was at one of the tables, talking to two fair-skinned men who were definitely not San Carlosites. I slowed my pace a bit. When he saw me he frowned deeply and said something to his two companions, who turned and gave me piercing looks. I simply nodded and walked out of the lobby and onto the sidewalk.

Things had quieted down even more out there, perhaps because the humidity had become oppressive. In fact, for several blocks in either direction there didn't seem to be any pedestrian traffic at all. The street was dark, lit only by the neon sign in the window of the hotel bar and the streetlight way down near the taxi stand. The ozone smell of rain was in the air, and I figured we were in for a tropical cloudburst.

I started down the sidewalk for the first of three taxis, immediately sweating through my shirt at the small of my back. What was Jean-Paul doing in that sleazy bar? Who were the other men he was with? Was there something bigger and more complicated at work here than I'd first thought? And did it have anything to do with what happened to Joel Kerner?

Half a block from the corner there was a gangway that ran along the side of the hotel, probably for laundry and deliveries and such. As I passed it I sensed a quick movement behind me, but before I could react to it an arm snaked around my neck, cutting off my breathing, and I was hauled off the sidewalk into the darkness.

The pain in my windpipe, added to the surprise, blinded me for a second. When I was able to see again, someone behind me still had his arm wrapped around my throat—someone who had eaten onions for dinner. There was a skinny, dark-skinned young man wearing a tattered sweatshirt dedicated to the glory of the University of Miami Hurricanes standing in front of me. The way he slowly waved the four-inch blade he held was almost mesmerizing.

"Give us you fockin' money, man," he said, making a very theatrical pass with the knife, close to my face. A stylist, he was.

The grip around my throat tightened, apparently as a punishment for my slight hesitation, and I was more worried about having my windpipe crushed than about being cut. If he didn't loosen up I was going to black out. I jerked my head back hard, and he let go as the cartilage in his nose crunched against the back of my skull. I lifted one foot and raked the heel of my shoe down along his leg, probably taking off most of the skin, and then smashed down hard on his instep when I got to the bottom. Sidestepping as he fell, I grabbed for the wrist of the knife wielder with my left hand.

He twisted away from me, but he wasn't fast enough to avoid the straight right shot to the mouth, which popped his head back. His eyes crossed, and he staggered backward, tripping over his own feet. As he went down he swiped at me with the blade, slashing the inside of my left arm. When he hit the ground the knife clattered away on the uneven paving, and I kicked it out of his reach. Then I spun around to face the one who'd been choking me.

He was bigger than the one I'd decked. He stood against the wall of the hotel, the foot I'd stomped on about six inches off the ground, a dazed expression on his face and blood streaming out of his nose. I stepped forward and drove my knee up between his legs, and he emitted a shriek so high-pitched that all the dogs within three blocks must have perked up their ears. He doubled over and threw up, too near my shoes for my liking.

The one who'd been waving the knife said something terse and guttural in Spanish, scrambled to his feet, and took off running down the alley.

I looked down at the other one. He was squatting against the wall with both hands clasping his crotch, his crushed nose at a funny angle. I could have beaten him senseless if I'd wanted to.

I nudged him with my shoe. "Fuck off,' I said.

I don't know if he understood English, but he understood that all right. He hauled himself painfully to his feet and started off down the alley, walking very strangely, kind of bow-legged, the way John Wayne used to when he got older.

I went back into the hotel and the desk clerk informed me that the nearest hospital was about three blocks away. He didn't seem very concerned, or even interested, that my coat sleeve was slashed and soaked with blood. In this neighborhood it was probably business as usual.

I walked to the hospital holding my left arm with my right hand, trying to stanch the flow of blood. When I got there, I found the building run-down and decrepit. The emergency room nurse called the cops, and after that I only had to wait twenty minutes before they took me into a cubicle where a doctor not much older than my older son disinfected the wound and put seven stitches into my arm.

Just before he finished a young policeman with skin so black it was nearly purple entered the cubicle and in very halting English asked me what happened. He made some notes, asking for a description of my assailants. My answers, I could tell, weren't satisfactory; it had been dark in that gangway. He snapped his notebook shut in exasperation, gave me his card, and told me to report to the police station the next morning.

That's all right, I thought, I was planning on going there anyway.

The hospital charged me a hundred dollars for the emergency care, and I was on my way. It had begun to rain, the hard, drenching rain of the tropics, and the asphalt beneath my feet was steaming. I took Joel Kerner's photograph from my ruined sports jacket, put it in my hip pocket, and dropped the jacket into a trash receptacle on the street; I figured someone else would be wearing it by morning, rip and bloodstain notwithstanding.

By the time I got to the cabstand, I was soaking wet and my arm was throbbing. I climbed into the first cab in line and told the driver to take me to the San Carlos Inn.

Then I handed him the card Eladio had given me. He looked at it, then back over the seat at me, grinning a mile wide.

"Eladio, sí," he said, and pulled out into traffic.

We rode out of town in silence. When we were back on the mountain road, he said, "So, señor. You have a good time, no?"

"Nifty," I said through gritted teeth.

CHAPTER ELEVEN

I awoke early the next morning. My arm was stiff and sore, but I could flex my fingers all right and figured no permanent damage had been done. There'd probably be a scar, but I was full of those already, some of them dating back to my football days. One doesn't play on the defensive line without getting banged up.

The barely postadolescent doctor who'd stitched me up had warned me not to let the wound get wet, so I ran a warm bath instead of my usual shower, using some of the bath salts the San Carlos Inn had supplied, and lay back in the tub with my left arm draped over the edge. I spent about fifteen minutes just luxuriating in it—an entirely different proposition from standing under the punishing needles of a brisk shower. It could be habit-forming.

The shirt I'd worn the night before was wadded up in the wastebasket, the left sleeve ripped and caked with dried blood. I slipped on another of my polo shirts, the light blue one, and the slacks I'd worn the night before, and packed everything else in preparation for my return flight, which was scheduled to leave at three o'clock that afternoon. The tropical sun was just beginning to burn off the heavy morning fog.

I opened the drapes.

There was a knock at the door, firm and masculine.

"Yes?" I called.

"It is Jean-Paul d'Arcy," came the muffled voice. "Your next door neighboor."

I was surprised, but not much. I opened the door.

He wore loose-fitting slacks and an eye-achingly strawberry red pullover, which was untucked, and leather sandals with no socks. The smell of too much Canoe wafted from him; a cologne I hadn't smelled in years.

"Bon jour, Mr. Jacovich." He not only knew my name but how to pronounce it, although we hadn't been introduced. Men like Jean-Paul d'Arcy have their own ways of finding out things.

"Bon jour," I said.

"Jacovich. A Slavic name. Slovenian, from the spelling."

"Very good, Mr. d'Arcy."

He inclined his head, accepting the compliment. "I heard your water running, so I knew you were awake early on this beautiful morning and decided to take the liberty of knocking. Would you care to join me for breakfast? In my room? Everything is ready."

"That's very kind," I said. "But I have lots to do this morning before my plane leaves, and—"

He reached behind him and took a small .22-caliber pistol from the waistband of his slacks. I should have known at once he was packing when I noticed he hadn't tucked his shirt in. The gun didn't have much stopping power, not like my own .357 Magnum that I kept in my desk drawer, or even the .38 police special I sometimes carried. But it's the weapon of choice for professionals who need to do close-up work. Wet work, they call it. And I had no doubt that M. d'Arcy was a professional.

"Please," he said, still smiling.

Well, I thought, as long as he asked nicely.

I slipped my room key into my pocket and went out into the hall, walking ahead of him. He'd left his door unlocked; he reached by me and turned the knob and it swung open.

The room was the mirror image of my own, except I'd opened the curtains to let in the morning sunlight and his drapes were drawn tightly shut. True to his word, he'd ordered quite a nice breakfast for two. On the table was a large tray, with a pot of coffee and another of hot water, tea bags, jam, bagels, cream cheese, and a nice assortment of beignets.

He gestured at one of the two chairs at the table with his pistol. "Make yourself comfortable."

"I'm never comfortable when I'm on the wrong end of a loaded gun," I said.

I sat down and poured some coffee; it was very hot and very strong. I selected a bagel and spread some cream cheese on it, the kind with chives—which I don't like, but what the hell, I didn't like being there in the first place.

He took the chair opposite me and helped himself to some coffee, too, using his left hand, his right being occupied with the .22.

"You've hurt yourself," he said, looking at my bandaged arm.

"No, somebody else did it for me."

"Perhaps because you were someplace you were not supposed to be—sticking your nose where it doesn't belong." He took a sip of coffee and beamed. "We French prefer strong coffee. I hope it's all right for you."

"Do you always issue invitations to breakfast at gunpoint, M. d'Arcy?"

"Only when someone follows me and I wish to know why."

"Follows you?"

"I saw you in town last evening." He picked up a beignet and took a bite out of it. "Surely that couldn't have been a mere coincidence."

"It couldn't have been anything else," I said. "I have no interest in you. I never laid eyes on you until yesterday, and I didn't even know your last name until you told me just now."

"Then what were you doing at the Hotel Antibe?"

"Is that the name of it?"

He nodded.

I fidgeted in my seat. "I was—visiting a woman," I said.

"A prostitute?"

I sighed. "That's right."

"Forgive me, Mr. Jacovich, but I find that extremely difficult to believe. I noticed you had drinks and dinner with the two young American women from Washington last night."

"That's right."

"Surely you realize either of them would have been more than happy to satisfy your desires. They're easy—both of them. That's what they came to San Carlos for—some anonymous and impersonal fucking. I'm afraid it's their idea of romance." He chuckled and took another swallow of coffee. "I had the blonde myself."

"Not very nice to kiss and tell."

"I'm not a very nice person." He patted his lips with a napkin. "So I don't believe you were in need of a whore at all. Unless you have sexual requirements that are—outside the norm? I wouldn't think so, though. You look so American, so ordinary."

"Thanks," I said, stung. "But I didn't want the prostitute for sex. I just wanted to talk to her."

He raised an eyebrow. "You could have saved yourself a ride into town, to say nothing of the money." He pointed at the bandage. "And been none the worse for wear, either. I'm sure one of those lovely ladies would have let you talk dirty to her—for nothing."

"I didn't say anything about talking dirty. Do you put a sexual spin on everything?

He shrugged. "It's a national characteristic. So I'm sorry, but I don't believe you."

I thought for a moment and decided I had nothing to gain by keeping the truth from him. And possibly something to lose—like my life. "May I take my wallet out of my back pocket?"

He put his other hand on the .22 to steady it. "As long as it's only the wallet, monsieur."

I opened my wallet, took out a business card and the photostat of my license, and handed them over to him. "I'm a private investigator from Cleveland, Ohio," I said as he examined them. "Eleven weeks ago a man from my area was shot and killed on the beach while staying at this hotel."

"I heard of the incident," he said, nodding. "Tragic."

"Yes, it was. At the request of his family I came down here to look into it. The young woman I visited last night—the prostitute—he was her client the evening before he died. So I wanted to talk to her."

Handing me my bona fides, he uncocked the pistol and returned it to the waistband of his trousers at the small of his back. "It sounds just bizarre enough to be true."

"It is," I said.

He smirked at me. "Monsieur Jacovich, I hope you'll pardon my saying that you are a hopeless naif."

I've been called many things during my checkered career, but this was a first. "Why?"

"Don't you know what the Hotel Antibe is?"

"You mean besides a whorehouse?"

He threw back his head and emitted a hearty laugh from deep down in his belly, showing me the gold crown on one of his back teeth. "My God, you *don't* know."

I waited.

"My dear friend, because of its very liberal laws—and a police department that defines 'corrupt'—San Carlos is a haven for every shady dealer in the world. And the Hotel Antibe is headquarters. Clandestine arms deals, drug smuggling, espionage. It's sort of a haven, a cop-free zone, if you will, for every international gangster and supplier of contraband in the world. The Mafia, the Chinese triads, the Japanese yakuza, the Colombian drug cartels. My God, you must have been the only person in the place who isn't wanted somewhere." He laughed again. "And yes, my friend, it is certainly a whorehouse as well."

"I can see why you were upset," I said, feeling very much the fool. "I must have screwed up one of those clandestine arms deals for you."

"You did, as you put it, screw up something—temporarily. But it was not an arms deal."

"You mean you have sexual requirements that are outside the norm?"

"Only in terms of quantity, I fear." He pulled out his own wallet, extracted a card encased in plastic, and tossed it over to me.

Jean-Paul d'Arcy—Inspector, INTERPOL, it read.

"I'm impressed," I said truthfully.

"Do not be. It's a job." He replaced the card in his wallet. "You said your plane was leaving this afternoon?"

"That's right."

"Pity. This is a lovely spot for a holiday. I trust your errands this morning do not include a return visit to the Hotel Antibe?"

"No."

"Good." He pointed at my bandage again. "It is no place for innocents." He sipped some more coffee. "Please. Finish your breakfast."

"I think I'm finished, thank you. All right if I go back to my own room?"

"Certainement," he said airily. "And I apologize for interrupting what will surely be a fascinating day."

I stood up and went to the door.

"Good luck with your little murder, Mr. Jacovich," he said.

My little murder. I suppose to men like Jean-Paul d'Arcy, all human life is cheap. I resisted wishing him good luck with his little dick.

After all, he still had the gun.

Chapter Twelve

I went to check out a few minutes later; the same smiling young woman was behind the desk. I tucked the receipt in my wallet and then went out on the patio to look for my pal Heriberto, to say good-bye.

I caught a glimpse of him ducking around the side of the bar shack; strange, I thought. I strolled back there and found him crouched under a palm tree.

"Heriberto, I wanted to—"

There was a swollen blue bruise under his eye.

"Hey," I said, "what happened?"

"It is nothing, señor," he said, turning his face away. He stood up. "I got to go."

"Wait a minute. Who did this to you?"

He shook his head, keeping his eyes averted.

"Was it Mr. Ybarra? The manager?"

"No, señor."

I stopped, remembering the ugly house dick glaring at us the day before when we came back from the beach.

"Was it that security guy?"

The boy looked up at me, eyes widening.

"It was because you were with me, wasn't it, Heriberto?"

His expression grew frightened, almost panicked. "Don' say nothing, señor. Por favor."

"Don't worry, Heriberto. You won't lose your job. And he won't hurt you again." I took two twenty-dollar bills from my roll and stuffed them into his shirt pocket. "This is for being such a good friend, Heriberto. I'm in your debt."

He tried to give the money back. "You don' need to give friends money, señor."

"Maybe I don't need to," I said, ruffling his hair. "But I want to, okay? Just between you and me."

He lowered his eyes, and I drew him to me in a hug. His strong young arms could barely meet around my waist. Just like Stephen, only with dark hair and dark eyes. "You're good people, Riberto," I said. "I'm gonna miss you."

I went back into the lobby, feeling mean and sour.

"You would like a taxi to the airport, señor?" the woman behind the desk said.

"Not just yet. I'd like to see the head of security, please."

I waited off to one side, my gut on fire. If a kid is punched around and slapped, he grows up thinking that's the way things are, and he punches and hurts others, and the cycle of abuse continues. Someone has to stand up for kids. Otherwise, it isn't fair.

Fair. That's why we have rules. Like Marko's, like the ones in baseball or football, rules only work when everyone follows them. If someone is going to break the rules, only a chump keeps playing fair.

The security guy appeared from the guest wing. "You wan' me?" he said gruffly.

"Yes," I said. "On a matter of some delicacy." He knitted his brow, confused. "It's a secret," I clarified. "Somewhere we can talk alone?"

He looked around. "The bar is not open yet," he said. "You wan' go in there?"

I set my garment bag on the floor near the desk and followed him into the darkened cocktail lounge.

He turned to look at me. "*Qué?*" he said.

I punched him hard in the left eye. He wasn't expecting it, and the blow sent him reeling back against a barstool. It toppled, taking the three stools next to it down with it in a kind of domino effect. He went down, too, all tangled up with the legs of the stools, and lay there looking up at me, almost in shock, a mouse swelling rapidly under his eye.

Now I was even for Heriberto, I thought. But even wasn't enough. I reached down and grabbed his shirtfront, hauling him to his feet. Several buttons popped.

When he was upright I slapped him across the face, once forehand and once backhand. The second one brought blood out of his nose.

"Listen, cabrón," I said, still holding on to his ruined shirt. "You listening?"

He bobbed his head, terrified the way most bullies are when someone stands up to them.

"Heriberto," I said. "If I hear you ever hit him again—or that he loses his job . . ." I took a deep breath. "You know the Hotel Antibes? In town?"

He nodded again.

"I have many friends at the Hotel Antibes. They won't like it if anything bad happens to Heriberto, comprende? They won't like it at all, and they'll blame you."

His good eye widened in fright.

"That wouldn't be good for you, would it?"

He wigwagged his head rapidly from side to side.

"So you better make sure Heriberto is okay, right?"

He nodded.

"Right?" I said, raising my voice and drawing my fist back again.

"Sí, señor," he said hoarsely.

"Bueno," I said, and shoved him backward. He tripped over the fallen bar stools and went down in a tangle again. I gave him one last hard look and went out into the lobby, picking up my bag next to the desk.

"I'll take that taxi now," I said. "Por favor."

The police station in Ciudad San Carlos looked like a police station in any small town in Iowa. Built of yellowish brick and cinder block, it was squat and ugly and bore the unmistakable look of officialdom. Outside on the small lawn a San Carlos flag snapped smartly atop a tall flagpole.

The desk sergeant and I had a language problem, I discovered at once. When I finally made myself clear to him, he picked up a telephone, said a few words in Spanish, and ushered me into the office of a Captain Sanabria, whom I took to be the man in charge, given the size of his lair and the ridiculous Graustarkian uniform he wore, complete with gold epaulettes you could have served a steak on.

He'd been waiting for me.

I took a seat opposite his big mahogany desk, putting my garment bag on the floor next to me. He patted the file folder he had before him. I could see my name upside down on the tab. "You've assuredly crammed a lot of excitement into your short visit to San Carlos, señor," he said in barely accented English. "I hope you will not return to your home with a bad impression of us."

Since I hated to disillusion him, I didn't tell him that my bad impression of San Carlos could fill a thick book.

"You are recovering from your injury?"

"What's a little scar?" I said.

"You are gracious. Please be assured that everything is being done to find and punish your assailants of last night. However, with random youth violence rampant on the streets . . . " He gave a rather charming little shrug.

"Suppose I don't think it was random, Capitán?" I said. "Suppose I think someone was really out to get me?"

"Then I would tell you that you are being a trifle . . . " He searched for the word for a few seconds. "Paranoid."

"You think so?"

He nodded. "This is your first visit to San Carlos, no? You know virtually no one here. Why would anyone deliberately desire to hurt you—excepting that they wished your wallet?"

"Maybe because I've been asking questions someone doesn't want answered."

He opened the folder and sifted through the sheets of paper

inside. "Yes," he said, "questions. In the unfortunate matter of young Señor Kerner."

I leaned back in my chair. "I'm impressed with your jungle drums, Capitán."

He raised an eyebrow.

"You seem to know an awful lot about me already," I said.

"We have the usual complement of criminals here, just like anyplace else in the world. Robberies, muggings, an occasional killing over money or gambling or a woman. But when a tourist is shot on the beach, it gets our attention. So some of my friends here on the island have been—*alerted.*" He leaned into the word. "To keep me informed of any activity or development related to that case."

"And is everything being done to 'find and punish the assailants' of Joel Kerner?"

He blinked. "Everything that is possible."

"What does that mean?"

"It means—confidentially, Señor Jacovich—that I believe the killer or killers are not on this island."

I waited for him to elaborate, and for a moment I thought he wasn't going to. We played who-blinks-first for a while. Then he picked up a cigarette case, opened it, and extended it to me. The cigarettes inside were brown and didn't look like anything I wanted to light up, so I shook my head.

He took one out, examined it as if it were a strange specimen of seashell, then lit it. The acrid stink of the smoke made me feel better about my refusal.

"Even though we are a sovereign nation here in San Carlos," he said, "we are tiny. Almost like a small town. As jefe of the policía, I generally know exactly what is going on here. We have had incidents before—but if it were any of my local bad boys, I assure you they would have used a knife. Just like the men who attacked you last night. Except for those that are out there in my own gun case, which I keep under lock and key, there is not a single shotgun of the type that killed Joel Kerner on this island."

"I assume you'd be notified if anyone brought such a weapon through customs?"

He nodded.

"Then how did it get here?"

His smile was downright avuncular. "I think you know, señor."

"By boat," I said, voicing my suspicions about the inlet on the beach. "Someone took a small boat into that little lagoon just south of the San Carlos Inn, got out and shot Kerner, and then sailed away again."

"That is what I believe too," he said.

"But where did they come from? The nearest island is at least eighty miles away, over open ocean."

"You know your geography," he said. "But there are many men skilled with boats. For such a one, it would have been a simple matter."

"I don't suppose you've checked with St. Albans to see who rented or chartered a boat?"

He took another puff of his noxious cigarette and waved the smoke away from his face. "Over two hundred and fifty boats were rented at St. Albans that weekend," he said. "More than half by Americans. It would be a daunting task to track each of them down—especially since it's entirely possible that the killer would use an assumed name."

"Why?"

He laughed. "Wouldn't you?"

I took out my pack of Winstons and shook one out; then I noticed him eyeing them hungrily. "Try one of mine?" I said.

He stubbed his own out with alacrity. "That is kind," he said. "American cigarettes are a luxury a poor civil servant cannot afford."

I didn't ask him how a poor civil servant could afford a desk the size of Vermont and a uniform with enough gold braid to outfit an entire marching band. I just gave him the Winston, grateful I wouldn't have to smell his brand anymore.

"Then wouldn't it make sense, Jefe, that the same person would hire those two thugs last night to take me out?"

"It is possible," he said. "In a poor country, everything is for sale." He made some notes on one of the pages in my folder.

"We shall take that into account should we apprehend the men who hurt you."

"If you think Kerner was killed by an off-islander, why is the official verdict that it happened in the course of a simple robbery?"

"Because," he said, "an off-islander would mean the case had international implications. So much bureaucracy, so many forms. We don't wish to become involved in anything international."

"And yet you have a hotel not ten blocks from here that's a virtual clearinghouse for international gangsters and smugglers. How do you explain that, Jefe?"

"I already have, Señor Jacovich," he said with an absolutely straight face. "In a poor country, everything is for sale."

CHAPTER THIRTEEN

It was nippy and raining in Cleveland again on Monday morning, with the wind churning up the surface of the river and whipping up stray papers so they flew around above it for the wheeling, cawing gulls to dodge. The temperature hovered just below sixty degrees, and the fine cold mist in the air was the kind that gets into your bone marrow and chills you from the inside. Just the ticket after twenty-four hours in the tropics. Welcome home.

Patrice Kerner was sitting in one of my client chairs. She wore one of her power suits, this one a medium blue that gave her olive skin an unattractive greenish-yellow tinge; she was more suited to fall colors, brown and orange and rust and yellow. She shuffled in her hands without really looking at them the expense sheets I'd submitted for my trip. That was because she was pretty shaken up by what I'd reported to her.

"I don't believe this," she was saying, shaking her head slowly from side to side as if that would make it go away. I felt a rush of sympathy for her—the truth isn't that easily banished.

"I'm sorry, Patrice," I said—we'd at least progressed to first names. "But from everything I learned down in San Carlos, your brother wasn't the random victim of a robbery and killing. He was the intended target. I'd bet anything the killer came from right here in town—or from somewhere else where Joel might have known him."

She compressed her lips to try and keep her emotions from spilling out again, causing little white lines to form above and below her mouth.

When she finally got herself under control she said, "Who would want to *deliberately* kill someone like Joel?"

"That's the question. Do you want me to stay on this and try to find out?"

She dropped her head forward on her chest, and mumbled an indistinct "I don't even know anymore" into her chest.

I gave her some time, but she didn't seem disposed to say anything else. "Let's look at it, Patrice. Now that we've more or less eliminated any San Carlos locals, asking around Cleveland is going to be a whole lot easier. But you have to remember that the trail is old, almost three months old—and cold. That's going to make it really difficult."

She raised her head to look at me.

I shrugged. "I can't make any promises."

"Promises . . ." she murmured.

"It's up to you."

She filled her chest up with air and held it there for a bit; then the breath rushed out of her. "Of course," she said helplessly. "I want to know."

"Then I have to ask you if Joel might have been into anything—hinky."

"What's hinky?"

I hesitated. Hinky is one of those street words, like skanky and skeevy and snarky, that is its own definition. I took a stab at it. "Suspicious. Not exactly kosher."

"How can you even ask?" she raged. "Joel was the most decent, honest—he wouldn't even take a stick of gum that didn't belong to him!"

"I don't mean stealing. I mean did he have anything to do with people who might be—questionable?"

"God, I don't know," she said, slumping in her chair. "Probably."

"Why do you say that?"

She looked up at the ceiling. "He was down at the courthouse all the time. That's where you run into a lot of—hinkys."

I suppressed a smile. Hinky was not, and has never been, a noun. "What about Pat Stranahan?"

"What about him?" she said. "He was Dad's friend, not Joel's."

"And he's not a hinky?"

She shrugged. "Not so's you could notice. Union politics get rough sometimes. But no more than anything else. The infighting in some big glamorous corporations would curl people's hair if they knew about it. I'm sure Pat Stranahan cut a few corners now and then. But he wouldn't have anything to do with Joel— or Joel's world."

"What was Joel's world, Patrice?"

"He just wanted to be a good lawyer and help people. He always said that insurance companies screw over the little guy, which is why he went into personal injury practice." She twisted her mouth. "He and I used to go round and round about the kind of corporate law I practice. He said I was just helping the rich get richer."

"Unusual for a kid born to the purple, isn't it?"

"That's just the way he was. So I can't imagine him ever getting involved with anyone on the wrong side of the fence. He was just too good. He was probably the—*goodest* person I know."

"But you said the other day that the two of you weren't really close."

"We weren't."

"Why not?"

"Sibling rivalry, I suppose. I was the older one, but Joel . . ." She squared the papers in her lap. "Joel was the crown prince."

I didn't say anything.

"God's favorite," she added. "I was named after my deceased maternal grandfather—at least, we have the same initial—which is a Jewish tradition. But when Joel was born, to hell with tradition. He was Junior, and supposed to be a perfect little Xerox of my father. The keeper of the flame, the bearer of the name. The white hope."

"That must have been a lot of pressure on him."

"It was." She cleared her throat, hard, to get rid of the frog. "But God, he thrived on it! He and my father were peas in a pod. Best buddies. Dad adored him from the moment he took his first breath, and the feeling was always mutual." She laughed the kind of mirthless laugh people affect when something is too painful to be funny. "My mother and I always were a little bit outside the picture frame."

"Did you resent that?"

"I learned to live with it. But it did create a distance between Joel and me. And between my father and me." She patted the papers on her lap. "It doesn't make me feel very good now, but that's the way it was."

"So you're closer to your mother?"

"Sure. But Dad was always king of the hill and emperor of the household. That made Mom and me subjects." Then she sat up and crossed one leg over the other, swinging it impatiently. "Why all these questions? What does any of this have to do with what happened to Joel?"

"I don't know," I said. "I never know why I ask a question until I hear the answer."

She squeezed out a grudging smile. "It's just the opposite with lawyers. They tell you in first-year law school never to ask a question in court unless you already know the answer."

I swallowed the dregs of my coffee. "Here's another one I don't know the answer to. When Joel was killed, your father made quite a bit of noise and stirred up things down at police headquarters. A natural response, I guess. Yet when I saw him last week, he begged me to stop looking. He even offered me money to stop. I'd like to know why."

"Me, too," she said, rolling her eyes toward the ceiling. "He raised hell with me about hiring you. I don't know, some people think it's easier just to go on, to heal, to allow the grieving process to work. I guess Dad wants that. He wants us to put Joel's death behind us and get on with our own lives."

"And you don't?"

She shook her head so hard that it mussed up her hair. "I can't live with not knowing—especially after what you've just told me."

"All right," I said. "Then you want me to stay on it."

The words came out like grapes shoved through a keyhole: "Whatever it costs."

She wrote me a check for the expenses and got herself together and left. I heard her heels clacking down the steps, and I went to the window to watch her cross the parking lot to her car, her shoulders hunched up and her purse held over her head, that futile, almost silly attempt people make to keep their hair dry in the rain.

Ed Stahl and I were having lunch at the small, intimate bar of Jim's River House, just steps from my office building. One of the most venerable restaurants in Cleveland, it sits right on the point of Collision Bend and caters to an eclectic lunchtime crowd. Rainmakers from the downtown brokerage houses sit cheek-by-jowl with warehouse workers from the Flats, and the occasional ink-stained wretch who finds his way down from the editorial offices of the *Plain Dealer* on East Eighteenth and Superior.

I say "his way" advisedly; not too many women lunch at the bar at Jim's, although Ray, the affable daytime bartender, would be more than pleased to see them. The dining room is spacious, with almost the same view as from my office window, but the bar is tiny, clubby, and decidedly masculine.

Ed and I were both having steak sandwiches and the delicious hash browns that are a house specialty. I know we were probably raising our cholesterol counts to dangerous levels, but in my years on this planet I've discovered only a handful of immutable truths, and one is that the only two things that really taste good are sugar and fat.

I told Ed everything that had happened so far in the case of Joel Kerner Jr.

"All the way to the Caribbean and you only stay twenty-four hours," he said. "You're a schmuck, Milan. You could have at least gotten a weekend out of it."

"Sitting around getting sunburned isn't my idea of a weekend."

"You couldn't tell it by looking at you," he said. "Rudolph the Red-Nosed Reindeer."

I rubbed my burnt nose. "Ever hear of a guy named Patrick Stranahan?"

He dumped enough steak sauce on his sandwich to float a kayak. "Pat Stranahan, Local 696? Sure. He's one of the last of the real old-timers in the labor movement. Kind of a dinosaur, really. Today your union executives learn their manners at Berkeley or the University of Chicago; Stranahan started out on the construction crews, dancing on a girder twenty stories above the ground. One tough little mick son of a bitch. He's old now." He belted down a gulp of Jim Beam, grimacing when it hit his ulcer.

"Is he a straight guy? Or bent?"

He shook his head. "Milan, I swear you sometimes sound like the pampered son of a white-bread family from some suburb like Avon Lake instead of a millworker's kid from Sixty-seventh and St. Clair. What's straight and what's bent? Everybody cuts a corner now and then—except you, maybe." He forked a hunk of hash browns into his mouth. "Union bosses are like high-priced lawyers or cardiac surgeons—you do what you have to do."

"That sounds like John Wayne in *Hondo*."

"It sounds like John Wayne in everything," he said between mouthfuls, "but that doesn't make it any less true. When the labor movement got started, things were pretty rough. There was wrongdoing on both sides." He pointed his fork at me and sighted down it. "But if there hadn't been some guys like Stranahan around to kick ass and bust heads, we'd all be working for slave wages and owe our souls to the company store."

"Any headbusting going on these days?"

"Some. Not so much. Times have changed a little. We're civilized now."

"What about mob ties?"

"Aw, Christ, Milan, give it a rest. You've had the mob on your mind for years, ever since you first butted heads with them. You blame everything on the outfit, from the Browns defecting to Baltimore to tornado warnings in Portage County."

"I never blamed a tornado on them," I assured him. "And I know damn well whose fault it is that the Browns moved."

"Fine. So you're a wonderfully open-minded human being.

Look. I'm not sitting here saying there aren't any corrupt unions anymore, or any corrupt guys in them, but for the most part they're on the up-and-up. Jimmy Hoffa's been dead a long time."

"You sure? He just might be showing up with Elvis at the local Dairy Queen."

He ignored me. "And even though labor has lost a few sharp teeth, most of the working people in this country can thank God for trade unionism."

He took out his pipe and pouch; the bar at Jim's is one of the few places left where no one much gives a damn whether or what you smoke. "What does Stranahan have to do with Joel Kerner?"

"Maybe nothing. He's friends with Kerner's father. I saw him at their house."

"So?"

"I told you about the hotel in San Carlos, though, Ed. It's Bad Guy Central for organized crime all over the world."

"Parts of Detroit are Bad Guy Central, too," he said, stuffing the bowl of his pipe. "But if you went there to take in a Pistons game and happened to get killed on Woodward Avenue, it wouldn't necessarily mean that organized crime was behind it." He lit up and was instantly enveloped in a blue-gray cloud. "Most crime is *dis*organized anyway."

I cut into my steak. "That's a little glib."

"Don't believe me, then," he said. "Go right to the source."

"Meaning?"

He sighed. "You know all the made guys in this town. You even go to dinner at their houses."

"Once!" I exploded.

"Whatever. You have a connection there."

"A pretty spiky one."

"Don't give me adjectives. I hate adjectives. They're weasel words."

"Did they teach you about weasel words in J school?"

"What they taught me," he said, "was the higher up you can go to talk to someone, the more likely you are to get something vaguely resembling the truth. And you're stupid not to do that, seeing as how you have a relationship with Victor Gaimari."

"I haven't even seen Victor Gaimari since last fall, or talked to him. I have a *relationship* with you. I have relationships with my friends. With my clients, my lovers, my children. What I have with the outfit is . . . "

He cocked a satanic eyebrow at me and puffed away. His pipe made a sickening, gurgling sound.

"A relationship," I admitted lamely.

CHAPTER FOURTEEN

I have to explain about Victor Gaimari.

Victor is number-two man on the organized-crime depth chart in northeastern Ohio. Number one is his uncle, Giancarlo D'Allessandro, who's old and frail and asthmatic and leaves the day-to-day running of the family business pretty much to Victor now. But he's still sharp mentally. He calculates every angle, weighing it carefully to ascertain how much profit might accrue from it. I've never known him to miss a trick.

But D'Allessandro never gets his name in the papers—that's part of his genius. Victor is the front guy, the one with the image. Handsome and fit, he looks like Cesar Romero did in 1942—dark mustache, big soft dark eyes, and a dazzling white smile that comes at you out of a year-round tan. All that and his considerable power and charm is enough to make him one of Cleveland's most eligible bachelors. He's a stockbroker, an Ohio State graduate, a patron of the arts, and gives generously to worthy causes.

He could also have both your kneecaps broken with just a phone call.

I first met Victor several years ago on a missing-persons run-down that turned into a murder. We didn't exactly hit it off. He made a veiled threat against my family, I punched him in the nose, and he had three of his goons beat me senseless. Since then our paths have crossed too many times for my comfort. I asked him for a favor once, and he's asked me for a couple. Guys like

Victor tend to keep score on those things. And somehow whenever I find myself up to my ass in alligators, Victor seems to be standing somewhere in the darker shadows.

His uncle, the don, thinks I'm the greatest thing since marinara sauce. Because I treat him with respect. That's big with the don, respect.

I don't dislike Victor, exactly. Over and above the personal charm I grudgingly cede him, he and his organization have standards, at least, and a certain convoluted kind of honor that sort of endears them to me in spite of myself.

So when I picked up the phone to dial Victor's number, it was with mixed feelings. I knew what he was, and that was hard to overlook—but he wasn't as bad as he might have been. And I needed his help.

His secretary at the brokerage put me through to him only with reluctance. She was there on that long-ago day when I punched him in the nose and has never forgotten nor forgiven me. It hurts, kind of. She's old enough to be my mother.

"Milan!" Victor said in that peculiar, almost girlishly high-pitched voice of his. "How delightful to hear from you!"

Not many people could actually say something like that without it sounding completely affected and phony. Victor pulled it off with ease and grace.

"How've you been, Victor?"

"I am well," he said. "Better now for talking to you. What's up?"

"I wonder if I could have a few minutes of your time? I'd like to run something by you."

"That sounds heavy."

"It might be. How's this afternoon?"

I heard pages flipping. "A bitch. Can you meet me for a drink after work? Five thirty at the Renaissance?"

I had to stop and think for a moment until I remembered that the Renaissance was the new name of the grand old Stouffer's Hotel on Public Square, right next door to Victor's office in Terminal Tower. Not so new, actually; it's been a couple of years now. But I still haven't gotten used to it.

Then again I have to catch myself to keep from saying things like icebox and phonograph and davenport. Ed says I'm retro—and he's right.

"That sounds fine, Victor."

"You're buying the drinks," he said.

I hung up, chuckling. Victor was trying to be a good guy. He probably had more money in his pocket than I had in the bank; making me pay for the drinks was his way of not rubbing my nose in it.

I kept thinking about Stranahan's attitude when I'd seen him at Joel Kerner's house. I couldn't imagine how it would fit in with what had happened to Joel Junior, but it nagged at me. I wondered who I could call that knew about the labor movement in Cleveland.

There was, of course, a union for police officers. I'd been a member myself. But law-enforcement people live in a world unto themselves, and I didn't think any gung ho union cop would have much information about Stranahan and his construction union.

And then I thought of Chet Tumbas.

A friend and neighbor of my parents in Slovenia, Chet Tumbas had come over to America at about the same time they had. He and my father had worked shoulder to shoulder on the floor of the steel mill, and when my father died, Tumbas became shop steward in his stead. I remembered him coming to my home, remembered even more vividly when my father had taken me to a union meeting and Tumbas had stood up and spoken passionately, even eloquently in his broken English.

I didn't even know if he was still alive. If he was, he'd be in his eighties, I calculated. I got out the telephone directory and looked him up. Sure enough, he was listed, on East Sixty-fourth Street, three blocks from the house where I grew up.

He answered, his voice low and guttural, raspy, like when you step on sand on a linoleum floor.

"Mr. Tumbas," I said. "This is Milan Jacovich. Louis Jacovich's son."

For a moment there was silence. "Louie's boy?"

"Yes, sir."

"Holy God!" he said. "Louie's boy! I don't see you for twenny years already. How you? How you doin' now?"

"I'm fine, Mr. Tumbas. I was wondering if I could come over and see you this afternoon?"

The alacrity with which he agreed almost broke my heart. Chet Tumbas had never married. As far as I knew, he had no family. And at his age, I imagined most of his friends were gone, like my father. He probably didn't get many visitors.

I drove up out of the Flats in a wet mist that beaded up on my windshield and headed east, past the plaza where the statue of Lincoln stands in front of the Board of Education Building. The statue had been paid for with the saved pennies of Cleveland schoolchildren and is said to portray the Great Emancipator delivering his Gettysburg Address. Just in front of him on the grass, a homeless man with a bewildered look was delivering an address of his own to an invisible audience.

Heading east on St. Clair Avenue, it struck me that though Cleveland is a city with definite eastern sensibilities and a midwestern work ethic, it is laid out more like the newer cities of the west, with broad, wide streets and an open feel, so unlike the narrow, almost claustrophobic main drags of Philadelphia or New York. Just one of the many things that makes it unique.

Things have changed little in the old neighborhood where I played and fought and grew up. The steeple of Saint Vitus Catholic church still rises over the squat frame houses, and most of the businesses are still Slavic owned, like Smrekar Hardware, Nosan's Bakery, and my old hangout, Vuk's Tavern. There are new and definitely non-Slavic additions now, including the Empress Taytu Ethiopian restaurant, which serves deliciously spicy food to those brave enough to try it. A lot of black families moved in when the more well-to-do Slovenians and Croatians deserted to suburbs like Euclid and Eastlake, but there was a familiarity to the streets that was comforting to me.

I stopped at Azman and Sons, a little mom-and-pop store that has been on St. Clair and Addison for as long as anyone could remember, and bought a six-pack of Stroh's; in the Slovenian community one doesn't come visiting without a small gift.

The house I was looking for was painted a light blue-gray with white trim. There were opaque white curtains in the windows, and displayed on either side of the door were the Stars and Stripes and the national flag of Slovenia.

I could hear a polka playing inside, a vinyl platter, not a tape or a CD—it had that scratchy, played-too-often sound. The Slovenes of Cleveland love the polka, or at least their own particular version of it. They dance it smooth and fluid, like figures in one of those glass globes that you shake and snow starts falling. I'm told that Poles who dance the polka tend to hop a little more, although recently the Slovenians have started hopping, too.

I knocked on the heavy oak door, feeling its solidity and strength.

After a moment it opened and Chet Tumbas stood there grinning, looking to my surprise just as I remembered him. He was almost as tall as I, probably had been taller when he was younger, before age had compressed his skeleton. He was more wrinkled, of course, with crepe paper skin at his jowls and underneath his eyes. His hair was white, clipped very short, and his earlobes were long and pendulous. He wore a pair of steel-rimmed half-glasses which made him tilt his head back when he looked at me.

"Louie's boy," he rumbled, nodding his head. "Yah. You look just like father."

"It's good to see you again, Mr. Tumbas," I said, and extended my hand. He pulled me to him in a clumsy embrace, his day-old stubble rough on my cheek, and pounded me on the back with the flat of his hand.

"Milan," he said into my ear, pronouncing it the old-world way, Mee-*lahn*. I didn't correct him as I usually do; to Chet Tumbas that was the right way to say it.

"Come," he said. "You'll sit."

He led me into a neat, tiny living room. Antimicassars, their lace yellowed with age, graced the back of overstuffed chairs. The rug that all but covered the hardwood floor was floral and a little faded. On the wall, in a place of honor over the small fireplace, was a framed color photograph of Ljubljana, the capital city of Slovenia. On the other wall was an inexpensive print of the Virgin Mary and the infant Jesus.

I offered the six-pack. "I thought you might be thirsty, Mr. Tumbas."

He beamed as he took it from me. "Good," he said. "T'ank you. Doctors say I shouldn't drink beer no more. You know what I say? I say nuts to doctors." He gestured at the largest and most comfortable-looking chair, the one facing the small TV set that perched on a wooden stand next to the hearth. There was a cable converter on the floor next to the stand. On the other side of the fireplace was the record player, an RCA at least twenty years old. "Sit. I get glasses."

He went through the equally tiny dining room into the kitchen, and I could hear him clanking around in there, taking glasses from the cupboard, and then the satisfying hiss of two beers being opened.

He came back with discount-store glasses and the two beer cans on a tray. Setting the tray down, he served me, and then he lifted the tone arm off the record, turned off the stereo, and sat down on the sofa, pouring his beer expertly, tilting the glass so there wouldn't be too much head.

"To Louie—your pa," he toasted, raising his glass. "And to your ma."

We drank.

"Your ma," he said, wiping the foam from his lips. "Mirijanna, yes?"

I nodded.

"Such a beautiful woman. Beautiful skin—like a peach." He ran the tips of his fingers over his own cheek. "A good woman. And dose eyes . . ." He closed his own, lost in a reverie.

"You look well, Mr. Tumbas."

"I'm okay," he said. "I'm—I don' know—eighty-two or somet'ing. So for eighty-two, I'm good." He looked at me and nodded approval. "You grew up a big boy. You look like Louie. Bigger than him, though."

"I guess I am."

"What you do now, Mee-*lahn*? You don' work in the mill?"

I shook my head. "I was a policeman for a while. Now I'm a private detective."

His bushy eyebrows lifted. "Like who is it—Barney Jones on the TV?"

I smiled. Any resemblance between Buddy Ebsen's Barnaby Jones and a real private investigator was strictly coincidental. "Sort of."

"I see him alla time on Nick at Night." He took another gulp and put his glass down on the coffee table. "You look tougher than him. Younger. Bigger. Is good work, like Barney Jones? You make money?"

"I do okay," I said. "And sometimes I get to help people who have troubles."

"Everybody got troubles, Mee-*lahn.*"

"I'm working on a case now. Maybe you can help me."

"Ah. That why you come see me." He shook his head. "I don' t'ink so. Not be much help to no one no more."

"You were active in the union when you worked at Deming."

He puffed up his chest proudly. "I was shop steward. Twelve year, I was steward."

"You knew all the labor people in town?"

"Not all. Some." His jaw jutted out like a speed bump in a parking lot. "Most."

"Did you ever run into a labor official by the name of Pat Stranahan?" He was in the construction union.

He brightened. "The Irish?"

"Is that what they called him?"

He nodded. "Sure! I know Stranahan. Good man. Tough. Not big, not like you an' me. But tough in his mind." He tapped his temple with a thick forefinger. "A man tough in his mind, don' matter how tough he is in his fists. Besides, the Irish don' need be tough in his fists. He got a guy do that for him."

"Who's that?" I said.

He screwed up his forehead, trying to think. "Big guy. Irish, too. Got crap all over his face. Little holes, like." He twiddled on his own cheek with his fingers.

"Pockmarks?" I said, remembering the man I'd seen at Joel Kerner's home, waiting for Stranahan.

"That what they call 'em?"

I nodded and took a sip of my beer. "Stranahan, was he honest?"

Tumbas rubbed at his nose. "What is be honest?" he finally said. "Everybody try to make a buck."

"He's a union official," I said. "Their job is to take care of the rank-and-file, no?"

He looked down, not meeting my eyes. "The Irish take care his people okay."

"But he made a buck or two on his own along the way?"

He shrugged.

"Stranahan is still active," I said. "He's the treasurer and business manager for his local. He handles all the money. Do you think he handles it honestly?"

Tumbas looked into his beer, swirling it around a little the way people do with a bourbon on the rocks. "He don' steal from his people."

"You sure?"

"Not that I ever hear. Oh, sometime he make side deals, maybe, you know? All them guys make side deals. But when he handle money belong to his men, he don' steal."

"If he's so honest," I said, "how come he needs a bodyguard? The guy with the pockmarks?"

He waved a huge hand at me. "So what? The president got bodyguards. Does he steal?"

I'd like not to think so. "Okay," I said. "How about a lawyer name of Joel Kerner? Big labor lawyer. Does he steal?"

"Mee-*lahn*," he said with patience. "I work on floor of mill, thirty-fi' years. Wit' these." He held out his gnarled hands. "I don' know lawyers. Lawyers for guys wit' suits. Not working man."

He was right, of course. What goes on in courtrooms and boardrooms and union offices is miles removed from the world of the rank-and-file, who get their hands dirty and their backs bent. They strike or not, as they're told, and paying their union dues makes them think they have a say in what happens in their own lives. Men like Kerner did indeed wear suits—expensive ones—and never even got their hair mussed.

I looked at Tumbas. He was still an imposing figure, despite his age, but there was a sadness in his eyes that got to me. A lifelong bachelor with no family, most of his friends, dead, like my parents. No job, no union position. He didn't have much motivation to get out of bed in the morning, I thought.

"How are you doing, Mr. Tumbas? Now that you're retired. You okay?"

He shrugged. "Sometime okay. I watch the TV a lot. Old stuff. You know, Barney Jones, Sheriff Andy. And mass on Sundays, always. Sain' Vitus." He finished his beer in one long draught. "I go down the union hall, hang around some days. Talk to the guys. Not so many left from the old days. I miss them sometime. Miss your pa."

I wanted to ask him if he had enough money, if he was able to live on his pension, but I didn't. He would have been insulted. Slovenians don't consider that kind of inquiry polite. Besides, with a paid-for house and car, and medical benefits from his years at the mill, his expenses were probably negligible.

"You have to keep busy," I said.

"Yah. You, too." He derricked himself up out of his chair and loomed over me, and for a moment I could see echoes of the powerful, lusty man he must have been in his prime. "This Irish. Stranahan. He does wrong with the money?"

"I don't know, Mr. Tumbas."

He shook his head. "He's a good man. Union man. He don' do wrong with the money. I bet not."

I got up, too. "I bet you're right," I said.

He went with me to the door and we shook hands.

"Mee-*lahn*," he called to me as I walked down the path. "You come back sometime, yes?"

"Yes," I said, turning to face him. "I will."

"You look like your pa," he said. "The way you hold you'self. You just like him, like Louie."

I do look like my father. He was better-looking, at least when he was young, and I'm taller than he was, but there'd be no mistaking the relationship if you saw the two of us standing together.

How much do I resemble him in other ways? Louis Jacovich never finished high school and I got my master's from Kent State, thanks to his saving for my education from the day I was born; he wanted better for his son than the grinding life of a steel mill. His command of the English language was on a par with Chet Tumbas's. He went to church every Sunday of his life, and I can't remember the last time I took communion or made a confession. He worked with his hands and his back and I make a living with my head—and sometimes my chin. He was happily married to my mother until he died, thirty-two years; my marriage lasted just twelve tumultuous years, and I've been through enough busted relationships since that I'm starting to believe that marriage—like auto racing and Brussels sprouts and going to the opera—is fine for other people but probably not right for me.

And yet I know that an awful lot of who I am comes from my father. He wasn't verbose and didn't pass out a lot of unwanted advice, but when he did talk I listened. He instilled in me the love of books and music—Slovenians love to sing—and every month he took two books in Slovenian out of the public library and read them slowly and carefully. By osmosis, I guess, he imparted to me the wisdom to know the difference between what's right and what isn't, and the courage to do something about it whenever I could. He could be pretty rigid, like me, and for a man of his limited education and sophistication he had a finely honed sense of the ridiculous; I remembered how his eyes would twinkle at other people's foolishness, although he never seemed to judge them— a trait I could use a little more of, I'm told.

Most of all, I think, he gave me a sense of pride in who I am, and a comfort in my own skin.

Not a bad legacy. I wondered whether twenty years after I was gone my own sons would be thinking similar thoughts about me. I hoped so.

I wondered how Milan Junior had done on that test.

I drove down the ramp, right across the river from my office, and parked my car in the subterranean garage underneath Tower City. Then I made my way up the escalator, through the food court and the huge atrium where a fountain sprayed dancing waters in rhythmic and artistic patterns, up a central staircase grand enough for an emperor's entrance, and past row after row of smart shops and boutiques to the lobby of Terminal Tower, which connected to the lobby of the Renaissance Hotel.

It's one of the most beautiful public spaces in town, with its marble fountain in the middle, its soaring ceiling, and its graceful arched windows that look out on the urban bustle of Public Square. People consider it Cleveland's front yard.

Victor hadn't arrived yet, so I went into the lobby bar, took a table back by the windows, and ordered a Bushmills on the rocks. When drinking with Victor Gaimari, having anything as mundane as a Stroh's makes me feel self-conscious, like a peasant who's been asked to tea with royalty.

Self-assurance seemed to radiate from him, gentle ripples in a charismatic pond, as he walked across the lobby and into the lounge like he owned the place. Like he didn't ever sweat or sneeze or have intestinal flu or get scuff marks on his highly polished Giorgio Brutini shoes. The way we'd all walk if we were as rich and good-looking and powerful and well-connected as Victor Gaimari.

"Milan," he said with warmth anyone might swear was genuine, "it's so good to see you." The high-pitched voice seemed to belong to a smaller man. "How are you?"

"I'm swell," I said, and extended a hand.

He shook it with both of his, put the topcoat that was draped over his arm on an empty chair, and glided gracefully into his own seat in such a way that his gray sharkskin suit wouldn't sustain a single wrinkle. Victor usually wears gray or tan to the office, as opposed to the blue, off-black, or charcoal suits he sports when seen around town of an evening with the daughters or ex-wives of the most socially prominent people in Cleveland at the kind of glittering events often reported by Mary Strassmeyer in "Mary,

Mary," her who's-doing-what column in the *Plain Dealer*. He gets his name in the paper a lot.

I hadn't seen him in a while, and I couldn't help noticing that there were a few strands of silver at his temples, and in his dark mustache. It looked good on him—but he was getting older, Victor.

Me too.

He ordered a Bombay Sapphire martini straight up with a twist, very dry, and we chatted for a few minutes about inconsequential trivia as people often do to prime the conversational pump. He asked about my sons. Usually when Victor mentions my family it sets my teeth on edge, but this time I even answered him genially. Maybe I'm getting mellow too.

It wasn't until after a second round of drinks had been called for that Victor said, "Milan, as much as it pains me, I know you didn't set this meeting up because you were longing for my company. And I do have somewhere to be this evening, so . . . "

Give him credit, he didn't just look ostentatiously at his watch.

"All right, Victor," I said, "I'll get to the point. Do you remember reading in the paper a few months back about a Cleveland man named Joel Kerner being killed while on a vacation down in San Carlos?"

"Of course. His parents and I know each other socially. And his sister. That was a terrible tragedy. I sent flowers to the memorial service." He nodded his thanks at the cocktail waitress as she set our drinks on the table and toyed with the delicate stem of his martini glass, his long, tapered fingers caressing it like a lover's. "How are you involved with that?"

"As you know," I said, "the police here have no jurisdiction over anything that happens in a foreign country. And the San Carlos authorities are calling it a random killing during the course of a robbery. That explanation doesn't satisfy Joel's sister."

"Ah, Patrice," he said. "A pretty woman. A little severe for my taste, but very pretty, wouldn't you say?"

"Yes, but that's hardly the point."

"So she's hired you to look into it?"

I nodded.

He sipped his drink as if a movie camera was focused on him, and rolled the gin around on his tongue. "Are you suggesting that I might have some involvement in young Joel's death?"

"I don't think that, Victor. A shotgun in the face isn't your style. But I know about San Carlos. About what goes on there. And I'm trying to put pieces together."

"Right," he said. "Like a jigsaw puzzle. I know that's how you operate."

"So maybe you can supply me with a few missing pieces."

"I don't know whether to be flattered or irritated that you'd ask me. But that's kind of the way our relationship is most of the time, isn't it?"

"It's nothing personal, Victor. And you know I'm discreet."

A vertical line appeared between his eyes for a moment. I had something on Victor, from a case I'd worked on a while back regarding a priceless piece of English porcelain. Nothing that would put him in jail, but if the word got out, it would make him look pretty silly. And to a man like Victor, that's worse than a legal problem; he has lawyers to take care of those.

"Do I detect the softest whisper of blackmail here?" he said easily.

"I think you know me better than that."

He laughed. Or at least he smiled and said "Ha ha," which is as close as Victor Gaimari ever gets to laughing.

"Let's just say," I said, "that in the past we've done each other favors, and we may again in the future."

He touched his mustache with the tips of his fingers, smoothing it down. Victor always preens his mustache when he's thinking. It's the sort of gesture a man makes when the mustache is new and he isn't used to it yet—but Victor has been wearing his for all the years I've known him. "All right, Milan. So San Carlos is the hangout for some bad boys. It's also a popular vacation spot for ordinary people from this area, some people in the Jewish community, a lot of people closely involved with the labor movement. I don't know why, exactly. Things like that just happen. A lot of Clevelanders, especially the Italians, go to Naples, Florida, for the winter. Why don't they go to Miami or Palm Beach or Port St. Lucie instead? Certain places attract certain people."

"What was Joel Kerner doing in San Carlos?"

He raised both his shoulders—not enough to ruin the drape of his suit, though. "From what I've heard, scuba diving, windsurfing, and jogging on the beach."

"That's all you know?"

"He didn't share where he went or what he did with me."

"Victor, don't jerk me around. All I want to know is whether he was in San Carlos for something illegal."

He took another taste of his drink and smacked his lips. "To my knowledge, no."

"He went to the Hotel Antibes the night before he was killed."

Victor showed no reaction other than a rather interested blink. He has long, dark eyelashes, so when he blinks it's noticeable.

"Are you familiar with it?"

"I've never been to San Carlos."

"But you've heard of the Hotel Antibes?"

He shrugged. "I've heard of Yellowstone National Park, too, but I've never been there either."

"Don't be glib."

"Don't tell me what to do, Milan," he said without heat. "I hate that."

We sat and looked at each other over our drinks, two men who could never quite decide whether to be friends or enemies, each of whom saw and recognized the potential threat in the other. Somebody could write a textbook about our relationship, I thought—because despite the ethnic differences, the diversity of lifestyles, and our very different values, Victor Gaimari and I are more alike than either of us cares to admit. Stubborn as hell, rigid, and neither of us suffers fools gladly.

"All right," he said genially, "so the Hotel Antibes is a hangout for some pretty unsavory people. But that doesn't mean everyone who goes near the place is unsavory. Young Joel Kerner was, as far as I know, as clean as McGuffey's reader. His father, well, that's another story. But Junior could have qualified for sainthood—or whatever the Jewish equivalent of sainthood is."

"How is Joel Senior not clean?"

"I don't know for sure," Victor said, "and I don't like rumors or innuendo—I get enough of them leveled at me. I haven't talked to Mr. Kerner about it, or anyone else, but he handles the investment of pension funds for several locals, and the word on the street is he doesn't handle them very well." He turned his head slightly to look out the window at the traffic. It was the end of the homeward migration, and people were streaming into Terminal Tower and the rapid station deep in its bowels, probably walking not quite as briskly as they had that morning before the workday had taken a serious bite out of their psyches. "It could be that the son went to the Hotel Antibes as a surrogate for his father, although that's a very doubtful scenario."

"Why?"

He followed the progress of an attractive, leggy woman past the window and across the street to the southwest quadrant of Public Square, which is dominated by the statue of General Moses Cleaveland, who founded the city in 1796, gave it his name, and then left, taking that extra *a* with him. "Kerner senior would have no business to transact in San Carlos that I know of. He does his rough stuff in courtrooms and boardrooms and union halls right here in Cleveland. Junior wasn't a tough guy. Not a negotiator. It wasn't his thing. His forte was sweet talk," Victor went on, watching as the woman crossed over to the southeast quadrant of the square where the Soldiers and Sailors Monument rises up into the sky like a dark finger. "You don't hear much of that in San Carlos—at least, not in the circles you're thinking of."

"Then what was he doing at the Hotel Antibes?"

As the long-legged brunette disappeared into the lobby of the British Petroleum Building diagonally across the square, Victor turned his attention back to me. "Did it ever occur to you, Milan" he said, "that the guy just might have wanted to get laid?"

＊ ＊ ＊ ＊ ＊ ＊ ＊ ＊ ＊

CHAPTER FIFTEEN

＊ ＊ ＊ ＊ ＊ ＊ ＊ ＊ ＊

Sure it had occurred to me. But it just sounded too facile, too coincidental. I wasn't going to write Joel Kerner Jr. off quite that easily.

I ransomed my car from the hotel garage and started eastward on Superior. It was getting dark out; the rain had stopped and the streets were so shiny it was hard to see the white lane markings. The rush hour, or what passes for a rush hour in downtown Cleveland, was pretty much over, and it only took me fifteen minutes to get home to the top of Cedar Hill. One of the advantages of living in this city is that you're never more than half an hour's drive away from anywhere you might conceivably want to go.

Victor Gaimari had been remarkably forthcoming, and I don't think it was because I had something on him that was potentially embarrassing. He probably did feel bad about Joel Kerner Jr.'s death—unless, that is, he'd been in some way responsible.

But I didn't think so. In all the years I'd known Victor, and with all the dirty deals I knew he'd been a part of, he had never, to my knowledge, had anyone iced. It's probably not out of any moral conviction that taking human life is wrong, but he's the type of man to consider murder simply too messy to bother with. He's more of a finesse guy, Victor.

He had gotten me thinking, though. Joel Kerner Sr. had possibly mishandled some pension funds, which would mean a lot of people might be mad at him. People that might be associated with Victor Gaimari and Giancarlo D'Allessandro. That was probably why Kerner had turned his home into a citadel.

I walked up the stairs, unlocked my apartment door, and found Milan Junior in the living room, reading *Sports Illustrated,* drinking a soda, and munching from an enormous bag of sour cream–flavored potato chips he had to have brought himself—I rarely have chips on hand.

"Hey," he said.

"Hey."

"Wanta go have dinner out?"

"What's the matter with my cooking?"

He looked at me through half-lowered lids. "Give me a break, okay?"

Since moving my office downtown from my front room, I've been entertaining visitors at home more often, and I'm not half-bad in the kitchen. But Milan Junior doesn't care about that. "Where's your mom tonight?"

"She and Joe went to some church thing. Stephen got stuck going with them."

Religion had been a point of mild irritation during my marriage to Lila. A Serbian, she'd been raised in the Eastern Orthodox church; my Slovenian upbringing had been strictly Roman Catholic. As often happens in situations like that, the kids got stuck in the middle. Milan Junior didn't much bother with church at all anymore, and Stephen dutifully followed his mother's faith unless he happened to be with me on a Sunday morning, at which time he'd ask me to take him to Saint Vitus.

Shoving an alarmingly large handful of chips into his mouth, Milan stood up. "Do you have a Chip Clip?" he asked.

I had to have him explain what a Chip Clip was before I told him no.

He closed up the bag and disappeared with it while I went into the bathroom to wash up. Although I've always been a very private person, I liked the idea of my son's dropping in unexpectedly after school. As a noncustodial parent I've often had to fight fears that my boys didn't care about me anymore, which sometimes rise up like bloody-mouthed demons in the night. I could imagine a scenario where Milan's popping in without notice might be awkward—if I had female company, for instance—but that happened so infrequently these days that I didn't much worry about it. For now, his surprise visits made me feel more like family.

I came out of the bathroom with my sleeves rolled up, and he stared pointedly at the bandage on my arm.

"A little accident," I told him. "Don't worry about it."

He frowned. "Did that happen when you were away?"

"Yes."

"I don't like it that you're always getting hurt, Dad."

I blinked rapidly, feeling my eyes begin to tear. "I got hurt worse than this every Saturday when I was playing football. I imagine you do, too."

"You've gotta be more careful, okay?"

I rolled down my sleeves. "I'm careful driving," I said. "I'm careful when I lift something heavy. And I try to be careful with other people. But you can't go around your whole life just being careful. Nothing ever gets done that way."

"You think you're Superman sometimes."

"You mean I'm not? No wonder the last time I tried to leap tall buildings with a single bound I fell on my ass."

He laughed in spite of himself, but he really wasn't amused. "You ought to find a safer job."

"Sometimes I think so too," I said. "Come on, I'm hungry."

We put on our water-repellent jackets and walked across Fairmount Boulevard in the mist to the Mad Greek. Half the menu is Greek, naturally, but the other half is East Indian. If you're the type of person who shares your meal with your co-diner, the Mad Greek sometimes produces interesting flavor combinations.

"I took the physics test today," Milan said after our food arrived at the table.

I knew he had. I was sure he had come over to talk about it. But respecting that curious and delicate balance parents must maintain with their children, I couldn't be the one to bring it up.

"It was a bitch," he said.

I nodded, busying myself with my avgolemono soup.

"I think I did okay. Not great, but okay." He waited a beat or two—my son is great at dramatic pauses. "But I'm not sure."

I looked up at him and gave him a tight smile. It was his way of telling me that he'd taken the test straight up, no "pony" written on his hand or his shirt cuff. The bubble that had been inside my chest collapsed, and I took a deep breath.

"When will you know?"

"Barr said he'd have the tests graded and back to us on Thursday." He fiddled with his silverware. "Will you be disappointed if I did lousy?"

"Sure. I want you to do well. But I would've been more disappointed if you'd copied the answers. You can always study harder next time. But once you start taking shortcuts, you chip a litle bit of your integrity away—and that's a nonrenewable resource. It doesn't come back."

He licked his lips nervously. "That's what I figured," he said, not looking at me.

The waiter brought us our entrées, lamb stew for me and a curry for him. He'd asked for it extra spicy.

"I'm just lousy at math, that's all," he admitted. "And physics is a lot of math."

"You can get along being lousy in math," I told him. "But you can't get along being lousy at life. So you're okay. You get an A-minus on that."

"Minus?" he asked, looking up quickly. "How come a minus?"

"Keep you from getting a swelled head."

As I watched him eat, pride pumping through my system because he hadn't succumbed to the very real temptation of cheating on an exam, I wondered if he had flirted, even for a moment, with the idea of telling Mr. Barr that one of the other kids had the test answers. I doubted it. Staying righteous yourself is one thing, and ratting out a friend is another.

I'm not sure I would have liked him so much if he had.

After Milan Junior went to bed in the spare room I always keep ready for him and his brother, I sat in the den with a Bill Evans solo CD playing, reading a paperback, smoking a Winston, and sipping on a Stroh's. Reflecting.

When my marriage to Lila came apart, I'd suffered a case of the galloping guilts, even though the divorce had not been my idea. I worried what might become of my sons in a "broken home." Would they wind up on the streets in a hunting pack? Would they resent me forever for leaving? Would their mother's almost immediate start-up with her new boyfriend give them a twisted and skewed view of the world and of relationships in general? And what kind of values would they wind up with?

But for all Lila's faults, she is a terrific mother. Her longtime live-in lover, Joe Bradac, had always treated the boys decently—possibly because he knows what I would do to him if he didn't—and their home life was relatively normal. As for me, I guess I hadn't been a bad father at that. I know I can be pretty tight-assed sometimes, and it's cost me over the years. The ultimate test, of course, is how your kids turn out, and I'm certainly pleased with mine.

More important to me at that moment was that Milan Junior was pleased with me. With the things I'd taught him.

With who I am.

I hoped to hell it would last, but I wasn't optimistic. I knew teenage boys. Some day soon I'd do something Milan considered stupid or old-fashioned or hopelessly dorky, and then the generation gap would widen again, and there wouldn't be a damn thing I could do about it.

Is there always unfinished business between fathers and sons, always circles to be closed? A competition, a psychological pissing contest, a desperate need for paternal approval? Turgenev wrote about it, and Dostoyevsky and Arthur Miller and Ross MacDonald and Saul Bellow. Even Rodgers and Hammerstein, in *Carousel*—"I wonder what he'll think of me. . . ."

What had Joel Kerner thought of his father? Was there a family dynamic there I was somehow missing? And if so, might it shed some light on his death?

Patrice had told me about as much as she was going to, I figured. And Joel Senior had let me know that he wasn't going to discuss anything with me.

Perhaps Pat Stranahan could tell me. He was, after all, a close friend of the family.

The question was, would he?

At eleven o'clock I switched on the news, keeping the volume low so it wouldn't wake Milan, who had turned into a restless sleeper in his adolescence.

It was a slow news day; not much held my attention. I waited for the weather forecast, and was sorry I did—the Doppler radar showed more rain heading for the North Coast the following day. "Thunder cells," the station's meteorologist said, pointing them out on the radar map. When I'd been a homeowner I'd welcomed the rain because it meant I wouldn't have to water the lawn. Now that I lived in an apartment and owned a building that was at least a city block from the nearest blade of grass, the rain just meant one more gloomy, gray day.

Turning off the set, I took the dirty ashtray into the kitchen, dumped it, put my beer bottle in the recycling bag, and dug out the telephone directory. I looked up the number of Patrick Stranahan's local and jotted it down on a pad, leaving it by the kitchen phone so I'd see it in the morning. Then I brushed my teeth, set the alarm so I could make Milan breakfast before he left, and got into bed.

I stared at the ceiling for a long while. When I finally fell asleep, I dreamed about my father.

CHAPTER SIXTEEN

Milan Junior and I had coffee and toast in the morning before he set off to school. It seemed very right, a perfectly reasonable, two-guys-together kind of thing to do—drinking coffee, reading the newspaper, and listening to the antics of Lanigan, Webster, and Malone on WMJI, who were calling someone who was having a birthday and reminding her about her most embarrassing moments. My son was particularly amused when the birthday girl confessed that she had made love in the swimming pool when she was seventeen and gotten caught by her parents.

It was a family moment for us, and it made me feel good. Never mind that when Milan finally left I felt a hollow place; I didn't know when he might come back.

The trouble with your kids growing up is that often they grow away at the same time.

I got dressed, and left for work, ripping the page with Stranahan's number on it off the memo pad and stuffing it in my pocket on my way out.

Once at the office I set a pot of coffee brewing, booted up my computer, and opened the Kerner file. Then I took out the set of index cards labeled with all the players in the Kerner case. I moved them around on the top of my desk, changing their positions in relationship to one another, trying to make some sense out of it. I suppose it comes from playing with jigsaw puzzles when I was a kid; there was one of the Grand Canyon I must have worked on for a month. But I couldn't make the pieces fit this time.

I set myself up with a cup of coffee and dialed the number of Local 696. When I asked for Stranahan, they told me he was in a meeting and couldn't be disturbed until at least eleven o'clock. I hung up smiling—at least I knew where he was.

I fooled around with the index cards for a while longer, but they still didn't speak to me. Finally I got bored with them, so I did some of the bookkeeping work that bedevils everyone who is self-employed, sending out past-due statements and the like, and filling out government forms.

At twenty minutes to eleven I turned off the coffeepot and made my way out of the Flats to the headquarters of Local 696 on Superior Avenue. I left my car on the street, since the gated parking lot required a card key.

The union occupied three floors of a well-kept old building. Their offices were furnished with neither flair nor imagination, but with a stolid practicality. If the pension funds were being misspent, it wasn't on lavish headquarters.

There were several large, beefy men wearing work clothes standing around in the lobby. I've often wondered whether the conventional wisdom that hard physical labor and exercise keeps you in good shape is true or not. If it is, why do so many construction workers have huge bellies?

The receptionist, a pug-nosed, brown-eyed redhead with two incisors twice the size of her other teeth, was one of those small-minded people who had been given a dollop of authority and made it the defining characteristic of her life. She seemed insulted that I was there bothering her. She told me that Stranahan was still in his meeting and assured me that he wouldn't see me without an appointment even when he was through, but I'd heard that one before and decided to wait anyway. I tried to pass the time chatting with her but since she'd failed her charge to keep strangers away from her boss, she was angry with me for stripping her existence of meaning and not interested in anything I had to say. I hoped Stranahan wouldn't be long.

Finally, at twenty minutes after eleven, four men came out of the corridor behind the receptionist's desk. One of them, a man of about seventy, wore a sports shirt hanging outside his pants, the better to camouflage his beer gut. Two others, somewhat younger, wore work clothes—heavy denim shirts, cords, and heavy steel-toed boots. One looked Irish, and the other was African-American. The fourth was Patrick Stranahan.

The Irish. I could see how he'd come by that soubriquet. The round face, the pug nose, and the ragged mustache made him look as if he'd be more at home in a shebeen in County Kerry.

The bad toupee didn't look any better under the fluorescent lights than it had at Joel Kerner's house, but the man himself was obviously more at ease here on his own turf. He was without a jacket, his shirtsleeves rolled up to just below the elbows, and was wearing a bright green tie that didn't go with the blue dress shirt. I tried not to think of what he must look like on Saint Patrick's Day.

He shook hands with the other three men and watched as they went out into the lobby to catch the elevator. Then he turned to me, smiling and frowning at the same time.

"I know we've met somewhere," he said. "Recently. Help me out here."

"Milan Jacovich. It was last week at Joel Kerner's."

"Sure it was." He cocked his head, like a pigeon listening for the whir of the hawk's wings. "You here to see me?"

The receptionist said, "I *told* him he needed an appointment, Mr. Stranahan."

"For a friend of Joel's, I guess I can make some time. Come on in," he said.

I seriously considered sticking my tongue out at the little redhead, but my sense of decorum got the better of me. I followed the union boss into his private office, which was furnished with a little more class than the reception room, but not much. A big window overlooking the street would have let in a lot of warm sunlight, had there been any. On the wall were photos of Stranahan shoulder to shoulder with a host of national and local politicians, from Hubert H. Humphrey to the current governor of Ohio, and several more of him with past Cleveland sports figures like Bernie Kosar, Lenny Wilkens and Joe Charbonneau.

"We seem to be out of coffee. I can have Molly make some more."

If Molly was the receptionist, I figured she'd spit in it before bringing it in. "None for me, thanks," I said. I gave him one of my business cards and told him what I was there to talk about.

Stranahan's face crumpled with what seemed like genuine grief. "God, I still can't get over that," he said. "I knew that kid when he was born. I was the first one outside the family and the hospital people to hold him, y'know. It was like losing my own son." He fell heavily into the chair behind his big desk. "I'm not sure I can help you, and I don't think I can even talk about it without breaking down."

I took a chair near the window and glanced out. There's a certain security in being able to look out a window and see where you've parked your car. "You're close to the Kerner family, then?"

He nodded. "For years. Decades."

"When I saw you at the house last week, you and Mr. Kerner seemed to be at the end of an argument of some sort."

His jaw got stony. "You never have disagreements with your friends?"

"All the time," I admitted. "Mind telling me what the argument was about?"

"You bet your sweet ass I mind! It certainly had nothing to do with Joel Junior."

"Did it have to do with pension funds?"

A muscle twitched under Stranahan's eye. "You're skating on pretty thin ice here, Mr. Jacovich. You have no official law-enforcement status and you're not a member of this union, or any other union, as far as I know. You're fucking around in stuff that's confidential—and none of your business."

"I'm asking because I'm grasping at damn near anything. This case has a lot of dead ends."

"Then you're wasting your time and Patrice's money," he said.

"It was a robbery that got out of hand. Gangsters. Bandits. You know how those people are down there."

"What people?"

He scowled at me. "You know the answer to that, and so do I."

"You mean Latinos."

"Hey, it's a different culture down there," he said. "It's not their fault, really. It's just how they are, y'know. They put a different value on human life than we do."

"I imagine," I said, trying to soften the edge in my tone, "that a San Carlosite or a Puerto Rican or a Honduran wants to live as much as you and I do."

"You know what I mean."

"I'm afraid I do," I said. "But let's say for a moment that it wasn't a random robbery, and that it was somebody from outside San Carlos who did it. Maybe somebody from Cleveland."

He patted at the front of his hairpiece. "Why would you think that?"

"I'm just supposing."

"Why don't you let the police handle it? It's their job."

"It's not their job when a crime is committed in a foreign country. That's why Patrice Kerner hired me."

"So?"

"So could you think of anyone who'd want to kill Joel Kerner Jr.?"

He shook his head. "No. He was a great kid."

"He wasn't a kid, Mr. Stranahan, he was almost forty years old. He must have made some enemies."

"If he did it's news to me. He and I didn't exactly play in the same league, y'know."

"Meaning he had nothing to do with the unions."

"Right," he said, nodding. "It broke his father's heart when the boy didn't follow him into labor law, but that's how it was. I understand that, y'know. Why he wouldn't want to. Joel casts a long shadow in this state."

"Is that why he has such a lot of security at his house? It'd be easier breaking into the mint."

"That's right," he said. "And it makes him feel better, don't you see? Most people who hire bodyguards or carry guns never have to use them, and that's a good thing. But it makes them feel better."

"Let's talk about that a minute. Do you think it's possible, since Joel senior is so well protected, that someone killed the son to punish the father?"

His eyes became slits, almost disappearing in his beefy face. "That's about the sickest goddamn thing I ever heard of. Holy Mary mother of God, where would you come up with a sick idea like that?" He clenched a fist on the desktop, and his voice got louder. "You read every day about gang kids killing people for a jacket, a pair of shoes, just for giving them what they thought was a dirty look. There's no respect anymore, for anything or anyone. Someone killed young Joel for what he was carrying in his wallet, and that's it, now!" He pulled the knot of his tie up closer to his throat. "What you're suggesting, that there was some sort of sinister plot going on—that's impossible."

"Did you ever read Conan Doyle?"

"Who?"

"Sir Arthur Conan Doyle."

His lip curled. "English, was he?"

"He wrote the Sherlock Holmes stories."

"Oh. No. I saw the movies."

"Well," I said, "Holmes always used to say that when everything possible had been eliminated, the only answer left was the impossible."

He crossed his arms defensively over his chest. "Listen, I don't have the time to sit here talking about books with you."

"I'm not talking about books, Mr. Stranahan. I'm talking about a young man you held in your arms as a baby who got most of his head blown off by a shotgun."

That shook him. "You play kind of rough, don't you? Play a little football once?"

I shrugged.

"I'll bet you were one mean son of a bitch."

"Not mean," I said. "Tough. Like I was supposed to be."

"Wusses need not apply, is that the way?"

"That's the way," I said.

"Well, let me tell you something, Mr. Jacovich. That's the way it is in the labor movement too. I can be tough when I want to. I didn't get where I am without being tough. And I damn well resent your whole attitude here. I loved that boy!" His eyes glittered with unshed tears. "I didn't see much of him the past few years. He grew up, got busy. That happens—different generations and all. But what happened to him damn near broke my heart, and to hear you talk about it that way is . . ."

He bit his lip, shook his head, looked down at his lap. "I never got married," he said. "I was too busy with my career, with making this union strong and healthy. It wouldn't have been fair to a woman, don'tcha see? So I never had children. The Kerner kids were like my own." He breathed a ragged sigh; big drops of sweat were forming across his forehead like a tiara that had slipped down too low.

He suddenly shouted. "So don't come poking around here where you've got no business with your questions and innuendos because I don't like it one goddamn bit!"

The office door opened, and I turned to see the pockmarked Irishman I'd assumed was Stranahan's chauffeur slipping in and leaning quietly against the wall, arms folded across his chest like the guardian of a seraglio.

"See what happens when you get me upset?" Stranahan said. "I holler. And when I holler Michael here gets upset. It's better if you don't get me upset." He rolled down his sleeves. "And you shouldn't get the Kerners upset either. They've had a tough time."

"Is that why you were arguing with Mr. Kerner at his house the other day?"

"That was business," Stranahan said, low and mean. "Business goes on."

"Were you arguing about pension funds, Mr. Stranahan?"

He looked at me for a long time. Then he stroked his mustache. "I don't have to talk to you at all. I don't even have to see you. I could have you thrown out of here—via the window."

Michael, the hard guy, stirred behind me, and I shifted my

feet so they were under me and I could get up quickly if I had to. But apparently things hadn't gotten quite that far yet, because Stranahan quieted his bodyguard with a look.

"Let the Kerners grieve in peace, for the love of Jesus," he went on. "Let them heal."

"I'm pretty sick of hearing that," I said. "The best way for them to heal and get on with their lives is to find out exactly what happened to their son, and why. How come Patrice is the only one who seems to realize that?"

"Because she's a damned overemotional woman!" he scoffed. "You know what the best thing for Patrice would be? To get herself a life. Find a husband, have some kids of her own."

"Welcome to the nineteen forties, Mr. Stranahan."

His face turned to granite. In spite of the ridiculous hairpiece and the out-of-date mustache, Patrick Stranahan was indeed a tough cookie. "In the nineteen forties, guys like John L. Lewis and Hoffa and Walter Reuther wouldn't have thought twice about what to do with a wise-mouth like you," he said. "We've talked enough, now. You can take my advice and back off of this, tell Patrice you've done your best. Or you can not. But you're a damn fool if you don't."

He buttoned his shirt cuffs and stood up. "Michael, see Mr. Jacovich out."

The pockmarked young man propelled himself off the wall like an Olympic swimmer making the turn at the end of the pool, winding up at my elbow.

"Don't touch me, Michael," I warned. "Don't put your hand on me. You won't like what happens if you do."

Michael didn't touch me, but he didn't back off either. Never taking his eyes from me, he said, "You want me to fuck with this guy, Mr. Stranahan?"

"Naw, it's all right, Michael," Stranahan said, once more in control. "Come on, Jacovich, I just lost my temper for a minute. Nobody wants to hurt anybody. Be a good fella. Go home. Tell Patrice you tried and couldn't find anything. Give her a break. Give her parents a break."

"Everybody wants a break," I said. "Who gave one to Joel Kerner?"

He walked over to the window. "That's a very painful subject for me, Jacovich," he said. "And I'm too busy to talk to you anymore."

Effectively dismissed, I went back out into the waiting room and then into the lobby. Michael followed me out to the elevator.

"You better not come back here," he growled as he watched me push the down button. "You won't be so lucky next time."

"You think you're that good, Michael?"

"Maybe, maybe not. But I could get ten other guys up here as good as me. Then where would you be?"

"Am I supposed to be scared?"

"No," he said. "You're supposed to be smart."

He waited until I'd gotten into the elevator and the door had closed. A polite and gracious host.

While I was unlocking my car across the street I looked up at Stranahan's window. He was standing there, staring out at me. I waved.

It hurt my feelings that he didn't wave back.

CHAPTER SEVENTEEN

The rainwater hissed beneath my tires as I drove through the manicured streets of Shaker Heights and turned onto South Park. There was no Japanese gardener in evidence on the lawn of the Kerner home this time, nor foraging robins on the grass. And in the gloom of the rainy afternoon the huge, brooding house completely surrounded by wrought iron fencing looked even more like a prison. Far away on another street the sound of a gas-powered mower was all that disturbed an unsettling silence.

I turned into the driveway, rolled down the window of my Sunbird, and pushed the button on the intercom. The box crackled with static, a little green light came on to replace the red one, and the same gravelly voice answered with a curt "Yeah?" Carl Cavallero.

"This is Milan Jacovich. I was here a few days ago. Is Mr. Kerner home?"

"No," the voice said, and the connection was broken.

Well, he'd answered my question. Nothing in the rules said he had to be polite. I waited a moment and pushed the button again.

"What?" This time there was an edge to Cavallero's voice.

"Jacovich again. Is *Mrs.* Kerner there?"

An exasperated sigh whooshed through the speaker like a chinook wind, and then it went dead.

I didn't know whether that was a yes or a no. Lighting a Winston, I sat in my car with the motor running for a few minutes listening to Dee Perry's mellow, low-pitched introductions to great jazz music on WCPN. I was burning even hotter than the tobacco. If you laid the stone walls I'd hit in this investigation end to end, they'd challenge the one in China.

When I finished the cigarette I was finished with waiting too. I was about to back out of the driveway when I saw the front door of the Kerner house swing open. Elaine Kerner came out, wrapped in a heavy cable-knit sweater, her arms crossed in front of her. She stood on the step for a moment, and then started down the driveway toward me.

It took her almost a minute to get from the house to the gate. It was a long driveway.

I got out of the car, hunching my shoulders to keep the mist from getting down my collar. She reached the gate and put both hands on the bars, clutching them white-knuckled, like someone locked in a cell.

"You shouldn't come here anymore, Mr. Jacovich," she said. "My husband would be very angry."

"I don't understand that. I'd think he'd want to know what happened to Joel as much as Patrice does."

"He just wants it to be over."

"And do you?"

She let her hands fall to her sides and looked down at her shoes. A tremor wracked her body.

"I'd like to help."

She sniffled. "You can't."

"I can if you'll help *me.*"

She shook her head and shivered again. Tiny drops of water were beading on the shoulders of her sweater.

"Can we go inside and talk?"

"No," she said. "That's not a good idea." She stared off into the distance through the bars. "No matter what you do, what you find out, it won't bring my son back. It'll only bring more pain. And trouble. I don't want that." She put a hand up to her throat. "I'm sixty-eight years old. I've lost a child. I'm losing everything. I can't take anymore. Leave me be." She raised her eyes to me;

the haggard grief behind them was like an ice pick in the heart. "I'll die if you don't. Literally. I'll die."

A big black Sedan de Ville pulled up beside my car in the driveway, purring so quietly I didn't notice it until it was almost on top of me. Joel Kerner Sr. got out—very quickly for a man of his age—leaving the door open. His face was red and angry, his fists knotted at his sides; I almost felt as if I'd cuckolded him.

"How dare you?" he roared. "I told you to stay away from here. How fucking *dare* you?"

"Joel . . ." Mrs. Kerner murmured.

"Do you want me to take out a restraining order on you to keep you the hell away from us?" Kerner fumed. "Is that what you want? Because I'll get one like a shot! I'll have you brought up on harassment charges. *Stalking* charges!"

"Joel, Mr. Jacovich is just trying to help."

"I don't want his goddamn help!" He flung himself at the intercom box and leaned on the button, relentless as a door-to-door salesman. After a moment the box crackled and I heard Cavallero's bored voice.

"Yeah?"

"Carl, get down to the gate right away!" Kerner barked into the box. Then he turned back on me with an air of angry satisfaction. "You can't go bulling your way into other people's lives, Jacovich."

"I'm trying to do my job. I was hired—"

"I don't care! Patrice made a big mistake going to you—a mistake that I want undone. Immediately! You mess with me, you'll live to regret it!"

Carl Cavallero came out the front door of the house and jogged quickly down the driveway like a man on a mission.

"Mr. Kerner, this isn't necessary."

"I'll decide what's necessary. What's the matter, you going chickenshit?"

"I'm not going to fight a man twenty years older than I am," I said, glancing at the quickly approaching Carl.

All of a sudden there was a small pistol in Joel Kerner's hand. The way he was waving it around, any pigeons flying by were in a lot more danger than I was, but I didn't like it anyway.

"Joel!" Elaine Kerner said, frightened. "Put that thing away right now!" It was as forceful as I'd seen her.

"I think your wife has a good idea, Mr. Kerner."

I thought about taking the gun away from him, which would have been relatively easy. But I was on his property, uninvited. "All right, Mr. Kerner. I'll go."

"Goddamn right you will," he said.

Cavallero got to the gate and opened it from the inside.

"What the hell's the matter with you, Carl, letting this guy hang around here?" Kerner demanded. "What do I pay you for anyway?"

Cavallero looked crestfallen. "Mrs. Kerner said she'd see him."

Kerner turned on his wife. His eyes were as red as his face.

"I'm sorry I caused a fuss," I said, and got back into my car.

"Next time you come near my wife or me," Kerner said, coming around to the driver's side of my car and sticking the pistol through the open window into my face, "I'm going to use this on you, and ask questions later."

That was one threat too many. I grabbed his wrist with one hand and twisted the .22 out of it with the other. It was as easy as I'd thought it would be.

"Next time you point a gun at me," I said, "you'll have to get your proctologist to remove it."

I broke open the gun, emptied the bullets out onto the floor of my car, and tossed it out the window onto the ground. "Wouldn't you feel better if you knew what happened to your son, Mr. Kerner?" I said. "Or do you just not give a damn?"

His head quivered as if with palsy, and he turned away.

Madder than hell, I slammed the car into reverse and backed out of the driveway onto South Park, almost creaming a young couple coasting by on their ten-speeds. The man's bike wig-wagged crazily and spilled him onto the street, which cost him only a little dignity, since he was well-protected with a helmet and knee and shoulder pads. He shouted after me that I was a stupid son of a bitch.

He might have been right.

❖   ❖   ❖

I was ripping mad. So far I'd been insulted, slashed with a knife, threatened with a gun, and generally insulted by everyone I'd come in contact with on the Joel Kerner Jr. case, including a bicycle rider I didn't even know. And I was no closer to cracking the case than I had been when Patrice Kerner first walked into my office and started to cry.

So I drove back to the Flats with care, not wanting to take my aggressions out on a bunch of innocent drivers, chewing over my day so far.

Both Patrick Stranahan and Joel Kerner Sr. had been so anxious not to talk that they were ready to sic their hired muscle on me. That made me wonder what they were hiding, and how finding Joel junior's killer would threaten either of them.

Patrick Stranahan had held the boy in his arms right after he was born. What could Joel have done since then to make Stranahan mad enough to kill him?

Nothing, I decided. Stranahan had seemed genuinely grief-stricken when he talked about it. Maybe union officers were better actors than I thought, but I doubted it.

As for Joel Kerner Sr. killing his own son, you read about things like that in the papers every day, but it simply didn't compute in the case of the Kerners.

But then why didn't he want me to lay his son's ghost to rest by finding the murderer? Why didn't Stranahan? What were they covering up that would lead them to threaten violence, for Kerner to pull a gun on me?

And what did Elaine Kerner mean when she said that she'd lost everything? Joel junior's death would be devastating, of course, but she still had Patrice. She still had her husband, her home.

Or did she?

Since nobody was disposed to talk to me about it, I might never find out.

When I got back to the Flats, Lolly the Trolley, the colorful little tour bus that shows visitors the highlights of downtown, was snaking its way down Old River Road, surprisingly full of tourists even on a chilly spring afternoon. Tourism, believe it or not, is way up in Cleveland the past few years, thanks to our new sports and entertainment venues. But the carrot-topped tour guide didn't point out to the sightseers a slightly fuming, red-faced private investigator who couldn't get a break.

Back in my office, I checked my messages. One of them was from a Mrs. Chrosniak, who said she wanted to make an appointment to get her teeth cleaned. There's a dentist down in Parma whose name is very similar to mine; I wonder if he occasionally gets requests to find missing persons or investigate insurance frauds.

Another was from Teri Levine.

It pleased me to hear from her. She was an intelligent, attractive woman, very appealing despite being under the thumb of a dominating mother. I wondered what she wanted.

I needed some more answers, so I called Ed Stahl at the newspaper but got his voice mail. "I can't talk to you now," his recorded voice said, "I'm busy writing my column—and that's what they pay me for. Leave a message."

I did as I was told.

Then I called Teri Levine back.

"Would it be possible for me to stop by your office tomorrow afternoon, around lunchtime?" she said. "I can be there by twelve thirty."

"Sure, no problem." I scribbled her name down in my appointment book. "Maybe I can take you to lunch."

She hesitated long enough so that I knew what the answer would be. "No," she said. "Not this time."

"Is anything wrong?"

"Everything," she said in that tentative little voice of hers. "I don't want to go into it over the phone."

"All right, then, Ms. Levine. I'll see you in the morning."

"Teri," she said.

"Teri."

Now what was that all about, I wondered.

Maybe she was as anxious to see me again as I was to see her—

but I didn't think so. I'm nobody's idea of a dream date. So it probably had something to do with Joel Kerner. Something she'd forgotten to tell me, something she'd suddenly remembered.

The phone chirped.

"Milan Security."

"Ed Stahl."

"Ed, thanks for calling back. How's it going?"

"I'm blocked."

"Excuse me?"

"I have writer's block," he said, as if explaining something scientific to a small child.

"I'm sorry. Have you tried hot baths?"

"It's not funny! I'm plumb out of anything I want to write about."

"Is that like Alexander the Great weeping because there were no more worlds to conquer?"

"*You* try coming up with twelve hundred words five times a week."

"If I could, I would," I said. "Instead I'm a down-at-the-heels investigator who needs some help from an old friend."

"With a deadline looking me in the eye I'd ordinarily tell you to go to hell. But anything to keep from sitting and staring at a blank page. What do you need?"

"Anything you can dig up from your newspaper cronies about Joel Kerner Sr. and Patrick Stranahan."

"You already know about them."

"I know who they are. I want to know what they're up to. Currently."

I heard noises that indicated Ed was lighting his pipe, thus violating the *Plain Dealer*'s no-smoking policy. "You think Kerner did his own kid?"

The hair on my arms stood up at attention, and I resisted a shudder. "I hope not."

"And I'm supposed to just walk around the city room and ask people like Jane Scott or Bud Shaw?" he said, naming the paper's septuagenarian rock music critic and a sportswriter.

"Like anybody. The business writers, people like that."

"And what if I uncover some evil cabal and want to do my column on it?"

"I'll personally shoot you."

There was a bit of a stage wait. "Kerner and Stranahan are very visible Clevelanders. They're news. If there's a story here, I'm damn well going to write it. It's how I earn the rent money."

"Ed, that would put a serious hitch in my git-along."

"We've each got a job to do." I heard him lip-smacking his pipestem. "You want me to ask around, or not?"

I grit my teeth. "Do it."

"Look, it's two thirty. I've got to file some sort of a column by seven o'clock or there's going to be a big blank space with my funny-looking picture over it. I'll do what I can."

"Great. Call me tonight if you find anything. I'll be home."

"Big swinging bachelor like you, of course you will," he said, and chuckled as he hung up.

CHAPTER EIGHTEEN

I arranged to meet Marko Meglich after work at Vuk's Tavern. Vuk's is on St. Clair Avenue, a few blocks from where I was born. My father used to drink there, and it's where I chose to have my first legal alcoholic beverage on my twenty-first birthday. The proprietor, Louis Vukovich, called Vuk by literally everyone except his aged mother, has forearms like Popeye, an enormous walrus mustache over which his nose hangs precariously like a melting ice cream cone, and a suspicious nature when it comes to strangers. I've known him as long as I can remember.

Marko was as comfortable in Vuk's as I; he spent his formative years running this neighborhood too, and like me, he learned quite a bit about life with his elbow on the hard mahogany of that bar.

I arrived first. Vuk nodded brusquely, bent down to reach into the cooler for a Stroh's, and brought it over. He knew no glass was necessary; I've been drinking in his joint for twenty years.

"Good to see you, Vuk," I said, looking around at the sports memorabilia that decorated the walls. There were bare spots where once he'd proudly displayed the colors of the now departed Cleveland Browns; he wouldn't put them back until the city got a team again. "You all ready for baseball season?"

He shrugged. "Since the Tribe lost Belle and Baerga and Lofton, I don't even give a damn."

We chatted back and forth about left-handed pitching and the dearth thereof until Marko walked in the door.

"It's the chief!" Vuk said, snapping out a salute the equal of any jarhead's. "How ya doin' there, Chief?"

Marko would probably have taken umbrage had anyone else said it; with Vuk, he knew it was simply rough affection. "Vuk, how'd you like me to trump up charges against you so I can take you downtown and bounce you off the walls a little?"

Vuk put a Stroh's in front of Marko. "It'd be a righteous bust— I bet on basketball games."

"I didn't hear that," Marko said.

It was just past six o'clock, and Vuk's was starting to crowd up as business wound down for the day and workers were set free. They were mostly male, mostly blue-collar, and almost exclusively Slovenian or Croatian. Of course at Vuk's they don't call it happy hour or the cocktail hour, or attitude adjustment. They just call it having a beer after work.

"You look tired, Mark," I said.

"I am. You know what I'm most tired of? Paperwork. I'm drowning in it."

"Isn't it kind of nice getting up in the morning and knowing nobody's going to take a shot at you?"

"Sure." He flexed his fingers as if they'd grown stiff from lack of use. "But I'm starting to miss being on the street."

"The price of success."

"I don't mean I'd want to be a uniform again, but piloting a desk sometimes makes me feel old."

"Don't all those very young women you go out with keep you feeling like a kid?" I asked, unable to resist the dig.

He actually blushed a little. "That's another thing," he said.

"What?"

He searched for the words. "I'm getting a little tired of running around, Milan. Tired of women who are too young to remember who Gene Wilder is. Tired of living alone." His face got red, and he fingered his dark mustache. "I—I miss being . . . married."

That called for a big swallow of beer. I wiped my mouth. "Wow. Who's the lucky woman?"

"Well, see, that's the problem. There isn't one. I haven't met just the right one yet. I'm looking around, though."

I gestured along the bar. "Not in here?"

He laughed. "No. God, no! I see this woman in the lobby of the Justice Center every so often. She's really pretty. Maybe in her late thirties. Big blue eyes. She looks—nice. You know? Just—nice. The kind of woman you want to sit down and have dinner with."

"So ask her. Doesn't she seem like she'd be receptive?"

He ducked his head. "We've smiled at each other a couple of times, but we've never talked."

"Why not?"

He blushed. "I've been picking up on bar bunnies, using the old, tired lines for so long, I don't know what to say when I really mean it."

"Say whatever you're comfortable saying. Like, 'You have the right to remain silent.' "

"Thanks for the help."

"All right, all right. Why not just start with hi and take it from there?"

"You think?"

"Come on, what've you got to lose? She probably won't chew your head off—you said she looks nice."

"She does."

"Well, then. 'Faint heart ne'er won fair maiden.' Go for it."

He grinned at me shrewdly. "When are you gonna start taking your own advice?"

Now it was my turn to look down. "When I see someone with big blue eyes in the lobby of the Justice Center."

We watched the local news on the TV at the end of the bar for a few minutes. The weatherman said we could expect more wet, gray weather. Marko said, "Is this drink for old time's sake, or do you have something you want to ask me?"

"Both," I said.

"I figured. The Joel Kerner thing?"

"It's hard. Cold trail and all that."

He nodded.

"I'll tell you one thing—it was a hit of some sort, and I'd bet it originated right here in Cleveland."

He looked away, lit a cigarette. "Could be," he said guardedly. "You know who Patrick Stranahan is?"

"The union guy? Sure."

"The Irish, they call him."

"Uh-huh. What's he got to do with a killing that happened two thousand miles away in another country?"

"I don't know. Maybe nothing. Maybe a lot. He does a lot of business with Kerner's father. You interested?"

"In an abstract way."

"Why abstract?"

He sighed. "I told you, Milan. It's not my jurisdiction."

"There may be a murderer walking around in your jurisdiction. You don't care?"

"Not enough to get my shorts in a twist. Look, I'm putting in overtime as it is, and my percentage of closed cases is getting lousier by the day. I don't have time to try busting squeals I'm not getting paid to bust, especially if I have to get in the face of someone as well connected as Stranahan when you don't have a shred of evidence against him."

"Well connected?"

"Milan," he said, "get a clue, okay? You know that whatever political power there is in this town that isn't black or Italian is Irish. And Stranahan is no shanty mick from the west side. He's an important guy, and he has important friends."

"And that makes him untouchable?"

"It makes me not want to poke him with a stick when I've got no reason to."

"No reason? I thought your job was to make the streets safe for the rest of us."

"The Cleveland streets, not the ones in San Carlos. Look, you bring me some sort of reasonable evidence that Stranahan did something naughty here in town, where my badge means something, I'll be all over him like white on rice. Otherwise . . ." He shrugged, turning his palms upward. "It's politics, Milan. I can't just show my ass when it isn't official Cleveland police business. I've got people I have to answer to."

"Funny, that's what Stranahan said."

"When?"

"It doesn't matter, Marko. It's not official business."

His eyes got big and soft, the way they used to when he was a kid and our football team lost a game. "That's lousy," he said.

I knew I'd hurt him, but all I said was, "Murder is lousy."

"You just don't understand the way it works, Milan. You don't understand politics. If you'd stayed on the job, maybe you'd get it."

"Then maybe I'm glad I didn't stay on the job," I said. I watched his brow furrow and his face darken. He turned away from me and slammed down the rest of his beer. Vuk started over. He took one look at the two of us, read the body language, felt the anger and resentment hanging in the air, and stayed away.

It's just as well. He wasn't going to sell either of us any more beer that evening.

What is there about good friends and loved ones that makes it easier to hurt them than perfect strangers?

There was no one in the world outside my immediate family that I cared more about than Marko Meglich. Yet he and I had been tearing at one another since the day we met and fought in the schoolyard.

Maybe we both knew that nothing would ever really get in the way of our friendship. But if I had become a welder, say, or a dentist like my near namesake in Parma whose phone calls I often got by mistake, instead of a private investigator whose goals frequently ran against those of a gold-shield homicide cop, that friendship would have run more smoothly.

In any case, I was feeling a little off-kilter as I went home and broiled myself a steak I'd picked up across the street at Russo's. I studded it with peppercorns and minced garlic. What the hell, I wasn't going to get kissed anyway. I microwaved some Tater Tots to go with it—I don't really like them, but they're quick—and washed it all down with a couple more beers.

Ed Stahl called just as I was finishing up the dishes.

"Well, I didn't get nearly enough for a story," Ed said, "so lunch is on you." If Ed ever had to pay for his own lunches, he'd probably starve to death. "Other than stuff you already know, I was able to mine two little tiny pieces of information about your buddies."

I pulled a yellow legal pad close and picked up a pencil. "Shoot."

"First, Stranahan. The Irish is on very shaky ground over at the local."

"Why?"

"It seems they'd committed to investing about three million bucks and change in a rehab project in the warehouse district. Stranahan, being treasurer and business manager, somehow misplaced it."

"Three million dollars?"

"He's been telling them not to worry, that he'll get it back in ninety days. But the owner of the building is twisting in the wind because he was expecting that money to fix up the building and then sell it. And the rank-and-file are mightily pissed too, because the project would have meant a hell of a lot of jobs for union guys. To say nothing of the pension funds they've been contributing to for years going swirling down the crapper."

"So everybody's mad at everybody?"

"Mad isn't exactly the right word. We're talking big numbers here."

I made notes furiously. "You think Stranahan is in any real danger?"

"Physical danger? Hard to say. It's not the fifties anymore. Nowadays people tend to take care of things like this in court."

I doodled an empty gallows in the left margin of the pad. I couldn't imagine my father or Chet Tumbas taking the business manager of their union to law for stealing their money. The discussion would have been a lot more personal.

"The only other thing is on Joel Kerner Sr.," he said.

I drew a line across the page beneath my notes on Stranahan. "I'm ready."

"Well, he's lived in that big house on South Park for thirty-some years," he said. "Paid off the mortgage quite a while ago. But just last month he put it on the market. Listed it at two point six million."

"I don't find that so unusual," I said. "It's a huge house. Their son is dead and their daughter is forty and living on her own. They don't need that much house, no matter how big the old man's ego is."

"No," Ed said, "but in addition to the house and a state-of-the-art security system, they have six acres of woods in the back. That kind of property on South Park goes dear. According to the real estate editor, the house is way underpriced. By about three quarters of a million, she says."

"So?"

"So the very very rich aren't in the giveaway business. They don't lowball their big expensive homes unless they need to sell in a hell of a hurry. Now why would a guy like Kerner need that kind of money in a hurry, d'you suppose?"

"Why indeed?" I said.

"The thing is, Milan, none of this sounds like it has anything to do with Joel junior. I've talked to some police beat guys, and the consensus is that it was a random killing that grew out of a random robbery."

That remained to be seen.

After hanging up, I settled into my big overstuffed chair, smoking and doodling more empty nooses dangling from gallows, and thought about Stranahan and Kerner. Maybe Marko and Ed and all the police beat reporters on the *Plain Dealer* were right, maybe there was no connection between the union's financial troubles and Joel Kerner's murder. There certainly didn't seem to be one. But if there wasn't, I had absolutely nowhere else to go, and I wasn't willing to accept that yet.

The phone at my elbow let me know that even after regular business hours, someone was thinking of me. It was as close to a warm-and-fuzzy as I'd come all day.

"Milan, it's Victor," came the high reedy voice through the receiver. "I'm so glad I caught you at home. Am I calling at a bad time?"

"Not at all."

"My uncle and I were wondering if we could buy you a drink."

"Now?"

He chuckled. "It's only nine o'clock. And we're down at the Vesuvio. It's five minutes from your place."

I knew where it was; I'd been there with Victor and his uncle before.

"It'll take me more than five minutes to get presentable, Victor."

"Don't worry about it," he said. "Be casual."

In a pig's eye, I thought. In all the years I'd known them, I'd never seen Giancarlo D'Allessandro wear anything but a dark suit and tie. Victor, too, except for twice when I visited his home on a Sunday morning and he was wearing sweaters that cost more than the monthly rent on my apartment.

Besides, in Cleveland, *formal* means black tie, *informal* means a suit, and *casual* is a sports jacket and tie. Anything less than that is sloppy. And that's how I was dressed at the moment, in jeans, disreputable running shoes, and an old Kent State sweatshirt.

Nevertheless, accepting an invitation from Don Giancarlo D'Allessandro was not something one waffles about. As politely and sincerely as it was delivered, it was nothing less than a summons.

I hung up and went into the bathroom to run my electric razor over my jaw. Then I put on a soft dress shirt, one of my collection of ties that all my women friends judge as "too wide," light tan slacks and a brown tweed jacket. I slipped into my oxblood loafers—they're the only shoes I own that are anywhere in the brown family—and headed down the hill toward Little Italy.

Ristorante Vesuvio is on Murray Hill, set well back from the street, with a narrow driveway and an unpaved parking lot in back. When I pulled in I saw the don's black Lincoln near the entrance. A hard-looking guy I'd never seen before leaned against the fender smoking a cigarette. After I parked, I had to walk by him to get to the door of the restaurant; he straightened up and gave me a long look, then relaxed again. He'd obviously been told I was coming.

Inside Victor and his uncle were at their usual booth, well back in the large, airy room. Between them and the door were two tables occupied by three big, dark-suited men each. One of them, John Terranova, I knew fairly well, considering that at Victor's behest he and two other men had beaten the stuffing out of me some years back. We'd had dealings since, none of them unfriendly, and while I couldn't really say that I liked him, we were on cordial terms.

"Whattaya say, Milan?" he said as I passed by his table. The other men didn't even look at me, just continued eating their pasta.

Victor stood up when I approached but waited for his uncle to greet me. The old man wore a black suit of uncertain vintage with a stained red napkin tucked into his collar. His lips were red-tinted from the special homemade wine he loved to drink. He motioned me to bend down to him and when I did so, he hugged me around the neck and planted a whiskery kiss on my cheek, the ultimate seal of Italian approval.

"Milan Jacovich," he said, showing his teeth. My name had never been easy for him to bend his Mediterranean tongue around, but he'd yet to mispronounce it.

"Don Giancarlo."

"Sit down here, sit down. Skoosh over, Victor."

Victor shook my hand. "Thanks for coming, Milan," he said. He sat back down in the booth and slid over against the wall, and I sat next to him.

"What you want to drink?" D'Allessandro said. "Some nice grappa?"

"No, sir. Maybe a brandy."

Victor turned and waved at a waiter, who bustled over to take my order. Except for Victor and his uncle's minions, the only other people in the restaurant were a couple finishing up their meal.

D'Allessandro smiled at me, his ivory teeth long in his shrunken gums. Each time I saw him he seemed to grow older and more frail. Since our last meeting he'd lost weight he could ill afford to lose, and the bones of his face stretched his skin tight. I knew he was on a low-fat diet and had had to give up his beloved espresso; they'd taken him off cigarettes years before. Home-brewed red wine was probably his sole remaining vice.

"How you been?" he asked me. "Okay? Your kids okay?"

"They're great," I said. "Thank you for asking."

"That's good. The good Lord, he don't bless me with kids. It's the only thing in life I really missed." The old man cocked his head to one side like a quizzical sparrow, as if he found it hard to believe anything in this world had been denied to him.

The waiter appeared with a Rémy Martin on a tray; the glass had been steamed and was warm to the touch. I was impressed.

"Victor tells me you been to San Carlos. Beautiful place. Beautiful beach." He made a sour face and touched his chest. "The food is crap, though. What is that stuff they have? Jerky chicken? Good name for it. You like it there?"

"Not much. I wasn't there very long."

"Can be a dangerous place for somebody don't know what he's getting into. Guys jumped you with a knife, Victor says."

I nodded.

"Animals. You go to kill a man for a couple of bucks he got in his pocket. Bunch of animals. No—*insects*. An insect would do that, a pissant. A beetle that eats shit." He took the napkin out of his shirt collar. He was wearing a red, white and green tie. "They hurt you bad?"

I held up my arm. "Few stitches, that's all. But I'm not entirely sure they only wanted my money."

The old man lifted an eyebrow.

"I think they were laying for me."

"Nobody knows you in San Carlos. Why anybody lay for you?"

"That's what I'd like to know."

The couple across the room got up and left, and all three of us watched them go. I inhaled the cognac fumes and took a sip. Powerful stuff.

"You know, Milan Jacovich," D'Allessandro said, "you go dangerous places, you stick your nose in dangerous things. That's when a man gets hurt. You listening?"

I was listening. D'Allessandro wasn't just talking to hear himself talk. He never did. The waiter came over and poured him more coffee. He looked balefully at it and then pushed it away. "What they call it, *dee*-caf. They don't let me drink real coffee no more. No espresso. This—this *dee*-caf—tastes like the water in a urinal."

The waiter whisked the cup away quietly.

"We got friends around town. They aren't our people, you know, not *famiglia*—but they're friends. People we do business with. A friend comes to me, he says, 'Don Giancarlo, I got a guy who's running up my arm. Can you do something?' I say, for my friend, I find out what's going on, at least. What's what. That's what you do when you got friends."

I nodded.

"You're our friend, too, Milan," Victor put in. "I want to make that very clear. There's no hostility here."

"Sure not," the don said. "Listen, when you wanted to know what's what, you called Victor, right? And sometimes we want to know what's what, we ask you. Right?" He sat back in the booth, looking very small and frail. "So."

"So," I said.

"The Irish."

"I thought it might be," I said.

"He felt that when you saw him this morning you were being accusatory," Victor explained.

"He said you practically accuse him of doing the Kerner boy," the don added.

"That's not quite the way it happened. I just asked him—"

"Listen, Milan Jacovich. Sometimes good people—and the Irish, he's good people, you ask his union boys—they find themselves in a corner and it isn't even their fault. The Irish, Stranahan, he's sucking wind right now, but I give you my personal word, he didn't do nothing bad."

The old man stopped and drew in a chestful of air; fifty years of smoking had left him without much lung capacity. He held the breath for a moment, then coughed it out. His eyes teared, and he dabbed at them with his napkin.

"Except exercising poor judgment," Victor finished for him. "And we've all done that. You, me—everybody."

"What kind of poor judgment? Mishandling pension funds?"

"It's confidential," the don said. "Got nothing to do with you."

I took another swallow of the cognac. "So what you're telling me is to forget about who killed Joel Kerner and back off Patrick Stranahan or else?"

D'Allessandro sat up straight, his eyes boring into mine like laser beams. " 'Or else?' Don't insult me."

"I meant no disrespect."

"You see too many lousy movies. 'Or else!' " he scoffed. "We don't do things like that. I ask you to come here, sit down like a gentleman, talk about some things. Nobody said nothing about 'or else.' "

"What my uncle means, Milan," Victor explained, "is that Patrick Stranahan is a friend of ours and he's in a little bit of a bind right now. We just wanted to know why you're leaning on him, that's all."

"I didn't lean, Victor. I'm talking to him because Joel Kerner Jr. has been killed, the police aren't helping, and his sister wants me to find out what happened to him. I'm sorry Stranahan is a friend of yours and that I upset him. I thought the Kerners were friends of yours, too—and I'll keep talking to whoever I need to talk to until I find out what I need to." I looked at the don, holding his gaze. "That's my job, Don Giancarlo."

The old man didn't say anything for almost a minute, but he kept staring at me, wetting his lips every so often with his tongue. Then he relaxed back against the padded back of the booth, and the wrinkled pouches of skin beneath his eyes crinkled up even more.

"Then do it," he said.

No one spoke for a while, and I sensed the interview, or whatever it was, was over. I got up out of the booth, finishing my Rémy with a flourish, which made me dizzy for a few seconds. "It was good seeing you, Don Giancarlo," I said. "And I thank you for the drink."

"Come here," the old man ordered. I bent down and he hugged me again, kissing my cheek.

When I straightened up, he said, "Hardheaded Polack, you."

"Slovenian, sir," I corrected him. "Hardheaded Slovenian."

I'm not sure, but I think he smiled.

CHAPTER NINETEEN

The next morning I stopped at Coffees of the World on Cedar and got a blueberry muffin and a coffee to go on my way to work. I drank the coffee as I drove down to the Flats.

My friendly drink with Giancarlo D'Allessandro the previous evening had unsettled me a little. He and Victor had assured me they were just asking, that no threat or sanction had been implied—although just knowing those guys was something of a threat. But I had to wonder what Patrick Stranahan was into if I'd rattled him so badly that he went to his friends on Murray Hill for succor.

I briefly considered calling Marko to tell him what had transpired but thought better of it. As a police officer, he naturally had little use for Victor and his uncle, and he and I had argued many times about my relationship with them. I didn't want to hear a lecture this morning.

But I was curious enough to do some more digging.

When I got to the office I made a pot of coffee and washed down the muffin with the first cup. Then I looked up the number for the Ohio Mercantile Bank in my Rolodex.

Rudy Dolsak and I have been friends almost as long as Marko Meglich and I have. Overweight and nearsighted as a kid, Rudy was a sports nut nonetheless, and in his position as equipment manager and assistant to the football coach both in high school and at Kent State, he had quietly worshipped the better favored and bigger-shouldered young men who were allowed to suit up on Saturdays.

But there is compensation for everything, and while Marko and I had been getting our brains scrambled on the gridiron, Rudy was studying business and economics. He was now executive vice president of the Ohio Merk, with a big new house east of Richmond Road in Beachwood, a Mercedes, and a son on the Kent State basketball squad of whom he was terribly proud.

We didn't see each other too often anymore; we traveled in different orbits. I'd tried to involve him in Ed Stahl's weekly poker games, but Rudy, being a fiscal conservative to the bone, suffers great pain when he loses twelve or fifteen dollars and not only gets no return on his investment but has to chip in for the beer and pretzels, so his appearances at Ed's Wednesday night soirees are at best infrequent.

He was always glad to talk to me, though—except when I asked him to bend the rules a little, as I did this morning.

"Aw, Milan, jeez! You know how I hate that crap!" he complained when I asked him for some financial information on Patrick Stranahan and Joel Kerner Sr. *Jeez!* sounded funny coming from a bank executive. "That's confidential information!"

"It might put a murderer behind bars," I said.

"Murder? Jeez, what have you got yourself into now?" He paused for a breath. "Kerner—the big labor lawyer? This have something to do with his kid getting killed down in the Caribbean a few months ago?"

"It might," I said.

"Might is pretty flimsy when you're asking me to break every rule in the book!"

"Okay," I said, "let's say it does. But you know damn well that I'll keep everything you tell me quiet."

He thought about it.

"Give me a break, Rudy. I'm hitting the wall on this one."

"How many times have I done this for you, Milan? A hundred?"

"More like six."

"Seems like a hundred." He sighed. "All right, but this is the last time. What do you need?"

"Nothing specific. Just an idea of the general fiscal health of the two guys I mentioned. Liquid assets, mostly."

"I suppose you need this yesterday?"

"Tonight will be fine," I said.

"You don't ask for much."

"Sure I do. What good are friends if they don't ask for anything?"

"Okay, well here's a payback. Rudy junior's starting at forward now for Kent, and they're playing two games at home next week. Tuesday and Thursday. I know he'd love to see you, he'd love it if you'd come see him play. He admires you so much. You and Marko are legends at Kent."

"Sure I'll come. How about I take you and your wife to dinner first? Make an evening of it?"

"That'd be really nice, Milan."

I hung up and looked around the office. Although the place was clean, it was untidy. I set to work straightening papers, putting things away, knowing I was going to have a very attractive visitor.

I'd run into several good-looking, available women since I became aware of the death of Joel Kerner. His sister, Patrice, his ex-girlfriends Patt Wolfe and Lois Scaravelli, even the two vacationers on San Carlos, Ann and Lissa. A couple of them had expressed an interest, if only for the night. Yet it was Teri Levine I kept thinking about.

Attraction is a funny thing, isn't it? There's no explaining why certain people touch us and others don't. Since my divorce from Lila, I seem to have some sort of homing device that draws emotionally unavailable women to me. For some men that would be just fine. Others, like me, want something more.

A minister in the Church of Religious Science had once told me we attract to our lives the people we deserve. Maybe I'm emotionally unavailable myself.

I didn't feel like it, though, now that Teri Levine was on her way to see me. I felt like I was fourteen years old, trying to get up enough nerve to ask the pretty girl who sat next to me in English class out to a movie.

She came in at twelve thirty, looking businesslike but very pretty in a blue wool suit, a white V-necked blouse, and a navy and red scarf. I dismissed the thought that she'd dressed up a little for me.

I smiled a welcome at her, but she didn't smile back, just nodded. I didn't think she smiled often, and I was willing to bet she had a beautiful smile that was going to waste.

I handed her into one of my client chairs and took the other one, turning it slightly to face her; our feet were almost touching, but I didn't want the desk as a barrier between us. Suddenly self-conscious, I cleared my throat.

"Are you sure I can't take you to lunch?" I asked. "Jim's River House is only steps away."

She shook her head. "I rarely eat lunch. Only when I have to, with clients." She shifted around in her chair. "I came because I remembered something I didn't tell you before. I didn't think it was important—and besides, it's a little personal."

I nodded, smiled reassuringly at her. I was afraid if I said anything it might spook her. She was as skittish as a week-old colt.

"And then I got to thinking," she continued, "that it might be important. What do I know about these things? So that's why I called you."

She opened the clasp on the small clutch purse in her lap, then closed it again.

"I told you that Joel was coming on pretty strongly to me while we were in San Carlos," she said. "I know it was just because I was the only woman there about his age, but—"

"You really have to start thinking better of yourself, Teri," I interrupted her. "A lot of men would be interested in you even if there were a hundred other women around."

The blush spread from the bridge of her nose outward.

"*I* certainly would," I added. "And I wouldn't be scared of your mother, either."

That got a smile out of her, and a little laugh too.

"I had an aunt, my Auntie Branka—she died a few years ago. She wrote the book on formidable old ladies, especially when it came to making me eat things I didn't want to. Like sarma—

stuffed cabbage." My gorge rose at the memory. "I hated stuffed cabbage all my life, but she fixed it for me every time I had dinner at her house, and she stood there until I ate every bite of it. So your mother doesn't scare me." I faked a frown. "She doesn't cook sarma, does she?"

She laughed again; then the smile faded. "Then that makes what I have to tell you even more embarrassing."

I'd been leaning forward in my chair; now I settled back and waited. She looked around, gathering herself, her eyes scanning the ceiling, searching the corners of the room up there. I hoped there were no neglected cobwebs.

It took her about thirty seconds to get started. "That last night, before Joel . . . " She shook her head to get rid of whatever word fluttered around in there. "The last night I saw him. He asked me to come to his room. To spend the night with him." She looked over at me quickly. "I didn't go, of course. I mean, what would I have told my mother?"

She had chewed off all her lipstick again, and now she was starting on her lower lip itself. "Besides, I don't think he really cared about me, I was just—convenient. So I said no."

"And how did Joel feel about that?"

"Most men are okay about it. They take no as a matter of course."

I smiled. "Most men are used to it."

"But Joel—got upset. Very upset."

"Upset?"

"Enraged, actually. He cursed and carried on, and then he just turned on his heel and stomped away. I was shocked. I mean, I felt like I'd been slapped. About half an hour later I saw him getting into a taxi outside the hotel. I don't know where he was going, but I could tell just by the set of his shoulders that he was still angry."

It wasn't going to be me who told her he'd gone into town for a rendezvous with a hooker.

"Later that night," she went on, "much later—Mother had gone to sleep, and I was sitting out on the balcony, just looking at the moon—I saw him come back to the hotel. He almost staggered when he got out of the taxi. And his head was down, his shoulders were slumped."

"Was he drunk?"

"I couldn't tell, but I don't think so. He wasn't weaving or anything. He just looked, I don't know . . . broken. He came back into the hotel and . . . " Her chin quivered. "I never saw him again."

I gave her some more time, but apparently that was it. I was disappointed; she hadn't told me a damn thing I hadn't known before.

"I didn't know whether that might mean anything to you," she said. "So I thought I'd better let you know."

"I'm glad you came."

"I guess San Carlos wasn't such a great idea," she said. "I didn't really think it would be."

"Why did you go?"

"Well, Josh Borgenecht called my mother and said Beachwood Travel had this deal with the San Carlos Inn, and so she jumped at it."

"Borgenecht called your mother?"

She nodded. "We've known his family for years. His father was president of a union before he died, just like my father. A construction local. So a lot of the big unions in town give him their travel business."

"A construction local? Was it 696?"

"I think so, yes." She cocked her head. "Is that important?"

"I don't know," I said. "It might be."

"Well, that's good, then." She stood up. "I should get back to the office."

I got up too. She started for the door and I went with her, but after several steps I touched her arm, stopping her.

"Teri, would you like to have dinner sometime?"

The blush spread again, and she didn't say anything.

"Don't you eat dinner either?"

"Sure I do. But, uh, why?"

"Why does a man usually ask a woman out to dinner? I think you're very attractive and I enjoy your company."

"You mean like a date?"

"Not *like* a date. A date."

"Well . . . " She fumbled with her purse again. "Uh, sure. I guess so."

I was going to suggest a specific evening, a specific restaurant. I never got the chance.

It happened so fast it's almost impossible to recount. There was the sound of breaking glass, followed immediately by a wave of searing heat that raced across the room, like the second shock after a nuclear explosion, burning the side of the face. Sheer instinct made me push Teri against the wall and cover her body with mine. Fire spread across the floor like liquid, ankle high, coming toward us like something living.

The overhead smoke alarm kicked in with a vengeance, its high-pitched shrieks adding a note of surrealism to the moment. I felt Teri shudder against me, and she let out a little moan. Mentally I gave her a whole bunch of points for not screaming.

We staggered together for the door, and I reached out, opened it, and literally threw her out into the hall. "Call nine-one-one!" I yelled, and yanked the portable fire extinguisher from its mooring on the wall and stepped back into the burning office.

The unmistakable smell of gasoline was almost as strong as the smell of smoke. I aimed the extinguisher at the spot where the flames had advanced farthest across the floor and sent a jet of CO_2 fog roaring out of the nozzle to smother them. Nearer the windows the concentration of fire and smoke was heavier. The straw-stuffed netting on the bottom of my client chairs was burning merrily, as was my jacket, which I had tossed casually over the back of one of them. The insulating strips around the windows were burning too, as if waiting for a lion tamer to coax one of his charges through them. I attacked those as best I could and tried to contain the rest of it until the professionals arrived.

The crew from Fire Station 21 was there to finish the job within ninety seconds—after all, they'd come from right next door.

* * * * * * * * *

CHAPTER TWENTY

* * * * * * * * *

$\mathbf{M}$y new office was a mess. Beirut-on-the-Cuyahoga.

I felt violated. Invaded. Under siege.

Surveying the wreckage I was angry, and more than a little scared that an attempt had been made on my life, but the most pervasive feeling was a kind of heartbreak. I'd only moved into this office the year before, and I'd loved its spaciousness, high ceilings, the spectacular view of the river and Tower City and Jacobs Field across the water. I'd even begun to like my computer—once I'd learned to work the damn thing.

The good news was that nothing important was really lost. The little refrigerator designed to look like an old-fashioned safe that I'd kept across the room in the space between the big windows was still intact, but the gasket around its door had burned, rendering it useless. The door hung open to reveal a collection of scorched cans of Stroh's and Pepsi that had exploded from the heat. Smoke and flame had turned the big filing cabinet nearest the windows a murky gray. Both client chairs were charred, and their vinyl seats had melted and dripped down onto the floor like tar, but they were holdovers from my old office and I didn't much like them anyway.

Workmen were hammering large sheets of plywood into place over the broken windows, effectively cutting off the view until I could get the glass people in to replace them. The hardwood floor which I had paid handsomely to have resanded and varnished was now scorched and splintered, and under about an inch and a half of water muddied by the flame retardant and the soot. It would have to be completely replaced, and the walls would need replastering and painting.

The whole river-facing side of the building would have to be rewired, as the electrical wires and plugs were burnt through.

I was glad I'd put most of my loose papers safely away before Teri arrived. I didn't know then whether my computer had been damaged by the smoke and water; as it turned out, it survived, living as it did against the wall behind the desk in what had been a fairly protected spot.

My tenant downstairs, the wrought iron company, had been untouched by the fire but had sustained a lot of water damage and a few broken windows of their own. The boss was not happy.

The entire building stank of smoke and probably would for a long time to come.

The regular noontime gang at the bar of Jim's River House had, at least, been entertained during their lunch hour. Several of them brought their drinks outside to watch what was going on. It was probably illegal to drink alcohol in the parking lot, but none of the Cleveland Police Department in attendance seemed too rigid about enforcing that particular law. They were too busy.

Marko Meglich was huddled over on one side of the room with the fire battalion commander, talking in low tones. His sidekick, Detective Bob Matusen, was chatting with three fire inspectors, who were picking through the debris on the floor with pincers and putting bits and pieces in large plastic bags. In their black fire coats, boots, goggles, and helmets, they looked like atomic mutants in a cheesy nineteen-fifties sci-fi movie.

Teri, pale and shaken, her blue suit covered with black smudges, was sitting in the hallway on one of the four metal folding chairs I usually kept in the storage room along with my expensive electronic equipment; the steel fire door I'd had installed had saved that room completely.

I was standing near my burnt desk, surveying the damage like a World War II Londoner returning to his home after the Blitz. It felt like I was trapped in a T. S. Eliot poem.

Bad as it was, things could have been worse. A lot worse. If the fire had started a minute earlier, when Teri and I had still been sitting in the client chairs, we'd both have been crispy critters. The side of my face felt hot, and my nose, already cooked medium rare by my walk on the San Carlos beach, itched annoyingly.

Marko left the battalion commander and came over to where I was standing. He looked pretty grim.

"You okay?"

I nodded.

"You're insured, aren't you?"

"Minus the deductible, sure."

He coughed away some of the smoke residue that was permeating everyone's lungs. "Chief Katzmiller seems to think it was an old-fashioned Molotov cocktail," he said. "Wine bottle full of gasoline with a rag stuffed in the neck. They found the neck of the bottle intact. Chief said that's where the glass is thickest."

"Was it at least a good year?"

"Not much chance of getting prints off the bottle, though," he said, ignoring me.

Matusen joined us, holding his pant legs up delicately to keep the cuffs from dragging in the water. He looked like a Victorian matron at the seashore.

Marko reached into my shirt pocket and took out the pack of Winstons. "Any ideas about who doesn't like you?"

"A lot of them," I said. I told him about Kerner, about Stranahan, even about Giancarlo D'Allessandro.

He lit the cigarette with a gold lighter. "It was the boys on the hill," he muttered, his mouth a thin slash across his face. "Your buddies. Your goombas."

"I don't think so. Not their style. I don't like them much. But they've always been square with me, and if they'd wanted me to back off they would've told me, straight. Besides, firebombs aren't their MO. It would've been one quick one behind the ear, from close up, with a twenty-two. You know that."

He turned without answering and I followed him out into the hall. The sound of hammering wasn't quite so loud out there.

Teri looked up as we came out.

"How are you doing?" I said.

She forced a brave smile. "I've stopped shaking."

"Ms. Levine," Marko said in his official, tough-cop voice, "can you think of anyone who might want to harm you?"

"For Christ's sake, Mark!" I said.

"I have to ask."

She shook her head. "I'm an architect," she said, as if it was inconceivable that anyone might want to kill an architect.

Marko raised an eyebrow at me and I shook my head.

"Someone from the arson squad will be in touch with you," he said. "This isn't my area."

"When in hell does it get to be your area?" I flared.

He looked at Teri, then back at me. "Why don't you see that Ms. Levine gets home all right."

"I'm fine," Teri said, and stood up.

"I'll drive you back to your office, then," I offered. "Or home, if that's where you want to go."

She unclasped and clasped her purse again, clearly distracted. "I can drive."

"Let us walk you downstairs, then," Marko said, all at once kindly.

I took her arm and we went downstairs, Bob Matusen and Marko following. She had lied to me a little bit—she was still trembling.

Because of the welding torches and acetylene tanks down in the wrought-iron place on the first floor, the fire department had arrived in hordes, several ladder companies. There were uniformed and plainclothes cops all over the parking lot, as well as several firemen dressed in black rubber raincoats and boots bumping into each other like Moe, Curly, and Larry in slow motion. It was the kind of scene you never imagine will take place on your own turf. Teri hesitated a step when we came out of the building. I figured the afternoon would from now on be a little piece of her nightmares.

"I'll call you," I said as she got into her car.

"Uh, I don't know. Uh, all right," she said shakily. She put the key into the ignition with a trembling hand and started the engine.

"I'm so sorry this happened."

"It's not your fault, Milan. It's . . . " Her laugh was more like a gasp. "It's just my luck."

She put the car in gear and drove off, kicking up some loose pebbles in the parking lot. Marko and I watched her go.

"Nice lady," he said.

"Uh-huh."

"You have something going there?"

I hunched my shoulders against the chill. "Not yet. And probably not after this."

"Too bad," he said. "The kind of woman who you'd like to sit down and have dinner with, you know?"

"I know."

The three of us watched almost wistfully as her car pulled out onto Scranton Road and drove over the Eagle Avenue Bridge toward downtown. I looked at Marko. Maybe my friend was changing, after all. Maybe in his early middle age he really was becoming more interested in women than in girls.

"Come around back with me," I said.

Out back was a small loading dock for the wrought iron company. The exterior of the building was a blank brick wall at the level of the first floor; the second floor, my office, was all windows overlooking the river. Fifteen feet of graveled drive, mostly utilized by trucks making pickups and deliveries, separated the building from the riverbank.

I walked around, my head down. The booted feet of the firemen had churned up a lot of the gravel, and the water had turned things to mud back there.

"If you're looking for a spent match, forget it," Matusen said. "There are probably a hundred of them on the ground down here—along with cigarette butts, Big Mac wrappers, beer cans, and used condoms."

He was right, there was a lot of small trash back there. Out of sight of the road, it was a place often used by derelicts and furtive lovers in warmer weather.

I let my gaze rake the area. I didn't find what I was looking for. "Mark," I said, "if you drove back here and threw a firebomb through my window in the middle of the day, would you hang around and wait to see what happened?"

He finished smoking my cigarette and flipped the butt out over the water. "I don't get your drift."

"I mean, wouldn't you just toss the bomb, jump back into your car, and get away in one hell of a hurry?"

"Well, I'd wait to see whether my aim had been good. After that, sure, I'd split."

I pointed at the ground. "No tire tracks. Not any new ones, anyway. If someone had peeled out of here that fast, there'd be a couple of deep, fresh ruts in the gravel, wouldn't there?"

"I suppose," Matusen said. "But don't forget, there's been a small army of cops and firefighters walking around back here. They've probably ruined the integrity of the crime scene."

"What page of the manual is that on?"

"Come on, Milan," Marko rumbled, "you know what he means."

"Sure. But they wouldn't have completely tramped down that deep a gouge. There'd still be some ruts left, some gravel that was churned up, wouldn't there?"

"So what are you saying?"

"Either the bomber came here on foot—"

"Pretty unlikely," Matusen offered.

"Agreed." I turned and glanced at the riverbank. "Or he came by boat."

Marko patted his mustache. "Could be."

"So why don't we find out who took their boat out this afternoon?"

"There must be twenty thousand small boats docked at all the marinas around here," Matusen said. "And they don't have to notify the authorities when they leave the dock, like you do when you own an airplane."

"Yeah, but how many people would go for a river cruise on a cold, wet day like this one?" I said. "You'd think someone would notice, one of the marina attendants or somebody."

"Maybe. Maybe not, though."

"And look, if he headed out toward the lake they would have had to raise the Conrail bridge for him. If he headed upriver he'd have to go through the swing bridge. Maybe the bridge-tenders could give us some sort of ID."

Marko took out his notebook and made some scribbles in it. "It's something to check out, I suppose. You'd better tell your theory to the arson squad guys."

"I'm giving it to you," I said.

"Yeah, but it's just a theory. You don't know for sure it was a boat."

"I don't know it wasn't little green men in a spaceship, either. Come on, Mark."

He looked exasperated again. "I told you before, this isn't my beat. I'm homicide."

"So if they'd killed me, you'd look into it, but since they didn't, it's none of your business?"

"Shit," he said, and took my pack of cigarettes from my pocket again. "You know how it works in the department."

I snatched the cigarettes away from him before he could take one. "Buy your own," I said.

"Don't get pissy with me, Milan. I've got a job to do, just like you."

"Somebody's trying to keep me from doing mine—permanently."

He went to the riverbank and stared down at the sluggish Cuyahoga flowing by. I came and stood next to him.

"Maybe there's something we can do," he said.

"What?"

Marko shook his head and grinned—just the way he had when we were ten and had bloodied each other's noses in the playground and then shook hands and became lifelong friends. He reached out for my cigarettes.

"You won't say until I give you a smoke. You're finally on the take, huh?" I said.

"One lousy cigarette is on the take in your book?"

"Two lousy cigarettes." I handed him the pack. "And that's just today."

He went through the ritual, cupping his hand around the lighter flame to protect it from the wind. Then he put the pack of Winstons in his own pocket, which brought the total to approximately ten lousy cigarettes. He nodded at Matusen.

"I want you to come with us to see a guy," Matusen said. "A snitch of mine. He can maybe point you in the right direction."

"A snitch?"

"Yeah. Doobie Lemp. His ass belongs to me. Doobie tells me what I need to know, and I keep him out of Mansfield. You'll get a kick out of him."

"I'm supposed to just leave my office open to anyone who wants to drop in and help himself?"

Marko tried to hide a smile. "Hire a security company to post a man here."

Matusen cracked his knuckles. "I need you to talk to this guy. This is right down his alley."

Marko threw an arm around my shoulders. "He sets insurance fires for money, Milan. He's an arsonist."

CHAPTER TWENTY-ONE

Marko, Bob Matusen, and I pulled up to a battered-looking house on Rowley Avenue—which most of its residents pronounce "Raleigh"—in the Tremont section of the city just west of the river. Several years ago there had been talk of "gentrifying" Tremont, with its old Victorian homes on small, block-long streets, but with the exception of a few trendy cafés frequented by the under–twenty-five set who've grown bored with the tinsel of the Flats, the neighborhood remains colorful if somewhat weathered, as blue-collar ethnic as it's been for the last fifty years.

On the way Matusen had told me a little of Doobie Lemp's background. Like me, he'd been in Vietnam. Unlike me, he'd spent most of his tour in the guardhouse. He'd worked in ordnance—explosives—but got busted for doing a little freelance work for some Saigon gangsters. After mustering out he'd put his expertise to good use, until he'd been nailed for setting a giant warehouse fire near the Slavic village area several years before. He'd copped a plea and sung like a canary, implicating the building's owner, who'd been looking for a big insurance payout, and Lemp got himself a reduced sentence. Ever since he got out of the joint, the Cleveland cops had him pinned like a butterfly specimen to a card. In exchange for information about what was happening on the street, they helped keep him alive and on the edge of solvency with the occasional double sawbuck.

I shivered as we climbed out of the unmarked police cruiser.

My coat was still back at the office, burnt to a crisp. "Are you sure he's home?"

Matusen snickered. "Sure he's home. He's a vampire—never goes out in the sunlight."

We mounted the steps and went into the vestibule. The old home, once a single-family residence, was now a rooming house. On either side of the hallway what must have originally been the living room and dining room were partitioned off by sliding plywood doors that had been stained to look like oak but weren't going to fool anybody. Several small piles of mail looked forlorn and neglected on a table at the foot of the stairs, and mounted on the wall was an ancient black pay phone. The place smelled musty and somehow transient.

We went up to the second floor and along the hallway to a door at the end. The smell of marijuana was strong. "The guy's a pothead?" I said.

Matusen hammered on the door with a beefy fist. "Why do you think they call him Doobie?"

There was a muffled response from inside.

"It's Matusen. Open up."

"Minute."

We heard scurrying around inside, and the sound of a window being yanked open. True to his word, it was a full minute before he came to the door.

Doobie Lemp indeed looked like a vampire. I'd never seen anyone with skin so pale, almost gray. It was just about impossible to guess his age. I knew he'd been in Vietnam, so he was probably in his forties, but he looked sixty. His sleeveless undershirt exposed his pitifully thin arms, which were both adorned with crude jailhouse tattoos, and his nearly hairless chest. His skin looked doughy, as if the imprint of your fingers would stay forever if you grabbed his arm, and his pupils were dilated, his eyelids drooping. On his feet were a pair of backless maroon carpet slippers that must have been thirty years old. He couldn't have weighed a hundred twenty-five pounds. The sour odor of sweat and failure and fear emanating from him almost masked the smell of marijuana.

"Who you kidding with the fucking open window, Doobie?" Matusen said. "We know you've been smoking muggles. You can smell it halfway down the block."

Doobie's face got grayer, which I wouldn't have thought possible, and with one quivering hand he pawed at his mouth. "First one a' the day, Mr. Matusen. I swear to Jesus. Just to get my heart started."

"Ask me if I care. Close that before we freeze our asses off." Matusen pointed imperiously at the window and Doobie fell all over himself shutting it. Marko shot me a disgusted glance.

"This here's my boss, Doobie. This is Lieutenant Meglich. He's a real shtarker down at headquarters, you dig? The first shirt. The main man. The stud duck. You understand?"

Doobie licked his lips, and bobbed his head so violently I feared whiplash. "Yessir. Yessir. Hah yew, Looten't? Proud t'meet you, sir." I think he briefly considered offering Marko a handshake but wisely reconsidered, especially since his own hands were trembling so badly. His speech pattern was what they call in Kentucky and southern Ohio a "briar" accent, short for "briar-hopper," a polite way of saying uneducated redneck boob. He was as rustic as E-I-E-I-O.

"So you know this is important, Doobie, right? Or the lieutenant wouldn't be here."

The poor little pothead struggled to keep his eyes wide open, his head snapping back and forth from one cop to the other like he was viewing a tennis match at warp speed. "Yessir. I surely do."

"Doobie," Marko said softly—and if Lemp had known him he would have known that meant Marko was at his most dangerous. He was taking the good-cop role for a change. "My friend here, Mr. Jacovich, he had a little trouble at his office down in the Flats this afternoon. Somebody threw a firebomb through his window." He shook his head sadly. "What a terrible thing to do, eh?"

Doobie looked at me with a kind of pity, then blinked at Marko. "It wa'n't me, Looten't. I ain't been outta this room all day."

"You got proof of that?" Matusen snarled, and Doobie cringed.

"Now, nobody said it was you, Doobie," Marko said soothingly.

"But a guy like you, with your connections—we just thought you might've heard something about it."

Doobie's eyelids were batting madly. "I didn't hear nothin'."

Matusen stepped forward, looming over the little guy like a tyrannical parent over a five-year-old. "Horse puckey. Any torch in this town gets a bid, you hear about it."

"I swear to Jesus, Mr. Matusen." He held up his hand, taking the oath. "It's been real quiet. Things've been real quiet the last couple weeks. I ain't heard nothin'." The whites of his eyes were showing all the way around his pupils. "On my mother's grave."

"Your mother doesn't have a grave, Doobie. She's turning tricks down in Covington." Matusen walked over to the stained sofa as though he was going to sit down, then regarded the piece of furniture balefully and remained standing. He took two twenties out of his pocket and held them between his second and third finger the way Bette Davis used to hold her cigarette. "Who's around that's using Molotov cocktails?"

Doobie blinked stupidly. "Huh?"

"Don't give me a headache, Doobie. Every torch has a different MO. Plastique, remote-control, electronic, whatever. Who are the guys in town who toss bottles of gasoline stuffed with rags?" He moved his fingers back and forth so the bills wiggled like the propeller on a beanie. "I want names."

"You gotta be funnin' me, Mr. Matusen."

Matusen growled low in his throat.

"I mean, nobody."

"Nobody what?"

"Molotov cocktails. Nobody does them no more. Lessen there's real flammable material inside the building, chemicals an' shit. No pro would use anything like a Molotov cocktail." He shrugged almost pathetically. "It ain't—efficient."

"Why not?" I said.

"Hard to control." He was warming to his subject now; as most experts do, he loved to talk about what he knew best. "Besides, all it'll do is scorch whatever it touches. See, it's the vapor that burns, not the liquid. Now if you put potato chips on the floor—"

"Potato chips?"

"Specially cheap ones, with lotsa oil. They burn like a mother."

That was a new one on me.

"A real pro, he'd do somethin' different. Classier. Like rewire the 'lectrical circuits and then squirt gasoline on 'em. But a cock-tail, shee-it, that ain't no way to torch a building. A cocktail, see, that's more like when you wanta deliver a message."

"What about when you want to torch a person?" I said.

Doobie Lemp's face went slack; he licked his lips nervously, pulled at his cheek with a thumb and forefinger. His eyes were batting like a silent-movie vamp's. "Nothin' like that," he said, shaking his head.

Bob Matusen took a menacing step toward him. "Like what?"

"No torch is gonna do a job if there's people inside. That's a whole new . . . " He searched for a word.

"What?" I asked.

"That's—murder." He pronounced the word with wonder and mystery. "A torch don't do murder."

"Something new and exciting every day," I said as the three of us drove back to what was left of my building down in the Flats. "My office burns down around me, and now I've met my first firebug."

"Get your terms right," Matusen chided me. "A firebug is a looney-tunes, a guy who sets fires for kicks. That's usually the only way he can get his dick hard."

"All firebugs are men?"

"All that I ever ran into. A torch, now, that's another thing. He's a professional, a kind of trained specialist."

"Who trains him?"

Matusen shrugged. "More often than not, the United States military. The point is, he gets the big bucks because he knows what he's doing. He burns down buildings for money, usually so the owner can collect the insurance. He doesn't steal, he doesn't do contract hits, and he's usually too nerdy to do any sort of mob muscle stuff. He's a businessman. Like Doobie told you, no self-respecting torch would fire a building if he thought anyone would be hurt. He doesn't want to be looking at murder one, no matter how much they pay him."

"So who tossed that firebomb through my window?"

"An amateur," Matusen said. "And not a very good one at that."

"How do you figure?"

"Because he was trying to kill you, Jacovich. If it was a professional who was any good, you and your lady friend would be blackened monkfish right now."

A real phrase maker, Matusen.

We pulled into the lot in front of my building. The big hook-and-ladder trucks had returned to the fire station, the lunch crowd from Jim's had either gone back inside or back to work, and only a few fire department inspectors were hanging around downstairs.

I opened the rear door and got out of the car, and Marko heaved his bulk out of the passenger seat.

"They may have been amateurs, Milan, but they weren't kidding around. You're damn lucky to be alive."

I stared up at my building. No damage was visible to this side, the side facing the street and the parking lot. I thought what an eyesore the blackened brick on the other side would be to the river traffic, especially when summer came, when the locals took their pleasure boats out on the river heading for Lake Erie, and the tourists enjoyed the sightseeing and dinner cruises on the *Good Time III*.

I quickly pulled my notebook out of my pocket and wrote *BOAT* in it in large, dark letters.

"I don't think your friends on Murray Hill are such good friends after all," Marko said.

"They've got nothing to do with it. It's either Kerner senior or Stranahan."

"You're pretty sure of that."

"Damn right I am."

"Pretty heavy names to be accusing."

"Don't worry, Marko," I said, and as angry as I was, I couldn't keep the teeth out of it. "I won't ask you to risk your ass with the higher-ups and help me out."

His back and neck stiffened. "That is so fucking unfair," he said, measuring his words out carefully and precisely, like they were ingredients in a recipe.

I looked away. The side of my face felt hot and sore where the fire had scorched it. "I know," I said. "Sorry."

"I'm a cop, Milan," Marko said. "A public servant. That means I don't do my own thing, I don't own my own building, and I don't make my own rules. Sometimes I don't like the rules much, and I bitch about them, about the courts, about letting scumbags off on technicalities. Sometimes I go home and drink myself shit-faced when a righteous bust skates because some cop didn't follow the rules and another bad guy ends up walking the streets again. But rules give us structure, whether we like them or not, and if cops didn't follow them we'd have anarchy." He took a deep breath, his broad chest straining the button on his suit jacket. "And that's what I took an oath to prevent."

I started to say something, but he held up a hand. I looked at it, remembering those hands catching passes on the football field, impossible catches, reaching out and pulling the ball down as if it were a shooting star passing by.

"You're the oldest friend I've got in this world," he went on. "And I don't want anything to happen to you. I'd be sick for the rest of my life if something did. But if I broke the rules, Milan—not penny-ante stuff like we all do sometimes, but big-time, like turning vigilante—I'd be worse than sick, I'd be useless. Because it's my job. Obeying the rules—and making sure everybody else does too. It's what I do."

He opened the car door. "Watch your ass," he said, and stuck out his hand. When I went to shake it he pressed my pilfered pack of Winstons into my palm angrily. Then he got into the car and Matusen pulled away, his rear wheels peppering me with a shower of gravel and mud.

I stared down at the crumpled cigarette pack in my hand. It made me want to give up smoking.

CHAPTER TWENTY-TWO

I retrieved everything I thought I'd need from the office and went home, spending the rest of the afternoon on logistics. I contacted the telephone company and arranged to have the damaged equipment repaired and all calls forwarded to my apartment. I called the glazier. The painter. The carpenter. The electrician. Someone who could put in a new floor. A cleaning crew to take care of the wrought iron people downstairs. A gravel company to spread new gravel in the ruined parking lot.

But first I called the insurance company that was going to have to pay for all of it. You can imagine how thrilled they were to hear from me.

I put my clothes in two piles, one for laundry and one for dry-cleaning, because they stank of smoke, and probably a little of fear, and then I showered off the dirt of the day under a needle spray that was almost too hot to bear, holding my bandaged arm away from the water to keep it dry.

I put on jeans and a T-shirt and went out into the living room, where I'd worked for so many years. I'd finally grown used to having a real home, and now it would be full of office equipment and files again, pressed into the service of commerce while the various repairs were being done down in the Flats. I imagined the building wouldn't be fit for human habitation for at least three weeks. More, if the repair people dragged their feet, didn't show up, or came at noon because somebody's uncle died. The mortality rate of uncles of contractors and subcontractors in Cleveland is extremely high, especially when the weather gets warmer.

Then I started to shake.

I've been shot at—several times. I've been stabbed, sapped, and slashed, and I've come within seconds of being injected with a lethal mix of cocaine and heroin. A killer once tried to run my car into the stone embankment on Cedar Hill. But no one had ever tried to cook me alive before.

I couldn't imagine a more gruesome death. Someone must have wanted me dead very badly. Someone who didn't know much about firebombs.

Good, I thought, that eliminates about thirteen people in the Greater Cleveland area.

I called Victor Gaimari to tell him what had happened. He sounded genuinely shocked and concerned.

"I'm going to ask around, Milan," he assured me. "See if I hear any rumblings about this. If I do, believe me, I'll take steps."

"I don't want you taking any steps. I'll take the steps."

"Why not just let us handle it?" he said, choosing his words with exquisite precision. "We're more—geared for things like this."

"Because I know how you take care of things. I don't want that. Besides, you and I are about even in the favor department. I want to keep it that way."

He sighed. "You suffer from the sin of hubris, Milan. Excessive pride."

"I went to college, Victor. I know what hubris is. And I like my hubris."

"You sure you're all right? How are you feeling?"

"Brand new. I just wanted to let you know what was going on. No big thing."

"It's a very big thing, Milan," he said severely.

After we hung up I slipped on a sweatshirt, to stop the shaking. Then I realized I'd spent my entire lunch hour watching my office burn, and the afternoon had been taken up with the visit to Doobie Lemp. I was ravenous.

All that was in the refrigerator besides liquids was a half pound wedge of cheddar I'd purchased the week before from Wendt's cheese stand in the West Side Market, and some coffee ice cream in the freezer compartment. There were a few cans of roast beef hash in the cupboard, and on the counter the half-empty bag of potato chips that Milan Junior had left.

Not exactly a feast, but I was in no mood to go across the street to Russo's Stop-&-Shop, and even less inclined to run down the block to Nighttown for something to eat. I decided to make do.

I opened the hash, spread it across a large skillet, and set it to sizzling. Then I grated some of the cheddar to go on top. If anyone had been around with an egg, I would have taken it away at gunpoint.

I put the hash on a plate with a handful of potato chips, opened a beer, and ate at my kitchen table, listening to Herb Score and Tom Hamilton call the Indians game on the radio. I could have watched it on TV, but somehow baseball is more the way it used to be when you listen to it on the radio, when you can't see the players' ten-thousand-dollar neck chains, their earrings, their multimillion dollar attitudes.

Rudy Dolsak called during the fourth inning. "How ya doin', Milan?" he asked.

That was his mistake. I told him.

"My God," he said, "that's horrible."

"Are you calling because you got the information I wanted?"

"How can you even think of something like that after what happened?"

"You're right, Rudy. I'll curl up into the fetal position instead and suck my thumb until the smoke smell goes away."

"You're always such a tough guy, Milan, aren't you?"

I sure as hell didn't feel tough. I felt vulnerable and violated and shaky, and what I wanted more than anything right then was a pair of comforting arms around me.

But I'm a realist, and there were no arms available—nor was there likely to be anytime soon. So I settled for tough guy.

"What've you got, Rudy?"

"Okay," he said. "First, Stranahan. He lives in a sixty-nine-thousand-dollar house on the near west side."

"Sixty-nine thousand? That's not much of a house."

"It was when he paid that much for it in 1968. It's probably worth five times that now. And it's free and clear—no mortgage. He's got some stocks, nothing unusual, and is part owner of a couple of industrial properties in the Flats and the warehouse district. His pension plan at the union is vested—naturally—and he's got about thirty-one thousand dollars in the bank, half in a checking account and half in CDs. His salary is eighty-two five a year, with another twenty or so in bonuses. Altogether he's worth probably three hundred thousand plus."

"And how much of that could he get his hands on tomorrow morning?"

"Hmm," Rudy said, and I could imagine his fingers flying over the keys of a pocket calculator. Rudy would no more go anywhere without his calculator than he would without his pants. "Sixty, seventy K maybe. Why? Is he going somewhere?"

"Not on seventy thousand. What about Kerner?"

"Ah, Kerner," Rudy said.

It seemed that Joel Kerner Sr. had about fifty-three thousand in the bank and another hundred twenty in negotiable securities. The bulk of his net worth—some four million dollars—was tied up in the big house on South Park, which he had purchased twenty-three years ago for a million six, and the mortgage had been paid off in full four years ago.

"So he's house poor," I said.

"How do you figure poor?"

"If not, why is he selling it? And for less than it's worth?"

"There could be lots of reasons," Rudy said. "Their kids moved out, so it's just the two of them there now, rattling around. That's a lot of house. Besides, it might be hard living there, after what happened to their son."

"That house has more security than a federal lockup," I said. "He wouldn't sell that off so easy. When a guy like Kerner gets the cash-flow blues, it's not because he's run up a big bar bill at Morton's. I think he needs money for something—something serious."

"Seven figures serious? Come on, Milan, what kind of an emergency could cost three million dollars."

"I think I know," I said.

I went to bed after the eleven o'clock news, which featured footage of my burning building, and immediately fell asleep. It was a white night, full of fits and starts and frightening dreams.

It wasn't any easier getting into Joel Kerner's home the next morning than it had ever been. The video cameras mounted on the gateposts swung toward me like artillery, their red eyes unblinking. When I pushed the intercom button, Carl Cavallero wasn't exactly hospitable. I informed him that I was going to sit out there with my car blocking the driveway until either someone let me come in or Joel Kerner came out. He warned me he'd call a cop. I encouraged him to do so, and after a few moments of static-filled silence he suggested that I wait. After a few moments the electronic gates swung inward, admitting me to the holy of holies.

When I got to the house, Cavallero was waiting in the vestibule. He let me in and then ordered curtly, "Lift 'em."

I lifted 'em. I liked being frisked even less this time, especially since he took no pains to be gentle, but I didn't want to start any trouble. Not yet.

Cavallero sent me into the living room, where Joel Kerner Sr. waited for me, wearing a multicolored sweater over khaki slacks. On the glass-topped coffee table in front of the sofa there was a half-empty coffee cup and a copy of the morning newspaper. A spring fire, perhaps the last one of the season, crackled in the fireplace, and Kerner stood with his back to it.

"I'm a Bible reader," he announced without any sort of greeting. "Ever since I was a child. The Old Testament, mostly. So I know all about the plagues the Lord visited upon Egypt." He ticked them off on his fingers. "Frogs, floods, boils, pestilence . . ." He dropped his hands. "I don't recall Jacovich. Somehow you were omitted from the Book of Exodus. Why do you devil me, Mr. Jacovich?"

"Because I want to know the truth about your son, even if you don't," I said.

He glanced at his watch. It was, not surprisingly, a Rolex, the sale of which could probably assuage the financial problems of most Americans. "I've asked you to stay away from here. Now you have precisely five minutes before I call the police, so I suggest you talk fast."

"All right," I said. "I think you're a panicky man, Mr. Kerner."

"Oh?"

"You've got a serious case of the shorts. Otherwise you wouldn't be selling your home for so much less than it's worth."

His body jerked as if he'd gotten an electric shock. "How do you know . . . ?"

"I know. Let's leave it at that. You need a big injection of hard cash—which means you probably owe somebody big-time."

He considered denying it, but then his shoulders slumped. Everyone finally reaches a point where the lying, the faking, the smoke screens and subterfuge become too much trouble; Joel Kerner Sr. reached it at that moment. "Why should that be any of your business?"

"Because I believe whoever is into you had your son killed as a warning that you'd better pay up."

He turned ashen, seeming to grow smaller before my eyes. His head sagged forward. He looked like an old, tired, frightened lion. "That's absurd," he said without the ringing conviction that had held him in such good stead at the negotiating tables and in the courtroom.

"And I think the same person tried to kill me so I'd stop looking."

His eyes opened wide. "What? What happened? I had no idea."

"Someone sent me a present yesterday—a Molotov cocktail, thrown through my window. So it's not a matter of me backing off anymore. I'm in for the duration, whether you like it or not. You can either help me considerably or you can get the hell out of my way."

He closed his eyes. "I'm very sorry that happened to you. Are you all right?" he asked, opening them again.

"I'm fine, thank you. I can't say the same for my office, though."

"Offices can be replaced. People can't."

"I thought for a while it might have been you," I said. "I don't anymore."

He turned and walked stiffly over to the sofa, sinking down onto it like a Victorian lady onto a fainting couch. "Thanks for the vote of confidence."

"But you're still on the hook with me. I want you to tell me who you owe."

He shook his huge head, almost sadly. "I can't."

"You have to," I said. "Who might be next if you don't? Patrice? Your wife? You can't buy enough security gizmos and bodyguards to keep them safe forever. Take a look at it, counselor. You're in deep water here, and I'm a guy with a life preserver."

Neither of us said anything for almost a minute. Kerner sat immobile, his eyes closed, almost as if he'd gone to sleep. Then he raised his head and looked at me. "Sit down, Mr. Jacovich," he said. "Please."

I sat at the other end of the sofa.

"Would you like something?" he asked, suddenly remembering his innate good manners. "A coffee? I can have Carl—"

"No, thank you, sir. Let's just talk."

The corners of his mouth played with a smile and then fumbled it away. "Talk. That's what I do best, isn't it? Well, it's a long story."

"I have nowhere to go."

"We share that, then. I have nowhere to go, either." He coughed a frog from his throat. "Have you ever found yourself backed into a corner? Mostly due to your own greed?"

"Greed, no. Sometimes due to my own stupidity."

He fluttered a hand at me. "Semantics. Well, then. As I'm sure you know, my law practice has been devoted to the labor movement here in Ohio. People don't pay a lot of attention to the unions anymore. There are those who'd tell you unions have outlived their usefulness. But the labor movement is what made this country great in the early part of this century, and I'm proud to say that I've been at the forefront of that movement my entire adult life."

"That's admirable, Mr. Kerner. But it's also made you rich."

"Is getting rich against the law?"

"No. Just against the odds."

"Rich is a relative thing. How rich is rich enough? How rich is too rich?"

"Unfortunately that's a philosophical precept I've never had to worry about."

"Well, I'll tell you. There's no such thing as too rich."

"If you say so," I said.

He ran both hands along the sides of his head, pushing his white hair back. His face had regained some of its color. "So about a year and a half, two years ago, I had an opportunity to make a lot of money. And I jumped at it."

I nodded.

"I'd been given a sizable sum to invest. It wasn't my money, but I was trusted to invest it wisely, for the benefit of everyone. Unfortunately I proved unworthy of that trust. Naturally there are a lot of people who are angry with me."

I waited for him to go on.

"These are decent people I've been dealing with—and I plan to make reparations. Every penny. That's why I've put the house up for sale."

I stayed quiet, hoping he would elaborate.

All he said was, "So there you are."

"Where am I?" I said. "You've told me nothing I haven't already figured out. Don't play games with me, because I almost died yesterday, along with somebody else who's completely innocent. I want the names and numbers."

He ran his fingers through his hair again. "I can't do that."

"All right, counselor." I leaned forward, picked up the morning's *Plain Dealer*, and opened it to Ed Stahl's column. "You read Stahl?"

"Every morning. Why?"

"Because when you read his column tomorrow, you're going to see your name. You like getting your name in the paper, don't you, Mr. Kerner?"

His face turned gray again.

"Ed's one of my best friends," I told him. "He helps me out sometimes when I need information, and I help him out—when I come across a story he might consider juicy. Your little tale of woe is just the sort of thing he can run with."

He started to protest, but I cut him off. "I've got enough to get him going. Then he—and a lot of other people—are going to start asking questions. A bunch of union guys whose pensions are in the toilet are going to get mad, and then all the security cameras in the world aren't going to help you."

He flinched.

"It's all going to come out in the end anyway. Except maybe someone else will have to die first. You want that?"

"Jacovich, you're trying to ruin me."

"I'm trying to save you."

He put his face in his hands. "I can't . . . "

"Joel, for the love of God, tell him!"

Elaine Kerner stood in the archway between the living room and the vestibule, with Carl Cavallero hovering uncertainly behind her. Her gray hair was uncombed and her wild eyes glittered with inner torment. I got awkwardly to my feet.

"Just tell him, Joel—and let there be an end to it!" she entreated him.

We stayed like that for a long moment, a frozen tableau. Then she crossed the wide expanse of carpet to sit beside her husband, taking his hand between hers. "I can't stand it anymore," she almost whispered, but she wasn't trying to keep me from hearing—it was all she could manage. "It isn't right. What possible difference can it make now?"

Cavallero started for me. "You want me to put him out, Mr. Kerner?"

"Don't, Carl," I said. "I have twenty years on you. I don't want to hurt you."

That didn't stop Carl. He kept coming, looking as if he'd actually enjoy the experience, and I entertained a small doubt as to whether I really could take this hard, weathered man.

"It's all right, Carl," Kerner told him, and waved a dismissive hand. Cavallero pulled up short, like a Doberman whose leash had just been yanked. He hesitated, then turned and left the room, casting one last look over his shoulder at me, which might have been defiance, or perhaps disappointment.

Elaine Kerner clutched her husband's hand, her eyes fixed on him. His head was down, and he seemed to be gnawing on the inside of his lip, chewing on a decision. He glanced up at her once, and then away, as if the sight of her was too painful. Then he looked at me from someplace in the nether reaches of hell.

"Take your coat off, Mr. Jacovich," he said.

CHAPTER TWENTY-THREE

Joel Kerner reached for his coffee cup with a hand that trembled conspicuously. Taking a sip, he set the cup back down on the saucer with an uncomfortable rattle. He looked at it as if unwilling to believe it had made such a racket. Then he settled back against the sofa cushion and gave Elaine a quick smile.

"I'm on retainer to several of the big unions in town," he said. "It's the main portion of my income. I handle all their legal affairs. I go to Washington several times a year, I draw up their contracts, I consult with their leadership." His chest swelled— even in extremis, Joel Kerner Sr. had a boundless ego. "I'm good at it. Ask about me in labor circles anywhere in this country. 'Joel Kerner is for the working guy,' they'll tell you. 'He's the best.'"

I had my notebook out, my pen hovering above the paper, but there was nothing to write down yet.

"What you may not know is that I'm very involved in the handling of union pension funds. Hell, some of those funds I helped set up in the beginning, helped structure. It's part of my job."

He was warming to his subject now, the old lawyerly instincts kicking in. "A pension fund is a way of investing the rank-and-file's money for them, so that when their working days are over they'll have enough to pay their bills, buy their medicine, maybe finance a vacation or a retirement home, and when the union handles it, that means that the corporations can't raid it and screw it up. It's a sizable chunk of money, and you could let it sit in the bank and accrue interest, but in today's economic climate that's irresponsible. There are better investments, greater returns. Part of what I do for the locals is to find those investments, negotiate the best terms, do whatever I can to help out the blue-collar guys that really pay my salary."

The only union I'd ever belonged to was when I was on the police force, and I was too much of a kid to know what they really did for me. I didn't last long enough on the job to have my pension vested, either. "Isn't handling the pension fund usually the job of the union treasurer?"

"Sure," he said. "But a lot of those union officers get themselves elected because they're popular with the workers, they're tough, they're strong. And because, well, they're good people, rank-and-file guys who know what it is to bust their backs in the trenches in order to feed their families. A lot of them are . . . unsophisticated. Especially about handling a lot of money."

"So that's where you come in."

"Right." He stopped then, his mouth working, as if he didn't have enough saliva to continue. "I need some more coffee," he finally said.

Elaine Kerner got to her feet. "I'll bring the pot. Mr. Jacovich?"

I gave in. "All right, I could use some, thanks. Black, please." She nodded and went out of the room.

Kerner lowered his voice. "This has been so hard on her. What happened to Joel . . . It's a terrible thing for a mother to have to live with." His eyes turned inward. "Or a father."

I gave him half a minute, and then I asked, "Is Patrick Stranahan the one you owe money to?"

"Not Stranahan, no. His union. Local 696. He gave me almost three million dollars in pension funds to invest. And I . . . " He drew a ragged breath. "I blew it."

"That's unfortunate," I said. "But it was an investment, wasn't it? Any investment, even in blue-chip stocks, carries a certain amount of risk."

"Yes, but that's not how it was. I was supposed to invest the money in a specific way—Patrick and I had agreed ahead of time.

The pension funds were supposed to finance the rehabbing of an old broken-down building down in the warehouse district. What with the big downtown resurgence in the last few years, new companies are moving in, and people are actually wanting to live down there."

I nodded.

"That investment would have come back to the union guys in the way of work too—hundreds of jobs over maybe a two-year period—in addition to whatever profits the money itself would accrue."

"But that's not where you invested it?"

Running a hand over his jaw as if he was trying to decide whether he needed a shave, he shook his head.

Elaine Kerner came back into the room with a coffee carafe and an extra cup on a tray. She served me first, then gave Joel Kerner a refill and resumed her place next to him on the sofa.

He slurped at the coffee. "I've done some shitty things in my life," he said, patting his wife's knee. "But I've never been so deeply ashamed of anything before."

"Tell me what happened to the money."

"I heard of a deal where I could get the principal back inside of eight months," he said, lowering his voice conspiratorially, "and then literally double my investment within three years. I thought if I could just put the union's project off a while, let their money work for *me,* then I could make three million dollars for myself, fast, and still have the principal from the pension fund to invest where we'd agreed." He dropped his eyes. "It was a lousy, unethical thing to do—and illegal—but I thought I could get away with it, and that everybody would profit in the end."

"But it didn't work out like that."

"No. I knew it was highly speculative—that's why the potential profit was so great. I was a damn fool. But I didn't do it for myself, I did it for my kids. So they'd have a nest egg, so they wouldn't have to work as hard as I did."

"Your children weren't exactly starving."

He put the cup down on its saucer and glared at me. "Don't you want your children to look up to you, Jacovich? To think that you walk on water? So that after you're dead they'll brag about you and say what a great man you were? My children adored me—especially Joel. I was the man he was always trying to be. That's a hell of a thing to have to live up to." A tear ran down his wrinkled cheek. He was either a very good actor or he'd bitten the inside of his mouth to make his eyes water—or else he was honestly moved. "And I even fucked that up."

"Joel," his wife said gently.

He ducked his head. "Sorry, honey." Then he looked up at me. "Lainie hates it when I curse."

The room was quiet, save for the popping of the logs in the fireplace. Kerner leaned forward, his hands and forearms on his thighs, and with his mane of hair and his fierce visage he once more reminded me of an aging lion.

"Joel found out what I'd done," he said sadly. "It really ruptured our relationship. He was madder than hell at me. He felt betrayed; his idol had feet of clay. His father turned out to be a four-flusher, a cheap embezzler. A crook."

"It wasn't that bad, Mr. Jacovich," Elaine Kerner said.

"Yes it was, Lainie! Damn it, don't soft-pedal it. Joel and I argued about it—had a huge fight about it at a party. And then when it all fell through, when the money was gone with a ninety-five-percent chance it'd never come back, he never forgave me." He brushed at his eyes. "Now he's dead—and he died with nothing but contempt for me. I have to live with that."

That perhaps explained Joel's sea change shortly before his death, his transformation from a loving and dutiful son to an angry, aggressive risk taker who couldn't commit to a relationship, who threw himself into martial arts with a vengeance, who sought the company of prostitutes and then cried afterward. So many people don't really like their parents. When those who grow up adoring them discover that they are bent and corrupt after all, it can be a tough adjustment to make.

I wasn't much older than Joel had been. I wondered what I would do if I were suddenly to find that my own father had been an embezzler, a philanderer, a thief, a liar. It would shake my very foundations, make me doubt who I am.

I swallowed hard. "Stranahan found out about it too?"

He bobbed his head up and down.

"Is that what you were arguing about the first time I came here?"

"Patrick was very angry," Elaine Kerner said. "He'd known about it for months, but we had promised we'd make reparations. We couldn't pay him back fast enough, so last week he gave Joel an ultimatum—a time limit."

"His ass was on the line too," Kerner said, finding his voice. "That money was ultimately his responsibility."

"That's why we're selling the house," his wife added, her eyes big and dark and almost too haunted to look at.

"You think all of this might have something to do with what happened to Joel," I said. "That's why you called the police off. That's why you tried to buy me off."

"I'm not proud of it," Kerner said. "I've lost my son, I'm losing my house—I just wanted to keep some shred of my dignity."

"Enough to let your son's killer get away with it? Stranahan certainly had reason for wanting to get back at you."

"Patrick Stranahan has been my friend for forty years," Kerner said.

"That didn't stop you from using his money for your own purposes. Why would it stop him from killing?"

"He's not a killing man, Mr. Jacovich," Mrs. Kerner explained. "He's a hard man sometimes. But he's not evil. It just isn't in him."

"What if it is?" I said. "What if he is capable of killing?"

"He's not."

"Even if he was trapped in a corner? Anyone might be. What if he killed your son, or had him killed, out of panic, or plain rage?" I watched as the two of them grew older in front of me, but I'd come too far to turn back.

"If I thought he was responsible for what happened to Joel I'd kill him myself," Kerner said.

I tapped my pen against my notebook, making little blue dots all over the page. "That might not be necessary, Mr. Kerner."

◦　◦　◦

It's maybe a three-iron from the Kerners' home in Shaker to the Stone Oven in downtown Cleveland Heights. I lucked into a parking place right on Lee Road; there was even forty minutes left on the meter, and I went in and settled by the window to enjoy a roast beef sandwich on Pugliese bread and a Diet Coke while I read the paper. Then at one o'clock I called Stranahan's local from the pay phone. The operator, who sounded a lot like my redheaded friend with the squirrel teeth, informed me with a sniff that Stranahan was out to lunch.

That was okay. If he'd been there he wouldn't have talked to me anyway.

I drove down Superior Avenue at a leisurely pace and parked across the street from union headquarters, right behind a car with two bumper stickers, one reading I LOVE LAS VEGAS, with a red heart in place of the word *love*, and the other I LOVE JESUS. One would think the two were mutually exclusive.

I smoked a cigarette and watched the foot traffic on Superior, what there was of it. Cleveland used to be a walking kind of town, even a strolling town when the weather was good, but not much anymore, except downtown, right around Public Square and on East Ninth Street. Now we build our cities around cars, not people.

After a few minutes I saw the big Lincoln Town Car that had been parked in front of Joel Kerner's house the week before turn into the small executive parking lot at the side of the building. I started across the street. Stranahan's driver, Michael, jumped out of the driver's side wearing a leather bomber jacket and a bright green nylon scarf, which made him look like an IRA terrorist. He hustled around to open the door for his boss. Stranahan exited the car with some effort, adjusting his long cashmere overcoat. He was patting fussily at his bad hairpiece when he spotted me.

"Goddamn, you again?" he said. "Take a hike. I got nothing to say to you."

"I've got plenty to say to you."

His eyes glittered and he looked at his faithful retainer. "Michael, make this guy disappear."

"Right, Mr. Stranahan," Michael said. He bent his knees and leaned forward on the balls of his feet, his hands up in front of him like a boxer's. But he held them far apart, like he was going to start in with body punches, leaving him wide open for all sorts of things. His technique might have worked late on a Saturday night in the Irish bars on the west side, but he was no pro.

"Wait a second, Michael," I said. "You better go call those ten other guys."

I'd guessed right. A real boxer wouldn't have led with a round-house right the way he did, which put him a little off balance. I stepped aside and let the punch whistle harmlessly past my shoulder, then grabbed his arm and let his own momentum carry him forward. I put my other hand on his elbow and pushed, bending his arm and jerking it up behind his back in a hammerlock. Then I slammed him face down across the still-warm hood of the Lincoln.

"Michael, Michael," I said sadly.

My big mistake was not looking behind me. Stranahan may have been old, but he could still punch, and his knuckles crashing into my kidney from behind buckled my knees—and hurt.

Without letting go of Michael's wrist, I turned sideways and backhanded the old man across the face. The blow startled him, and he staggered backward and sat down hard on the concrete. Michael struggled and I gave his arm a little tweak that made him whimper.

"I don't want to do it this way, Mr. Stranahan," I said, "but I will if I have to. It's your call."

Blood trickled out of the side of Stranahan's mouth, and he wiped ineffectively at it. "My call is, I give a holler and there'll be so many guys all over you, you won't know whether to shit or go blind."

"You better make sure they kill me. Otherwise you'll be doing your talking to them."

He frowned his puzzlement.

"About mishandling pension funds."

Michael struggled a little, and I pulled his arm higher up his back. Any higher and he'd be able to scratch his head from the rear. He grunted in pain and subsided against the sleek hood of the car.

Stranahan blinked at me. "What do you know about pension funds?"

"Enough to hang you high. So you'd better talk to me."

He got to his feet clumsily, his long overcoat getting in the way. I had knocked his toupee slightly askew; he started to raise his hands to set it right and then stopped, embarrassed. He looked like a sad clown.

"Let him up," he said.

I looked down at my captive. "Michael, I'm going to let go of your arm now. Throw another punch at me and I'll break it."

Michael growled.

"Forget it, Michael," Stranahan said, and I felt Michael relax. I released his arm and he straightened up, leaving a smear of saliva on the Lincoln's shiny hood. He wiped his mouth, killing me with a glance, and I thought for a minute he was going to try me again. But his shoulders slumped and he backed away.

"You should die with a hard-on," he said. I hadn't heard that one before.

"So talk, Jacovich," Stranahan said.

"Not in a parking lot. Come on, Mr. Stranahan, let's go someplace and I'll buy you a drink."

"I'm particular who I drink with," he said. "We'll go up to my office."

"I don't think so," I said, thinking of Michael's ten friends. "Neutral territory."

Reaching inside his overcoat, he pulled a snowy handkerchief from the breast pocket of his suit jacket and dabbed at his mouth. "You play rough," he said, looking at the bloody linen.

"You have no idea. How about the Mardi Gras? I'll drive."

"I don't like being squeezed," he said.

"Most people don't."

He crumpled the handkerchief into a tight ball and shoved it into his coat pocket. "Let's get it over with, then."

"My car's across the street," I said.

We started walking toward it, with Michael following us. I turned to him.

"I don't like you," I said. "You can't come to my party."

He thought about making something of it, but Stranahan stopped him. "All right, Michael, just go on upstairs. I'll be back in a bit."

Michael turned away, heading toward the building, his shoulders slumped, his head down like a whipped dog's.

"It's been thirty years since anybody's had the balls to put their hands on me," Stranahan said as we crossed the street.

"It's good for you," I said. "Teaches you humility."

We got into my car and I pulled out into traffic. It was only three minutes to the Mardi Gras, just off Superior on East Twenty-first Street. The bar is kind of a Cleveland tradition, and many of the *Plain Dealer* editorial staff hang out there.

I parked in an unpaved lot directly across the street. I got out first; Stranahan stayed in the car for about twenty seconds. When he emerged, his toupee had been set straight once more.

The Mardi Gras was redecorated a few years back. From your standard minimalist grunge tavern it's evolved into something lighter and more airy, with half the walls hardwood and the other half painted a flat gray. The murals and paintings have a vague New Orleans motif, and over the bar is a long tubular black light that must have been resurrected from the sixties. It turns everyone's face purple.

A loud, happy guy in a white polo shirt sat at the bar with a more serious man in a gray suit, and between them a faded-looking redheaded woman with high, fragile cheekbones. Farther toward the back, a lone black woman in a cerise business suit was drinking a beer and studying *Crain's Cleveland Business,* making notations in the margin with a pencil.

We sat in a booth along one wall, and a weary waitress took our order. I had a Stroh's and Stranahan asked for a Bushmills, neat. Nobody said anything until the drinks were served.

"Your health," I said.

"That's a good toast, because I wouldn't give a bucket of warm piss for yours."

"Is that why you had someone toss a firebomb through my window yesterday?"

A deep vertical crease appeared between his eyes. "What the hell are you talking about?"

"I think you know."

"I think you're full of crap! What firebomb?"

"You own a boat, Mr. Stranahan?"

"Who the hell has a boat in a climate where you can only use it three months a year?"

"Somebody who came sailing past my office yesterday afternoon and air-mailed me a Molotov cocktail."

"You're saying you think I did it? Why would I want to do that?"

"Maybe it was a message—stop poking around. Or maybe you were trying to kill me."

"If I wanted to send you a message, it'd be a hell of a lot more direct. Michael wasn't kidding when he said he could get ten guys to bounce you around." He stretched his neck, pulling at his collar. "And as for the other—I don't kill people."

"No?"

"No! Hey, listen, what the hell you want from me?"

"A few facts. Because somebody's dead, and two other people almost were. And one of them was me. And that makes me uptight."

"I don't know anything about that," he said sullenly. "And I resent the implication. That's actionable, you know."

"Right, sic your lawyer on me. I'm quaking in my boots." I took a pull of my beer. "You gave Joel Kerner three million dollars out of your local's pension fund to invest in rehabbing a building in the warehouse district."

He didn't say anything.

"It's not a question. Kerner told me already, so let's not play games."

"All right, I did. So what?"

"So Kerner didn't do what you told him. He invested the money somewhere else and lost it all. Now he's scared, so scared he's turned his house into a fortress. The only thing missing is Secret Service guys with walkie-talkie buttons in their ears. He hardly goes out anymore. What's he scared of?"

"Why don't you ask him?" Stranahan said, and belted his whiskey down. He grimaced, putting a hand to his cut lip, and chased the whiskey with a sip of ice water.

"I think he's scared of you, Mr. Stranahan."

"Me?"

"That's right. That's why he's trying to sell his house quick, for less than it's worth, to repay you. You're in trouble, deep trouble because of him. That money is ultimately your responsibility, and you blew it. You're the one that'll have to answer to your membership if you don't get it back. You've got every right to be sore at him."

"*Sore* at him?" His one-bark laugh was without mirth. "I'd like to kill the son of a bitch." Then his ruddy face flushed darker. "That's only a figure of speech."

"It is, huh?"

"Think about it, Jacovich," he said, "in practical terms. The man owes me three million dollars. If I kill him, he can't pay it back, can he? And I'm out three million. I may not be a rocket scientist, but I'm not a moron either."

"That makes sense. But maybe if you killed his son instead, with the implied threat to the rest of his family, it'd give him a little more motivation."

His face grew even more flushed, darkening to a kind of rich burgundy color. "If I were twenty years younger I'd clean your clock for that. I held that boy in my arms when he was two weeks old. Killing him would be—incongruous." He pronounced it "in-con-*grew*-ous."

"I've heard your Baby Joel stories before. They won't wash."

He hunched over the table at me, the muscles at the sides of his jaw jumping. "Listen!" he hissed. Then he wiped his mouth, turned, and signaled the waitress.

He waited without speaking until he'd been served another Bushmills, which he downed in one gulp. Then he shook his head in great sorrow. "Holy Mary mother of God, you've got me drinking in the middle of the afternoon." He coughed and took another gulp of water. I'd have been willing to bet he'd been drinking in the afternoon for fifty years.

"Listen," he said again. "I'm no saint, God help me. I admit that. I've done some bad things. In the early days, when the local was trying to get a foothold, I beat guys up, or had it done. When I was younger, and full of the devil, I was kind of a rat with women." He nodded for emphasis. "And I've done the same damn thing Joel Kerner did," he confided, lowering his voice. "I took money that didn't belong to me, sure, union money, and made a profit out of it. But I got away with it, because I was smarter. Nobody ever lost a penny because of me. I paid back everything—and made a lot of money for the local too."

He drew himself up against the back of the booth. "But on my mother's grave, I wouldn't kill anyone. For any reason."

"Not even three million reasons?"

He slammed his fist down on the table, making the glasses jump. "You think I'd walk up to Joel Kerner and say, 'I just killed your son, now give me my money'?"

Because it was midafternoon and not too crowded in the Mardi Gras, only four people, plus the waitress and bartender, stopped what they were doing and turned to look at him.

"Take it easy," I said.

His hands were quivering, and when he spoke, so was his voice. "I swear to God, I couldn't kill anybody. Certainly not young Joel. I cared for him—for that family."

His eyes were shiny wet, and all of a sudden I believed him. And I told him so.

"That's supposed to make us best friends?"

"No," I said. "But it'll get me out of your face for a while."

"Thank God for small favors."

"Who do you think did kill Junior, Mr. Stranahan?"

"Ah, God," he said, wiping at his eyes with the paper cocktail napkin. "I wish I knew."

"But you don't think it was just a mugging either, do you?"

We ordered another round of drinks and sat there quietly for a while. The people at the bar returned to their own pursuits, the businesswoman picking up her newspaper and the two men trying to convince the redhead that her boyfriend was cheating on her and she should repay him in kind, preferably with one or both of them.

"I should be getting on back," Stranahan said at last. "I've got a local to run."

"First tell me about the time you did what Joel Kerner did with the pension funds."

"Why?"

"Because I'm down a blind alley here, and I'd like to understand the way things work."

"What the hell," he said after a moment. "It's all yesterday's news now." He put both hands flat on the table. "It was about fifteen years ago. I had about a million two of pension money that I was supposed to do something with. I heard about a real estate development out in Solon. The developer was undercapitalized and had run short of cash before they'd completed their first phase, so the terms they were offering were too attractive to pass up. In seven months I got the money back, with a thirteen-percent profit."

"Which you put in your pocket?"

He nodded. "And then I took the original money and put it in high-yield bonds. It was win-win. Or win-win-win, actually. The tract got built, and a lot of our guys went to work on it, I might add. That was part of the deal. The men made money on the jobs, the union made money on the bonds, and I made a neat little bundle. Everybody was happy, nobody got hurt. But that's because I was smarter than Joel."

"In what way?"

"I was dealing in real estate. You can't hardly go wrong with real estate, and I knew it. But Kerner, he really took a flyer." He looked at the ceiling in the barroom for succor. "Who in the name of the Blessed Virgin is dumb enough to speculate in oil stocks? I'll tell you who. Joel Kerner."

A fuzzy, many-legged insect ran up my spine. "Oil stocks?"

"Can you believe the gullibility of the man?"

With my finger I traced the letter *M* in the condensation on the side of my glass. There had been an oil stocks salesman in San

Carlos when Joel died. After a week of frustration, things were beginning to coalesce inside my head. It was about damn time.

"Not Republic Oil, by any chance?"

His eyebrows arched in surprise. "How in hell did you know that?"

Chapter Twenty-four

We walked across the street to the parking lot and I unlocked the passenger door so Stranahan could get in. Then I went around to the driver's side, and as I bent over to open my door I saw a movement behind me out of the corner of my eye. I whirled around.

Michael stood there, and although he didn't have the advertised ten other guys with him, the two he had seemed like more than enough. I silently cursed my incredible carelessness for letting him hear where I was taking Stranahan. Both of the other two were bigger than he was, and older, and their potbellies belied the hard muscle beneath the fat. They looked mean, but not as mean as Michael. He held a baseball bat clutched in his hands, and his little pig eyes glittered. It was a big one, probably the thirty-eight-ounce Ken Griffey Jr. model.

"I see you brought some help, Michael," I said. "Aren't you going to introduce me to your friends? Which one is Beavis?"

His forehead knitted in puzzlement, and it took him about twenty seconds to catch up to the insult. Then he lowered his head like a Cape buffalo about to charge and took a few steps toward me. "You son of a bitch!" he said, and swung for the left field fence.

I turned away and fell backward, instinctively throwing up my arm to protect my head. The bat glanced off it, hard, popping the stitches from the knife attack in San Carlos, the wound breaking open like a ripe melon. I felt a thousand tiny needles pricking me and warm blood running down my wrist.

The swing had caused him to lose his balance, and when my foot shot out and I slammed my heel against his knee; the knee gave beneath him. He screamed, cropping the bat, and went down on his side, squealing like a pig and clutching his leg.

The other two were unarmed as far as I could see. They started advancing on me, one from each side. Since my left arm was relatively useless, I threw a straight right at the guy coming from that side. It caught him flush in the nose. Bone and cartilage crunched against my knuckles as his head snapped back, and he made a sound like someone biting into a rotten apple, putting both hands up to his face. Blood spurted from between his fingers.

Before I could turn to confront the other one, he hit me on the side of the head, between my eye and my ear, with a fist about the size of a catcher's mitt. That it must have hurt his hand like hell was little consolation; the world turned cockeyed and I felt myself falling. As soon as my knees hit the damp ground, he kicked me in the stomach with a steel-toed work boot, and my lunch rushed up to the back of my throat. I was lucky at that; if his toe had hit a rib, it would've cracked like a pencil.

Stranahan got out of the car as fast as his age would permit. "Hey, knock it off!" he commanded, just as the big guy was drawing his foot back for another kick. "Marty, cut it out!" Everyone froze.

Stranahan came around to my side of the car and helped me up, inadvertently grabbing my mangled arm and sending a surge of agony all the way up to my neck.

"What the hell's the matter with you?" he barked at his three forlorn muscle guys. "You crazy or something, doing this on your own hook?"

"He broke my fucking knee!" Michael blubbered, writhing around on the damp ground.

"He broke by dose," the second one mumbled through his bloody fingers.

Still seeing the score of a Bach fugue dancing in front of my eyeballs, I turned to the guy who'd sucker-punched and kicked me.

"How about you, Marty?" I said. "You okay?"

He gave me a nasty grin. "Sure. You never laid a glove on me."

"That's what I thought," I said, clenching my good hand, and I threw my fist into his jaw with all the force I had. He dropped like a sack of mulch, which almost made up for the fact that the impact jolted my nerves all the way up to my elbow. Now both my arms were throbbing.

I turned to Stranahan, who backed away from me, holding both hands out in front of him ineffectually, as if he was trying to stop an onrushing train. "Hey, come on, now! I had nothing to do with this. You know that. We had a truce."

"You forgot to tell your troops."

He glumly surveyed his three soldiers—two on the ground and the one still standing but bleeding into his hands—and shook his head in wonder. "You're one tough son of a bitch, Jacovich."

"Don't ever forget it," I said.

Dr. Ben Sorkin is one of a disappearing breed of general medical practitioners. He's been my family doctor ever since I came back to Cleveland from Vietnam. His office is in one of those modern, blocky medical buildings not far from Josh Borgenecht's travel agency in Beachwood. The corridors always smell vaguely of disinfectant. Ben and I were college chums at Kent State, which is why I could just walk in without an appointment and get my minor injuries taken care of, saving myself a trip to the emergency room.

It wasn't the first time Ben had patched me up on a moment's notice. His receptionist knew me at a glance and gave me a big smile, and I wondered why it is that women wearing white uniforms always melt my heart.

I went into Ben's inner sanctum, bracing myself for a scolding, and I took off my car coat, sports jacket, and shirt, all of which were caked with dried blood and probably ruined. The Joel Kerner Jr. case was playing hell with my wardrobe; I made a mental note to bill Patrice Kerner for a new one.

"What happened this time, Milan?" Ben said with a trace of annoyance. Ben can be an old lady sometimes and vigorously disapproves of my lifestyle. For some reason he seems to think it's better to carry a stethoscope than a .357 Magnum.

I gave him the Cliff's Notes version.

"My God," he said, looking at the wound in my arm, which was oozing something I didn't want to think about around the loose threads of the torn sutures, which resembled the frayed cuffs of an old pair of work jeans. "Who sewed this up the first time, the guy at the Shell station?"

"Third World medicine," I told him, wincing as he probed the cut.

He ran his fingers over the side of my head, which had swollen up in a most unattractive way. "You're going to have a beautiful purple bruise tomorrow."

"It'll bring out my blue eyes."

"Were you knocked all the way out?"

"No."

"Then there's probably no concussion. You're just lucky Slovenians have such hard heads."

"You've got to be tough to dance the polka."

He swabbed the cut on my arm with a stinging antiseptic, which would be a good way to persuade prisoners of war to tell the enemy the strength and location of their units. "I'll have to sew this up again, of course. Are you going to gut it out or do you want something for the pain?" he asked with a straight face.

"Sure I want something for the pain!" I hollered. "This isn't a movie."

"Your whole life is a movie," he said. *"Pulp Fiction."*

He went to a drawer and took out a vial of liquid, then sucked it into a syringe. "When are you going to get yourself a desk job? One of these days I'm not going to be able to put you back together, you know." He jabbed the needle into my arm with what I took to be undue relish. "How many of these little incidents will it take before you decide you're in the wrong business for a forty-five-year-old man?"

"Forty-three," I corrected him. "And I used to get banged up a lot worse than this every Saturday playing football. Hell, there was a fullback at Akron that used to hit harder than that guy did."

"Must have been the last time the Zips hit anybody hard," he said, a reference to Akron's less than stellar won-lost record the past few years. He pulled the needle out. "Give it a few minutes. Your arm will start to tingle and then go numb."

I reached over for my sports jacket and pulled my Winstons out of the pocket.

"No, God damn it!" he said, snatching the pack away from me. "You're not going to smoke in my office!" He threw up his hands. "I never saw anybody with a death wish quite like yours before."

"A death eater," I said.

"What?"

"Just thinking out loud."

By the time I got out of Ben's office it was almost five o'clock. Too late to check out any of the things I wanted to. Besides, my head was pounding and my hand hurt, my kidneys ached and my arm stung and throbbed. I was in no shape or mood to do anything efficiently. I went home.

I took my shirt off and threw it into the trash, tossed the sports jacket and car coat onto the ever growing dry-cleaning pile on my closet floor, and put on one of my vast collection of Kent State sweatshirts. Then I brewed some tea; I was feeling entirely too fragile for coffee or beer. I gobbled down two of the codeine tablets Ben had given me for my headache and sat down in my den. I didn't bother with the six o'clock news—the night before I'd been treated to videotaped shots of my own building burning, and I didn't want to see it happening to someone else tonight.

Which reminded me of Teri Levine.

I'd thought about her a lot in the past twenty-four hours or so, thought how close we'd both come to dying. I'd thought other things about her too.

I picked up the phone at my elbow and tapped out the first three digits of her phone number, then hesitated. I put the receiver back into its cradle.

What if Mrs. Levine answered the phone, breathing fire and sulfur like any mother dragon might if a man even so much as glanced at her daughter?

I touched my bruised head gingerly. That afternoon I'd been punched and kicked and attacked with a Louisville Slugger. In the past few days I'd been knifed and nearly incinerated. One would think I'd be able to handle even such a formidable adversary as Dalma Levine. Well, I could. I was damned if I'd let her intimidate me.

Much.

I redialed, this time going all the way. I was ashamed at the flood of relief I felt when Teri answered the phone.

"I'm calling to find out how you're doing," I said. "No after-effects?"

"No," she said, her voice low and guarded, as if she was trying to prevent someone from overhearing. To me it sounded sexy and mysterious. "I just had a bad case of the shudders last night is all. Are *you* okay?"

"I'm okay. A little inconvenienced by having to stay away from my office for a while, but okay. Except right now I have a headache the size of Indiana."

"How come?"

I thought about telling her, then didn't. It would sound too much like whining. I've never liked whiners, and I was starting to fear I was falling into the habit. "It was nothing. I'm fine, really. I just don't feel much like reading tonight. Or eating, either. I'm just glad that you're all right. I was worried about you."

"Oh. I'm okay."

Awkward silence punctured by the sound of two people breathing into their telephone mouthpieces.

"Look," I began, and then had to clear my throat. I felt like I was fourteen again. "Uh, yesterday—what I said. I'd really like to see you sometime."

"You would?"

"Very much."

Her voice grew even softer, more breathy. "My mother would have a fit."

"I'll bet she'd deal with it if she had to."

"Mother's had a tough time. . . . "

"I know," I said, "but you can't make it up to her by not having any life of your own." I rubbed the nape of my neck. The pain in my head was causing me to hold it funny, and my neck and shoulder muscles were starting to stiffen up. "We don't have to go pick out a silver pattern or anything. Just dinner."

She didn't say anything right away. Then I heard another voice in the room with her—her mother, I was sure—and the pattern of her breathing changed. She said, "I've got to go now. It was sweet of you to call. I hope your headache gets better."

After I hung up, I took my teacup into the kitchen and stood at the sink brooding about mothers. Teri's, specifically, who was so busy feeling sorry for herself that she'd kept her daughter under heavy wraps for her entire life.

And I brooded about fathers too. Like Joel Kerner Sr., whose greed and perfidy and corruptibility had turned his son's feelings from adoration to anger and a sense of betrayal, and who had turned his son himself into a death eater, a man who found it difficult to cope with things like dating and committing. About how parents can so easily ruin the lives of those they love the most—their children.

Without even realizing it.

I ran more water into my cup and boiled it in the microwave, then dunked my used tea bag in it. The codeine I'd taken for my headache was kicking in; it was helping, but I was a long way from comfortable. I emptied half an ice cube tray into a towel, twisted it up, and brought it and my tea back into the den, where I sat down, holding the ice first against my bruised face and then on my equally bruised arm.

In my mind I ran through the affairs of the day. Michael and his two beefy compatriots had distracted me from business for a while; throbbing head and aching arm or no, it was time to reflect.

Patrick Stranahan had given Joel Kerner Sr. a huge hunk of his local's pension fund to invest in a downtown building. Kerner had instead pissed it away on oil-well stocks being peddled by Harry Channock of Republic Oil.

The same Harry Channock who just happened to turn up on a package tour to San Carlos on which Joel Kerner Jr. had been murdered. And who'd neglected to tell me he'd done business with the victim's father.

It was too damn convenient. I couldn't quite make anything fit yet. But I knew I didn't like it.

I was vaguely aware that my stomach was rumbling—it had been a long time since my sandwich at the Stone Oven. But I knew there was nothing in the refrigerator even vaguely appealing, and I felt too banged up to go across the street and shop for dinner at Russo's. Sitting in a restaurant was out of the question. So I decided to skip dinner. At six foot three and two hundred thirty pounds, I didn't figure I was going to waste away to nothing anytime soon.

I scribbled some notes on a yellow pad I dug out of a kitchen drawer. It was funny—I'd used this apartment as an office for years. Now that I had moved my business down to Collision Bend, though, it felt peculiar working here again. I doodled empty gallows all over the margins of the paper.

The ice cubes had begun to melt, and I threw them and the soggy towel into the sink. The ache in my head was now a low murmur, and while my arm still throbbed and Ben Sorkin's new stitches were still sore and tingling, the pain was bearable.

I sat down in my big chair again with my eyes closed, hoping I'd drop off to sleep. It didn't happen. There were too many things bouncing around inside my brain, things about Harry Channock and Patrick Stranahan that I wanted explained tomorrow.

After about thirty minutes, the doorbell rang.

I was instantly alert, my apathy melting away. Someone had tried to kill me two days in a row—and that wasn't counting the knife attack in San Carlos. What was to say they wouldn't try again?

"Hang on," I yelled, and got down my .38 police special from its nesting place on the top shelf of my hall closet. Checking the load quickly, I went to the door, the weapon held down next to my thigh.

I stood to the side of the door in case anyone had ideas about firing a shotgun through it. "Yes?"

"It's Teri," I heard through the wood. "Teri Levine."

I opened the door. She stood in the hallway with a paper sack in her hand, the shoulders of her Bogart trench coat speckled with the light rain that fell outside. Her hair was damp and stuck to her forehead. She wore very little makeup that I could see.

"I was worried about you," she said.

"Come on in."

She did, pushing her wet hair off her forehead. Turning to face me, she saw the gun. "I don't think you'll need that," she said after several seconds.

"Sorry. I'm a little edgy these days." I put the .38 back on the shelf.

She took in the living room with a glance as she shrugged off her coat. Under it she wore black jeans and a white blouse. Not designer jeans, but the kind you'd wear to sit around the house and watch television.

"This is a great apartment," she said. "I've noticed the building from the outside when I drive down Fairmount, but I've never been inside before." She handed me her coat and shook out her hair with her fingers. "It suits you. Masculine and minimalist."

I laughed, hanging her coat in the closet. "Is that a nice way of saying I don't have enough furniture?"

She put a hand up and touched the bruise on my face with cool fingers. "Ooh, nasty," she said. "Tomorrow that's going to be a real lulu."

"Gives my face character."

"You've got plenty of that already." She handed me the bag. "Here. You have a microwave?"

"Sure. What is it?"

She didn't answer, so I opened it up to find a Rubbermaid container with a yellowish frozen mass inside.

"You said you weren't eating, and I got concerned. You have to keep up your strength."

I took a closer look. There were carrots, noodles, and matzo balls visible in the yellow block. "Chicken soup?"

"What can I say? It's in my genes. It was in the freezer and I thought you might like it."

"I like that you brought it."

We looked at one another for a minute.

"Aren't you going to heat it up?"

I went into the kitchen and put the container in the microwave, setting the timer for five minutes. "Can I get you a drink?" I called out to her. "Wine? A beer?"

"No thanks."

I came back into the living room to find her sitting on the sofa and paging through the latest *Sports Illustrated*.

"You're a sports fan."

"I played a little football when I was a kid."

She nodded. "Who do you root for now that the Browns are gone? The Ravens?"

"Not with my dying breath."

"Me either. I even hate their uniforms. That purple—yuck!" Smiling, she went back to the magazine.

"I have to admit, this is kind of a surprise, your coming here tonight."

She looked thoughtful. "Kind of surprised me too. My mother walked in while I was talking to you. I guess you heard her." She put the magazine back on the coffee table. "She got really pissy about it."

"And?"

"And it made me mad. It made me mad when I thought about all the other times she's kept me from living my life. It made me think about Joel Kerner."

"What about him?"

She shrugged. "I don't know. It was just a vacation flirtation. It probably would have come to nothing. But I never got the chance to find out. I've never gotten the chance to find out—anything."

She stood up, shoving her hands into the back pockets of her jeans, and went over to the window to look out at the traffic heading up Cedar Hill. "Tonight when she wanted to know why you called—she grilled me like I was a suspect in a bank heist—I thought that if I let her push me around one more time, I'd never get to find out about you either. So I told her I was going out, and when she asked me where, I said it was none of her business." Turning away from the window to look at me, she smiled with one corner of her mouth. "She did the whole wounded-dove guilt thing. But for the first time in my life I don't even care."

I went across the room to stand close to her. From the street, if anyone bothered to glance up, we probably looked very romantic, framed that way in the lighted window.

"It's great that you're so nurturing with her."

"I'm a nurturer—didn't I bring you chicken soup? At least that's what my shrink tells me."

"You see a shrink?"

She chuckled. "If you had my mother, wouldn't you?"

"You're entitled to a life too. Part of a parent's job is to see to it that their kids have a better time of it than they did."

"I guess I have to do that for myself. That's why I'm here."

We stood there face to face for what seemed like a long time. Then I drew her close and kissed her. Her mouth was gentle, soft, and tasted every bit as good as I'd thought it would.

She stepped back, catching her breath. "I didn't come over here to sleep with you. Not tonight."

"What is that, chapter one of the Girl Code? No sex on the first date?"

"Is that what this is? A date?"

"I don't know what it is. Fifteen minutes ago I didn't know you were coming over."

She gave me her crooked smile again. "Let's just see how it goes, all right?" She put her arms around my neck. "That doesn't mean I don't want you to kiss me again."

I did. It was a more serious kiss this time. I ran my hands down her back, cupping her buttocks in my palms, and she pressed against me. We were a good fit.

The moment—or rather the minute, because that's about how long we kissed—was interrupted by a harsh beeping sound from the microwave in the kitchen.

She pulled away from me. "Eat your soup," she said.

CHAPTER TWENTY-FIVE

Teri Levine made damn good chicken soup.

It was the old-fashioned kind, with onions, garlic, carrots, and a few globules of golden fat floating on the top. I remembered the taste the next morning as I drove down to the Flats under a sky that was actually threatening to be blue later in the day.

I could still taste her kisses, too.

I got to my office building at about nine thirty. Seeing the ruins where I might have been immolated sobered me completely, driving all thoughts of chicken soup and kisses to a holding cell in the back of my mind.

I went upstairs to chat with the cleaning crew that was mopping up inside. Of course they told me why they couldn't do what I'd asked them to in the time they'd promised, at least not for the price we had agreed upon in advance. I didn't have much of a bargaining position, and they knew it.

The glaziers had replaced the broken windows the day before, but I hadn't been able to convince the painters, the plasterers, or the people who were going to redo the floor that I was in any sort of a hurry, so they were all scheduled for the following week. Service companies in Cleveland, the people who do repair work and home and office makeovers, are by nature an independent sort, and it does no good to get tough or to threaten to call another company when they don't show up or suddenly raise prices on you.

You either live without their services or you suck it up.

Tony Radek, who owns the wrought iron company downstairs and whose physique resembles a fireplug, was at his desk when I walked in, the inevitable cigar in the side of his mouth. Tony had been smoking cigars twenty-five years before the Generation X-ers decided they were as de rigueur as designer martinis and abs-crunching machines.

"Jesus, Milan," he said, looking up at his water-ravaged ceiling, "does this happen to you a lot?"

"No. I was a virgin when it comes to firebombs."

He took the cigar out of his mouth, and examined the end, which was nasty and spitty. "Well, at least you're here to talk about it. When the corporation owned this building, whenever I wanted to talk to them I got the chick who answered the phones. With you I got a landlord I can bitch at face to face." He allowed himself a rare smile. "You didn't get hurt, though, that's the main thing," he observed, his innate decency shining through the gruff blue-collar facade. He looked at the bruised and swollen side of my face, which this morning was the purple of an early evening sky after the rain. "Or did you?"

"Unrelated incident. I think."

"Some job you got," he said, and put the cigar back between his teeth; he favors the left corner of his mouth. "Well, I'll kind of keep an eye on that cleaning crew for you."

That gave me a certain security; I had heard Tony driving his workers as ruthlessly as the guy who used to keep the galley slaves rowing with the mallet and the whip—and they were his brothers.

I went outside and strolled around to the back of the building to stand and look out at the Cuyahoga. It was the color of a Heineken bottle this morning; the warming temperatures had greened it, along with the buds and leaves that were beginning to make their appearance on the trees planted in front of the fire station. The gulls were having their daily organizational meeting out over the water, wheeling and screaming. I turned around and regarded my second-floor window with an analytical eye. If someone had thrown the Molotov cocktail from a boat, he had to have possessed a pretty good arm.

I refused, however, to consider Green Bay Packers quarterback Brett Favre a viable suspect.

I had a better one.

I got back into the car and drove the five blocks to the headquarters of Republic Oil. As I approached the door, the sun burst through the overcast, startling me. We hadn't seen sunshine on the North Coast for months. An omen, perhaps, of illumination and enlightenment?

Nah.

Harry Channock was wearing a yellow shirt and brown slacks held up by a pair of improbable red suspenders that didn't quite match his crimson tie. He didn't look very dangerous, but I'd been around long enough to know that killers don't always look like the bad guys in a Martin Scorsese film.

When I came in he was leaning back in his chair reading the business section of the morning paper. By his elbow was half a powdered-sugar-covered doughnut on a greasy paper bag. Some of the white stuff clung to Channock's upper lip.

"Well, look who's here," he said, tilting his chair upright. "The shamus." He pronounced it *shah*mus.

He shuffled some papers around on his desk, shoving the doughnut to the side. "What happened to your head there? What does the other guy look like?" Another thudding cliché—Harry Channock must have had a whole file drawer full of them.

"So," he said cheerily, "sit down already."

"It's your chair." I sat down on his spindly director's chair and heard the wooden frame groan under my weight.

"What can I do for you this morning? You want to buy an oil well?"

"You weren't very forthcoming with me the other day, Mr. Channock. You never told me that Joel Kerner Sr. was one of your investors."

He knitted his brow and put his hands flat on the desk blotter, as if he was afraid it would fly away like a magic carpet. "Why should I tell you that? It's not your business."

"A man invests three million dollars with you, and you lose his money. Then his son gets killed in San Carlos, and you just happen to be staying in the same hotel."

"Coincidence."

"Don't crap around with me. You could be in some serious trouble."

"How do you figure?"

"The police don't believe in coincidences."

He tapped the blotter with all ten fingers, the way Oliver Hardy used to. "So are you saying I killed the Kerner boy?"

"I'm asking for an explanation. One I can believe."

He nodded gravely, then took a bite of his doughnut. "Suppose I don't want to give you one."

"You have powdered sugar on your mouth, Mr. Channock."

"Oh. Thanks," he said, and brushed at his lips with tobacco-stained fingers. There will be a brief pause in matters of life and death while we take care of the social niceties.

"I'm a little pressed for time," I said after a long wait.

He wrestled with his decision for a while longer, then said, "Okay, let me set you straight on a few things. First of all, I didn't 'lose' Kerner's money."

"No?"

"The money's still in place. It's just taking a little more time than I thought it would. We're close, though, damn close—or so my people there tell me. Bringing in an oil well, it isn't an exact science. I mean, it's a science, but a lot of it depends on luck and gut instinct."

"Your instinct is at the cleaners this week?"

"I'm a salesman, not a scientist. It's not my instinct we're talking about. We got drillers, geologists, engineers—"

"But you took the three million."

"I didn't pocket it, for God's sake. Look at me, I live in the same house in University Heights for twenty-eight years. It's no mansion, it's three bedrooms with a finished basement. I drive a 1991 Grand Am. I got no bank accounts in Switzerland or the Cayman Islands, and even if I did, I'm an old cocker and I've got nobody to leave it to. I eat TV dinners five times a week, my best wristwatch cost thirty bucks, and believe me, I got no tootsies stashed in a condo someplace." He wrinkled his nose. "My big luxury, I got HBO and Cinemax on the cable."

"You did get a commission on Kerner's money, though."

"That's how I make my living. A man has to put food on his table, no? Look, I never told Kerner it was a sure thing. Sure, I sold him. That's what I do—sell. And I never said the money was gone for good, just that it was going to take more time."

"And more money?"

He dusted the sugar from his hands. "Oil shares aren't like buying General Motors stock. They're high-risk. Kerner knew that going in."

"So tell me how you just happened to wind up on the same excursion as his son. And don't give me that crap about coincidence."

He folded his hands in front of him, a third-grader trying to impress the teacher. "Okay, so it wasn't a coincidence. It was a mistake."

"A mistake?"

"Sure. I thought it would be the old man on that trip, not the son. I was as surprised as anybody when I got there and found out it was the kid."

"I don't understand, exactly. You went to San Carlos deliberately to see Kerner?"

"Right," he said. "I knew he was pissed at me. I knew the kind of trouble he was in. I wanted to try and convince him that if he could come up with some more cash, maybe half a million or so, that it would expedite the oil exploration and he'd get all his money back quicker."

"Why not just call him on the phone here in Cleveland and save yourself a trip to the Caribbean?"

He ducked his head. "He wouldn't return my calls. He'd got his tits in a wringer and he figured it was my fault. I can't blame him for that, really. So I thought if I caught him on vacation, when he was relaxed, maybe I could talk him into it. Convince him that we're all on the verge of making big bucks. Really big. I tell you, it's this close." He held up a thumb and middle finger half an inch apart.

"So when you got there and found out it was Junior, not Senior . . . "

He snorted that back-of-the-nose, sinus snort again. "I said the hell with it and tried to enjoy my vacation. Any excuse to get out of Cleveland in the winter."

"You didn't try to hustle the son?"

"What good would that have done me? A personal injury lawyer? They make good money, but I didn't figure I could get half a million bucks out of him. No way."

My sore arm was thumping with every heartbeat, and I flexed my fingers to take some of the ache away. It didn't work. "I'm puzzled about one thing, though," I said.

"What's that?"

"What made you think Joel Kerner Sr. was going to be in San Carlos?"

He rocked his flattened hand at me, like a raft on white water. "I have my sources."

"You'd better give them up right now, or a couple of cops will be down here in ten minutes, and they won't ask you as nicely as I am." It was a hollow threat, but I was gambling Harry Channock wouldn't know that.

"What, this is nice you're being?"

"Compared to them I'm Mother Teresa."

For the first time he seemed nervous, uncertain. "I don't want to get anybody into trouble . . . " he said hesitantly.

"Them or you. Take your pick."

He patted his palms together gently, like Eddie Cantor singing "Ma, He's Making Eyes at Me." Thinking it over.

"My travel agent," he said, squeezing out the words. "A guy by the name of Josh Borgenecht."

I felt an adrenaline rush. "How do you know Josh Borgenecht?"

"He's also my landlord. He owns this building and one in the warehouse district, and he's losing his ass on both of them. His agency does a lot of business with the union people—his father was a big labor mucky-muck—and with the Kerners, too. He was the one that called and told me Kerner was going on a trip to San Carlos."

"But Senior, not Junior."

He shrugged. "Like I told you, it was a mistake."

"But why did Borgenecht think . . . ?"

I closed my eyes, envisioning in my head the San Carlos passenger list Janice Futterman had given me: Harry Channock. Joel Kerner. Dalma and Teri Levine. . . .

Joel Kerner.

Not junior, or senior. Joel Kerner.

"And Borgenecht is your landlord?"

Channock nodded. "Sure—if he doesn't lose the buildings by default."

The jigsaw puzzle pieces inside my head shifted around, and all of a sudden they all fit together. "Holy shit!" I said, sitting bolt upright in the rickety chair—which was one quick move too many. It finally buckled under me, and I wound up sitting on the floor, tangled up in chair legs and canvas.

"Hey, my chair!" Channock protested.

Embarrassed, I hauled myself to my feet and dusted off the seat of my pants. "Don't say I didn't warn you," I said.

I walked up the narrow metal stairs to the bridgetender's shack over the Eagle Avenue Bridge, perhaps a hundred fifty yards from my office building, experiencing a moment of giddy terror as I looked over the thin steel railing, which was all that separated me from the Cuyahoga River some sixty feet below. A grizzled, wiry-looking man near sixty stood at the top of the steps waiting for me.

"Bob Talty," he said gruffly, sticking out his hand. "The department called and told me you were coming."

He led me across a catwalk into the cozy little shack twenty-five feet above the roadbed of the bridge. Inside were two large banks of buttons and lights, a desk, a chair, and a space heater which was sending out merry waves of warmth.

"Ever been up here before?" Talty asked.

I shook my head.

He explained the buttons and lights to me. It was remarkably uncomplicated for so perilous an operation as raising a thirty-ton bridge.

"See those?" he said, pointing to light stanchions at the sides of the bridge. "They put those in to light up the bridges for the bicentennial. What they didn't think about was, they shine right in the operator's eyes at night. They fixed 'em a little bit afterward, though, so it's okay now."

"How often do you have to raise the bridge?" I asked.

"During the off-season, we do maybe eight, nine lifts a day. In the summertime when everyone is running around with their pleasure boats, maybe three times that."

"What do you do in between?"

He laughed. "They took the TV sets out last year, but that didn't bother me any. I read. A lot. And . . . " He opened a folder on the desk. "Genealogy is kind of my hobby. I've been tracing my family tree, clear back to Ireland in the last century. It keeps me occupied, all right."

"You keep a log of the boats that come through here?"

"Sure," he said. He flipped open an old-fashioned ledger, full of the names and numbers of boats, times of day, and dates. "Every time we do a lift, we record it. Sometimes the coast guard wants to see it, so we have to be ready." He chuckled. "It's just as much trouble to do a lift for a sailboat as for a six-hundred-fifty-foot ore boat."

"What about when you don't do a lift? When a smaller boat goes underneath—a power launch or something?"

"We don't pay much attention to that," he said.

"How many bridges are there that have to open for every boat, no matter how small?"

"Three. Willow, the Conrail bridge out by the lake, and the swing bridge. The guys on the Conrail, they have to coordinate with the trains, so there's sometimes a big wait there. Summertime you might see ten boats waiting to get out onto the lake, and another ten on the other side, coming back."

"So they'd have a record of every boat?"

He nodded.

"You saw the fire trucks over across the street day before yesterday?"

"Sure did. Don't often get that kind of excitement right outside the window."

"That was my office that was on fire."

"Aw," he said, looking abashed. "Sorry. I didn't mean—"

"That's okay," I assured him. "You didn't happen to notice a small boat go under the bridge right around that time, coming from that direction, did you?"

He scratched the white stubble on his chin. "Can't remember. Like I say, we don't pay much attention to the little guys we don't have to lift for." He cocked his head at an angle. "You think that boat might be connected to your fire in some way?"

"I wouldn't be a bit surprised," I said.

There are a lot of private marinas in the Cleveland area. They dot the shoreline of Lake Erie, mostly on the west side of town, and both banks of the Cuyahoga. Boating is an expensive hobby, but the lure of the water is strong, and our lakes and rivers are magnets for all kinds of pleasure craft, from sailboats to the power boats real sailors refer to as stinkpots.

I decided to check out the closest marina first. I don't often get that lucky—such investigations are by nature tedious and tiring—but one has to begin somewhere.

Besides, I thought, would anyone be dumb enough to undertake a sail-by bombing if he knew that when he made his getaway he'd have to stop and wait for a bridge to be raised—and that the bridgetender would write down the registration number of his boat?

The small marina just upriver from my office is accessible by car from Scranton Road, an area that ninety percent of the local residents have never explored. There isn't much for the tourist, unless you like old industrial plants and warehouses. I do, as it happens, which is why I moved Milan Security down there in the first place. The industrial section of the Flats, where a hundred years ago Irish laborers lived in makeshift shacks clinging to the edge of the riverbank, and where now most of the architecture remains untouched by modern progress, seems to me to be a definitely Cleveland kind of place.

The marina attendant came out of his office smoking a cigarette. He wore a shirt and tie under a Browns jacket that helped to camouflage his little beer gut; obviously, like many ardent Cleveland fans, he was in denial about our football team's dumping us. When the morning had begun, I hadn't known exactly what I was going to ask him. After talking to Harry Channock, I was afraid I knew too well.

"Which one is Mr. Borgenecht's boat?" I said.

He looked suspicious. "Why?"

"I'm thinking about buying it."

"He didn't say nothing to me about that."

"Well, no, he wouldn't have," I explained. "I met him at a party last night and we got to talking boats. I'm in the market, so he suggested I come down and have a look at his, and then we could talk about it."

He reached under his jacket and scratched his armpit. "I can't let you take it out or anything without him."

"I understand that."

He let me squirm for a while, another little man with a little authority wanting to milk it for all it was worth.

"I guess it's okay."

He led me out onto the dock and pointed at a low-slung Maxum 2000 Bowrider runabout, with seats for four in the main body of the boat, and two more forward of a walk-through windshield.

"That's Borgenecht's there," he said.

"Nice little boat."

"It needs a lotta work. The engine does. He don't take care of it like he should. What's he asking for it?"

"We never got around to that."

He sucked on the cigarette, exhaled the smoke in two jets through his nostrils, and then arced the butt out over the water. "Well, don't say nothing about this or I could get in trouble. But the thing is, if you're serious about buying a boat, you could do better. I could show you one or two, both of 'em owned by buddies 'a mine. Be a better buy."

Sometimes it seems to me that everybody is on the hustle. "Does Mr. Borgenecht take it out often?" I said.

"Not as much as he use'ta."

"Has he taken it out recently?"

He scratched again, this time vigorously enough to kill whatever he was hunting. "Coupla days ago. But that was the first time since last summer."

I tried to feign interest, but the fact was I didn't give a damn about the boat. I'd already learned what I came for—that Josh Borgenecht had a boat, and he'd taken it out the day my office had been firebombed.

But why would Josh Borgenecht want me dead? I hadn't been *that* big a pain in the ass.

The attendant gave me his card, scratching his home number across it in pencil, and told me to call him as soon as I was serious about a boat.

He didn't know how serious I was.

I drove back to Collision Bend and went into Jim's to use the pay phone. Not having access to my own office was getting to be a drag. Maybe I'd have to break down and get a cellular one of these days, but I still figured that I wasn't so damn important that the earth would go spinning off its axis if someone couldn't reach me every minute of the day or night.

Elaine Kerner answered the phone.

"Joel is lying down, Mr. Jacovich," she said with a hint of apology. "He's been under a lot of stress."

"I'm sorry, Mrs. Kerner. I just have to ask him one quick question."

"I hate to disturb him. . . ."

"I'm afraid it's really very important."

She sighed. "Just a moment, then," she said, and put me on hold.

It used to be that only large companies put you on hold, but now the new and advanced telephone technologies allow people to be just as rude in their own homes as the federal government or IBM or some ten-syllable downtown lawfirm.

At least I didn't have to listen to canned music while I waited.

After a moment there was a click on the line, and Joel Kerner said, "Haven't you done enough?" He didn't sound as if he'd been sleeping. "I've spilled my guts to you as much as I'm going to. Now don't call here again."

"This may be the last time I bother you, Counselor, but it's terribly important, and—"

"To whom? What's important to me is that you leave my wife and me in peace. Who the hell do you think you are, calling up here and acting like it's a matter of life and death?"

"As a matter of fact, it is. My life, your son's death. Do you understand me, sir? I don't give a damn what you've done or who you owe, or about anything about you, unless it relates to who killed your son and who tried to kill me."

His breath came loudly over the phone. "Lainie said you had one quick question. Ask it, and then leave us the hell alone."

"The pension funds from Stranahan's local that you gave to Harry Channock, the ones you were supposed to invest in downtown real estate—"

"I already told you about that," he said testily.

"Was the owner of that real estate Joshua Borgenecht?"

"It was DB Properties, yes. That's Borgenecht's company. What the hell does that have to do with—" he was saying as I hung up the phone.

I stood there for a moment, my hand still on the receiver, and my elation quickly dried up and blew away as a glum realization hit me low and hard.

I was pretty sure now that I had my killer. The question was, what in hell was I going to do with him?

CHAPTER TWENTY-SIX

"**M**rs. Levine, this is Milan Jacovich calling. The private investigator?"

I clenched the receiver tightly in my fist. I hadn't been so lucky this time; I'd reached the mother instead of the daughter. I should have waited until the next day and called Teri at her office, where, I could only assume, her mother didn't answer the telephone.

"Yes," Dalma Levine said. It wasn't a question. She wasn't going to make it easy at all.

"May I speak to Teri, please?"

At least twenty irreplaceable seconds of my life ticked away in the ensuing silence. I said, "Mrs. Levine?"

"She's told you everything she knows about that San Carlos business," Mrs. Levine said at last.

"That's not what I want to talk to her about."

Another long stage wait. "What *do* you want to talk to her about?"

"It's a personal matter."

Her voice, which had been frosty to begin with, turned subarctic. "I don't want you having personal matters with my daughter, Mr. Jacovich. She's a good Jewish woman. And I'm sorry to say this, but you're not our kind."

"If 'your kind' condemns people without knowing them, just because they happen to have different backgrounds and beliefs, then I'd say that was a compliment."

Her intake of breath was sharp, shocked. I heard Teri protest in the background, then Dalma must have put a hand over the mouthpiece; all I could make out were muffled, angry voices. I stood there in my kitchen, holding a can of beer, feeling worms of sweat trickling down my sides. I wanted very much to hang up and even more not to.

Finally Teri said into the phone, "Milan, I'm sorry."

"So am I. I think I was a little rough on your mother."

"It doesn't matter." She raised her voice and added, "I'm really glad to hear from you." I got the feeling it was directed at her mother as much as at me.

It made me feel good that she was standing up for herself. It was important. "I just wanted to thank you again for the chicken soup. It was very thoughtful."

"That's why you called?"

"Uh, no."

"Good."

"I'm finishing up my investigation . . . "

"Tell me." There was eagerness in her voice, and a little fear too.

"I can't. Yet. Anyway, I should be all done by this weekend, and—"

"Saturday night? I'd love to."

I laughed. "I can't offer you homemade chicken soup."

"Then you have to take me someplace wonderful. Someplace where they never even heard of chicken soup."

"Johnny's Bar on Fulton?"

"Marvelous," she said. "I've heard about it for years, but I've never been there."

"It's my favorite restaurant," I assured her. "I'll pick you up at seven."

She let a few too many beats go by before answering. "Uh, why don't I come to your place?"

"No, I'm from the old school. I like to call for my dates."

"But—"

"I don't like sneaking around, Teri, and I don't want to start out that way with you. We're not doing anything wrong, and I don't want to hide it. I think I can handle your mother. I'm a big boy."

The sigh on the other end sounded like relief. Then she chuckled. "I've noticed that. I hope some of your strength rubs off. All right, then, seven o'clock at my house. Just one thing, though."

"What's that?"

"Don't show up with a corsage, okay?"

There. That was done, or it would be on Saturday night. My first date in months. I was feeling elation and nervousness and apprehension about Teri's family situation all at the same time, and while it made me happy, there were other, more important things I should have been thinking about.

I took my beer into the den and sat down in my leather chair, trying to refocus my thoughts on Josh Borgenecht.

It would take an experienced sailor to make the trip from St. Albans to San Carlos, and although Lake Erie probably posed fewer threats than the Caribbean, Josh Borgenecht was a boat owner and probably knew his way around in the water.

That was strike one.

From what Janice Futterman had told me at the travel agency, Josh was one of those people who manage to kill every opportunity they touch. Losing the promised shot in the arm from Local 696's pension meant he couldn't rehab his building in the warehouse district, and that would put him in serious financial trouble, if it didn't bankrupt him. He'd lose the building, perhaps, and maybe even the one in which Harry Channock plied his grubby little trade. And since it was Joel Kerner Sr.'s fault the money got spent elsewhere, Josh had a perfect reason to want him dead—revenge.

That was strike two.

Josh told Harry Channock that it was Joel Sr. who was going on vacation because that's what he thought. He'd sent Channock down to San Carlos so there would be a likely suspect handy, and then he went down to St. Albans, rented a boat, took it over to San Carlos, and shot Joel Jr. himself, in the fog-shrouded half-light of that deserted dawn beach, mistaking the son for his father.

Someone on San Carlos must have tipped him off about the

early morning jogs. Eladio? Ybarra? The security guy at the San Carlos Inn?

It didn't really matter anymore. Strike three, called.

Because I was getting too close to the truth, and because Josh had obviously been in touch with both Patrick Stranahan and Joel Kerner Sr., as well as with Harry Channock, and knew that I was, he had powered his boat up to the riverbank at Collision Bend and heaved a bottle of flaming gasoline through my window, either to kill me or to warn me away. Janice Futterman had said he'd played quarterback in high school—he had the arm for it.

And that was an extra strike I didn't even need.

Now what was I going to do with all that information?

Unless I could prove that Borgenecht was the firebomber, a doubtful posit, the Cleveland police had no interest in him. I harbored no faith that San Carlos had an extradition treaty with the United States, either, so telling the authorities down there what I knew would be a plentiful waste of time. And I couldn't even give the story to Ed, because without proof Ed wouldn't write it and the paper certainly wouldn't print it.

I was at a dead end.

But I couldn't just let a killer skate—it went against everything I believe in and stand for. And besides, there was always a chance that he'd try to shut me up again. The next time he might even do it right.

I pulled my yellow pad toward me and doodled an empty gallows again—but try as I might, I couldn't seem to fit Josh Borgenecht's neck into the noose.

Vuk's Tavern was rocking.

Not that there was any rock music playing. Vuk wouldn't hear of it. When there was music at all in there, it was generally Frankie Yankovic and his polka band, or else something from the Glenn Miller–Tommy Dorsey era, Vuk's own personal choice, even though it probably cost him some revenue from the jukebox. The last rock music Vuk had listened to was Little Richard back in the fifties, and that had sent him around the bend. "All that screaming," he said. "You didn't ever hear Sinatra scream. Or Rosemary Clooney. They didn't have to—they could sing."

Nobody would have listened to music anyway on that particular evening. The rain we'd experienced for almost a week had let up, the Cleveland Indians were playing at home and beating the Red Sox, big. Vuk had unplugged the jukebox and turned the game up, and though his usual clientele was mostly male, tonight there were several couples present and even one or two unescorted women, come to watch the Tribe in the warm comfort of a circle of friends and fans. Nearly everybody was smoking, and the air in the bar was blue with it. Vuk moved as quickly as I'd ever seen him, drawing beers, pouring shots, washing glasses, the tattoos on his thick forearms rippling. Perspiration sheeted his high forehead, and he looked almost happy.

Jim Thome and Manny Ramirez had already homered, Omar Vizquel was three for three, the Tribe led by seven, and it was only the fifth inning. That's the kind of thing that makes Vuk's rock. Everyone present had probably drunk one beer too many by way of celebration, and the decibel count was uncomfortably high.

If I'd known the Indians were going to stage a blowout, I would have elected to meet Marko Meglich someplace more quiet.

We were as far as we could get from the blaring television set and the raucously good-natured crowd who'd gathered to watch it, way down at the end of the bar, where it curved like the handle of a shepherd's crook.

"All right, Milan," Marko said, patting beer foam from his mustache. "I agree. Borgenecht is probably your perp. But there isn't a damn thing anybody can do about it."

"Why not?"

There was a cardboard box full of little plastic straws on the bar, and he reached over for one and began bending it into half-inch lengths. "Nothing has changed here. The crime was committed in a foreign country, outside our jurisdiction. Even if he cops to it, we can't arrest him for it."

"What about firebombing my office? That's a crime, isn't it?"

"Sure," he said. "But no judge will sign an arrest warrant without any evidence."

"I'll bet if a forensics guy went over that boat, he'd find traces of gasoline."

"Probably so. You'll find traces of gasoline on every other power boat in the marina, and even a bad lawyer would point that one out." But we'd need a warrant for that, too, and what judge will issue it, especially on someone from a heavy union family like the Borgenechts? Without any really compelling reason, that'd be political suicide in this town. Judges need the votes of the labor movement, just like presidents do."

"I think we've got a good argument for probable cause."

"Maybe. But it'd be a waste of time, even if we get the warrant."

"So we know the guy's a killer and we just let him walk around?"

Marko signaled Vuk for two more beers. "Let's say I arrest him, okay? And let's say—there's no chance, but just for the sake of argument—let's say that San Carlos was willing to extradite him."

"Why is there no chance?"

"Because to them he's a foreign national, and so was Joel Kerner. It's gotta be nothing but a big pain in the ass for them not to just let it go away quietly. But let's say they bring him back for trial."

"All right," I grumbled.

"And they prove that he was on St. Albans when Kerner was killed—eighty miles away on another island."

"That wouldn't be hard."

"Probably not. And let's even say that they can find a guy, barely speaks English, who runs a boat-rental outfit on St. Albans and who's going to remember—by the time this gets to trial we're talking at least a year or two after the fact—who's going to remember that Borgenecht rented a boat from him."

"Not impossible."

"But nobody can prove he took the boat, crossed eighty miles of ocean, and blew Joel Kerner away on the beach in San Carlos. Where did he get the shotgun?"

I shrugged. "Any kind of weapon is easy to come by," I said. "Especially a shotgun. You can pick it up in any sporting goods store."

"And bring it through customs?" Marko shook his head. "The way airport security is these days you can't sneak a nail file past them, much less a shotgun."

"He got it on St. Albans, then."

"Well, being a foreigner, he sure didn't pick one up in a gun shop. So he probably bought one on the street somewhere, illegally. Right?"

"Right."

"Prove it. Go find a guy who sells illegal guns and get him to testify. And while you're doing that miracle, why don't you see if you can't make us both twenty-one again?"

"I wouldn't be twenty-one again if my life depended on it," I said. "Which reminds me, how're you doing with the lady in the lobby of the Justice Center?"

He seemed genuinely touched. "Hey, thanks for asking, Milan. Really. I talked to her after you told me to. Just said hello, and we got to chatting, and next week we're going out to dinner." He looked almost childlike. "She's . . . I don't know, she's different from the women I've been seeing lately. She's real easy to talk to."

"They are after they've been out of high school for a few years," I said. "You might even like grown-up women."

Vuk came down the bar and put two beers in front of us. "The Tribe brought their hittin' shoes tonight, huh?" he said. "Where'd you get your nose sunburned like that, Milan? You look like Bozo the Clown." He walked away without waiting for a reply.

I reached for my beer. "I can't prove it, Marko. About Josh Borgenecht and Joel Kerner. I can't even prove he did my office."

"Then there you go," he said.

We watched the ball game for a while, not saying much. In the seventh inning Mo Vaughn hit a three-run homer for the Red Sox, which still left the good guys ahead by four but sobered the crowd in the bar considerably. When manager Mike Hargrove came trotting out of the Indians' dugout to summon Paul Shuey from the bullpen, it was almost as hushed as Saint Vitus at High Mass.

"Why don't you jerk his chain?" Marko said.

"Mike Hargrove?"

"Borgenecht. You've already got him scared enough that he tried to toast your office with you in it. Lean on him, rattle his cage a little. Force his hand."

"What good would that do?"

"If he tries again, then we can arrest him."

"But not for murder."

Marko shrugged. "Not unless he kills you."

"That supposed to be funny?"

"No, factual. Look, I know you want him for murder one, but you can't have him. I'm sorry as hell, but he got away with Joel Kerner. And unless we can find an eyewitness—which you know damn well we can't—we can't even get him for the torching. So the only way we can nail him is if he goes for you again."

"Isn't that entrapment?" I said.

"It is if I do it."

"You mean you're not going in with me on this?"

"I'm not getting my ass shot off before my first date with Ruth."

"Ruth," I said. "Even her name sounds grown-up."

"Besides, I told you before, Milan—"

"Yeah, yeah," I said. "Rules. It doesn't seem fair that the rules protect the bad guys though."

He picked up his beer. "Show me in your contract where it says life has to be fair."

A shout went up from the crowd at the bar as Matt Williams lined a home run into the left-field seats. Vuk smiled beneath his mustache and washed some more dirty glasses; Indian homers hype beer sales.

"Just be careful, Milan," Marko said, taking a cigarette out of my pack and lighting it. "For my sake. What good is Sundance without Butch?"

"So what you're saying," I thought out loud, "is that I should stick a hook through my back like a minnow and toss myself into the water as bait."

Marko took a deep, luxurious drag and exhaled the smoke into the already polluted air. "Part of the cost of doing business," he said.

CHAPTER TWENTY-SEVEN

It was almost as if the Indians' heavy hitting the night before had been the official kickoff to actual spring weather, because the morning dawned bright and sunny, the temperature flirting with seventy degrees but not quite making it. I awoke before seven and showered and shaved, noting sadly that my nose was finally starting to peel from my day in the San Carlos sun. Some long-ago lover had left a jar of moisturizing cream in my medicine cabinet, and I slathered it on my nose, hoping to camouflage the damage. The swelling on the side of my face had gone down some but was now an alarming Crayola shade of yellowish-green.

I was colorful, if nothing else.

I drove down to my office. Now I had a name and a face to put to the firebomber, and someone at whom I could direct my anger. And I was mad as hell, in an ice-cold way. Mad and determined. Josh Borgenecht wasn't going to get away with torching my office—and he wasn't going to get away with murder.

I went upstairs to talk to the work crews about the repairs being done. The place was beginning to look almost habitable again, and Tony Radek, whose space had been fixed up before mine, was in what was for him a remarkably good mood. He even invited me to help myself to his coffee instead of picking some up at one of the nearby diners.

It was not yet nine o'clock. I used Tony's tattered White Pages to look up Josh Borgenecht; I found he lived in a middle-class area of Shaker Heights, not far from his travel agency.

Sitting at Tony's desk, I dialed the number. A woman answered the phone. Her flat vowels were the hallmark of a longtime Clevelander, and her voice told me she was somewhere over sixty.

"May I speak to Josh Borgenecht, please?"

"I'm sorry, but he's already left. May I take a message?"

"Is this his mother?"

"That's right," she said.

Damn! Why do killers have to have mothers? I suddenly lost a little of my edge. "Uh, this is Milan Jacovich." I spelled it for her. "Could you tell him I took a look at his boat yesterday, and I'm very interested?"

She paused. "Is he selling the boat? I didn't know that."

"We're just talking about it at this point," I said. I gave her my home number, thanked her, and depressed the button for a few seconds. I didn't like using an elderly lady.

I released the button and listened to the new dial tone. Tony gave me a sideways look from across the room, wondering, I suppose, if I was going to tie up his phone all day. I tapped out another seven digits.

"You have reached Beachwood Travel," a recorded female voice said. It didn't sound like Janice Futterman; lower, younger, sexier, it promised untold vacation delights. I imagined it must be the blonde. "Our office hours are from ten A.M. to five thirty P.M., Monday through Friday. Please leave a message and we'll call you back. Thanks."

The final word sounded arch and cute, like *thinks*.

At the sound of the beep I identified myself. "This message is for Josh Borgenecht. I was just wondering if, being a travel agent and all, when you go away someplace, say, St. Albans, do you get a discount on the air fare? Call me." I left my number on the tape and hung up.

He'd left the house at about eight and wasn't due in the office until ten. Maybe he'd gone somewhere for breakfast. Or maybe he was going to stop by and try to kill me again on his way to work. There's always something interesting to do in Cleveland.

Then I looked up DB Properties, Borgenecht's real-estate holding company, but there was no listing. It didn't surprise me. A guy like Borgenecht, with a serious cash-flow problem and hanging on by his fingernails, couldn't afford to maintain a separate office. He probably kept it in his hat.

Rattle his cage, Marko had suggested. I was trying.

Tony Radek reclaimed his desk and phone and I drove out of the Flats, east on St. Clair Avenue until I got to Addison Street. I stopped and got two large containers of coffee and a bag of assorted pastries from Nosan's Bakery and took them over to Chet Tumbas's house.

"I was in the neighborhood," I said, "and I thought you might like to have some breakfast."

He might have been happier if I'd handed him a million dollars—but not a penny less. We sat and chatted for more than an hour, and he reminisced some more about my mother and father, and the good old days at Deming Steel. I enjoyed talking to the old fellow; now that both my parents and my Auntie Branka were gone, Tumbas was one of my last links to the old country. As I grow older, my yearning to visit Slovenia someday—Ljubljana and Maribor and the seaport of Potoroz—has grown more keen. Thank God Slovenia has been spared the ravages of civil war. Maybe I could ask Josh Borgenecht to arrange my itinerary.

I left the rest of the pastries with him, drove back to Cleveland Heights, and did a major shopping at Russo's before going up to my apartment, picking up all the things I'd run out of while I'd been all wrapped up with the Kerner case.

I was going to see Teri on Saturday night. And Marko had a dinner date with his Ruth from the Justice Center the next week. Were both us lonely bachelors turning the corner?

It was almost noon. When I walked in the door laden with paper bags, my answering machine was blinking. After I put the groceries on the kitchen counter and refrigerated the lettuce, milk, butter, and beer, I played back the messages; four of the six were hang-ups. I pushed the little high-tech button on the machine to find out what numbers the other calls had been made from.

They were all the same. Beachwood Travel—at twenty-minute intervals. I looked at my watch. He was almost due again.

I smiled. Sweat a little bit for me, Josh, I thought.

I took out the tape with my standard outgoing message and recorded a new one especially for Josh—if anyone else called they'd think I'd lost my mind.

Looking out the window at the point of the Cedar–Fairmount triangle, I saw the mail carrier trudging across the street toward the big office building next to the Mad Greek. I went down and retrieved my mail from the slot, shuffling through it as I walked back upstairs. Bills, junk mail, requests for contributions. No personal letters, though. There rarely are. I'll bet if I had an E-mail address people would send me little messages every day.

That's why I don't.

In the corridor outside my apartment I heard my telephone. I went inside, but I let it ring four times, waiting for the machine to pick up.

"Hi, this is Milan Jacovich," I heard my own voice saying. "My good friend Ed Stahl of the *Plain Dealer* is doing a travel piece on beautiful tropical St. Albans. So if you've been there lately, he'd love to talk to you. Otherwise, leave a message at the beep."

After the beep came exasperated staccato breathing, and then the caller hung up. I figured that by now Josh Borgenecht really had his knickers in a twist.

Now he knew that I was home, or at least that I'd been here long enough to change my message. I wondered if he'd pay me a visit, and whether he'd come with evil intent.

I put back the tape meant for the rest of the world and waited. Outside the sun went away and it started to rain again. Hard.

Borgenecht must have gone out for lunch, because he didn't call again until almost two o'clock.

"This is Josh Borgenecht," he said in a low voice when I answered the phone.

"Josh," I said. "How nice to hear from you."

"What's the idea of calling up and upsetting my mother?"

"I didn't mean to upset her. I just left you a message."

"I've been getting your messages all over town. Stranahan

called me, and Harry Channock, and the guy from the marina. I've got a good mind to call the police and file a harassment charge."

"Good idea, Josh," I said. "By all means, call the police."

There was a long pause, almost half a minute. I heard him swallow hard. "What's going on here, Jacovich? Just what is it you think you know?"

"You really want to discuss this over the phone?"

"No," he said. "I don't. I think we should meet."

"I'll come over to your office."

"Don't be a goddamn fool."

"Okay," I said. "Your call."

Another pause.

"Remember Shorty's Diner?"

"In the Flats? Sure."

"Meet me in the parking lot," he said. "Eleven o'clock tonight."

A little warning light flashed on behind my eyes. "Why the cloak-and-dagger stuff? Why not somewhere public?"

"Are you being deliberately stupid?" he said.

"Not anymore, Josh."

"Look, I'm trying to make this worth your while."

"Worth my while?"

"You know what I'm talking about, Jacovich. You won't be sorry."

I doubted it at the time, but I had no idea how sorry I would be.

I waited until three o'clock and then called Victor Gaimari at his office.

"Milan," he said. "How's it going?"

"It's going," I told him. "Victor, have you ever run into a guy named Josh Borgenecht?"

He thought for a moment. "I used to know a Phil Borgenecht—know of him, anyway. He was a union official, one of the Cleveland locals. He died several years ago. Why?"

"Josh is his son, I think."

"Is he a bad boy, Milan?"

"I think he might be."

"Does this have something to do with Patrick Stranahan?"

"Indirectly," I said. "Don't worry about it."

"I do worry, though. I worry about you. I worry about Stranahan. You want us to get involved in this?"

"No!" I said. "God, no. I'm just fishing. Forget I even asked."

"You sure?"

"I want your word on it."

"You've got that, then." I could hear a smile in his voice. "But you know that we look out for our friends. All you have to do is call. We're here for you, Milan."

I hung up, sudden unease eating at my gut. How had it come to this? How had I become a friend, a pet of the Cleveland mob? I didn't want them to be there for me—it made me feel creepy.

Maybe Marko Meglich was right. Maybe I was too chummy with them, calling them for information, having drinks with Victor. I've always prided myself on drawing lines I won't cross, but maybe somewhere along the way I had allowed those lines to become blurred and even to start disappearing.

I was going to have to work on that.

"Shorty's Diner?" Marko and I were sitting at the bar of Sterle's Slovenian Country House on East Fifty-fifth Street, drinking Slovenian beer. It was the middle of the afternoon, and they only had one other customer, who'd obviously been there since lunchtime and wasn't paying us a damn bit of attention. "Shorty's has been closed for years."

"I think that's the idea," I said. "I did what you said, Mark, I rattled his cage. I think he's going to bite now."

"I think so too. Just like we figured it. Well," he said, "for God's sake, watch your ass."

"Watch my ass? I was kind of hoping you'd be there to do it for me."

He took one of my Winstons and lit it. "Like I told you—if I get involved in this, it's entrapment."

"If you're not going to be there, then what's the point?"

"The point is, you can file a formal complaint on him for attempted murder and I can go pick him up."

"What if the 'attempt' works?"

He turned his head and blew out a jet of smoke. "You're a big boy, Milan. You've always been able to take care of yourself."

"I don't believe this," I said. "You know we've got a killer here, you know he's going to try for me, and you want me to wait till he does and then file a complaint?"

He looked away, studying the cloud from the lungful of smoke he'd just expelled. "I'm not a free agent like you. There's a certain way we've got to do things. And this isn't one of them."

"You mean to tell me that I just got a killer all riled up and coming after me, and you're going to leave me twisting in the wind?"

"If you want a righteous collar on the guy."

"I want to live through the night," I said.

He made X's on the serviette with a fingernail. "You got a cellular?"

"No."

"That figures. When are you going to jump into the twentieth century?"

"The century is almost over," I said, "so why even bother?"

He reached into his jacket pocket and pulled out a little telephone, folded up to the size of a pack of cigarettes. "Here," he said. "Take this with you when you go to see Borgenecht. I'll be at my desk at the Third from about ten thirty on. I'll stay there all night, if I have to. You know the number. Just dial it when you need me, and I'll come running."

I looked at the phone in his extended palm. "And that's it? That's all?"

"It's all it can be. You don't want the guy to walk on a technicality, do you?"

I took the little toy and put it in my own pocket. "I wonder whether Butch Cassidy ever called the Sundance Kid for backup on a cellular phone."

He looked genuinely saddened. "That Butch and Sundance stuff—it was just a silly dream, Milan."

"Apparently," I said.

* * * * * * * * * * * *

CHAPTER TWENTY-EIGHT

* * * * * * * * * * * *

At one time, Shorty's Diner had been a happening place. When the fifties diner craze had been in full throttle, Shorty's, located on Old River Road beneath the Veterans Memorial Bridge, was where you took your kids for their birthday parties or where you took a date for a hamburger and a soda if the glitz clubs in the Flats were not to your taste.

When it closed a few years back, there was much talk of converting it into something else. A "gentleman's club"—read topless bar—had been proposed, and an upscale restaurant, but none of those plans had materialized, and now it's just a shell that people hardly give a glance as they pass by on their way across to the west bank.

It was pretty quiet down in the Flats. It was a weeknight, and the relentless rain was keeping all but the most dedicated party animals at home. It was ten minutes to eleven when I drove onto the rubble-strewn area that used to be Shorty's parking lot and peered out through the strokes of the windshield wipers, but no one was around. That's a failing of mine—being early to everything.

I turned the engine off and unbuckled my seat belt. Across the river the lights of the Nautica complex, with its dance clubs and eateries, were bright and cheery. On this, the east bank, it was quiet and dark. Occasionally a car would drive by on Old River Road, but none stopped or even slowed.

Josh Borgenecht said he'd make it worth my while. Was he

going to offer me money to keep my mouth shut? How much did he think Joel Kerner's murder and the burning of my office was worth?

But I didn't think he would make me an offer. First of all, since Borgenecht had a bad case of the shorts, I doubted he'd be able to come up with enough cash for any sort of a bribe. And it seemed to me that the more logical progression would have been to try to pay me off first and then attempt to fry me if I refused.

That's why I brought my .357 Magnum with me, nestled uncomfortably under my left arm. Just in case. A loaded weapon and a cellular phone—I was well equipped.

I rolled down the window a little so I could smoke. The rain drummed its own rhythm on the hood and roof of the car. This was the part of my business that I hate—the waiting.

A few more cars went by. So did a few more minutes. At ten past eleven I was beginning to wonder if he would show up at all. That's when he suddenly materialized on the driver's side of my Sunbird.

I hadn't expected him to come on foot. He was wearing a long black raincoat and a silly-looking rain hat, and in his gloved hand was a Sig Sauer automatic, which was pointed at my head.

"Don't move, Jacovich, or I'll shoot you right here," he said. "Put your right hand on the steering wheel where I can see it."

I did. I was in no position to argue.

He stepped backward a few feet. "Now open the door—slowly—and get out."

I was so angry with myself for being taken unawares, I didn't have room to feel afraid. I got out of the car, leaving the door open so the dome light stayed on, hoping to draw some attention if anyone came driving by.

"Clasp your hands at the back of your head," he said.

My cigarette went *pish* as it hit the puddle I was standing in. I put my hands where he told me to.

"Now kick the door shut."

He was smarter than I gave him credit for. And cooler. But then when you've killed once, doing it again probably seems easy.

I nudged the car door shut with my foot. The rain was pummeling me, running down my face into my eyes, making it hard to see. "You expect to get away with this?"

"I got away with it before." He shoved the gun into my stomach and patted me down. It took him two seconds to find the Magnum. He reached in beneath my coat and removed it, putting it in his pocket.

"You know, Josh, you're not very good at this. First you kill the wrong man, and then you try to burn me up and don't even come close. You're as inept at murder as you are at everything else."

"Don't piss me off, Jacovich. I can make this easy and fast, or I can make it hurt." With the gun he gestured toward the incline behind the building, where the pilings of the bridge were sunk into the bedrock. "Move."

I walked across the parking area toward the hill, with Borgenecht following close behind. The mud sucked at my shoes. "Your passport is going to show you took a trip to St. Albans the week young Joel was killed," I said.

"So what? There's nothing that says I was anywhere near San Carlos. The only one who knows is you—and you aren't going to tell anybody."

"I've already told somebody. The police."

"If they were going to do anything about it, they would have by now."

"Are you silly enough to think I haven't talked to the police about you?"

"Proof," he said, stepping back so I couldn't reach him. "They'll need proof. They don't have a case and you know it." He snickered. "It really grinds you that I got away with it, doesn't it?"

"Are you going after Joel Sr. now? This time do it right?"

"Somebody had to pay," he said. "I needed that pension money. I could have really made that building into something. It would have been a real cash cow. I'm ruined without it."

"You were going to kill Kerner just to get even? Jesus . . . "

"I'm sick of rich people like Joel Kerner crapping all over me. They've been doing it all my life." He gestured with the muzzle of the gun. "Up the hill," he ordered.

He was going to walk me up out of sight of the road and shoot me. Then he'd probably drive my car off somewhere and leave it, and no one would find me for days. It was a lonely place in which to die.

"You can't go around killing people when things don't go your way, Josh."

"Shut up," he said, and poked me in the back again, harder.

I started up the incline. The ground was pure mud, interspersed with shards of rock and cement, and it was tough going. I slipped and fell to my knees.

"Come on, come on, get up," he growled.

I stood upright, feeling the cold wetness through my pants. My hands were covered with mud, too. "Your mother must be real proud of you."

"Shut up about my mother."

We were about halfway up the incline, directly above the building that used to be the diner, when all of a sudden the whole world got brighter. A spotlight pierced the darkness from down in the parking lot, lighting up the rain. It wavered slightly, as if someone was pointing it by hand. Both Borgenecht and I froze where we were in a grotesque game of statue maker.

"Hold it right there," came a familiar voice through a bullhorn.

Marko. He'd come through for me after all. I found I had been holding my breath—I let it out in a rush.

"You all right, Milan?" he called.

"I'm fine."

"Throw down your weapon, Mr. Borgenecht."

Josh Borgenecht's face was the ghastly color of expensive stationery. His eyelids fluttered wildly as he looked from me to the spotlight, shielding his eyes with his free hand.

"Drop it right now!" Marko ordered.

Borgenecht cast a quick look at me, then whirled and fired five shots down the hill. The light wavered, then fell to the ground.

I lunged at him, hitting him in the middle of his back. I'd been above him on the grade, and the impact sent him falling forward. My arms wrapped around him, and clawing with one hand for the automatic, I rolled with him down the hill, picking up mud along the way, bouncing over shards of rock and cement that ripped and abraded the skin on my legs and hands.

We finally came to a stop against a concrete bridge piling, banging into it hard. He struggled in my bear hug, trying to turn around to face me. He was almost as big as I am, and strong. I grunted with the effort of holding him.

He jerked his elbow back and smashed me in the face—right where it was already most bruised and swollen. It hurt like hell and made my head swim just long enough for him to break out of my grasp. He scrambled to his feet and turned on me, his back against the piling.

I was still on my knees. I lunged forward and butted him in the crotch with my head. His scream cut the night, and he doubled over. I stood quickly and batted the Sig Sauer out of his hand, and it slithered down the muddy slope.

Borgenecht staggered away and stumbled down the hill with me after him. I caught up with him just as we reached the parking lot and tackled him the way I'd been taught back when I tackled people for fun. The thought that a defensive lineman was sacking the quarterback flashed into my mind and then was gone.

When his right leg hit the ground I heard a sickening pop. I'd heard that sound before, on the football field, and I knew he'd just blown his knee out. He screamed again, even louder this time.

I flipped him over on his back and drove my fist into the side of his face, putting all my weight behind it, feeling his jaw crunch beneath my knuckles. He went limp, and I didn't figure he was going to be causing any trouble anytime soon. I reclaimed my Magnum from his coat pocket and put it in my own.

Then I got to my feet and went unsteadily over to where the spotlight lay on the ground, illuminating the side of Shorty's Diner. Marko was on his back cradling his 9-millimeter Glock in his bloody hands. A big hole in his chest pumped blood ominously, making a sucking sound with each breath he took.

"Did we get him?" he said weakly, trying to move his head.

I knelt down next to him. "Marko. Oh, Jesus, Marko . . ."

"I couldn't let you down, kid," he croaked. "Couldn't let you do it—alone. Fuck the rules sometimes."

"Don't move," I said. "Don't try to talk." I searched frantically in my pocket for the cellular phone, fumbled it open, stabbed unfamiliar buttons, trying to activate it. When I got a dial tone I punched out 911.

"The way it always—should have been," he said between gasps. "Butch—and Sundance, huh?" His entire body was wracked by a convulsion, and blood and saliva came out of his mouth.

"Police officer down!" I screamed into the phone. "He's shot! We're at Shorty's Diner on Old River Road—send an ambulance!"

"Waste—taxpayer's money," he said. "Trained me—not to do that." His voice was no more than a wheeze, as he gasped for breath, for life. "Give me—cigarette."

"Hang on," I said. "Just hang on, Marko."

"Shit. I'm not—gonna make that date—with Ruth."

Hot, bitter tears streamed down my cheeks. "Sure you are. Just take it easy now, Marko. Don't talk."

I pried the gun loose from his fingers and cradled his head in my lap.

"We get him?" he rasped.

I glanced over at Borgenecht. He was still down, still out, not moving. Maybe I'd killed him. I hoped so. "We got him, Marko. Oh God, hang on, pal. The medics are on their way. Jesus, hang *on*."

He coughed violently, emitting a gob of bloody phlegm, and I held him tighter, rocking him like a baby.

Through the hiss of the rain I heard a far-off siren, a mournful wail like a wolf in the dark, lonely wilderness, that might have been the ambulance coming for Marko.

It wasn't going to make any difference.

He reached up, his bloody fingers clasping my shoulder with surprising strength, squeezing hard. Then his hand went limp and dropped to his side. And my oldest and best friend, the Sundance Kid, my teammate and childhood chum, died quietly in my arms.